So Last Century

Stories 1900–2000

Charles Nevin

The Book Guild Ltd

First published in Great Britain in 2023 by
The Book Guild Ltd
Unit E2 Airfield Business Park,
Harrison Road, Market Harborough,
Leicestershire. LE16 7UL
Tel: 0116 2792299
www.bookguild.co.uk
Email: info@bookguild.co.uk
Twitter: @bookguild

Typeset in 11pt Minion Pro

Printed and bound in the UK by TJ Books LTD, Padstow, Cornwall

ISBN 978 1915603 128

British Library Cataloguing in Publication Data.
A catalogue record for this book is available from the British Library.

For Liv, for all and always

Contents

1907

Tum-Tum Trouble

Bertie took a deep draw on his last Corona y Corona Super Toker and contemplated the past day from the comfort of his four-poster. Breakfast had been acceptable, particularly the chicken, steak and scrambled eggs with truffles. Lunch pretty much up to scratch: the rabbit curry, wild boar and rum baba more than acceptable. Dinner adequate, eight courses, good that Elsie Thornfield had remembered his penchant for boned snipe, even if she had been a bit stingy with the accompanying foie gras and Madeira sauce. Still, that had left more room for the oysters, caviar, plovers' eggs and grouse.

Not a bad haul of those last little blighters, actually: good driving, 400 in all, 80 bagged by him, would have been more but couldn't rush lunch. Bridge had gone well enough, despite a few tricks cashed too early and some bad penalty doubles. Terrible partner, Elsie, not a patch on Alice. Pity about Alice's cold. Wouldn't want to catch anything himself if he could help it, though, feeling the old tempus fugiting fairly rapidly recently, in bed by one o'clock tonight.

He stubbed the cigar out, half smoked, and turned off the table lamp. There was the sound of someone shifting on the other side of the door in response to the dying of the light. That would be his detective, Raab, a man of immense discretion and impressive obsequiousness; or possibly one of his policemen, or his valet, the diminutive but determined Hancock. It was difficult to obtain access to Bertie at night, if not invited. His one constant companion was his pet terrier, Caesar, who slept on a nearby chair.

Sleep normally came quite easily. Bertie's was not an immoderately troubled conscience, and he found being King of England a great aid to equanimity. Foreign relations were an increasing concern, though, especially in the matter of his two nephews, the completely crazed Kaiser and the stunningly stupid Tsar, both of whom would have been far better suited to the life of eccentric landowners safely pottering around somewhere in west Sussex.

But both were being neither too mad nor idiotic at this particular moment, so there really ought to have been nothing to halt the royal progress towards its first mighty reverberation (he had once asked Alix if he snored; 'Oh, no, Bertie,' his adoring, eccentric, endlessly forgiving wife had replied, 'you purr like a tiger.'). He and Caesar always made fine concert, their alternating snores producing a continuous blast like an asthmatic siren.

True, he was in Yorkshire, which was not the most favourite part of his vasty empire. Something a little unforgiving about the inhabitants, he felt. He remembered that his mother claimed to have been offered the bill after a lunch in Leeds. And they were always looking at you in an unimpressed, oddly superior way, including the loaders, particularly the head man today, Boycott. Probably the result of too much East wind, he decided, and went no further: Bertie was a good reader of people, but as uninterested in motivation as he was in moderation.

There was a loud thump outside the door which confirmed that Raab was on duty, as the detective was given, rather tiresomely, to falling asleep and off his chair. Drat the fellow, thought Bertie, before turning to the real cause of his unease, a problem that seemed to have dogged him since he first discovered the delights of intimate indiscretion with not entirely suitable participants, beginning with the lusciously naughty Nellie at the Curragh all those years ago, and proceeding with any number of ladies not his wife and most often somebody else's. (Alice's husband, Colonel Keppel, was particularly understanding about his comely wife's position as Bertie's current and long-standing *maitresse-en-titre*.)

If Bertie had consulted an increasingly influential doctor in Vienna, he might have come to realise that this bent was almost certainly a reaction against his mother's worship of both marriage and her humourless husband. But even had the thought occurred, he would not have pursued it, as he was perfectly content with arrangements that allowed him to exercise the prerogative of the prince throughout the ages, pleasure without responsibility.

Almost. There were certain recurring little problems, the inevitable upshot of engaging with bewitching accompanists who by definition also enjoyed risk and so from time to time abandoned former friendship and fealty to indulge in a spot of the ugly activity they preferred not to call blackmail.

These attempts were generally meant either to regain his affections or settle debts. The chosen instruments were usually letters that Bertie had written in happier times. But although he was an enthusiastic correspondent, he was also a discreet one; the letters were mostly to arrange trysts and were carefully ambiguous. It normally required only a visit by one of his private secretaries to settle the matter: the perils of social ostracism and bad publicity would be explained, an appropriate emolument made.

But the present complication was different, and had come up on his first night at Thornfield Hall. As was the custom, his fellow guests had been carefully vetted, but Bertie did like to make new acquaintances, especially from the fairer regiment. Thus, the presence of a Mrs Adler, and Mr and Mrs Eynsford Hill. Elsie had vouched for them, although, if she were to be entirely honest, she had left arrangements a little late and had become anxious to find company fit for a king, especially one with, how shall we say, certain standards. Standards with which Elsie was well acquainted as a former intimate of Bertie (whether this had been with the acquiescence of her husband, Lord Thornfield, was impossible to know, as he had not been heard to say anything intelligible since Balaclava).

Their dalliance, for that was what it was, had petered out due to Elsie's incurable inability to keep an appointment and Bertie's eye falling elsewhere, as usual. But he was very good – apart from the exceptions mentioned – at keeping old flames flickering in a friendly fashion. Indeed, as he grew older, and lazier, and ate even more, indoor activity of the more energetic kind held less appeal than a little light flirting and a lot of cake.

But he had not entirely lost his eye, and that eye had been immediately taken by both Mrs Adler and Mrs Eynsford Hill. Mrs Adler was dark, shapely and alluring, while Mrs Eynsford Hill was a truly striking example of the English Rose, from her perfect strawberry and cream complexion to her accent, as clear as the Kennet on a Sunday summer's morning.

It did not take long for a veteran connoisseur to decide which lady would be more susceptible to his approach. A few minutes with each before dinner favoured Mrs Adler. She was American, a type Bertie had always relished, with a career behind her, according to Elsie, in the opera, one of the few art forms Bertie appreciated, probably because, like him, it was larger than life and loved extravagant costume. Mrs Eynsford Hill was indeed beautiful, but he couldn't quite place her type or her conversation; she also had a husband in tow, and although Eynsford Hill affected a monocle and lacked a little in the chin area, always promising signs of a Lord Thornfield-like persuasion, one never quite knew.

The routine was well-rehearsed: in among the polite discussion about various arias and artists came the almost casual reference to the graciousness of Elsie in providing such excellent quarters on the first floor and their exact location, followed by the subtlest of enquiring looks beneath the most imperceptible of raised eyebrows. Mrs Adler displayed a most charming mixture of demurely growing realisation, interest, amusement and future promise. On retiring, Bertie made certain customary arrangements involving the discreet withdrawal of his staff and, sure enough, not long after he had put his light out there was a knock at the door of the bedroom.

The king, feeling a revived thrill of his old chief interest, shushed Caesar, moved through to the door and opened it to reveal Mrs Adler in the most becoming of night attire. 'Oh,' she said, 'but this is not the bathroom! Forgive me, Your Majesty!' The change of tone that accompanied the last two words was allied to an impressed look down at Bertie's mid-region. This was indeed an impressive area – the king had long been known as Tum-Tum with cause – but the way in which Mrs Adler managed to convey by her glance and tone that she was referring to another protuberance altogether under his nightshirt was highly encouraging of what might follow.

It seemed entirely natural for her to enter the bedroom and then sit by Bertie's side on his bed and, quite soon afterwards, for the royal hand to find that of Mrs Adler. The deep meaningful stare into her really rather fetching amber eyes was meant to combine attraction, admiration and passion with just a hint of regal mastery but met a slight hesitation and gentle withdrawal of her hand.

'There is something we must discuss, Your Majesty,' she said softly.

'Bertie,' said Bertie, going on to mumble about practical arrangements and precautions, all that sort of thing, very sensible. 'No, you misunderstand me, Bertie. I would like you to pay me £50,000.'

'Good lord,' said Bertie. 'You're a damned pretty woman, Mrs Adler, but that's a bit stiff!' He also noticed, slightly to his surprise, that the size of the amount had made him rather more so elsewhere. 'It can cool a man's ardour, too,' he lied, employing a sheepish look that had worked somewhat better when he was younger.

'Call me Irene, Bertie. You misunderstand me again. I don't want the £50,000 for allowing you to make love to me. I want the £50,000 to destroy some photographs.'

Bertie, a short-fused man at the best of times, was getting cross, and also conscious that he was striking a less than regal note in his nightgown. But it was also clear that the ravishing Mrs Adler was exciting him in a way he had imagined long lost. And this, he realised, was not only on account of her very proximate embonpoint, but because of the delicious unscrupulousness of her attentions. As has been noted, though, he had been in enough similar situations not to give too much away at such an early stage, and so decided on bluster.

'Photographs? What puffering photographs? Who the deuce are you? I thought you were a friend of Elsie's!'

'Well, in a way. More a friend of a friend of a friend. Your Elsie is a friend of Skittles and Skittles is a friend of Blondine who is a friend of Arlette who is a friend of Hector, the friend of mine who took the photographs.'

Bertie now had an inkling of the direction in which matters were travelling. Catherine Walter, known to all as Skittles because of her one-time employment in such an alley, was a remarkable throwback to the days when girls of ordinary origin could use their beauty, wit, and availability to parlay themselves into the highest society. She was, in short, London's last, antique word, courtesan. Bertie knew her very well, though not so well since he had become king. He also knew that connections of hers who sounded French were not necessarily a good sign. So, deciding on a spot of diversionary action very much suited to his present (and most insistent) inclination, he toned down the indignation and dropped his voice. 'Let's talk about this later, shall we?' he said, in what he imagined to be a throaty, irresistible whisper, and made a grab for Mrs Adler.

She evaded the lunge with practised elegance; Bertie just had time for a shimmering vision of trembling bosom before he toppled forward and planted his face in the mattress.

'That would be such fun but this is rather pressing, Bertie dear,' she said, calmly. 'Do sit up and I'll tell you. Hector had one of those concealed cameras hidden on the bookshelf of your room at *La Chabanais*. The results were most interesting. I must say that for a man of senior years, your performance and technique on the *chaise d'amour* seem most impressive.' Mrs Adler now stood in front of Bertie and surveyed him with a half-smile which he still contrived to find stimulating; for a moment, he was hopeful she might be about to take off her night robe. Instead she went to one of its pockets and produced a print. 'Look, hold it under the light. Good, isn't it? Aren't there actually two girls there? What *is* that one doing? And isn't that your tattoo?'

Bertie scanned the photograph with what he hoped was *insouciance*, even *ennui*, but wasn't. It certainly looked like him at his favourite Paris haunt a few years ago. He'd never taken much notice of books, and definitely not in his specially dedicated room at Europe's swankiest bordello. The photographer had thoughtfully made sure his royal coat of arms over the bed – such a good joke, it seemed, at the time – was in view. In the foreground was indeed his chair of love, especially constructed to aid the fuller, veteran figure in any number of ways, at least three of which were on display. It was fairly well-known, too, that Bertie had acquired a tattoo of a crusader's cross on his arm on a trip to Jerusalem; less advertised was the tiger on his right buttock, which the passage and gravitational pull of the years had left with a pronounced squint.

Again, past experience helped, along with a certain amount of previous pondering on just such a moment. 'Ah, Irene,' he said, hoping to strike a disappointed but understanding tone which would impart worldly wisdom and even a hint of amusement, and which he imagined was lent an extra touch of sophistication by his slight but detectably German way with English. 'You are not the first delightful and handsome woman to attempt to extract funds from me. You are the first with a photograph, though. Very resourceful. But, tell me, who do you think will publish this? I'll tell you: no one will publish this. They wouldn't dare, on grounds of decency alone.'

Mrs Adler looked not one whit disconcerted. 'And your wife?'

'I'm afraid you do not understand the relationship between me and the Queen. Alix is, as you will know, very beautiful, but she is also very eccentric. She is deaf, but with me, she is also blind. She decided when we met that she was deeply in love with me, and that therefore I could not possibly do any wrong. And so it has remained despite all evidence to the contrary. It is my blessing, and penance. Show her that photograph and she will simply refuse to believe it is me.'

'Really? I'm told she's very jealous of Daisy and Alice,' said Mrs Adler, a tease in her voice as she listed the latest of Bertie's close friends, the Countess of Warwick and the said Mrs Keppel.

Bertie was enticed into a brag. 'The Queen becomes troubled only if she thinks I am in love with someone else. That is not the case with Alice, who mostly stops me from becoming bored. Women are so much more entertaining than men, aren't they? I thought for a little while that I was in love with Daisy but, in the end, she was a little too unpredictable. I need complete predictability where my affections are concerned,' he said, oblivious to the rather obvious contrast with his side of the bargain.

He now went for a little-boyish plea for sympathy. 'It's not as easy as people think, you know, Irene, being a king. There are constant challenges, tribulations, demands, concerns for all his people from which a monarch needs – deserves – consolation and companionship. You are a clever woman, you will understand the rewards for providing such solace and support. So, come on, why don't you drop these silly little plots and sit back down next to me?'

Any blackmailer worth his or her viperous implacability would have been impressed with Mrs Adler, who did not falter but instead went to her other pocket. 'Very well, Bertie, I regret we cannot do business on my original terms. This is the second photograph. You will see it features you again, and this time, very clearly, what you might like to term your little, ah, how shall we say delicately, *Bertie*. In short, if you'll pardon the phrase, it's exactly the sort of little thing to make a chap a laughing stock if it were to be widely circulated, wouldn't you say?'

Mrs Adler had scored. Bertie was a proud man. He was proud of the way he had endured his insufferable father, and, much more lengthily – much more! – his insufferable mother. He was proud of the rapport he had built up over the years with the public, his instinctive understanding of what it wanted from a king (if not from a prince). He was proud of his political instinct and astuteness, whether at home with foxy fellows like Rosebery and Asquith, or abroad, where he had been using his family connections – Victoria's children had clambered onto most of the European thrones – with aplomb to applause.

But, despite all this, and for reasons he wouldn't have been able to explain even if he'd thought about them (come in again, Herr Dr Freud), he was proudest of his reputation as a ladies' man. That reputation, built up over so many years, and with so many beauties, had survived intact, despite the cooling of his ardour noticed earlier. And to have it held up to scorn now...

Apart from that, he had always been serially underestimated. Time would tell if the beauteous Mrs Adler had made the same mistake. For now, the king betrayed little. 'A trick of the light, I'd say. Not sure what anyone would make of that. And you want £50,000 for it? I admire your cheek, my dear.'

'Actually, Bertie, there's something else. I'd like to be a duchess. I've been doing a little light reading and discovered that there hasn't been a Duchess of Portsmouth since Charles II's mistress. Quite apt. Give me that and the £50,000, and I will give you the photographs. Think about it, Bertie.'

Mrs Adler turned to leave. In profile she was perhaps even more magnificent. 'I don't suppose,' said Bertie, 'there's any chance of a little jig-a-jig before you go?'

There hadn't been.

And, two days and some achingly polite exchanges later, even the imperturbable Bertie was growing concerned, mostly at his inability to come up with a solution to the Adler Matter, as he now termed it. The ridicule point had been well made: Bertie was so sensitive to it that he felt unable even to consult with his private secretary, Spry, a highly efficient, intelligent but slightly supercilious fellow whom he already suspected of not taking him entirely seriously. The pity was that Spry's predecessor, Sir Francis Howerd, would have been precisely the man to take command. Such a shame that he had fatally overexerted himself with a rating after the last Spithead Review. Still without a solution, Bertie finally drifted off, and dreamt about his mother and cold trout.

THE NEXT MORNING, AFTER BREAKFAST, AT WHICH HE HAD managed the porridge, sardines, grilled cutlets, coffee, hot chocolate, bread, butter and honey but passed, unusually, on the curried eggs, Bertie found himself in Elsie's marvellous rose garden, undistracted by the blooms, scents and high light of a Yorkshire summer morning. It was a rare moment alone, without even Caesar, now being taken for a walk by the less than enthusiastic Hancock, who found the terrier rather smelly. The faithful Raab stood at a distance, thinking about pork chops. Solitude was not something Bertie enjoyed at the best of times, but he needed it for another unpopular activity, deep thought. The regal brow was clouded, and not just by the smoke from his inevitable cigar. This was because, in the chatter, chaff and general communication of the not-that-interesting, he had heard Mrs Adler confide to Elsie, as he was meant to, that she would be forced to take her leave tomorrow, since a vital matter had arisen that required her attention in London. She would, she said, be seeking an audience with the king later to make her farewell.

It was at this fateful moment that Freddy Eynsford Hill entered the rose garden. His mood was in sharp contrast to that of his monarch. For Freddy was that singular specimen in the upper reaches of Edwardian society, a man still in love with his wife. Not the sharpest of men, Freddy, but a loyal, reliable fellow whose path through life was eased by the support of his beautiful wife's connections. It was her suggestion that he took a turn in the garden while she readied herself for the rigours of the day and Freddy, obedient as ever, was now sauntering through the garden while singing a cheerful little ditty about larks and lilacs being particularly prevalent when his love was near. A topical ad-libbed attempt to include roses was not a great success, but Freddy didn't care, especially as he was now being hailed by Bertie.

'Eynsford Hill, isn't it?'

'Rather, Your Majesty, sire!' Freddy sketched something between a bow and a curtsey as his monocle fell out. The king waved this away with his cigar hand.

'Met your wife. Charming.'

'Gosh, I should say so! An absolute pippin, the mull in the mulligatawny. What she sees in young Freddy is a mystery, but I've been as head over heels as a giddy aunt since I first clapped the old mince pies on her!'

Bertie, despite everything, was surprised to find himself warming to Freddy, even if he didn't quite follow all he was saying. The king could be a terrible snob but he liked the energy of the young. There was something familiar about this one, too, in a good way, and his dress for the shoot was beyond criticism.

'Mince pies!? What on earth are you blathering about, sir?'

Being artless has its advantages; many would have been taken aback to be talking to the king, but this didn't occur to Freddy. 'Sorry, Your Majesty, it's the new small talk. Mince pies – eyes, do you see? Killing, isn't it? Elizabeth is a whizz at it.'

'Elizabeth?'

'My wife, Your Majesty. Elizabeth Eynsford Hill, the darling poppet that she is.'

Bertie was as surprised by this as by anything else about Freddy: he had thought Mrs Eynsford Hill far too cool and correct for slang. He made one of his usual mental notes in the disproportionately large area he reserved for that sort of thing. But there really was something about Freddy.

'Do I know your father, Eynsford Hill?'

'Well, to be honest, Your Majesty, I haven't the foggiest. I never knew him, and the mater is pretty oyster-like on the matter. All I really know is that it was a whirlwind romance and that he was eaten by a lion on the honeymoon, which put rather a dampener on things, as you might imagine. And that's about the top and copper of it, I'm afraid… oh, yes, sorry, copper bottom, top and bottom.

Really, thought Bertie, Elsie does know the most extraordinary people. But then, he reflected, so did he. And he liked the cut of this open, enthusiastic young fellow's jib. A plan was beginning to form in the monarchical mind.

'Tell me, do you like risk?'

'Risk? I should say so! If there's any derring to do, Freddy's your man! Ask anyone about Eynsford Hill and the Boat Race. Only last month I took on the Gran Paradiso Challenge and triumphed!'

The king was impressed. The seeds of a misunderstanding were sown. Bertie thought Freddy was indicating participation in the Oxford and Cambridge rowing competition, while he was, in fact, referring to the high jinks that tended to take place following it in the evening. Nor was he talking about conquering that legendary alpine mountain but rather the establishment of the same name in Old Compton Street whose Challenge involved standing on one's head and drinking a bottle of champagne while being tickled under the chin and elsewhere by an exotic dancer.

'Hmm. Any experience of the clandestine?'

'Absolutely. I quite often have a go and I'm pretty good at it even if I say so myself!'

Again, confusion: Freddy was talking about the latest dance imported from France. Bertie had already decided, on instinct but rightly, that Freddy was a man to be trusted. He now felt, wrongly, that he was the man for a daring mission.

'Good. Would you be prepared to undertake a mission of the utmost delicacy for me?'

Freddy had by nature a positive attitude and was most eager to be amenable, even if his comprehension sometimes wasn't quite up to snuff. This had won him the heart, against the odds, of his wife, but it had also led to several, popular Freddy word, 'scrapes'.

'I should cocoa, Your Majesty! How can I be of service?'

'Listen very carefully. Do you know Mrs Adler?'

'Yes, indeed, the corker with the mysterious air?'

'Precisely. She has some things of great value to me, and I want you to steal them.'

Freddy, as we say, though sunny, was not bright. There are, all the same, certain suggestions and situations that provoke a ripple in the most tranquil and untroubled of waters. That ripple, eventually, caused Freddy's eyes to open very wide indeed, with the inevitable consequence for his monocle, while his jaw simultaneously took off in a southerly direction. Bertie, observing the marked similarity to a baffled bream, had a momentary doubt about his man, but instantly dismissed it in preference for swift, decisive action.

'A little irregular, I know,' he now told Freddy. 'But, I have to tell you, Eynsford Hill, Mrs Adler is more than a little irregular herself. She may be beautiful, but she is not a good woman. Not an honest woman, Eynsford Hill. She has some photographs which in some lights could pass for photographs of me. They were taken in Paris at an establishment I might have visited a few times. Reckless of the truth, but mindful of the embarrassment they might cause me, she is demanding a large sum of money for them. I want you to go to her room and take them.'

'Gosh. What larks, eh?' said Freddy, a little doubtfully. He had sneaked into a few bedrooms in his time, but mostly to make apple-pie beds. Nevertheless, this was the king. 'Right-ho, Your Majesty. Under the cover of darkness, eh? In and out like a mouse?'

Bertie was encouraged. 'Exactly. I shall arrange for Mrs Adler to find it necessary to leave her room some time after the party retires. You will be waiting, concealed, and will enter the room and retrieve the photographs, which you will return to me here tomorrow morning. Clear?'

Freddy felt much reassured by this regally crisp confidence. 'As mud, sire. Daring, decisive action. I'm your man.'

'Good. No one must know about this, not even your wife. I haven't told my closest staff. It is a matter, obviously, of the utmost delicacy and discretion. Let us have no further communication until tomorrow. Good luck, Eynsford Hill.'

The king turned and left, relieved to have acted. Freddy for his part brimmed with pride, wonder and anticipation. A more reflective character might have also felt extreme apprehension tinged with blind panic; so perhaps Bertie had indeed made the right choice. Neither of them had spotted a man wearing a fairly obvious wig hiding in the shrubbery.

THE DAY PROCEEDED MUCH AS ANY OTHER WHEN KING Edward VII was at a shooting party: feathered elimination accomplished with a joyless determination sustained by extravagant amounts of sustenance. Only a socialist would have suggested that the exercise was invented to give those with nothing to do something to do.

Elsie, certainly not at home to any misgivings of that sort, was feeling rather pleased with the way the royal visit was proceeding. It was all ridiculously expensive, of course, but the Risings had done remarkably well out of the discovery of coal to the south of their large estate just after they'd bought it for a song from the Rochesters following the fire; so well, in fact, that Edward Rising had been able to become the first Lord Thornfield. None of the staff had been too drunk, and the guests had turned out really quite well, mostly on account of the stimulating beauty of the two newcomers, the Mesdames Adler and Eynsford Hill. A pity Mrs Adler was leaving tomorrow, but Elsie had watched her taking leave of Bertie and making her excuses, and he had still seemed much taken with her; indeed, if Elsie read it aright, and she knew the form, matters might be going further before tomorrow's departure. She sighed, but with resignation rather than regret: life with Bertie had been demanding. Not that she wouldn't mind a bit more excitement now, she thought, looking across to the other side of the room where Lord Thornfield gently slumbered as most of the party, including Freddy, clustered around either the luminous Mrs Eynsford Hill or the lustrous Mrs Adler, before the King commanded the inevitable game of Bridge (mostly so he wouldn't have to talk to anyone too much).

Bertie called time a little earlier than usual, about half-past twelve. Within an hour of the company retiring, Fairfield Hall was sleepily silent, apart from Freddy, Bertie and Mrs Adler. Freddie had not had long to wait before his wife fell into her usual deep and contented sleep; he then tiptoed along the corridors in the gloom towards Mrs Adler's room. All was going well until a floorboard close by creaked so loudly under his feet it sounded like a wild cry – these old houses! – but he had quickly slipped behind a convenient suit of armour just before Mrs Adler came out of her room, surveyed the empty corridor, and went back in.

Freddy waited, keeping alert by trying to remember past winners of the Gold Cup at Ascot, an event he rarely missed. By a remarkable coincidence, he was just building to the stunning victory by Persimmon, Bertie's horse, in 1897, when Mrs Adler came out of her room again and began to make her way royalwards. Even at this moment of high tension, he couldn't help noticing what a terrific popsy she was.

Well. Whither? The meeting in Bertie's room, or Freddy's entry into Mrs Adler's? Royalty must take precedence. Procedure followed that of her earlier visit, down to Bertie's stirrings, and his attempts to have her sit next to him on his bed as he suggested once again that she 'should forget this silly little shenanigans and have a bit of fun'. Rebuffed once again, he began a slightly stilted discourse on the original Duchess of Portsmouth in order to give Freddy enough time to search the aspirant's room. Mrs Adler seemed a little impatient and unwilling to listen, even when Bertie went into some fascinating detail about the royal yacht that had been named after the original Duchess, 'Very nice little sloop, apparently, beam 21 feet, draught 10 feet, it was actually called HMY *Fubbs* because that was Charles II's nickname for her. It means plump or chubby, which was fashionable at the time, not like you, of course, Irene. Launched in 1682, had a long career, two rebuilds...'

Mrs Adler placed a hand on his arm, raising fresh hope in the eternally springing monarch. 'This is all very fascinating, Bertie dear,' she whispered in her most low and attractive American drawl, 'but what about the more pressing matter of my £50,000?'

Bertie reverted to bluster, mentioning that these things took time to arrange, it was a lot of money, would she be satisfied with £25,000 if he chucked in another couple of titles, Marchioness of Margate, for example, and Countess of Canvey…? Mrs Adler remained unimpressed; Bertie suggested they have a series of meetings to finalise matters, dot the i's and cross the t's, that sort of thing, afternoon tea, some delightful intimacies…? 'Bertie, I am going now. I shall require the money next time we meet in exchange for my charming photographs. If you do not have a banker's draft or equivalent then, I shall circulate them. Good night, I shall be leaving before lunch.'

Bertie was worried about giving Freddy enough time, and saw a neat coincidence of objectives. 'Don't go just yet, Irene, I don't suppose there's any chance of a spot of the old rumpscuttle first?'

There wasn't.

Freddy, meanwhile, wasn't having a lot of luck, either. Sensibly, especially for him, he had decided on a methodical search, starting with the most obvious place, Mrs Adler's bureau, then moving on to her dressing table, then chest of drawers. This entailed a lot of drawers, Freddy's fingers were not the nimblest, and he kept losing count. Having finally drawn a blank, he was approaching the wardrobe when he heard the floorboard outside in the corridor give that same moan as before. Mrs Adler was returning! Many men would have panicked: Freddy certainly did. He decided, if his thought process can be so dignified, to hide in the wardrobe. This would have been a more successful ploy, if, on flinging the door open, he had not discovered Lord Thornfield inside. The peer placed a finger to his lips but showed no signs of moving to one side to allow Freddy in. Freddy quickly closed the wardrobe door and rushed to hide under Mrs Adler's bed. This, too, would have been a more successful ploy if he had not discovered the man with the ill-fitting wig already hiding there.

Mrs Adler entered, pensive. Freddy was nowhere to be seen. He had taken the other route usual in such scenes, leaving through the window which was now being closed by Mrs Adler, pensively. His plight, though, was not as desperate as one who had not attended a certain type of public school might suppose. Many a time after a dormitory raid at dear old Tweeton Freddy had found himself on such a ledge. The challenge now, as always, was to find the right window to climb back through. Lack of knowledge of the geography, the difficulty of counting on his fingers in such a perilous position and the traditional outcome of such scrapes were all against him. The voice that came from the bed as he climbed into his room of choice was not that of dear Eliza. 'Well, hello,' said Spry.

Freddy, understandably, froze. 'If you're after a touch of adventure, I'd be more than happy to oblige,' said Spry. 'And don't worry, I've seen through the dumb ox act. Come over here beside me, big boy.'

This was not a choice favoured by Freddy, who had somehow contrived to remain remarkably and uncomplicatedly orthodox despite Tweeton. After a substantial pause, he moved into default setting, looked down at his watch and made rapidly for the door, declaring as he went, 'Gosh! Is that the time?! Really must dash! Lunch soon? Pip-pip!'

The return to his own room was never going to go well but he excelled even himself by falling over the dressing table stool and clutching at the table's lace covering as he went down, bringing Eliza's brushes and other accoutrements crashing after him.

'Strike an illumination, who is that gaining access to my chamber unannounced?' shouted Eliza, her exquisite diction and eccentric grammar splendidly unaffected by alarm.

'Sorry, darling, did I wake you?' responded Freddy, a touch redundantly.

'Lord love a duck, Freddy! You did not half give me a right turn! Pray tell of what you have been doing of?'

Freddy, as we have seen, was no artist of artifice, especially after such an escapade; he proceeded to tell his darling wife everything.

'Well,' said Eliza, 'you do appear to have manoeuvred yourself into something of a cheese and pickle, my dearest. I expect Eliza will have to sort it, cushty.'

Freddy stared at Eliza with the awed and adoring look she could not resist. 'Do you really think you can, mine own? The old crowned head happy, vicious villainess vanquished, that sort of thing?'

'I've got my dear father out of far worse than that, the shifty old soak. I shall attend to Madame Doodah on the morrow. Now let us turn the old trotters northwards and get some bleeding kip.'

BREAKFAST DISCLOSED THE FAMILIAR GAGGLE AROUND ELIZA, punctuated by the usual delighted guffaws from the males and bright but puzzled smiles from their mates as Mrs Eynsford Hill gave English her unique treatment. Many rumours surrounded her provenance; the latest was that she was from southern Lancashire, where, allegedly, all spoke in this entertaining way. Eliza, aware that none of the society she mixed in would ever visit there, mildly encouraged this. (There was the Earl of Derby, who lived just outside Liverpool, but, apparently, although he did speak to the locals, he never listened.)

In the midst of it all, while her admirers were held by the way she sipped her tea from her saucer, Eliza was studying Mrs Adler, who commanded a smaller but possibly more sophisticated group, closer to Bertie. The monarch himself, who was dressed in Hancock's favourite shooting choice, a Norfolk jacket with just a suggestion of fuchsia amid the russet, preferred to concentrate on his heroic input in silence, aided by Elsie, who knew this, and Lord Thornfield, who was not disposed to break it in any case.

His Lordship appeared entirely undisturbed by his time in Mrs Adler's wardrobe. Bertie, on the other hand, while maintaining an impressive rate of steady ingestion, particularly of the grilled cutlets, was also trying to attract Freddy's attention. Freddy, unsurprisingly, was doing his best to evade the regal signals, and had opted for a half-smiling, steady gaze at his sausages.

What Freddy generally referred to as 'a sticky moment' could not be long delayed. The king rose; the rose garden beckoned.

As the breakfast party broke up, Eliza whispered, beautifully aspirated, to Freddy, 'Here, F, I have clocked that Adler bird heretofore. Leave it to old Eliza.' She then laid a dainty index finger alongside her fine retroussé nose, and winked. Somewhat buoyed, Freddy prepared to encounter his liege.

Who was not in any way a mirror of the Yorkshire sun suffusing Elsie's prize specimens. Anyone tapping Bertie's barometer would not be leaving home without galoshes. As Freddy approached, he waved away Spry, who left giving Freddy his second wink of the day, and it was only nine o'clock. Raab stood at a discreet distance, ignoring the man with the ill-fitting wig, now supplemented by an obviously false nose, who was once again hiding in the shrubbery.

'What-ho, sire!' Freddy aimed for the carefree, not necessarily a good tactic in the circumstances. But just as faint heart never won fair lady, the ones that do are not necessarily deeply sensitive to the emotions of others.

'Yes, yes, Eynsford Hill,' snapped Bertie, noticing once again in spite of himself Freddy's similarity in looks to someone he couldn't quite place. 'Where have you been? Have you got the pictures?'

'Not exactly, Your Majesty.'

'What do you mean? Have you got them or haven't you?'

'Well, to be perfectly frank and above board, no.'

'No? No! What happened?'

'I'm afraid the lady in question returned to her room rather sooner than I expected, so I didn't have time. I don't know where she'd been, but she mustn't have enjoyed it because she'd clearly scarpered as soon as she could. Sorry, sire, left. I must say, if I was the roving kind, which of course I'm not, because who would be when you're married to the most beautiful and terribly clever knee of a bee in England, but if I was, I'm pretty sure the old Eynsford Hill magic could have detained Mrs A for a touch longer than five minutes! What do you think, Your Majesty?'

'Never mind that now. What are you going to do? She will be leaving shortly.'

Even Freddy could see that the king was agitated; if the way he was pounding the palm of his left hand with his right fist wasn't enough of a clue, there was also the slight but insistent twitch to the right eyebrow, and a rising colour that it was sounder not to blame on the cutlets.

'A minor hitch, sire, worry not; it will all be tickety-boo in the twitch of a heifer's wotnot. I detect doubt, but worry not. I mean I would possibly be a bit jumpy myself, doing a touch of the alternate foot hopping, if it was just old Freddy, but I'm delighted to tell you that Elizabeth has now taken over the case and will shortly be interviewing the Adler. Expect resolution and success on the jolly old instant! Mrs A is toast!'

'Toast!? Your wife! What can she possibly do? I'm now beginning to regret my decision to ask you for help, Eynsford Hill. I'm going to leave now, because I don't want to lose what little is left of my temper, and I have a lot of birds to kill. Raab!'

'No, Your Majesty, I don't think you understand about Elizabeth. Not only is she radiantly beautiful, she is also wonderfully shrewd, or "sharper than the toot on a rozzer's whistle", as she so colourfully puts it, ripping little sweet pea that she is. Her family is of a deuced eccentric turn, don't you know. She has had a more lively time of it than many, and spent some time working in direct floral marketing. An aunt died in suspicious circumstances, which had quite an effect on her, as it bally well would, wouldn't it, sire? All to do with the theft of a straw hat as she puts it and I understand it, which isn't always the same thing.'

'The theft of a straw hat?! Raab! Eynsford Hill, I've taken a liking to you for some unknown reason, but you do talk the most absolute rot. Ask Mrs Eynsford Hill to come to see me for tea. Let's hope she makes more sense. Raab!'

Bertie stalked off, bent on avian execution, trailed by Raab, who was not built for speed. Freddy nodded amiably at him as he passed. 'Mornin'. Pukka day for bang-bangs, what?'

Raab grunted, torn between following his king and being courteous to someone who, no matter how he appeared, had just been in audience with Bertie.

Freddy lowered his voice. 'Something I've been meaning to ask you. That chap over there, the one with the wig, false nose and vivid facial scar, in the shrubbery, the one Caesar is now peeing on. I keep seeing him around. Who is he?'

'Ah, yes, sir, you don't want to be worrying yourself about him. That's Holmes, one of my chaps. Keen, but some way to go in the disguise department, as you can see. Can't fault the way he's dealing with Caesar, though, hasn't moved a muscle, has he? And he's better than Watson, the red-faced bloke who spilt hot soup all over Lord Thornfield at dinner last night. Tough old bird, mine hoste, isn't he? Didn't seem to feel a thing. Nothing escapes me, sir.'

'What do you make of Mrs Adler?'

'Charming woman. Taken a bit of a shine to me, as it happens. Lovely smile. You can always tell the genuine ones. Must be off now, sir. Got to keep an eye on the beaters. I've a bet with Boycott that the Russian count will hit at least five of them today. You shooting, sir?'

'No, no, you carry on, old chap.'

Freddy didn't like to mention that he had been advised by the same Boycott in the very strongest terms not to bother turning up today after he had somehow contrived to wing an owl. Instead, he took a stroll through some more of Elsie's gardens. Emerging, after quite some time, from the ornamental maze, he espied Mrs Adler coming out of the Hall and climbing into the estate brougham, clearly on her way to Heathcliff station. The car began to climb the moorland drive, watched by Cummings, the butler, and one of the footmen, Jenrick, as they compared empty palms disappointedly.

'Wotcher,' said Eliza, pronouncing it with the same careful dignity and precise modulation she allowed even her most colourful turns of phrase. Freddy jumped. 'Crikey, Eliza! How *do* you do that? One moment I am alone and palely loitering as a cloud or daffodil or whatever, the next – poof! – you're there!'

'Came in very handy when one wished to evade the attention of the Old Bill in my previous calling, it did. Anyway, I don't think we will be troubled by her nibs any further.'

'Eliza, you really are the eel in the jolly old jelly! How on earth did you manage it?'

'Well, it's a little complicated to explain to you, Freddy. You'd better just Adam and Eve it, my darling diamond delightfully dopey geezer.'

Freddy didn't always completely understand what Eliza said to him, but he generally got the drift, and this sounded good on the whole. 'Tiptop. You've got to explain it to the king, anyway. He wants to see you for tea. I must say he seemed more than a little mobbed up about things, which was a tiddly touch hurtful after all my gallant efforts last night.'

'You did very well, Freddy. I've just dressed it up a bit, put a bow round it, that sort of ticket. Sound. You just leave old Bertie to me. He'll be grinning like a creamed-up kitty when your old E has finished with him. Now I'm off to the shoot lunch. Coming?'

Freddy had not revealed his Boycott boycott, and said he had some letters to write. Eliza, previously unaware of this unlikely accomplishment, smiled quizzically (but fondly) and left the young hero in search of a discreet sofa upon which to recover from his recent overexcitements.

ON HIS RETURN FROM THE SHOOT, BERTIE DISCOVERED THAT Mrs Adler had left. The day had been moderately successful – another four score of grouse for him, plus rabbit pie, devilled eggs, cold pigeon, truffles and trotters – and only three beaters winged, all flesh wounds. Hancock eased him out of his clothes and into his bath with clucking fuss and perched on a low stool alongside, holding a tray with a cigar and a brandy, rather in the manner of a dissolute nurse. Bertie's cigar was lit reverentially. He took a sip of the brandy, and continuing to stare in front of him, said, 'Anything doing here, Hancock?'

'Nothing much to detain us, Your Majesty. Mrs Adler left while you were out frightening those birds.'

'Hmm. Did she say anything of interest?'

'Not so much what she said as what she didn't do, Your Majesty. No tips for anyone, including Cummings the butler. He's very miffed. Touch uppity if you ask me. Apparently he was at Barnard Castle before coming here but left because he didn't see things quite the same way as everybody else up there. Or down here, come to that.'

Bertie wasn't really listening, his mind being on the recently departed and apparently stingy Mrs Adler. What did that mean?

'Mrs Eynsford Hill and I will be taking tea, Hancock.'

'Yes, Your Majesty. The mauve smoking jacket with the comfortable trousers? That's usually a successful combination, especially when teamed with the primrose cravat. I understand Mrs Eynsford Hill is rather modern, Your Majesty. Where will you be, Your Majesty?'

'Lady Thornfield has set aside a parlour for us. Perhaps Cummings can tear himself away from his disappointment to tell you which one it is. The trouble with servants like him is that they start to think they're in charge.'

A little later, Eliza was duly ushered into the parlour. Elsie's choice of decor was still determinedly that in favour when the old Queen was in her pomp, so the room was packed with bewildering clusters of overelaborate chairs surrounding so many occasional tables crowded with ornaments that it closely resembled one of the new emporia patronised by those who had to buy their own furniture. The effect was accentuated by Bertie's instruction that the curtains should be drawn against the late September sun in order to present him in the best (lack of) light.

Many – the very many – who had gone before had found this kind of audience initially intimidating and always imposing, but Eliza, as we have seen, was a little different, and showed not the slightest sign of concern when the Emperor of India invited her to share his sofa for their interview *à deux*.

Bertie, as we have also seen, was not a man to be undistracted by a fine-looking woman. 'Mrs Eynsford Hill, how delightful to see you. I'm happy for this opportunity to get to know you better. I don't think we'd met before this splendid visit to Lady Thornfield's?'

'No, indeed, Your Majesty, we had not. Although I'd seen you quite a few times as you was on your way to the opera in Covent Garden.'

'You enjoy the opera, Mrs Eynsford Hill? I'm very fond of it for the spectacle, but I also like it because you can disappear for half an hour or so and return to find yourself with no more of an idea of what's going on than when you left. Or you can leave for good, same thing, won't miss much as they always die. And for some odd reason it's not in English.'

Eliza responded with her usual enthusiasm and unique mixture of perfect enunciation, eccentric grammar and informal vocabulary. 'I couldn't agree more, Your Majesty. I was otherwise engaged in Covent Garden, but as far as I'm concerned you really cannot be improving upon a sing-song round the old joanna. You shot very well today, by all accounts. Everyone at lunch was most complimentary, including the Russian count. My, but he can shift a few, can he not? I am prattling on, though, as you will want to know about Mrs Adler.'

'Indeed I do. Your husband is a lively young man who has earned my trust. But I fear he was not yet quite ready for the mission with which I entrusted him. Nevertheless, he was entirely, even touchingly, confident that you would be able to resolve my little difficulty, Mrs Eynsford Hill. I, rightly or wrongly, was a little dubious that such a beautiful and clearly innocent young woman would have the requisite skills, subtlety and experience, but Eynsford Hill was adamant. "Sharper than the toot of a rozzer's whistle", was the way I think he put it.'

'That's my Freddy, Your Majesty. Only on nodding terms with his onions sometimes, but in this case, entirely correct. I had an interesting early life for one of my station, before I was taken up by two gentlemen who introduced me to the finer things in life and made me what I am today. One, a professor, was particularly helpful. The other was a colonel, and rather nicer. They continue to support me to this day.'

'I hope no advantage was taken.'

'Bless Your Majesty, no. They were on the other omnibus.'

'The other omnibus?'

'Ah, Your Majesty! You have knocked around a bit. The other omnibus – the professor and the colonel liked each other, a lot. A lot.' Here Eliza winked at her monarch; this was a first, but it did help him gather her meaning.

'But I'm rambling on again. Mrs Adler. I thought I'd seen her before as soon as I clapped the old mince pies on her. And soon I was sure.'

'I'm not sure I entirely follow. You knew her in America?'

'America? Bethnal Green, more like. I mean, she's tarted herself up a lot since then, but at one time Irene Trotter was a bit of a girl, if you follow my meaning, Your Majesty. It was about that time she became acquainted with my father, which never worked out well for anyone, believe me. Mrs Adler, funnily enough, was either my second or third "stepmother", I really can't remember which, as my father has had at least six of them, a bit like your old Henry, although Dad wasn't quite so formal, and he didn't bump any of them off, either, so far as I know, and I don't know all, especially as he's now turned up his toes, that's right, he collapsed, croaked and carked after Just Deserts came in 50/1 at good old Ascot.'

Bertie's impatience was just about being held in check by Eliza's beguiling beauty and extraordinary turn of phrase. 'I'm sorry, Mrs Eynsford Hill, but the point of this?'

'Forgive me, Your Majesty, I've gone off on one again, haven't I? No, the point of this is that Irene Trotter now Adler is definitely the one who done my poor old aunt in for her new straw hat.'

Bertie saw a chink of light. 'Ah, Eynsford Hill was recalling the same incident, done her in?'

'Ah, like I say, Your Sire, I was not moving in quite the same circles in them days. Done the old aunty in, knocked her off, murdered her, all for the sake of a bloomin' straw hat. It was a nice one, though. Irene hasn't recognised me, as, like I say, I have moved up more rungs than a window cleaner since then I have. Anyway, as the actress said to the bishop, when we had our little palaver this morning I suggested that she might not want the world to know she isn't Irene Adler of New York, mezzo soprano, but Irene Trotter of London East, straw-hat coveter and suspected aunt eliminator.'

The king had never been hailed for his patience, even with a beautiful woman. 'Yes, yes, Mrs Eynsford Hill, but what about the, ah, photographs?'

Eliza's enunciation remained unruffled. 'All sweet. The problem that my Freddy, and perhaps even you, Your Majesty, begging your regal pardon, did not really get your noddles round is that getting the photographs is all very well, but what you've got to make sure is that Ma Trotter doesn't print and circulate any more from the negatives. So I suggested that my griff put the mockers on her griff and I'd stay as schtum as a harp with no strings so long as she stayed the same. I would be happy to bet Mayfair against Mile End that you won't be hearing from that particular piece of personage again.'

Bertie's recent exposure to both the Eynsford Hills had much sharpened his comprehension of the 'new small talk', and this, allied to his acute interest in the subject matter, allowed him to deduce that Eliza had indeed taken care, cushty, of the matter, although he was still a little sketchy on 'griff', 'schtum' and 'negatives'. Nevertheless, much relieved, he allowed himself to move seamlessly (as he saw it) into best-throaty-Bertie-choked-by-emotion seduction mode.

'My dear Mrs Eynsford Hill, your country is in your debt. Your king is in your debt.'

Said king now moved a little closer to Eliza and gazed into her eyes with a look he judged to be sensitive, friendly, grateful and irresistible. Eliza gazed back with a look he judged to be sensitive, friendly, grateful and unresisting. Bertie went for the Bertie lunge and found his face snuggling in soft, yielding contours. Unfortunately, for the second time in as many days, it was furnishings rather than flesh, as Eliza had also artfully evaded her rampant ruler.

She was, in truth, rather tickled to discover that Bertie, although legendary for his ways with women, was no more sophisticated in his approach work than many another ruddy-faced gentlemen after a few on a Friday night down the old rubadub. She judged it wiser, though, not to reveal this, relying instead on the truth.

'Your Majesty, I really am tremendously flattered but I am sworn to another. My Freddy might not be everyone's cup of cheering char, but I love him. I love him because he is kind, generous, sweet and he loves me.' (She might have added that Freddy had not even taken her hand until their sixth meeting, but again exercised her better judgment.)

'Other women might want someone masterful and dashing and exciting, but I want someone to rest his head on my knee, warm and tender as he can be. That is abso-bloomin'-lutely lovely, and that is what I've got with my Freddy. Like I say, it's true that when they were handing out the old cogitating clobber, Freddy was at the wrong hatch, but his hatch was the one for goodness and heart and sweet simplicity, and that, Your Majesty is why, although honoured by your attentions as any woman in her right mind would be, I must ask you to excuse me. Because I love my Freddy, Freddy Eynsford Hill!'

'Did someone call?' It was also true that Freddy had an enviable aptitude for sleep, and, if not interrupted, could push out the old zeds right around the clock, especially if his previous engagement had interrupted them as much as they had the night before. Hence his sudden rising now from a sofa in the far corner of the parlour whither he had retired (much) earlier.

'What ho, Liza! Your Majesty, splendid to see you again! Fancy meeting you like this! I was reading a fascinating article on women's suffrage and must have dropped off.'

Freddy came bounding over, leaving several occasional tables wobbling dangerously. 'Hello, my darling,' said Eliza enthusiastically. The king, beginning to feel his grasp slipping and wondering whether he was asleep himself, patted his waistcoat absently.

'Do have one of mine, sir!' said Freddy, producing his cigarette case and flipping it open. It was a particularly exuberant case, a wedding gift from the late Mr Doolittle, who had come into some little money from an American trust on the recommendation of one of his wife's mentors, Professor Henry Higgins. Opposite the row of cigarettes sat two small photographs in the manner of a locket. Bertie, refusing a cigarette in favour of a large cigar, noticed that one of the photos was of Eliza, but it was the other that took his attention.

'Who is that, Eynsford Hill?' he asked, with more than usual interest for someone who had spent a life feigning, and often failing to feign, polite interest.

'That is dear Mama, Your Majesty, taken when she was younger.'

'Tell me, was your mother ever a governess?'

'Indeed she was, sire, before she married Papa. Miss Catherine Chrism, bringer of wisdom to several noble families before she arrived at Wilde Hall, Herts, and into the heart of its son, the late and tragic Hereward Edward Eynsford Hill.'

'Good lord,' exclaimed Bertie, sitting back down on the sofa, heavily. 'As I live and breathe, Catty Chrism!'

Freddy was taken aback, and slightly sideways as well. 'You know Mama, sire?' he said

'Yes, I did know her,' said Bertie, now pulling furiously on his cigar. 'But I haven't seen her for 30 years.'

'For 30 years? That's a jolly coincidence – I'm 30!'

A fittingly pregnant silence fell on the three as they pondered, with varying success, the implications of this revelation. It was broken by the parlour door being flung open and the sound of a loud voice which betrayed a childhood in one of Europe's northern kingdoms.

'Bertie!' cried Queen Alexandra, for it was none other than the Consort herself, the beautiful, elegant and unusual Princess of Schleswig-Holstein-Sonderburg-Glucksburg. 'Surprises! The confounded Royal Train broke itself again coming up one of these sticky Yorkshire hills, so I thought I would take the opportunity to see my wonderful Bertie and travel on to Balmoral tomorrow. And who are these young people being?'

'Alix!' cried Bertie, weakly. A man who lived by routine, even for his adventures, could only take so much excitement in one day. He climbed to his feet, a little unsteadily. 'How marvellous to see you. You didn't think to send ahead? We could have prepared for you!'

'Now, Bertie, I know you don't like your routine upset, but we were so close to you, weren't we? I did send young Lieutenant George Mainwaring on ahead to alert Elsie but there was a misunderstanding and he was attacked by one of your undercover detectives who leapt out at him from the ha-ha. The shock was so great that it brought on his stammer, with the result that he couldn't explain himself, and your man, House or some such, threw him in the wine cellar, where Elsie has gone to rescue him. I'm not sure how useful Georgie will be if he has to order an attack, but there you are, he does look very fine in uniform, splendid calves. Now come on, who are these young people?'

Bertie looked meaningfully at Freddy and Eliza nudged him in the ribs. Freddy, contrary to the expectations of both, rose to the challenge, or, rather, bowed to it. 'Freddy Eynsford Hill, Your Majesty, and my wife, Elizabeth.'

Eliza dropped a very elegant curtsey, and all might have gone well but for the Queen's hearing: 'Bill? Ein afford bill? They're charging you here, Bertie? What has happened to Elsie? Didn't you tell me they gave your mother the bill here in the Yorkshire once?'

Bertie was grimacing his way through this misunderstanding; Freddy was still frozen in mid-smile after his introduction exertion; it fell to Eliza to try to straighten matters out. 'No, Your Majesty – Eynsford Hill, not bill. Do you remember the phrase that is a great aid to English elocution? "There are hardly any high hills in Holstein". An old friend taught it to me, along with something about Spain I cannot now remember. But of course Your Majesty has no need to improve her elocution.'

'Euston? No we came from King's Cross. Which reminds me, Bertie. I saw that Mrs Adler at Heathcliff Station, waiting for the next railway south. She was having a long wait and didn't look so happy about it. She was on the opposite platform but she didn't seem to hear me when I shouted across to her. Strange, as she came to see me recently. Young Mainwaring effected the introduction.'

Bertie sat back down on the sofa. The Queen, apparently oblivious to the *haut frisson* she had sent round the small gathering, sat down in a nearby armchair. 'Odd woman. She said she knew of my interest in the photography and wanted to present me with some photographs of you. I had mislaid my spectacles but thought it was best to humour her, so I looked at them and told her they were absolutely lovely and charming and showed you proudly erect and that you looked splendid mounted. She seemed to be expecting a different reaction for some reason, but left them behind. They're still around somewhere, I think, or I might have used them as postcards.' The Queen gave her husband a bright smile and continued. 'You're a little pale, Bertie, haven't you been with your birds today?'

Bertie was indeed a touch pale, and also, by turns, pink, at this fresh instance of Adler treachery. The Queen was now telling Eliza about the Schleswig-Holstein Question and the Prussian perfidy that had stolen these two delightful duchies from her beloved Denmark, before rapidly moving on into some disobliging remarks still at maximum volume concerning Bertie's nephew, 'that crackpot shred of sauerkraut, Willie, who will bring us all into trouble one day. Do you know when he was a little boy he bit both his uncles in the leg during my wedding?'

Eliza sympathised over the loss of the duchies, and the Kaiser, allowing that it did all seem, as she put it, 'a right how's your father... Mind you, at my wedding, Pa took a proper purler and was laid out in the aisle as stiff as a workhouse board. Too much gin.'

'Thin? Much too thin? You should have seen my great aunt, Wilhelmina, the Grand Duchess of Elsinore! She was so thin we had to keep asking her to turn 90 of the degrees so we could see her! And then there was Uncle Vitus, the Bishop of Copenhagen, what a dance he led us in...'

Freddy's lids were beginning to droop. Bertie went out into the rose garden. Caesar followed. Lord Thornfield rose from a seat in a far corner and beckoned his monarch in courtly fashion. The pensive peer then produced two large cigars from his case and two larger brandies from under the seat. The king sat down beside him and the two men sipped, smoked and stared in silent companionable communion. Eventually, Lord Thornfield said, 'Women, eh?' Bertie grunted in assent. 'Marvellous creatures,' continued the suddenly if comparatively voluble peer. 'Should get the vote. Certainly get mine.' Bertie grunted again, then said, 'Take a very big fight for that to happen.'

Elsewhere, Boycott was easing off his boots, Cummings was secreting more silver, Hancock had finished ironing his socks and now had his nose in a rather entertaining book by the young up-and-coming author, P G Wodehouse. Spry was writing his weekly despatch to the German secret service, Watson was discreetly guiding Holmes out of the maze, sensibly ignoring the now supine and completely out for the (Russian) count, and Elsie was trying to calm Mrs Medlock, the housekeeper, who was having to cope with the sudden descent of the Queen and her entourage. Back in the garden, Raab, at his usual discreet distance, was thinking about sausages, while the king and his nobleman had returned to synchronised puffing and mute reflections which produced pensive looks remarkably similar to that worn by Caesar, sitting next to them as the Yorkshire sun began to set in peace, and all too soon, alas, on peace.

Afterword

Some of this is true.

KING EDWARD VII (1841–1910), *known to his family as Bertie after his first name, Albert, was – is – a difficult character to pin down, conveniently label. He was, by turns, and often in the shortest space of time, kind, unkind, sensitive, insensitive, thoughtful, thoughtless, irascible, attentive, snobbish in small ways, generous in larger, intensely loyal, dismissive, wise, and foolish.*

He was a stickler for protocol, correct dress and medals who bowed to servants and allowed himself to be addressed by his mistresses' children as 'Kingy' and played games with them involving racing buttered toast soldiers down the stripes of his trousers. He owned large estates but would picnic by the side of the road. He mixed happily with Jews, and was far more critical of Russian pogroms than his Government. He hated rudeness to Indians, but opposed self-rule for them. He seemed essentially English, but spoke it like a German, rolling his 'r's. He was as happy, if not happier, in the company of women, but opposed votes for them. He had numerous pets, including Caesar, but slaughtered prodigious numbers of birds and animals.

It's possible to see this reflecting the deeper conflict between personal privilege and public duty that continues periodically to trouble our monarchy; a conflict that is the result of the irresistible introduction over centuries of regulation and consistency into personal will and whim, the evolution from absolute to constitutional, the introduction of consent by the ruled to be ruled.

Bertie shifted the balance to duty decisively, but where his strong sense of it came from, and how it matched his extravagant appetites is as unclear as what changed the young Prince Henry into the old Henry VIII, a similar figure in more ways than the physical. The easy answer is, of course, Victoria and Albert, his extraordinary parents. But their sense of duty was predominantly to themselves. Bertie somehow acquired one to his country, and passed it on to his descendants with one obvious exception, his namesake, Edward VIII.

And so he mixed any number of genial and attentive dedications, openings and plantings all over the country with any number of flirtations, shoots, games of baccarat and bridge all over the country in the houses of courtiers at their great expense, and in at least one case, ruination. Our story is set in the rebuilt former home of Mr Rochester, employer and more of Jane Eyre; in reality, the king shot grouse every September at nearby Bolton Abbey, the Yorkshire home of the ridiculously wealthy Devonshires of Chatsworth.

I have given him a valet, a secretary, a detective and a couple of policemen. It was not unknown for him to travel with two valets, a footman, a brusher and more policemen, often mingling in plain clothes, and then there was a lord-in-waiting, a lady-in-waiting and two equerries, all with their own servants. Kaiser Wilhelm, who did behave that badly at Bertie's and Alix's wedding and continued in much the same vein for the rest of his life, also had two hairdressers to accompany him, one responsible solely for the upward sweep of his moustache, much to the the entertainment of Alix, who disliked him even more than did Bertie: 'the fool!'.

When Bertie finally came to the throne, in 1901, at the age of 59, he proved over the next ten years to be a far more sensible constitutional monarch than his capricious mother, despite her having steadfastly, unreasonably and insecurely limited his role as Prince of Wales. His part in achieving the important Entente Cordiale between Britain and France was exaggerated, but still *influential because of his charm, shrewdness and relation to most of the crowned heads of Europe.*

He was bluff, prickly and relentlessly lowbrow, probably thanks to the ridiculously rigorous educational regime Albert insisted upon for him. He rarely read a book, preferring to turn the library at Sandringham into a skittle alley. He loved the opera, but the social aspects of it seem to have been at least equally important; he is also said to have complained at a more avant garde offering that he had been woken up four times by 'that infernal noise'.

His loss of virginity with Nellie Clifton – 'his fall', as his horrified parents put it so significantly – was almost directly responsible for Albert's death after the insanely overanguished consort caught a cold on a walk while he was lengthily remonstrating with his son, leading to typhoid fever and death. Bertie's womanising continued relentlessly thereafter; you can make of what you will that his paramours tended, unlike his lissom wife, to be ample, exemplified by the social adventuress and celebrity, Lily Langtry, and even matronly, as with the aforementioned Alice Keppel.

Perhaps flavours, vignettes are the best way of conveying this contradictory man. Some writers have disapproved of his practical jokes; I'm rather taken with one played on his pompous friend, Lord Hartington, who had been having an affair with the aforementioned and glamorous courtesan, 'Skittles'; when he and Bertie visited Coventry, the then Prince went to a lot of trouble to have a bowling alley included on the tour for no other reason than for the mayor, so instructed, to tell Hartington that the Prince had asked for it as a tribute to His Lordship's love of skittles. In Biarritz, where he spent much time as his health weakened, the authorities had limited the town's beggars to two blind unfortunates who every day rattled their cans at the king's approach, betrayed by a barking Caesar; and every day, the king contributed with the same comment: 'a demain'. My favourite, though, would be the newspaper photograph of the king in earnest conversation with his prime minister, Henry Campbell-Bannerman. 'Peace or War?'

read the caption. In fact, as Campbell-Bannerman later revealed, 'The king wanted to have my opinion whether halibut is better baked or boiled'.

PRINCESS ALEXANDRA VON SCHLESWIG-HOLSTEIN-SONDERBURG-GLÜCKSBURG, Queen Consort of the United Kingdom and British Dominions and Empress Consort of India, was the Danish princess selected for Bertie by his parents. Alix, as she was known, the eldest daughter of the heir presumptive to the Danish throne, was one of a very small pool of eligible partners for Bertie; she was seized upon by Albert, even though Denmark was not an ally of Britain, which favoured the German claim to Schleswig Holstein. This remained a loud and continuing exasperation for Alix when Prussia forcibly annexed the Duchies the year after she became Princess of Wales in 1863.

Hers was another contradictory character. She was loud – she became increasingly deaf – in support of her native country, but almost completely silent on her husband's philandering. It is impossible to ignore the uncanny similarities with a later Princess of Wales, Diana: both were greatly admired for their beauty, both were extremely popular with the public, and both had to contend with less obviously advantaged rivals who, most remarkably, were closely related: Alice Keppel and her great granddaughter, Camilla Parker Bowles.

It's difficult to assess Alix's appeal from photographs (she herself was a keen early photographer), although often she looks ready to break into broad amusement; the few moving images are quick snatches of her comings and goings, taken from too respectful a distance. But the acclaimed grace is there, along with the limp from a knee complaint that she accommodated so well that it became known as the Alexandra Glide, and was even copied by other society ladies.

Bertie and Alix had six children; the eldest and youngest, Albert Victor (Eddy) and John, both died young, Eddy of influenza at 28, John of a seizure associated with his epilepsy at 13. Eddy was not particularly bright, but does not deserve to have been named without convincing evidence as Jack the Ripper on the basis of his alleged homosexuality. He was certainly active sexually, and unwisely, but his taste seems to have been for the opposite rather than the same. There have been similarly inaccurate claims that John was hidden away for shame. Between them came the future king, George, and three princesses kept close by well into their twenties, unkindly – and unfairly – known as The Three Hags. Alix's mothering was of the Diana persuasion: bathing them, reading to them, tucking them up and kissing them goodnight, affectionate, undemanding. There were complaints about unruliness from the stuffy, including, inevitably, Victoria, who nevertheless was charmed by her daughter-in-law, mostly.

When Bertie lay dying, Mrs Keppel showed Alix a letter Bertie had written hoping she would be allowed to visit him in his last hours; Alix, rather splendidly, allowed it. Mrs Keppel was hysterical, Alix showed the calm of the stunned. She refused to allow his body to be taken away for eight days, but conducted herself magnificently, travelling behind the king's coffin as it was taken to Westminster Hall for the lying-in-state, and kneeling beside it at the funeral in Windsor (Victoria had hidden away from Albert's).

The royal advisers were at a loss to compose a message to the nation from her. She solved it by writing her own: 'From the bottom of my poor broken heart I wish to express to the whole nation and our kind people we love so well my deep-felt thanks for all their touching sympathy in my overwhelming sorrow and unspeakable anguish… Give me a thought in your prayers which will comfort and sustain me in all I still have to go through'.

One other glimpse, at Sandringham, when the Queen caught sight of Bertie and Mrs Keppel dismounting in stately fashion after a carriage ride: Alix was so suddenly struck by the advancing years and girth of the pair that she called a lady-in-waiting to the window and burst into laughter.

IRENE ADLER is, of course, 'The Woman', the only female to have bested Sherlock Holmes. She appears in one of Sir Arthur Conan Doyle's tales of the Great Detective, A Scandal in Bohemia, which has certain similarities to the story above. She was indeed supposed to be an American-born opera singer, but if she did marry Alfred Doolittle, the dustman father of Eliza, this is the first time it has been mentioned. Others have claimed Holmes was in love with her, but Dr Watson expressly denies it. You will notice, for the first time, that a gentle liberty has been taken with chronology as well as much else to permit the affectionate Doyle cameos.

ELIZA DOOLITTLE is, of course, the leading character in George Bernard Shaw's Pygmalion and its musical adaptation, My Fair Lady, based on the Greek myth of the sculptor who fell in love with his creation, brought to life as Galatea. Eliza is a Covent Garden flower girl taken up by a cantankerous professor of phonetics, Henry Higgins, who transforms her with the help of a fellow speech expert, Colonel Pickering, into a flawless enunciator capable of passing herself off as a member of the highest society. FREDDY EYNSFORD HILL is the young man who falls helplessly in love with her. The play was, and is, widely popular, but Shaw disappointed many with its rather inconclusive ending, in which neither Higgins nor Freddy quite gets the girl. Ever since, there have been attempts to hint more strongly at a Higgins triumph, but these were always fiercely resisted by Shaw, mostly, it is claimed, because it was based on his platonic or at any rate unfulfilled love for his leading lady, Mrs Patrick Campbell. He even went so far as to later write an afterword explaining that Eliza does marry Freddy. No one, as far as I know, has offered my bold solution, which has Higgins and Pickering as gay, thus leaving Freddy with a clear field. 'On the other omnibus', however, is derived from a popular Liverpudlian expression demonstrating yet again that fair city's subtlety and elegance. I have remained fairly faithful to play and afterword otherwise, as in the number of Eliza's 'stepmothers' and the demise of her aunt and the disappearance of the straw hat. But I really couldn't see Eliza and Freddy, as per Shaw, running a florist, and there is no mention of Mr Eynsford Hill senior, on safari or elsewhere; Miss Chrism, too, has wandered in, almost, from 'The Importance of Being Earnest'. I feel sure the mischievous and Shavian Mr Shaw would have approved, eventually.

Elsewhere, Bertie did have a tattoo of a crusader's cross, but not a tiger, and he did have such a room at the legendary Parisisan brothel, Le Chabonais, with his coat of arms over the bed and a large copper bathtub boasting a half-woman-half-swan figurehead. He liked to fill the bath with champagne; after Le Chabonais closed in 1951, it was bought by Salvador Dali for 112,000 francs. The large sex aid mentioned, a siege d'amour, was made by Louis Soubrier, a cabinetmaker of the Rue du Faubourg Saint-Antoine.

The faithful Caesar, bereft at Bertie's death, followed his master's funeral cortege, moving the hearts of all except the Kaiser, who objected to giving the dog precedence. He lived with Alix until his death and was buried at Marlborough House with this inscription, 'Our beloved Caesar, the king's faithful and constant companion until death and my greatest comforter in my loneliness and sorrow for four years after'.

FURTHER READING:
Bertie, A Life of Edward VII, *Jane Ridley*
Edward VII, The Last Victorian King, *Christopher Hibbert*
Pygmalion, *George Bernard Shaw*
A Scandal in Bohemia, *Arthur Conan Doyle*

1918

Gus Hits the Front

I WAS IN THE RED CROSS HOSPITAL IN ROUEN WONDERING about my luck because there wasn't much else to do. Still it was a lot better than the one in Amiens where I went first after the stray Boche shell landed too close to us and did for my officer. Made a bit of a mess of the car as well. It was one of the old Sunbeams but I'd grown quite fond of it. I quite liked the officer, too. I was taking him to Brigade HQ and he was chatty, unlike most of them, who don't take much notice of us drivers. Young, of course, still excited by it, the noise, the mud, the worse, even the waiting and the routine and the odd foray into no man's land to try to snatch a Fritz which never worked but was supposed to be good for morale anyway even if we lost a few while we were at it.

We'd been giving Mametz a good old pounding in preparation for another big push which if it was like the others would give us a few yards if we could hold them. My officer, Lieutenant Bentley, had been out on one of these mad night trips, and the anxious brass were eager to talk to him. They never did. The big push didn't go so well, either. But he wasn't to know that, poor sod, lying there and looking about 14 apart from the blood and the stare. He'd been saying how much he was looking forward to a good pint and a warm fire on an English autumn evening before it hit.

The car was tossed onto its side and over, crushing him. I was thrown clear, lots of glass cuts and concussion and a mouth full of the inevitable mud. When I came round, that's when I saw him. I sat there, staring at him, until the ambulance came along. 'Room for one more inside?' I said, feebly in more ways than one. They took me to Amiens and a ward of moaning and crying for mothers mixed in with the odd shriek from another nightmare and the suddenly empty beds that didn't stay empty for long.

But I was talking about my luck. I've always helped it along, if you know what I mean. Before this whole shitty shooting match began, I knew a bloke, Sid, Sid Knowles, nice chap, chauffeur to some son of the Earl of Wotsit, kept the motor in one of those mews in South Ken. Anyway, Algy or whatever he was called never got up before 11, so it seemed a good idea for Sid to teach me to drive his swanky Crossley in the mornings. Not many of them about, not many cars at all, then, but I could see it would be a useful string to my bow, especially as I wasn't in what you might call reliable employment.

Ha, reliable employment! There's a laugh: I was on the halls. A comic, pathetic monologues and a cheery song. Percy Perks, the Perky Pierrot, that's me. No, don't worry, I've hardly heard of me myself. Just one of the many trudging round the Metropoles, Empires and Hippodromes and Alhambras, on the bit of the bill no one reads, one of the ones nobody's really bothered about while they're restless waiting for the names; not much dosh, but the freedom to be yourself, and to starve a lot. To tell you the truth, it was the fidgeting and moving and talking and lack of attention I really didn't like, not the jeers and such. If they threw something, that was a compliment, believe me.

So I learnt how to drive off Sid during one of my starving spells – the legits call it resting, but that's not what it was for us. Sometimes for a laugh I'd sit in the back of the car and wave graciously to pretty girls as we passed by. But back to my luck and helping it along: when the war started, I was just over 30 and single, again. And I didn't need old Lloyd George's brain to work out that it wasn't going to be over by the panto season or that you really didn't want to be right up at the front. I was on at the end of the Grand Pier, Weston-super-Mare, you probably know it, big old place, interesting audiences, ice cream everywhere, particularly revolting kids, the summer season was coming to an end. I went down to the recruiting office in town and played my two aces: driving skills and varicose veins. The veins kept me out of the infantry and the driving got me referred to the Army Service Corps. They tested me on a four-ton lorry at Grove Park, and I just about got through. Three weeks later I was in France.

You know the score out here, or perhaps you don't. Fertile ground for a comic, obviously, except your audience doesn't normally keep getting killed, it being me that usually dies. I wanted to do my bit, but I also wanted to live. I know there's some who are against it, and there's more as it goes on and the allies don't seem quite what they're cracked up to be and the Germans seem a bit more. You don't have to be over here for very long to work out there must be better ways to stop a mad sod like Kaiser Bill. If you're not convinced, if you're still caught up in the romance and nobility of fighting for dear old England, try driving an ambulance. Try driving some of the poor shaking bastards up to the front in a London bus, what a laugh. Try driving what's left of them back to the field hospitals. Try driving on top of a load of ammo.

The brass do try to pretend they know what's going on but they haven't a clue. I'm not sure who could in this mess. Everything's changed. The guns got bigger and the men got smaller. It's all mixed up: the new stuff, tanks and airplanes alongside horses and London buses. And us poor bastards bang in the middle of it. But in some ways there's terrific efficiency, especially in supplies and provisions and feeding the machine and tending the poor bloody wounded and dying. Oh, yes, sorry, not everything's changed, we're still dying.

But I don't really blame the generals. It's like going on stone cold at the Adelphi, Attercliffe, on a Friday night – definitely not recommended. Besides, the gold standard for a driver out here is to get a job chauffeuring them. Jack Smith drives The Chief, old Happy Haig himself, a very cushy number, I can tell you, and his double declutching isn't a patch on mine. His jokes aren't as good either but he tells me The Chief doesn't have much of a sense of humour. *Quelle surprise*, as the natives say here.

My jokes have been quite useful as it happens. Quite a bit of entertaining goes on in France, you know. As I said, there's a lot of waiting behind the lines in the rest camps as the lads do turn and turn about up in the trenches. Almost since it started, professionals have been coming out from home on a mission to cheer us up. Organised by an actress, remarkable woman, Lena Somethingorother. Singing, excerpts from plays, all very high falutin' and uplifting, but strangely moving, too. Most of the lads have never been inside a posh theatre or heard the classic stuff, but they love it. Reminds them of home, I suppose, and makes them feel they're bothered about, thought worth it. And there's something about imminent death that does help you concentrate, as I seem to remember somebody almost saying. One of the first things I saw, in this big hangar in the docks at Havre, was Macbeth. Bloody marvellous. Especially that bit about life being a poor player that struts and frets his hour upon the stage. You'd have thought it would be a bit close to the bone, but sharing seriousness can be soothing, I find, at this late stage.

That's not to say there isn't broader stuff as well. The civvy performers get surprisingly close to the firing line, doing their stuff in barns, huts, tents and the open air, but they can't get everywhere, so there are all these concert parties made up of the men themselves. And officers. I'd have thought that alone would have put the kibosh on it, but one of the rummest things of this very rum show is that the brass encourage it. You can see it's terrific for morale, but even so. One of the revue sketches is entitled 'In the Trenches, 1967', showing the last Tommy and the last Fritz in trenches only inches apart, with the German using the Tommy's bayonet periscope as a shaving mirror. Haig's seen it, too. No, didn't laugh. But the top rum of rums is the large amount of men dressing up as women. Really. I know there aren't enough of the correct variety but there's more to it than that, innocent, not innocent, intended, obvious, unspoken, just another bit of the organised insanity that's got us by the short and curlies out here.

So I don't blush to say that I've developed quite a line in female impersonation myself. I'm a touch on the stocky side, admittedly, but I don't go for the glamour, more the laughs. My double hitch of the false bosom and affronted stare always go down well, along with some heavy eyebrow lifting and lip pursing. Christmas at Drury Lane when it's all over, I don't think. I'd like to do a bit more, but drivers are in demand.

Which was what I discovered in Rouen, where I was ticking off the time until I was taken back to Blighty, home and safety (bugger beauty). But then this captain arrived at the end of the bed. All chirpy. He told me the medics had determined that I was available for light duties, and he had a whizz of one for me. 'You were on the halls, weren't you, Perks?' he said, which I warily allowed to be the case. 'Then you're just the man to drive him round!'

'Who, sir?' I said, even more warily.

'Gus Pinner!' he said, triumphantly. Well, I thought, Gus Pinner. One of the biggest draws in the game. 'Gus Pinner – Almost a Gentleman', as he was billed. One of those big fellows who uses his grace to appear ungraceful and ungainly; a grin and a laugh you couldn't help grinning at and laughing with; terrible conjuring tricks that go wrong, worse jokes: everybody loved Gus. Captain Welsby was beaming at the thought of Gus as he told me the great man had wanted to come out to cheer everybody up, and the Army had been delighted to oblige (as long as he wasn't allowed anywhere near The Chief).

Gus was arriving next week, and it would be my job to drive him around, along with the Captain, who was to be liaison officer, road manager and nanny rolled into one. 'I know we're going to get along splendidly, Perks,' he said, adding that he had recently had quite a success as Kitty in his division's production of *Charley's Aunt*. The whole thing would be a breeze, he said: old Gus wanted to get as close as he could to the front line, but you're quite used to that, aren't you, Perks, should all go like clockwork, teamwork, that was the thing.

I recalled that they'd said very much the same before Ypres. I was also struggling a little with how *Charley's Aunt*, a play I happened to know relied heavily on said aunt being a man, would go with chaps also playing the rest of the female cast. Still, they tell me Shakespeare got away with it, and Captain Welsby did have a good figure. More of a problem was Gus Pinner. Comics, however loveable on stage, can be a little, how you say, difficult, off it (not me, of course). And I knew that in the profession, Gus was legendary, the full set: grumpy, mean *and* liked a drink.

'Have you met Gus, sir?' I enquired as matter-of-factly as I could. 'Good lord, no, but everybody knows Gus, don't they? Anyway, it's all sorted and settled, orders given. You're to be in Boulogne next Tuesday, with car. It's going to be great fun, Perks, can't wait.'

And there I was, next Tuesday, orders, warrants, requisition received and fulfilled, sitting in a fine Crossley very similar to the one I'd learnt on with Sid in the mews at least, oh, a century ago now. We were at the dockside, watching a troop ship disembark. The Captain was sitting beside me, accompanying himself with swagger stick banging on the dashboard in a jaunty version of 'Pack Up Your Troubles In Your Old Kit Bag'. As it happens, I knew Felix Powell, who'd written it. I'd been on the same bill a couple of times with his troupe, The Harlequinaders, before the war, and I'd come across him in France a couple of months ago. I congratulated him on the success of his song, and he looked at me in that Welsh way and said (this is a milder version) that there were times he didn't altogether appreciate hearing it. As the Captain continued, I knew what old Felix meant. Not the surest way with a tune. Luckily, there was now an interruption in the flow of nervous or resigned khaki off the boat as a tall figure in a fur coat and battered boater pretended – or perhaps didn't pretend – to trip coming off the gangplank onto dry land. Gus Pinner, for better or worse, was here.

GUS WAS ACCOMPANIED BY A RETINUE OF SQUADDIES, SOME OF whom were carrying his baggage, and some of whom were just smiling. They were rapidly called away by their NCOs, but not before Gus had given them a tip – 'Keep your socks dry. I said socks!' I know, but Gus laughed his laugh and they went off happy. I was contemplating his baggage, which consisted of a holdall and a battered tin trunk marked, 'This belongs to Gus Pinner. Vicious dog inside'. Ho, ho, I thought, and you're right, there was a certain amount of professional jealousy involved. But you don't survive on the halls at all if you don't think you're good enough to make it big even when all the evidence is pointing to the big sign saying Exit. In the absence of any move from Gus, or the Captain, who was still pumping his hand and smiling in that gormless fashion which is obligatory when meeting famous people, I picked up the trunk to put it on the back of the Crossley. 'Crikey,' I said, 'this is heavy!'

Gus noticed me for the first time and said, 'Well, it would be, it's got a dog in it.' He then lifted his arm and barked up his sleeve. Gus and the Captain both found this hilarious but, obviously, made no move to help.

'This is Lance Corporal Perks,' said the Captain, when he'd finally recovered himself. 'He was on the halls himself before this show.'

'Really?' said Gus, without a tremendous deal of interest. 'What line?'

'Yours,' I said. 'Comic. Percy Perks, The Perky Pierrot,' adding quickly before he did, 'don't worry, I've hardly heard of me myself.'

'Ok, Percy,' he said, 'be a good lad and don't drop the trunk.

It's got all my props in it as well as the dog. And don't forget my holdall.' The holdall, unsurprisingly, clinked. Gus and the Captain got in the back of the car and we were off.

I have to say that the trip went very well at first. You couldn't fault Gus for enthusiasm: it didn't matter where it was, in hangars, halls, barns, YMCA huts, even in a giant mine crater up on Vimy Ridge, Gus was giving it some and more. He'd asked to be close to the action and the Army was delivering, not always to the delight of yours truly. And you couldn't question his guts, artificially stimulated or not: he developed a pained response to shells landing in the vicinity that treated them as a kind of criticism of his act. The boys were in stitches.

Quite often, we'd be moving along to our next engagement and he'd spot a platoon along the road, have a word with Captain Welsby and I'd stop, sharpish. 'Here!' they'd shout. 'It's old Gus! How are you, Gus! What you doing here?' And Gus would be out at them, lapping up the love that the great ones need to breathe. In some ways, his caper was perfect for this sort of thing: asking a Tommy to take a card, any card, then coming up with completely the wrong one, the old rueful innocent smile, riots of laughter, same when tapping the top hat with the magic wand and the rabbit's still there. My duties included feeding the rabbit, which I didn't mind as it was terrific to watch a master so closely, even if he didn't take any notice of me. The insecurity of the comic, I believe they call it, although it's never bothered me, as apparently you have to be successful before you get it.

There is of course plenty of drink available out here. The war's fuelled by it – rum for us, schnapps for them on daily ration. I sometimes wonder how long it would last if everyone was sober. As well as the rations, there are the innumerable *estaminets* in the towns behind the line where the troops rest up. Scruffy little bars with a certain rustic charm, and lots of drink. Gus lapped it up, you might say. But he was a professional drinker and kept himself together pretty well; how much he was distracted by well-wishers helped, too. Like most big drinkers, it came out in other ways, particularly his meanness. God, he was tight! I remember a long argument in a for once quiet *estaminet* in Aubigny over the change. Gus insisted Le Patron had left him short and couldn't be persuaded otherwise in any language. Eventually, he came out with this deathless comment that I shall remember to my dying day, which seemed closer then than now, 'Listen, Monsewer. You have to comprend – this isn't about the principle of the thing, it's about the money.'

That was Gus. Professionally and personally, I still think he was best with a curtain. I lost count of the number of times he set the house in fits before he even came on. After the big introduction, the lights went out, and there was silence, which got the first laughs. Then you could hear him stumbling around in the dark. More laughs. Then the loud mutter in the familiar Gus tones, 'I must be in a cupboard.' Everybody doubled up and doubled it again when Gus eventually managed to appear and surveyed them with that half-baffled grin followed by that laugh.

Tramecourt, Arras, Le Quesnoy, Albert, Bapaume, Amiens and more, more shows by the roadside, more shows in chateaux, commandeered for rest and admin, more shows in battered halls and converted canteens, and, twice, car abandoned, shows in the trenches, one interrupted by shells and triumphantly resumed to cries of, 'Good old Gus!' At first I stayed with the car, but by now, grudgingly, Gus had allowed me in a little, bemused stooge with rabbit, straight man bringing props for want of a glamorous assistant, that sort of thing. And, to cue up his close and encore, if there was room and time, me and the Captain as a couple of floozies went down a storm, particularly when Gus came on behind us and started doing some complicated business involving bad juggling which was actually rather skilled. The Captain did seem to be enjoying it rather a lot, but that's not a problem for me, not where I'm coming from. I've had that Siegfried Sassoon in the back of my car; as touchy as hell, but as plucky as pluck with it, in the habit of charging enemy trenches on his own. Not called Mad Jack for nothing, either, although to me, as he rattled on nineteen to the dozen, he seemed rather more sane than most about this madness. Did I mention that I got my stripe so that I could be permitted to address an officer? It was really quite useful for finding out where they might want to go, for instance.

Gus didn't want to go home, but it was time. Just as well, as with this combination of alcohol, adrenaline and adulation, something had to give. What none of us expected was that it would be our front line. Gus's last show was his nearest to the front, east of Peronne, before back to Blighty by way of a final big encore at Boulogne, shows at the Number One Base Hospital and the big convalescent home. Me and the Captain had gone particularly well, I thought, already imagining being spotted by some big shot at Boulogne.

Early the next morning, the shelling started, shaking us out of bed and towards the windows of our billet in the battered town. It felt like the biggest bombardment I'd ever been around, the sky alive with red stabs of flame and the sound like every drum in every hall in England had sounded at once and kept on sounding. We hunkered down to wait it out. Gus was all for making a run for it, but Captain Welsby was dead against that: he said the bombardment would go on and on and it was much too risky. What we didn't know was that this was the start of a new Jerry tactic, short (well, shorter) intense shelling targeted on our big guns and communications posts rather than a lengthy bombardment of the front line, which would then be followed by a sudden attack with overwhelming numbers. So it might or not have been a good plan to scarper when, after a few hours that seemed even longer than the wait for applause in Yorkshire, the shelling seemed to have stopped.

We were making for Albert, the main supply town well back from the front. But it was difficult to tell, given the thick fog and the smoke from the guns with just a hint of mustard gas. You'll know that sinking feeling when you begin to wonder whether you're going exactly the wrong way. What a how's your father! Tommies retreating, Tommies advancing, orders being shouted this way and that; absolute bloody mayhem. The fog got thicker and we were forced to stop. We just sat there as figures loomed up, down and everywhere, with the panic of the unexpected just as thick as the mist and the crackle of small arms and the thump of mortars punctuating everything. Funnily enough, it reminded me of that performance of Macbeth in Havre and the battle scenes where all is confusion and Macbeth is about to buy it. We didn't realise at first that the latest figures to suddenly appear were Boche. And by the time we did, they were surrounding the car. Obviously, we would have been a more unusual sight on a normal kind of day, but still. Gus's fame had clearly not crossed the Rhine; even so, the Huns, pumped-up and bursting with the excitement of the advance, paused as they stared at a man wearing a fur coat and boater (Gus always insisted on travelling in character). But it was only for an instant; then we were ordered out of the car. I must say that Gus and the Captain were very dignified, in their respective ways, while I found myself in my character: ''Ere, mind my paintwork!' was the way I put it. Boche soldiers were flooding past; an officer materialised, and although he had little English and we had less German, the Captain, being that sort of sensitive toff, had excellent French, as did his counterpart: it became clear that Gus was being considered a very important personage indeed, as otherwise he wouldn't have been accompanied by an officer and driven by a chauffeur in such a smart vehicle. So smart that we weren't going to be allowed to keep it. Our things were taken out, and it was driven away by a Fritz who, to my irritation, seemed quite a good driver.

Predictably, I suppose, Gus was enjoying himself. I had noticed a marked increase in consumption even for him during the morning, and he had now taken to addressing the Germans in a guttural gibberish which had them intrigued in spite of themselves. 'Svine gut burp dansk schuttermutter!' was one of his more intelligible efforts. His trunk, not unnaturally, was arousing a lot of interest, too. 'Vot is zis dog?' demanded the officer, slowly reading Gus's fabled inscription on the lid. Gus did his bark up his sleeve, but for once no one laughed. The officer was beginning to get a little irritated: after all, he was part of the spearhead of a major attack. Gus, of course, didn't care. 'Zere is also ein rabbit in zere!' he shouted. I'm afraid I'm not up to describing a scene featuring a tall man in a fur coat and a boater shouting nonsense at a group of invading Huns who had stopped to listen while the rest of them poured by on either side. But he was right: there was a rabbit in there; that's where we kept him in his little cage when we were travelling, with some hard tack. That was why there were air holes, although Gus used to say they were for the dog. The officer ordered the trunk to be opened and Gus went through a lot of the opening it a touch, barking and then slamming it shut routine. This took some nerve in the middle of a major German offensive: Gus was brave, barmy, drunk, and rather magnificent. He opened the trunk after the officer gestured with his pistol a second time. The Germans crowded round and spotted the rabbit: '*Das kaninchen!*' Bayonets were produced and it looked like the pot for poor Herbert Asquith, as Gus had christened him.

But you do learn about people in a crisis, don't you? It was Captain Welsby's turn: 'Do not touch the rabbit!' he thundered, and the Fritzes, used to the tone if not the language of command, instantly complied. The German officer, impressed and further convinced of the importance of his capture, called several men, and as far as we could tell, ordered them to take us off. Two of them carried the famous trunk, which the officer had clearly decided was of great importance. It was a strange group making its way across the battlefield, with Gus maintaining a calm, slightly arch, dignity as he walked ahead of his trunk, oblivious to the noise and the clamour of cries and gunfire and the poor bodies, twisted, contorted, macabre, grotesque, a dead audience. We were also continually coming across large numbers of live Tommies who had been taken prisoner, but now there were no cries of 'Hello, Gus!', just dazed puzzlement on strained faces.

Eventually we arrived at a farmhouse which was acting as a forward command post. I say farmhouse; it was more of a ruin, hammered, crashed and crushed by them and us several times over. All was barking orders and bustling soldiers bucked and buoyed by the thrill of success; from there we were put in a truck and driven some distance, reasonably well, to one of the chateaux that serially dotted the area and which in more idle moments had caused me to think that the French Revolution couldn't have been so much of a surprise. This one was clearly the zone headquarters, very nicely appointed in that French toff way, reminded me of the Tower Ballroom, Blackpool. We waited for some time in a room with deep windows and fussy chairs, until the double doors opened and another officer entered. He announced himself as Major Heinrich Strasser and addressed the Captain in English that was a touch better than mine. The Captain, very formal, said he would not provide any information about us, save that Gus was a civilian whose only purpose in being out here was to provide entertainment for the troops. Gus, who had been dozing, his custom between engagements, now produced his pack of cards and was about to offer the Major a chance to pick one when the Captain indicated firmly that this might not be the moment. 'So,' said Major Strasser to Gus, beaming in a disturbing way, 'if you are an entertainer, you will have to entertain us! Let us see just how good you are. Tonight!' I could see the Captain hesitating at this, clearly thinking about succour to the enemy and such, but Gus, of course, was more than game. 'Wunderbar, General,' he said. 'Zis vill be very gut, ja!' The Major's beam froze slightly and became even more disturbing. Gus, noticing but not caring, bashed on with an even stronger approximation of a German accent. 'I vill give you a top hole show, ja, ably aided by my vizzbang of an assistant here! Now, tell me, mein Herr top General, do you have any schnapps?'

All this time being ignored or at best vaguely tolerated, and now he chooses his moment to pay me a compliment. And involve me in this high command performance. The Captain was looking his look at me, but you know how it is with us – a booking and we're anybody's. Gus's mood must have been catching, because I found myself doing a soft shoe shuffle ending with coming to attention and a smart salute. 'Really, Perks,' said the Captain.

'All right, Perce, no need to overdo it,' said Gus.

'Good – or should that be gut?' said the Major. 'Major General von Klinkerhoffen will be here and should be in an excellent mood. Schnapps and wurst will be arranged in the meantime. Until tonight, gentlemen.'

The Captain wasn't happy, but a bit of that might have been because he wasn't appearing. Schnapps and wurst consumed in the varying quantities you might expect, we were reunited with Gus's trunk and Herbert Asquith, who seemed unmoved by his brush with death. We talked over what we might give the Germans; I suggested I might do the whole thing in drag, and rather to my surprise Gus agreed, with reservations. 'But stick to looking after Herbert Asquith and try not to overdo those double takes and all the tit-hitching business, Perce. They've not come to see you, you know.' I thought of pointing out that he was unlikely to be a top draw himself but decided our future might depend significantly on how he went down and I didn't want to affect the confidence which was already being heavily sustained by schnapps. The Captain, meanwhile, was wistfully eyeing the female costumes in the bottom of the trunk.

There was quite a house in the chateau's grand hall, more gilt and mirrors and an atmosphere of excitement that Gus thought was for him but was pretty obviously because the assembled audience, a mix of officers and ordinary Fritzes, were geed up by the big advance that had raised hopes they might not lose this war after all.

A star shows why when things aren't going well. Gus was a horrible man in many ways, but my goodness he worked that night! I know Herman is not renowned for his sense of humour, and I could see that the idea of a terrible magician was puzzling some of them, but the mad bugger took them on headfirst and won, eventually, mostly. I don't really blush to say I did my bit because it was mostly by accident. After mucking and mugging about, Gus as usual succeeded in making Herbert Asquith disappear and reappear in the top hat, held him up, and as usual passed him to me, whereupon, not as usual, I dropped him. Well. Herbert was off round the hall faster than Kitchener after a recruit, evading two attempts by me to catch him, which I finally managed with a flying dive bang in front of Major Strasser's chair, dress all over the place and legs showing much too much, if you follow. The place went wild! Gus was teed off, of course, but I was used to that by now and it had been a long time between rounds.

Immediately after it was over, we were escorted back, me still in full drag, to meet Major Strasser in the same room as before. This time, though, the Major had no less a personage than Major General von Klinkerhoffen with him. The General was one of your typical Prussians, duelling scars, scowl as usual expression, monocle, bog-brush haircut, the lot. 'So,' he said, in excellent English, 'two very pleasing performances today. One by our troops, and one by you gentlemen.'

The Captain blinked hard while Gus continued to pull faces in one of the wall mirrors. The double doors were now opened by a lance corporal with droopy moustaches and a sour expression bearing drinks. 'You are surprised,' said the General. 'But I know England well, and when I return, which obviously will not be long now, I look forward to visiting your wonderful music halls again. What laughs I've had there!'

Blimey. The Lance Corporal handed us drinks, and Major Strasser joined in with a bit of oily and unconvincing stuff about how much he'd enjoyed it, too, a fine example of 'your wonderful English sense of humour', and how he looked forward to seeing it again when Gus had practised a bit more. Noticing that this wasn't going down terribly well with Gus, he quickly turned to the Lance Corporal. 'Well, *Korporal*? You've in England been – what about the show? Interesting, yes?'

'Yes, sir,' replied the Lance Corporal. His face remained impassive but his eyes betrayed a passion he was not sharing. Major Strasser pressed him. 'Come on, *Korporal*!' he said teasingly. 'What did you make of England? Speak freely!'

The Lance Corporal's English was halting, but still far better than my German. 'I did not enjoy it, sir. The British are smug and think themselves very superior. And they think everything funny, like children. The part I was in was poor, but they liked to joke about it not change it. And they had no respect for authority. That is why we will win this war, sir! He who would live must fight. He who doesn't wish to fight has not the right to exist, sir!' The Lance Corporal was now staring ahead of him with a fixed look on his face as if he was somewhere else.

There was the same sort of silence that sometimes greeted one of my less successful jokes. It was broken by the General, who had been taken aback by his soldier's passion: 'A fine speech, *Korporal*. What is your name?'

'Hitler, sir!' responded the Lance Corporal.

'Well, *Lanzenkorporal* Hitler, laughter has its value, even if the British do take it too far. Their frivolity is all very well in its place, which is the music hall, where these gentlemen come from. But you are correct, they also allow it to invade their judgment about more important things. They like leaders with wit and charm, which is usually a mistake, as it often disguises flaws. But neither do they appreciate the more fanatical type, those who pursue their ends to the end whatever the cost, which is even more dangerous. What say you, gentlemen?'

'Ask my agent,' said Gus.

That's the thing about comedy, isn't it? It disarms. In this case, even I could see that the General was having a crack at the Kaiser and that both the Major and the Corporal realised it even if they couldn't quite follow all he was saying. But disarming allows the avoidance of the inconvenient. Recognising it, the General laughed an attractive laugh, made more so by its ruefulness. 'Very good, Herr Pinner! I will be there when you grace Wilton's again.'

The General turned to me. 'And you, sir, or should I say madam?' He then winked at me, which is quite a feat while wearing a monocle. 'There were parts of your performance which reminded me of that promising young comedian, Percy Perks, the Perky Pierrot.'

Well. Astonished or on the floor having just been slapped with a wet haddock? But concealing my gasted flabber like a real pro, I managed a quick, 'The very same, General,' before sketching a curtsey and elaborately rescuing a sideways stumble.

'Ja, ja, right, Field Marshal,' interposed Gus, quickly. 'He's a good boy but with a lot to learn. Any chance of our being allowed to relax for a bit? Artistry can be exhausting, mein gott, mein papa, mein everyzing.'

'Of course, for tonight. But a plan is beginning to form. How would you like to be an international attraction, Herr Pinner? You could perform for German, British and French audiences while we mop up the last pockets of allied resistance. I regret that in this instance you will not be able to consult your agent. There will also be certain limitations on your liberty in return for copious amounts of schnapps and wurst, things that will not be available in our otherwise excellent prisoner-of-war camps.'

Captain Welsby had gone quite pale at this outrageous suggestion of treachery and collaboration with the enemy. But Gus had played the Glasgow Empire. He held up his hand to stay the patriotic broadside the Captain was about to deliver. 'An interesting proposition, mein vonoberperson. Let me retire to consult with the rabbit. He's usually all ears.'

'Ha, again very good, Herr Pinner. The Corporal here will arrange for an escort to your quarters, or in this case, should I say thirds?' I know, I know, but not bad for a German, and again unexpected, so I'm afraid I couldn't resist a snigger. We were taken to a large room containing nothing but three bunks and the famous trunk. I took Herbert Asquith out and let him wander around a bit while Gus and the Captain had the disagreement they'd been waiting for.

THE CAPTAIN WAS SPLENDID, I THOUGHT, RIGHTEOUS indignation mixed with sorrowful regret at such appallingly bad form. He was slightly built but he now showed a commanding presence. 'Gus, there is a time and place for levity and entertainment. That back there with the General wasn't it. We have a duty to show and share solidarity with our country and our comrades as we struggle to defeat this dastardly attempt to impose a Hunnish dictatorship on the free nations of the world. I say nothing of the effects on your standing and the affection in which you are held if you take this despicable and cowardly course of action: I ask you instead to take a stand for all that is good, right and proper... for England!'

Gus smiled at the Captain, but not in a friendly way. 'Bollocks,' he said. 'Did England help me fight my way from the arse end of Kennington and one room shared with a mad bad father, endless brothers and sisters and a mother who stayed drunk because that was the only way she could stand it? Was England up there on the stage with me when the bottles and the rotten fruit were flying rapidly and in tight formation? Was it buggery! England didn't and doesn't care about me any more than it cares about the other poor sods it rules round the world and expects to slave away for buttons and washers and less to keep people like you, Captain, in the positions you have never even stopped to wonder if you deserve. Why should I do anything for England?'

Captain Welsby, unsurprisingly, was taken aback, but rallied. 'So why did you come out here?'

Gus took another swig from his schnapps bottle. 'I didn't come out here to support one side of our late and blessed monarch Queen Victoria's cosy little family against the other, or to keep people like you in charge, Captain. I came out here because for one thing there's not so much work with a war on, and for another because I thought these poor helpless lied-to and terribly led bastards deserved a bit of laughter before they pointlessly sacrificed themselves. And because no one else can do it like this drunken, shambling and apparently completely daft mess called Gus Pinner can do it. Am I right, sir?'

'By god you bloody are, Gus,' I said, surprising myself with my force. Must have been the schnapps. The Captain was pale, and silent.

'And I'll tell you something else. I am my own performing monkey. I am not going to be a performing monkey for this shower. I've met that General's type before, a lot. Enjoy slumming it, but don't really want to know you, would be amazed to think us equals in any way. The creepy corporal knows more than he does. I've just bought us some time. We've got to get out of here, sharpish.'

'How?' asked the Captain.

'Blimey, you're the officer. You tell us.'

Captain Welsby visibly pulled himself together. 'Yes, yes... camouflage and deception!'

I looked blank. Gus was back at the bottle.

'Camouflage and deception. We should be able to get out, because with this offensive there's so much coming and going a few more isn't going to make any difference. As long as nobody recognises us, we'll be all right.'

The schnapps seemed pretty good for inspiration. 'Let's all go in drag!' I almost shouted.

Gus smiled – smiled! – and the Captain frowned. 'It's a long shot, but it might just work!' he said. (Well, yes, I know, but that's the first time I ever heard anyone say it.) 'You're in drag already, Perks. Most of the place has seen you in it. You change back into uniform. Come on Gus, let's dress!'

There are some advantages to being a comic: not least is that no one takes you seriously, which is probably why the escort hadn't bothered locking the windows, on a first-floor room. The Captain looked at his most fetching, while Gus looked like, apart from Gus, a cocktail of every theatrical landlady who'd ever put me up, a mixed memory.

I think one of those famous German strategists has said that military success depends on the ability to improvise; as this is equally true for the musical theatre, it was clear Captain Welsby had missed half his calling. After we had eased ourselves the few feet down to the ground outside, the Captain and I peeped round the corner to the front of the chateau while Gus leaned against the wall, humming 'If You Were the Only Girl in the World' quietly to himself.

'Do you see that, Perks?' hissed the Captain.

'I certainly do, sir, a Mercedes 16/40 horsepower, 3945 cc, four cylinder, L-head engine, leather clone clutch, 451 gearbox and shaft-drive, wheelbase 3.25 metres, maximum speed 85kph, which is about 50 miles an hour, lovely little bus, isn't she? Must be the general's staff car. I'd love to have a go in that.'

'That's the bloody point, Perks! All we've got to do is take care of the driver, and we're away.'

Said driver was peacefully asleep at the wheel while waiting for his master. We left Gus propped against the wall, now humming 'It's a Long Way to Tipperary', and made our way to the car, the Captain sensibly and silently, me in that exaggeratedly stealthy stage villain fashion. Unfortunately, I made a touch too much noise extricating the crank handle and had to duck down as the driver came to. The first thing he saw was the Captain, who, although I might be biased, did look a real cracker. The Captain was just tickling him under the chin when I came round behind my fellow driver and employed the handle in its popularly alternative usage.

'Right, get his clothes off and put them on!' ordered the Captain, who was gleaming with the excitement of it all. Well,

I'm not exactly unused to putting on costumes, but I do draw the line, and a smelly Kraut uniform which was still warm was well past it.

'Don't give me that look, Perks! Get on while I help Gus into the car.'

Gus loaded, the driver hidden, me changed but still wrinkling my nose, we moved off, expertly driven if I do say so myself. I don't know whether the Germans were particularly relaxed that night, drunk in every way with victory and its heady possibilities, or whether escape was something they weren't used to guarding against at the chateau; whatever, we were able to swish up its long drive, past any number of huts and outbuildings, without encountering a single person until we arrived at large ornamental gates which, we were delighted to note, were open for convenience.

I WAS JUST ABOUT TO PUT MY FOOT DOWN WHEN WE WERE flashed with a torch by a soldier emerging from the ornate lodge which had been built to resemble a large dovecote. I would still have gone for it, but Captain Welsby was cooler, more sensible, and told me to stop. The soldier with the torch proved to be none other than the lance corporal with unfavourable views of Blighty, which was the first piece of bad luck we'd had since being captured.

'Leave the talking to me,' said the Captain, again unwittingly starting a fashion. The lance corporal approached, all his attention taken, unsurprisingly, by the two exotic occupants of the back seat. But anyway that's something you must have noticed with chauffeurs and drivers: nobody ever notices them.

The Captain was, as ever, magnificent, giving what must have been the performance of his life, a fluttering, enticing, come-hither gush of coquette and vamp and husky French. I couldn't understand a word of what he was saying, and, as it happened, neither could the lance corporal. Bemused by the Welsby onslaught, he called for backup. Two more German squaddies came tumbling out; one was a French speaker, again not the best break, while the other took up position in front of the Merc.

The Captain proceeded as before, with the squaddie struggling to get a word in while this high-pitched vision kept repeating 'invitees!' and 'les Officiers Allemagnes très importantes!' Meanwhile, the lance corporal, who still hadn't recognised us, now turned his attention to Gus. I thought this was going to be the end until I began to realise, however unlikely it might be, that the dour fellow was rather taken with drag Gus. Gus, being Gus, was much quicker on the uptake: he swiftly came to comic attention and was soon enjoying himself terrifically, going into full panto dame, coy and come-on in rapid and repeated succession. Language could have been a difficulty, but it soon became equally clear that the corporal wasn't interested in talking, more in invading. I knew Gus by now; there was nothing he enjoyed more than a risky performance. So while the Captain was manfully (if you see what I mean) maintaining his dignity with the French speaker, Gus allowed the corporal to lean into the car and kiss him. Not only that, next, the Corporal, who was really rather aggressive, started, clumsily, unbuttoning Gus's blouse clearly in the hope of enjoying what looked a magnificent bosom.

It all happened very quickly after that. Gus's bosom was in fact Herbert Asquith, who now bounded off pursued by the two German squaddies while the corporal recoiled and stood quite stunned. This time I didn't wait for the word of command but got out of there as quickly as the Merc could. As we sped off, I could see the lance corporal in the rear mirror, right arm lifted in surprise, almost in farewell. Gus was laughing fit to bust. 'That was brilliant! Those moustaches didn't half tickle. What a very strange little chap! I dare say he hasn't finished causing trouble, not that one. Poor old Herbert Asquith, though. I'll miss him, best rabbit I've ever had, and I've had a few. The Marquis of Queensberry was a bit of a bugger, I can tell you, terrible temper.'

There was a huge amount of traffic on the road, mostly motor and horse-drawn stuff, all heading in the same direction, which was obviously the way to go if we wanted to get back to our lines. The trick, as the Captain put it, was to know when to abandon the car and take to our heels. The approaching dawn made the decision for us, as we were clearly unlikely to survive close examination. So we pulled off the road into another of the villages racked and ruined by the lumbering destruction and got ready to have a go at making it over to our lines.

The Captain, who still looked rather fetching, had been noting the bustle, hubbub and all the other signs and tempos and noises of war: he reckoned we were only a couple of miles from the action. The question was how far our boys had been pushed back by yesterday's attack. Gus, who still didn't look rather fetching (unless you were an odd German corporal), was occupied in his other activity between engagements, sleeping like a baby.

First light revealed a fog even thicker than yesterday, so it didn't surprise me when the Captain decided we should have a crack immediately. I don't remember much detail about the first part of our advance, except that Gus was grumbling and I had taken the German uniform off, leaving me back in our uniform. The Captain had thought about taking off the drag, but decided it might have some surprise value if we did run into trouble. 'You'll just have to take your chance, Perce,' he said. It wasn't much consolation that it was the first time he'd ever called me by my first name, but I did feel surprisingly bucked up all the same. We would move in 50 yard stumbles, wait, listen and move again. There was movement all round us, and time after time we just had to lie doggo as German troops moved past, often in wagons, not a good sign. Shell holes were useful, of course, and you couldn't be too fussy who was keeping you company, more dead, theirs and ours, poor, poor buggers, poor lost boys.

Gus had stopped grumbling and was holding up remarkably well. We were out there for what seemed hours, and was. Then, in the early afternoon, something really rather wonderful happened. The thick fog began to lift and there before us, about 100 yards away, was a British position. Captain Welsby, calm as ever, told us to move steadily towards it, with our hands up; he took the front. We were spotted about 50 yards away. A great ragged, whooping cheer went up, which seemed a touch much until I turned and saw Gus was waving his giant bloomers in the air. Even the Captain had to smile at that. Gus then took his wig off and waved the bloomers some more. More cheers, and now cries of 'Fuck me, it's Gus Fucking Pinner! Hello Gus!'

What a moment in a war! What a moment in a career! One of Britain's favourite comedians coming in from no man's land dressed in drag and waving his bloomers! Top that with an encore!

So it was then, of course, that Gus suddenly clutched at his heart as if he'd been shot, and dramatically fell to the ground. The Tommies went wild, with more cries of 'Good old Gus!' and, 'It wasn't me, Gus!'

But he didn't get up to take his applause. When I got to him, it was clear he was in a bad way. 'Dicky ticker, Perce. Not feeling too perky. It was fun, though, wasn't it? That fucking corporal!' He grimaced and went quiet. The Captain hovered, anxious and oblivious to his drag look, wig still in place, and skirt. And the noise and the laughter carried on. That Gus Pinner! What better release when you're nervous and frightened and waiting for the enemy and you can't see any of your own troops on either side of you? Good old Gus!

But Gus was struggling. And as he fought, I realised I loved the daft silly mean old goat. I really did. He looked at me and tried a smile. 'Goodbye, Perce. You're not that good, you know.'

I know he was making to wink, I know he was. I'm sure he was. I am.

THERE'S NOT MUCH MORE TO TELL. THE BRITISH POSITION was a redoubt which had held when the German swept through. We managed to retreat with them and got to the Somme just before the bridges were blown up. You'll know that the German attack stalled. You'll probably know, too, that Captain Welsby went on to win the VC. Posthumously. Charged a German machine gun position on his own to draw the fire from his men. Me? Nothing so dramatic. Carried on driving until the Armistice. After that, Sid and me opened a garage in Thorpe Le Soken. Doing well enough. Finally got a wife, lovely girl, smashing little boy. Sorry? No, didn't really fancy going back on the halls after that. You might say they died with Gus, out there by that redoubt. Bloody funny, but not really, how it turned out with the little corporal, though, wasn't it? I can see Gus's face now.

Afterword

Entertainment for the troops during the First World War has received scant attention, especially when compared with that paid to the efforts of ENSA and such names as Gracie Fields and Marlene Dietrich in the century's second outbreak of organised mass madness. The first professional concert party, organised by the famous husband and wife duo, Seymour Hicks and Ellaline Terriss, and featuring the later legendary Gladys Cooper, arrived in Boulogne in December 1914. They were followed throughout the war by many others, most of them in troupes organised by the redoubtable Lena Ashwell, the theatrical grande dame mentioned by Percy. There were also touring repertory companies putting on one-act comedies and, in response to demand, more serious material, such as the performance of 'Macbeth' in Le Havre which he so enjoyed.

Large halls and even theatres were well employed; closer to the front, the YMCA organised huts at the base camps for refreshment and entertainment. Even nearer to the fighting, one of Lena Ashwell's actors remembered, 'The concert was going splendidly and Charles Tree was singing, "Oh, no, John, oh, no". Precisely on the last note a 9.2 about 100 yards behind us spoke, and landed over heads with a crash! I am proud to say that not one of us so much as blinked. It set the Tommies into torrents of laughter and cheers.'

'To stand as we often did', wrote Lena Ashwell, 'on some piece of rising ground to watch regiment after regiment going down from camp to entrain for the line, to watch those thousands

going forward with a smile to death, sacrificing for an ideal, for freedom of small peoples, for an empire in danger of destruction, for Country, for Home, for wife and child, that women might not be ashamed of them, that God might know that they can play the game, who can describe that?'.

Gladys Cooper gave them 'Gunga Din'. Penelope Wheeler read Euripides in the Sergeants' Mess. Ellaline Terriss watched as Ben Davies, a popular tenor of the time, sang 'Land of My Fathers' to a Welsh regiment about to go up to the front. The men had been called to attention by their Colonel, Lord Ninian Crichton-Stuart, and as Davies sang in Welsh in the pouring rain the men took up the refrain. Within a week, the Colonel and many more were dead.

This is a letter to Lena Ashwell written by an NCO at Boulogne in June, 1917:

'Madam – in the name and on behalf of the NCOs and men of the divisions of the Third Army, who have had the good fortune to be in this base camp at this time, we beg to express to you our deep appreciation of the concerts with which today and on a previous occasion the members of your party have been good enough to entertain us. They have brought to us recollections and suggestions of "Dear Old Blighty". We confess we would rather listen for ever than go back to the horrid Orchestra of War, but they have helped us to realise again that we are fighting for the Empire, Home and Beauty, and for all that they mean in the life of mankind, and, therefore, we shall go back from our rest to our work with firmer will and stronger purpose to pursue our struggle to a victorious end, and secure for the world a just and enduring peace'.

Such was the superior entertainment. The concert parties formed by the troops themselves were widespread, highly popular, *and of varying quality and taste (the In the Trenches, 1967, sketch is authentic, including Haig's attendance). They were full of music hall performers after conscription was introduced in 1916 and married and older men were called up. One such was Felix Powell, mentioned by Percy, who did indeed write 'Pack Up Your Troubles In Your Old Kit Bag', one of the most popular and least cynical of the wartime songs of the period. You can decide on the irony of his later killing himself. The first verse before the famous chorus tells of a cheerful fellow, Private Perks. Thus Percy.*

An unexpected consequence of the troop concert parties was, in the absence of the real thing, the popularity of female impersonators. One of the most famed was a young Canadian who has come down to us only as Kitty O'Hara, described by a major who watched one of his/her performances as 'impossible to think of... as anything else but a delightful flapper'. Kitty, the major continued, had been over the top nine times 'without receiving more injuries than such as were caused by being blown about by shells on three different occasions'.

Such performers were rare, prized and in demand. The ambitious captain commanding the 51st Highland Division's pierrot troupe, for example, felt so hampered by his current impersonator's 'deep voice and large hands' that he offered two specialised machine gun mountings in exchange for a more fetching private from the Highland Light Infantry. Negotiations broke down but the private found himself transferred to the 51st's artillery anyway after influence was exerted at the highest level.

Possibly the most famous entertainer to visit France was SIR HARRY LAUDER (1870–1950), pint-sized purveyor of a kilted jolly and sentimental Scottishness, singer of hugely popular songs such as 'I Love a Lassie', 'Roamin' in the Gloamin' and 'Keep Right On to the End of the Road'. An indefatigable tourer of Britain, its colonies and the USA, by 1911 he was said to be

77

the highest paid performer in the world, although not all were in thrall to his cocky charms. When the First World War broke out, he became as prominent a recruiter and promoter of it as Rudyard Kipling, raising large amounts of money for the war effort and using his shows to persuade thousands of young men to volunteer, with inevitable consequences. Almost as inevitable was that both Lauder and Kipling would lose their sons in the fighting.

Lauder's trip to France was one way in which he dealt with his fierce grief. He was determined to visit the grave of his son, John, and to entertain as many troops as close to the front as he could. In 1917, he achieved both, as he recounts in his memoir, A Minstrel in France. It is a remarkable book, written in an artless, easy style, full of dialect and unflagging in an unquestioning support for the war that sits uneasily with the consensus now and the growing disillusionment then. But there is also raw pain, bravely set down in a time which much preferred restraint. This is part of his account of visiting his son's grave: 'I flung myself down upon the warm, friendly earth... I wanted to reach my arms down into that dark grave, and clasp my boy tightly to my breast, and kiss him'. Lauder was knighted for his war effort, which included setting up a fund for disabled veterans as well as the jingo. A rumour arose that his son had been shot by one of his own men, but this can safely be put down to the envy that seems always to accompany celebrity.

Gus Pinner's trip to France is based on Lauder's, but he owes nothing to the other's character. Lovers of last century's comedy will immediately recognise TOMMY COOPER (1921–84), but it is not an entirely faithful portrait. 'Almost a Gentleman', for instance, was the catchphrase of BILLY BENNETT (1887–1942), a master of mock-pomposity and an influence on later comics as diverse as Spike Milligan and Cooper himself. Bennett served with great distinction in the First World War, being awarded the Distinguished Conduct Medal and the Military Medal. The boater *and fur coat belonged to Bud Flanagan (1898–1968), stalwart of the once wildly popular but now largely (and possibly deservedly) forgotten Crazy Gang. Flanagan served in the First World War under his real name, Chaim Reuben Weintrop; he took his stage name as revenge on a hated sergeant-major. Tommy Cooper collapsed and died on stage and screen during a performance of 'Live from Her Majesty's in 1984'. Thinking, not unreasonably, that it was part of his act, the audience laughed. The principle and money remark was his.*

Lauder's trip was managed by a Captain Godfrey, who accompanied him. Rank, charm, courage and efficiency would be the only similarities he shared with Captain Welsby.

The First World War has been exhaustively examined and analysed; the events described take place against the setting of the Kaiserschlacht, Kaiser's Battle, the German Spring Offensive of 1918, masterminded by General Erich Ludendorff. It employed the tactics described – intense, targeted artillery followed by sudden attack from storm troopers – which had proved successful on the Eastern Front and taken Russia out of the war, freeing divisions to face the Allies in the West before the imminent arrival of overwhelming numbers from the United States. It succeeded initially, helped by the clumsy response of the British command. But once the Germans had broken through across the Somme 20 miles into Allied territory, there was nowhere for them to go: they did not have the manpower or resources to maintain their supply lines or surround the Allies. This essentially futile and entirely characteristic exercise took a terrible late toll: more than half a million casualties on both sides. For the British, the brunt was taken by young men, friends and neighbours such as those drawn from the cotton mill towns of Lancashire. The 66th East Lancashire Division, one of ten decimated, alone suffered 7,000 casualties out of a paper strength of over 12,000 in one week as it retreated from east of Peronne to the outskirts of Amiens. And this was just the first in a series of German offensives that spring and summer, which all petered out in the same way. The effect on Lancashire from the war was devastating. In all, it's estimated that the cities of Manchester and Salford lost 22,000 men killed and 55,000 wounded between 1914–18. Manchester, Salford, Rochdale, Oldham, Wigan, Bury, Blackburn, Bolton and their like had hardly recovered by the outbreak of the Second World War and the startling success of the German blitzkrieg, learnt from the failure of 1918.

ADOLF HITLER was indeed a lance corporal in the German army during the First World War, spending half of the time at his regiment's headquarters, but I am narrowly compelled to concede that this was in Fournes-en-Weppes, at the northern end of the German front rather than the southern, where our action takes place. Mostly a despatch runner, he was at Ypres, Arras, the Somme and Passchendaele. It has been claimed that he stayed with his aunt, Bridget Hitler, in the winter of 1912–13 at her home in Liverpool. Bridget had married Adolf's half-brother Alois, who was working as a waiter in the city. She later wrote a memoir, 'My Brother-in-Law, Adolf Hitler', in which she laments not being a positive enough influence on him, particularly in encouraging his English. Anyone wondering why he never mentioned this stay should know that he was dodging service in the Austrian army at the time, not something he would be keen to advertise later. Bridget's credibility is slightly undermined for me by her claim that she persuaded him to trim his moustache into that familiar truncated smudge, when it is clearly still luxuriant and drooping in his army photographs. I do not know whether he was attracted to large, mannish women, but obviously I have my suspicions.

FURTHER READING:
Death of a Division, *David Martin.*
A Minstrel in France, *Harry Lauder.*
Theatre at War, *L J Collins.*
Memoirs of an Infantry Officer, *Siegfried Sassoon.*
Modern Troubadours, A Record of Concerts at the Front, *Lena Ashwell.*
English History 1914–85, *A J P Taylor.*

1925

The Cat's Pyjamas

A PRETTY AVERAGE NIGHT AT THE CAT'S PYJAMAS, actually, so far: one duke, an earl, a baronet or two, some oldest sons, more younger ones; a group of cavalry officers, at least one Grand Duchess and two more minor representatives of European royalty; some wealthy men of less certain origin, without their wives, naturally; a smattering of politicians, Tory, equally naturally, who are on easy terms with the wealthy men. They are all in white tie but some of the wealthy men are less wealthy than they were, some more, easily distinguishable by their air of success or slight desperation, and the eagerness with which Mrs Kitty, dear Mrs Kitty, such fun, greets them.

All are very loud, but they need to be, to be heard over the vigorous syncopations of Albert and His Original Orpheans, the house band. And all of them are more or less rogues, of course; some are cads, too, and some worse, which the oldest sons and younger sons find rather exciting and fun, but not quite as much fun, top word, as the girls, the popsies and the dollies, the dancers and the dalliers, none of whom are ever going to be taken home, naturally. Not like the ones over at the table by the band, in that flapper party, very fast and bright young marrieds and not-just-yets with beaux of various enthusiasms.

It's after 10.30 now and things have begun to rev up with the arrival of the after-theatre crowd and, of course, some of the recent objects of their attentions, the stars, bright and brittle, striking and smiling until no one is looking. Albert, poised above the dance floor, greets them all with a beam and a bow without missing a beat of his ivory baton, which is rather more than can be said for most of the energetic efforts on the crowded dance floor. Mrs Kitty, a delightful Irish lady of certain years and assisted colouring, skilfully seats the famous faces in an order of such subtlety that it is imperceptible, almost.

Guy Graves sees it, his companion doesn't quite yet. This is Willa Wellington, who has just started a job on London's Calling, the gossip column on the *Daily Hail*. Guy Graves, who looks as though he was born in white tie, not Waltham Forest, also works on the column, and has done for a little too long. 'The Cat is always good for a snippet, worth keeping in with Mrs Kitty,' he tells her. 'Noël's just arrived, but don't neglect the old boys, always good for a line, love to see their name in print, makes them feel they're doing something instead of measuring out time in glasses of Kitty's overpriced imitation bubbly.'

Guy, though still young himself, does not take an entirely unjaundiced view of his occupation. He is still working on the sensational novel that would relieve him of it, tentatively entitled *A Fistful of Grit*. Willa is uncertain of her new career path – Uncle Hugo had somehow made it sound more respectable, more literary – but excited none the less to be amid this, The Cat's Pyjamas, and these extraordinary people, so unlike anything encountered at a concert.

'Old ones like that?' she shouts over Albert's latest effort, pointing at a small man at a crowded table with smiling sad eyes whose jacket clearly thinks he's an imposter.

'Exactly,' replies Guy. 'That's Jimmy White, broad northerner, property, promoter, boxing, racing, more ups and downs than the Grand National. Knows a lot, likes a pretty face, that's one of his up-and-coming boxers with him, next to Tallulah and Fred Wragg, the jockey, Sheffield lad.'

'Oh, is that Tallulah Bankhead? She's quite famous, isn't she? Look, she's dancing on the table! Isn't that one of those scoop thingies?!'

'It will be a scoop the night Tallulah doesn't dance on the table.'

'I can see I've got a lot to learn, sorry.'

'Don't worry, I'm not paying your wages. You'll soon pick it up. There's Sophie Tucker over there with Prince Carol of Romania and Winston Churchill. How did you get the job, by the way?'

'My Uncle Hugo knows the editor. Told him I was very interested in social matters, which I am, reform, the role of women, trades unions, things like that, but he obviously thought it was this kind of social matter, so here I am. Tallulah is kissing that large girl now.'

'Same as dancing on the table. That chap over there seems very interested in you.'

Willa looks over. 'The young fellow with the bored look with the flappers?'

'No. That's Evelyn Waugh. Another Oxford dissolute, but a bit louder, nasty streak. Wouldn't bother, won't ever amount to much. The one I'm talking about is alone, further over, at ten o'clock.'

He is older than Waugh, and not much like him in looks. His are better. But both have a lack of ease: Waugh's proposes the defensive arrogance of promise with the clock ticking; his is of the man who does not quite fit. His white tie is that vital touch too careful, his hair just too neat, as if he has it cut daily, which he does. But his smile, now full on at Willa, is unexpectedly warm and openly intimate.

She rather likes him. 'Who is he?'

'I don't know. Something about his jib suggests American, but he's not the usual type you get in here. They're either villains or bumpkins, but all are rich. You should wander over, might be interesting.'

'Can one do that? He is rather good looking, though.'

Guy is surprised to feel a tweak of disappointment. 'Hmm, looks a bit bland to me. But you can introduce yourself to anyone in here, don't worry. I'd be wary of more than two facial scars, though. And I would definitely advise avoiding the small swarthy fellow sitting on the other side of the dance floor, as he appears to be wearing spats with white tie.'

Willa walks over to greet her admirer, past a burst of laughter from Noël's table, and is gratified to get a smile from Albert as she passes the band, together with a wink from the double bass player.

Her admirer rises to greet her, smiling that smile again as she introduces herself, which is pretty brave for her. 'Hello, I'm Willa Wellington of the *Daily Hail*. I'm looking for interesting people to talk to.'

He smiles, with not a bad attempt at ruefulness. 'Well, I don't know about interesting. But I'd love to talk, providing you're not one of those scandal chasers we have in New York.'

'You're American! How exciting! I'm not a scandal chaser. At least I don't think I am. In fact, between you and me, I'm not really sure what I'm doing, as I've only just started this job.'

'You certainly don't look like any of the ones I've seen. Where are you from? And is that elegant sport your beau?'

'No, no, that's Guy Graves. He's on the column I'm working for, London's Calling, too. He's just showing me the ropes, and do I need it. I was at Newnham, hardly left my rooms, my Uncle Hugo says I now have to see a bit of the world beyond Hampstead.'

'Interesting. I'm an Oxford man myself. Champagne?' He has a little trouble catching the waiter's eye but asks for a bottle of Mrs Kitty's bubbly. 'Speed would be appreciated, old sport,' he says, handing the man a pound note. Willa is surprised to see Mrs Kitty herself bringing the drink over. 'James, here you are, my darling!' coos Mrs Kitty in an accent that will veer from Dublin to London via the Mersey. 'I see you've met our young newspaper friend, the one who's going to write nothing but gushing praise and admiration for my little club.' She opens the bottle with a practised twist and offers to fill their glasses.'

'But isn't it a little late to serve champagne?' says Willa, blinking behind her round tortoiseshell spectacles, rather fetchingly, James thinks.

'Bless me, it's fine for honorary members like yourself, and especially for one of my favourite suppliers.' She fills the glasses after this approximate and incorrect interpretation of the licensing laws and swishes her way back across the club with a smile and a sally here and there before sitting down with Guy. The club is now brim full, a crush emphasised as the dance floor clears for the cabaret, announced by Albert in excited European tones, 'Laydyees and Gennoomen-er, The Cat's Pyjamas is veree proud to present... The Rocky Twins!' Two wonderfully slim, soigné, indeterminate but identical dancers in immaculate evening dress make their way to the floor and begin to hoof along to a medley from Albert featuring, of course, Noël's songs. Sitting at the best table surrounded by acolytes and one earl, Noël does his famous royal acclaim gesture, palm turned up and out, twice; later, the Rockies, who, however improbably, are Norwegians, will return in wig and frock to even wilder applause. So this is twenties London, where governments of contrasting stripe rise, fall and meld in accord with the frantic confusion of the times, where the economy retreats to gold while skirts rise and hair shortens, where codes giddily collide and no one is quite sure where he, she or whoever stands when the music stops, and no one wants to look back, or ahead.

'Mmm, I could get to like champagne,' says Willa. 'Did Mrs Kitty say you supply it?'

'Not exactly. I export and import whisky from the States which is not being drunk because of prohibition. Not a life's career, but I've still plenty of time to find my true and sober course in life. If I don't fall wildly in love and do something stupid, it should all go swimmingly.'

'Gracious, are you what they call a bootlegger? I knew Oxford was laxer than Cambridge, but I didn't realise they went in for that sort of thing. Which college were you at?'

James tells her he was only there for a short time on an arrangement made for US Army officers after they'd seen service in France. His lowered voice as he confides the name of his college coincides with particularly high kicks from the Rocky Twins and is lost in the acclaim. He says he is not a bootlegger, unlike the small, swarthy man in spats on the other side of the dance floor, he says, who is called Mr Colombo, and is not a man to mix with socially.

Guy is interested in James. 'He doesn't give a lot away, my lovely,' says Mrs Kitty. 'Some people say he's not as nice as he seems, and they suggest that the time he says he spent at Oxford was mostly confined to the station platform. They also say he killed a man, and not in the war.'

Guy, who fancies himself a hard-bitten newspaper man, is surprised to discover a protective feeling. 'You do get the most wonderfully exciting crowd in here, Kitty. I'm certainly going to get a paragraph out of Monsewer Eddie Gray and Edwina Mountbatten. And who would have thought Neville Chamberlain could do the Black Bottom? What's James's surname again?'

Mrs Kitty gives Guy a look which attempts arch coquetry but achieves more of a leer. It is something about the rouge. 'Now, now, dearie, you're not going to embarrass Kitty, are you? I get enough trouble from the killjoys and puritans over the fun we have here without being linked to dodgy Americans, no matter how interesting and attractive. Why don't I introduce you to the Rocky Twins instead? Leif and Paal are lovely boys.'

Guy glances over at the twins, who are now giving their unique interpretation of 'If I Was the Only Boy in the World', with gestures. He decides that the readers of the *Daily Hail* must be content to wait to learn about Norway's gift to cabaret. He also decides that Willa has spent long enough with James. He salutes Mrs Kitty and walks over. 'Time to be moving on,' he tells her. 'I'm popping over to The Giddy Limit. The Prince might be in.'

Willa may have had one champagne too many. 'I'm very happy here, Guy,' she says, brightly. 'James is most interesting, and has promised to introduce me to all the Americans in here except Mr Colombo.'

'She'll be fine, old sport,' says James. 'Plenty of material here. Over there, for instance, are Miss Eudoria Stubb and, next to her, the one drawing the cork with her teeth, is Miss Adeline Tumbleweed, respective heiresses to the cod-liver and tinned sausage empires of the same names. I'd be delighted to take Miss Wellington to meet them. They have robust views on the average English earl.'

Guy is upset but determined not to acknowledge any advantage to the American interloper. 'Very well,' he says, affecting the fine insouciance that only seems to work in romantic comedies. 'Goodnight, Willa. Goodnight, Mr…?'

'Gatsby,' says James.

Shortly after Guy leaves, a shot rings out in The Cat's Pyjamas. This is rare but not unprecedented, so the incident is treated phlegmatically by most of the guests, after a sharp but simultaneous scream from The Rocky Twins. The shot came from Mr Colombo's table and was of course intended for James. It misses and gouges a furrow out of the top of the grand piano, ending up embedded in the back wall, acknowledged by Eric the pianist with a full glissando across the keys before he returns, without missing a beat, to the band's lively interpretation of 'Running Wild'. Miss Kitty gestures to Arnold, who she terms her 'membership secretary'. Arnold, a very large man with several almost equally large 'secretarial assistants', informs Mr Colombo that his temporary membership has been revoked for attempting to permanently deprive a fellow member of key benefits, and escorts him and his guests from the club. Mr Colombo accepts his expulsion with some grace, which cannot be said for his associates, who flex their shoulders under the tight suits with bulges in time and with chagrin, and mutter over the same shoulders various incomprehensible remarks reported by Arnold as closely as he could to be 'moider', 'crummy joint', and 'don't ever come to Chicago, you bum'. Willa, gripped by it all, turns to James to discover he has disappeared. Enquiries prove fruitless; no one seems to have noticed him leave, or indeed arrive; Mrs Kitty smiles vaguely and pleads being rather busy.

GUY SAUNTERS INTO THE OFFICE OF THE *DAILY HAIL* around noon the next day. He is feeling a little delicate, having left The Giddy Limit not that many hours ago after dancing too many dances with several girls who'd danced with the Prince of Wales but proved disappointingly discreet about his conversation beyond reporting an unfailing interest in how far they had travelled to be there. The editor of the column, Peter Dempster, a man on whom he used to model himself more enthusiastically than he does now, has already left for lunch. Willa is busy finishing off her account of the thoughts of Miss Stubb and Miss Tumbleweed. She is quite pleased with it, believing it to be a good match with London's Calling's style:

> *What comes to mind when YOU think of cod liver oil and tinned sausages? Not – I'll bet! – two American beauties just hankering for noble husbands! But then YOU haven't met Miss Eudoria Stubb and Miss Adeline Tumbleweed! Miss Stubb's father is none other than Hiram P Stubb, the "Cod Liver King" of Beaver Dam, Wisconsin, "Sort it with Stubb's!"; Miss Tumbleweed's "poppa" is the legendary Sidney W Tumbleweed, of Steam Boat Springs, Colorado, purveyor of Sid's Steamboat Sausages – "Feed your man from the Can!"*
>
> *Miss Stubb and Miss Tumbleweed are both in London, "looking," as Miss Stubb puts it, "for a man, honey, but not just any man, a real life Earl or Count or Duke, any of that as long as they shoot straight and own a castle."*

Miss Tumbleweed said they had so far been unsuccessful in their quest: "Some of these guys are so wet it's not surprising they've got a moat. Come on, boys, we want some nights with some of you knights!" We met the delightful and very lively couple at the famous Cat's Pyjamas club, where things certainly go with a bang!

Guy wanders over, wincing at the noise of Willa's typewriter. He looks over her shoulder and looks at the copy with as much concentration as the noise in his head allows. This, together with his surprise at Willa's style and his relief to see no mention of the ghastly James Gatsby, explains why he doesn't explore the full implications of her last sentence. 'This isn't bad, you know,' he says. 'Come on, let's go and have some lunch at the Criterion to celebrate.' There is something about Willa's enthusiasm, earnestness, effortless unsophistication, and, let's be honest here, stunning good looks, that have turned the suave boulevardier's knees to blancmange and set his heart to thump.

A Hanky Panky expertly mixed by the Criterion barman, Alphonse (aka Alfie Cropper) restores his equilibrium. Willa is surprised to find she has a strong head for strong drink, and feels rather fine after last night. She tosses back her cocktail, relishing the bracing taste of Fernet Branca.

'Do you know,' says Guy, 'you're not bad, for a girl.' This is a mistake. He is not used to the feeling which so deliciously dominates his thoughts and extends down to the tingling in his toes. So he has fallen back on the lazy facetiousness that especially irritates girls who do not wish to be treated as an audience but as an equal.

Willa looks at him through her spectacles. 'Thank you, Guy. I'm very grateful for your help. And I'll just have to work much harder to overcome my great disadvantage of not being a man.'

Guy might be a touch pleased with himself, but one does not travel from Waltham Forest to Mayfair without maintaining a vigilant self-awareness. So it is a pity that he chooses, again, to tease rather than sympathise, imagining this to be somehow attractive. 'Don't worry, I won't hold it against you, as the bishop said to the actress. It's not your fault.'

'No, it's not my fault. It's not my fault that men hang on to imaginings of superiority essentially based on a greater physical strength which doesn't really help that much in pushing pens and buttons and hitting keys and seems mostly to have led them to mostly pointless deaths on one battlefield or another. Which reminds me that they don't seem to have done very well in charge, do they?'

Guy goes for the hat-trick of errors: 'Now calm down, my dear, let's not get too emotional.'

Willa, who is already calm, smiles. 'Oh, that one. Women can't be trusted, the dear little things, because they can't control their feelings like men. But perhaps a few more feelings might have saved millions of lives in France, don't you think?'

Guy loses control. 'Actually, my brother died in France.'

Willa says, 'So did mine.'

The arrival of the waiter with their *saumon ecosse pochée* couldn't be more timely. Lunch, as you might imagine, continues stickily. The weather has to work hard. But Guy finds he cannot be angry with Willa, and as the standard bearer for her sensible sex she feels an obligation to behave well. Matters ease considerably over the *crepe suzette,* and Guy makes her laugh with his stories of Peter Dempster and his legendary approach to expenses. 'They could see why he would want to buy the Nawab of Patak lunch, but couldn't understand why he had to feed his elephant too. What they didn't know was that there hadn't been a Nawab of Patak since 1582!'

They return to the offices of the *Daily Hail* in better mood, Guy realising he is not dealing with some biddable flapper, Willa that she likes him perhaps more than she did. The rhythm of a daily newspaper is beginning to pick up as the evening deadlines begin to concentrate minds. The clack of the typewriters is becoming more intense, louder. Messengers scurry, answering cries of 'Copy!' from editors with rolled-up sleeves and furrowed brows. Occasional curses can be heard, lamenting the challenges of the English language, not always met. Peter Dempster is doing his expenses. He looks up when Guy and Willa enter. 'Guy, dear boy! Lovely stuff on the Prince of Wales and the Countess of Ormskirk being chased by the Earl's out-of-control new motor mower. Willa, a delight to see you again. You clearly fitted right in at The Cat's Pyjamas, loved it. Tell you what, why don't you go again tonight, same sort of thing. Readers love a taste of the naughty high life. I'm popping off to the Oxford Union, Stanley Johnson's proposing the motion, "This House Believes Out-Of-Work Coal Miners Could Make Themselves Useful as Quarry for the Christ Church Beagles", should be close, excellent expenses in prospect. Guy?'

'Oh, you know, first night of Edith Sitwell's new piece, "Cornice, Stucco, Megaphone", could be fun, she's threatening to kick Beverley Nichols hard if he turns up, then on to the Miss Charleston contest at the Up and Down, judges Wee Georgie Wood and George Bernard Shaw. Usual sort of night, but you never know.'

Jimmy white beckons Willa over to his table. 'I saw you in here last night, didn't I, love? With Guy Graves. You one of his debutantes? I'm Jimmy White, Lancashire lad, bit of this, bit of that, tolerated as long as I've got some brass. Have you met my friends? One jockey, one boxer, and one viscount, in that order. Isn't that right, my lord?'

A man who looks like a boxer nods vigorously and smiles without his eyes. 'Absolutely, Jimmy, old boy, yours till the last penny.'

A man who is a boxer slaps Jimmy on the back. 'Great man is Jimmy. Looks after a bloke does Jimmy.'

'Until you lose,' says the jockey, and everyone laughs, the uneasy laugh when drink meets truth.

'I'm a journalist as well, Mr White.'

'But you're a lass.'

'You'd be amazed what we can do. Take me, I can think as well as cook.'

Much laughter, more genuine this time. 'She's got you there, Jimmy boy!'

Jimmy joins in gleefully, a little to Willa's surprise. 'That's a good one! I thought I'd left all the sharp women up north. But what are you doing mixing with the likes of us, young woman? Shouldn't you be reading a book?'

'There you go again, Mr White. Is it only intelligent men who are allowed to enjoy themselves?'

'There's me as well, I'm having a good time.' Jimmy White winks at his coterie, who laugh along.

'Any more bubbly, Jimmy?' asks the Viscount.

'Come on, Mr White, you're no fool,' says Willa, with an

earnestness he hasn't come across for some time. He sends for more champagne. His table's limited attention span has now been distracted by the arrival of the golden Guinness sisters, Aileen, Maureen and Oonagh, looks, cachet *and* cash, with Mrs Kitty and at least six young interchangeable aristocrats in their wake and Albert and his baton bobbing up and down like a seal in a swell.

'No, I'm not a fool. I know what's what. And I know that all this isn't going to last. Prices going up here, prices going up everywhere, worst of all in Germany. The market can't keep rising for ever, there'll be a reckoning. And the first to go will be types like me, risk-takers, big borrowers, flash harrys. I've spent the last 20 years disproving what they say where I come from, that you don't get owt for nowt. I've mixed with nobs, better than this lot here. I'm even on nodding terms with royalty in here but not out there. They won't let me in their enclosure at Ascot but they'll take my brass in here.'

He looks at Willa, the sad eyes direct. 'But you don't want to talk about that, you want a snippet about who's walking out with who and who old Jimmy White is with and what he's up to next, you know, the colourful northern chappie who calls a spade a bloody shovel.'

Willa is excited, sips her champagne and brushes her fringe out of the way. 'But I do want to hear this stuff, Mr White, thanks, Jimmy. I'm very interested in social change. I want to write about it eventually.'

'Don't worry, love, you've got time. You think it might be happening when you see the mix of all sorts and mongrels and nobs and snobs in here, but like I say it's not happening out there. The old order's fighting back. The Home Secretary, Joynson-Hicks, old Jix, people laugh at him, but he's no fool, believe me. Church feller, abstainer, huge energy, great speechifier and a hound for publicity. Thinks all books but the Bible are potential hiding places for smut, as if you can't find that in the Bible, and he thinks places like this are the worst, drink and excess and breaking the licensing laws, he says, but what he really thinks, even if he doesn't know it himself, is that these places are breaking down and threatening the old order, from the top, not the bottom, much easier, and he's right.'

Jimmy White pauses. Albert and his boys are playing a lively little number of his own composition, 'Shepherd's Market Rag'. The floor is full, tables thinned to small huddles like Jimmy and Willa. She feels his charm, and his disillusion, cheeky chappiness dropped. 'What do you think will happen?'

'Soon, he'll be shutting these places down. Watch out for raids, they're coming. Best way out of here is through the band door next to the stage and out of the dressing room window into the back alley. Pays to know these things, you'll find. But if you're talking about proper change, that won't happen unless there's another war, and that'll come even though they'll fight like hell to avoid it, because they know what it means. Any rate, I probably won't be around to see it. Aye, aye, I'm off!'

Jimmy has spotted activity at the other end of the club, the entrance. Mrs Kitty is remonstrating, with extravagant gestures, as a group of people tries to enter. A whistle blows, the music stops and the guests make the mistake of moving towards the policemen, some in plain clothes, coming in. A few canny ones like Jimmy go the other way, following the band. The police start taking names and escorting guests out. Willa is torn between escape and duty. She is not committed enough to journalism to get arrested, and is in any case too sensible.

She moves to the band door. A middle-aged woman, conservatively dressed, has just come out of the ladies' and is frozen in alarm. 'Where's everybody gone? What's happening?' she says to Willa in a northern accent softer than Jimmy White's.

'I think it's some sort of a raid thingie. That way to get arrested, this way to escape!'

'A raid. Goodness gracious, no one told me! Why didn't anyone tell me?'

'Well, I'm not very experienced in this kind of thing, but I don't think telling people in advance is part of it.'

The woman is now seriously agitated. 'You don't understand! They should have told me! My husband should have told me! This is intolerable!'

'It's certainly a mess. But I'm not hanging about. Do you want to come with me? I know a way out.'

The woman, still shaking her head and complaining loudly, follows Willa. She follows Jimmy's directions, and after a short wait behind several of the band, who are delaying their exit for a quick drink (the double bass still flirting), Willa and the woman are out in the alley and in Lisle Street, walking towards Leicester Square among the usual throng making for home after a less exciting night in the West End. The woman, calmed by escape and the cool air, thanks Willa. 'My dear, I'm so grateful. I don't know whatever I would have done if I'd been arrested, my husband would have been livid. I shouldn't have gone to the club in the first place, but my old friend Georgie and her husband Teddy said it would be fun and make a change to all the fusty evenings I'm used to at the moment. How can I possibly thank you?'

Willa, demonstrating again why she has a lot to learn about the darker arts of journalism, fails to take note of this interesting eyewitness account, and shakes her head. 'Don't mention it, happy to help. You'll pick up a cab in Leicester Square, goodbye.'

'Thank you. But if you would ever like a cup of tea or some such, do get in touch.' She fiddles in her bag, they exchange cards, she walks briskly away. Willa moves over to a street lamp and examines the card she's been given in the light. 'Lady Joynson-Hicks', it reads. Willa thinks for a bit and then realises she has saved the wife of the Home Secretary from arrest in what can only be described as compromising circumstances, viz drinking alcohol outside the permitted hours.

WILLA IS AT HER TYPEWRITER BETIMES THE NEXT MORNING and has already done quite a lot when Guy arrives. They are the only two in the London's Calling office and there is that awkwardness that always affects two people who are attracted to each other but haven't quite worked out what to do about it. 'Hello!' says Willa, a little too brightly. 'How did it go last night? Did GBS cut a rug with the Charleston?'

Guy thinks about cool but goes for rueful. 'Sadly not. Turned out it was in fact Jorge Bernardo Shore, a department store proprietor from São Paulo who took a violent dislike to Wee Georgie Wood and awarded the prize to Lady Emerald Cunard by mistake. And Beverley Nichols didn't turn up to Edith Sitwell's recital and I'm left with the discordant triangle struck vigorously and repeatedly by Virginia Woolf echoing unpleasantly inside my head. You?'

'Rather exciting, actually. There was a police raid at The Cat's Pyjamas.'

'Crikey, that's terrific! Good story! Of course you got yourself arrested?'

'No, I managed to avoid it by escaping through the back. It makes a thrilling story.'

There is a silence. 'Hmm, that wasn't too clever, Willa. You could have written about being arrested, night in the cells, thrilling personal account, innocent journalist among all these society figures. Still, you've got a list of everyone who was fingered?'

There is another silence. 'No. I suppose I should have done that.'

Guy has the chance to play the seniority superiority card, but he must be in love. 'Don't worry, I can get hold of that for you, I know someone at Vine Street.'

Willa blushes, which makes her even more attractive to the smitten hack. 'Oh thanks, Guy, I'd be lost without you!'

Guy's turn. A meaningful pause is ended by the arrival of Peter Dempster. 'Everything tickety-boo? Predictable vote at Oxford last night. Tally-ho, I'm off to lunch with Gally Threepwood, trying to drum up interest in his memoirs, promising some ripe stuff about his sister, Lady Constance Keeble of Blandings and her early days, escapade involving a Bulgarian sailor in Frinton, apparently. Great man, Gally, he'll be happy to say our lunch was in Deauville. Pip-pip!'

The telephone rings. 'Willa Wellington?'

'Yes, hello?'

'It's Grace Joynson-Hicks.'

'Oh, yes, hello.'

'Please do not publish anything about last night until I've had a chance to speak to you. Can you come over now?'

'Of course.'

'I'll be waiting, thank you.'

Willa replaces the receiver, aware that Guy's attention is on her, which it would have been anyway. She finds herself hesitating to tell him about Lady Joynson-Hicks, partly because she should have mentioned it already, partly because Guy has already exposed her ignorance of cunning journalistic practice, and for some reason it's more important than ever to impress him; and partly because she finds herself uneasy about cunning journalistic practice. 'I'm just popping out,' she says to Guy, who smiles his rare smile, the genuine one. He makes promising noises about Vine Street, and carries on trying to make gold from the base metal that is Virginia Woolf's triangle.

The Joynson-Hicks have a smart house in Westminster, supported by the money Jix has made from a career as a solicitor assiduously concentrating on the most lucrative aspects of law. Willa is ushered into a reception room, furnished with the Victorian clutter Jix finds sympathetic. Lady Joynson-Hicks is standing by the fireplace, pale, agitated, and repeatedly touching her throat in the accustomed manner of a woman in high peril and emotion.

'Miss Wellington, thank you for coming so promptly. You can imagine how I felt when I read your card and realised you were a journalist. I didn't think women were journalists. I won't beat about the bush. If you publish that I was at The Cat's Pyjamas last night, it will ruin my husband. Innocently enough, I have let my husband down. You as a woman must understand that there is no higher duty than to one's husband! He must be protected from ridicule and charges of hypocrisy! I appeal to you as a woman – don't publish!'

Willa is moved, but not necessarily to Lady Joynson-Hicks' advantage. 'Lady Joynson-Hicks, I sympathise with your predicament, but I cannot agree with your views on husbands! There is no reason beyond outmoded and damaging convention why men and women should not be equal. There is no reason beyond outmoded and damaging laws why husbands and wives should not be equal!'

'As it happens, Miss Wellington, I agree with you. But the position is different with husbands in the public eye. Journalists and gossips and, I'm afraid, most of the general public, do not allow the wives of famous men to act according to views which may differ from those of their husbands. That was part of the contract I made with my husband before our marriage.'

She gives Willa one of those smiles that begs for agreement, and motions for her to sit down. They take opposing chairs. Willa asks, carefully but in surprise, 'You contracted to do that?'

'Well, no, not legally, although he wanted to, along with some other silly things such as obligatory but cheerful attendance at his public meetings. I was in love, and he can be both charming and masterful, but nevertheless he had to accept my assurance that I would never do anything to harm or embarrass him. And that if he wanted such in writing, he would have to look elsewhere for a partner.'

'Bravo. And did you get a similar assurance from him? And is harm or embarrassment to him worth more than your principles and independence?'

'No, I didn't. And I can assure you that some of the things he has supported and causes he has taken up – the crusade against supposedly pornographic novels, for example – have caused me exasperation and embarrassment. I don't know whether you know, but I come from a leading Manchester family, with all the free thinking that great city encourages. I love books! I love novels! If Lorenzo Lawrence wants to write about cunts and bore us even further with more pricks and gamekeeper-chatelaine fantasies, that's up to him and his readers in the privacy of their own book. And as for *The Well of Loneliness*, Jix has discovered lesbians even later than Queen Victoria. And now these raids! It's my fault, of course, he seemed charming when we were courting. But I expect that's what they all say.'

She looks wistfully at Willa, who is beginning rather to like her, and proceeds gently because of it. 'I got acquainted with a little law at Cambridge, Lady Joynson-Hicks. There wasn't much else we were allowed to do except read. So I know that when one side behaves outrageously the other can void the contract. Why don't you stand up to him?'

'Stand up to whom?' A prissy-looking man has appeared in the doorway. It is, of course, William Joynson-Hicks. The very Jix himself. 'I'm sorry, my dear, I didn't realise you had company. I've just come over to pick up some papers I was working on last night. I'm off to the Commons now.'

He smiles at Willa with a smile that she recognises from older men of a certain gauge. 'I don't think I have had the pleasure,' he says, with a smile that is never going to go well with a remark like that.

'This is Miss Willa Wellington, William,' says his wife, who has made a decision, possibly swung by the smile. 'Miss Wellington works at the *Daily Hail*. I met her last night at The Cat's Pyjamas.'

Jix is many things, including contradictions, but, as the House knows, he is nimble on his feet and under pressure. The smile disappears instantly, but he betrays nothing else, and pulls up a chair to join the conversation.

Willa is a junior to his senior but she is pleased to discover a coolness under fire. She too makes a decision. 'Yes, sir, you certainly caused some excitement at The Cat last night. All those arrests! All those notable people! It was very lucky I was able to help Lady Joynson-Hicks… effect an exit. What a story that would have been – Home Secretary's Wife Arrested!'

Jix smiles another smile, the careful one. 'Although "Newspaper Helps Home Secretary's Wife Escape Arrest" has a certain popular allure as well,' he says.

Willa lets this pass. Lady Joynson-Hicks, seemingly as unperturbed as her husband, continues. 'We were having a very interesting conversation before you arrived, William.'

'Oh?'

'Yes, it was about a wife's obligations to a husband.'

'What, not to embarrass him or harm his career, that sort of thing?'

'Yes, and how those obligations might be affected by his behaviour.'

'I see. You mean if he doesn't warn her that she might embarrass him, no matter how unlikely it might be that she frequented a club the police were going to raid?'

'You're a member of several such clubs yourself, aren't you, William?'

A touch of fluster, speedily dismissed, but not quite speedily enough. 'Indeed... indeed, but strictly for political purposes, and I would be shocked – shocked! – to find that illegal drinking was going on in any club of which I was a member.'

He looks calm, just about, to Willa, but Lady Joynson-Hicks knows he is unused to this sort of challenge at home, and she can tell, also, that he is irritated because it is interfering with his thinking about how to defuse Willa and her dangerous knowledge.

'Talk also moved on to the different interests of husband and wife,' says Willa. 'And how it is important that if one partner has to put up with views he or she finds a little extreme, so should the other.'

Now both Sir William and Lady Joynson-Hicks are in the dark as to where this is going, a worse problem for the politician and lawyer whose essential and comfortable modus operandi is knowing what comes next.

Unsurprisingly, then, Jix tries to take command. 'Interesting, interesting. But tell me, Miss Wellington, are you proposing to publish a story about Lady Joynson-Hicks and her presence in all innocence at The Cat's Pyjamas, where she categorically infringed no laws?'

He smiles the careful smile again but overreaches himself. 'And, of course, you don't drink alcohol, do you, my dear?'

Lady Joynson-Hicks is now, despite everything, enjoying herself. 'Well, I do have the occasional glass of champagne and the odd milk stout, don't I, William? And there was that time in Nice. On the terrace. It was rather hot, and the night was young and the scent of bougainvillea almost overpowering, but even so. You must remember, William.'

Some silences are easy and comfortable. This one is not. Willa, admirably self-controlled for one so young, uses it to avoid answering Jix's original question. 'Actually, Sir William, my main purpose in visiting today was to gather more material for a very important article I'm writing on women and equality in post-war Britain.'

'Goodness me, that's a serious topic for a slip of a girl,' says Jix, before realising he shouldn't have.

'Thank you, Home Secretary, but I'm not convinced that physical traits and reproductive function have a predominant influence on the intellect. I will allow, though, that age tends to give advantage, but not in all cases. The case I'm particularly interested in, for instance, is men being able to vote at the age of 21 and women not being allowed the same privilege until they're 30. I'll concede that Lady Joynson-Hicks might be able to bring more experience than I when she chooses whom to vote for in the next election, but I simply won't have it that a woman of 30 is somehow equivalent to a man of 21. I met a few of the latter at Cambridge and I laugh at the notion. Ha!'

Willa makes a very good job of that derisive exclamation. Jix, a keen orator himself, is impressed, and anxious to rescue himself from the slip slip. 'Yes, an interesting point, Miss Wellington.' He smiles in what he hopes is an avuncular, sage way but isn't, and continues, 'Let an old war horse with some experience of the way these things work advise you. Our precious and ancient democracy has evolved in a stately, calm and considered manner without any of the unpleasantness experienced elsewhere. All will come right in time when it is the right time, mark my words.'

'But, Sir William, I have the strongest feeling that *this* is the right time. I'm sure you know that the second reading of Mr Whiteley's private members' bill calling for the voting age for women to be lowered to 21 comes before the House today. And think how marvellous it would be if only there was some way that you, the Home Secretary, could be persuaded to speak in its support!'

'Yes, wouldn't that be wonderful, William?' says Lady Joynson-Hicks.

And, remarkably enough, this is what transpires in the House of Commons that afternoon. The bill fails but Sir William Joynson-Hicks, apparently off the cuff, and without consulting his Cabinet colleagues, has committed the Government to lowering the voting age for women at the next general election. Which is probably a better example of the way our precious and ancient democracy works.

CELEBRATION IS IN THE AIR AT THE CAT'S PYJAMAS. MRS Kitty knows that she will be closed down by the magistrates at her upcoming hearing, that she most likely faces a spell in Holloway, and that the police are unlikely to strike a second time in the same place on the next night, so she is determined to go out with a bang. All and every London is present, including Noël, Gertie, Ivor, Siegfried, Talullah, Oonagh, Eudoria, Adeline, perhaps the Prince of Wales – really, who can tell in this crush? – Jimmy, his chum Tommy Beecham, still looking for an orchestra, Evelyn, Sebastian, Charles, Julia (both Flyte and Stitch), Brenda, Tony, but definitely neither Mr Gatsby nor Mr Colombo. Guy and Willa are squeezed in at the back and having a happy shouted conversation over Albert's latest offering, 'Will You Be True, Yes or Noo, My Coochy Coo?' Guy, purely as a good colleague, earlier finessed Willa's account of last night's raid together with a list of the arrested and charged, most of whom seem to be back tonight. He is now staring admiringly into her eyes behind the spectacles.

'Do you know Willa,' he says, 'you're going to be a great journalist. Energy, style – Fleet Street will be at your feet!'

'I'm not so sure, Guy. I'm not so sure, either, that you would be quite so impressed with me if you knew about what else happened here last night.'

Albert is now guiding his band through a slow number, 'Mayfair Lady, Bet You Make Bethnal Green'. 'Tell me more,' says Guy, 'I'm all ears and an encouraging smile.'

'I didn't escape on my own last night. I was with Lady Joynson-Hicks.'

Encouraging smile turns to wide open mouth. 'Lady Jix was here!? What a story!? And it's not too late for tomorrow's paper. But we'll have to be quick!'

'No, Guy. We can't. That's how I got him to make the speech in favour of lowering the voting age. I went round to see her and he was there. She told him she was here – she's actually quite a good egg and sound on a lot of things, including him – so I seized my chance to get him to support women.'

'Did you promise him you wouldn't write about her being here?'

'Not exactly, but he took the point.'

'This is a really big story, Willa! Hypocrites, one rule for the rich, Jix's wife cavorts in club he's had raided, it's funny, scandalous, important and we've got to write it! This will make both our names!'

Guy's excitement is infectious. He also looks wonderfully boyish and appealing. Willa's will wobbles. But not for long. Wellingtons may give, but they do not sunder. 'No, Guy. I cannot do it. It would be dishonest and dishonourable. The women's vote is far more important than a passing scandal involving a pompous arse which is going to hurt his blameless wife far more than it hurts him.'

Guy stares at her. Surprise, stupefaction and the questioning of what he works for are chased across his face by awe, amusement, attraction and the arrival of a thought he finds more and more enticing. This, truly, is love, which conquers all.

'Maybe you're right… you could be right! You are right!' he tells her and himself. 'There are bigger things than here-today-gone-tomorrow ructions and frictions, the feeble idle doings of the pointlessly rich and the richly pointless.' He is warming, nay combusting, to his theme. 'I refuse to prostitute my gifts in the quotidian chronicling of emptiness any longer. Anyway, it will all be much better in a book full of anger and scorn and witty indignation. I shall resign immediately and concentrate on completing *A Fistful of Grit!*'

It is Guy's turn to be admired, as he stands tall, eyes blazing in the hubbub, apologising occasionally in the English way when other revellers bump into him. Willa regards him with new awe and fresh admiration. 'Oh, Guy! How romantic! I shall resign as well to devote myself to the cause of equality, truth and justice.'

The couple embrace, and then kiss, lingeringly, steaming up Willa's spectacles and dishevelling Guy's tie, which normally he doesn't like. Albert has moved on to 'Ponders End Blues'. The bass player is winking at another girl tonight. Mrs Kitty breaks open another bubbly. There will be more but not many before she welcomes guests to The Cat again. Noël and Evelyn and Talullah have just said something crashingly funny at exactly the same time at separate tables and three roars rush up and rattle the old place. Will it ever be better than this? Guy's book will be a success; he will write many more, and they will sell but never quite touch Evelyn or Graham G or even Anthony P, mostly because there is an amiability about them, born of happiness with Willa, who will be a Labour MP, as doughty and devoted as the 1930s and 1940s will need, and one of the two per cent who are women. She serves on several committees with her friend Grace Joynson-Hicks; Guy still has lunch (paying, of course) with Peter Dempster from time to time in any number of alleged exotic continental venues, some of which, funnily enough, he will later visit in reality and uniform, Captain Graves, MC. But for now, for this moment, for Guy and Willa, wrapped in each other and surrounded by beautiful faces, fine minds and some dark hearts, The Cat's Pyjamas, the brittle, flashy Cat's Pyjamas, really is exactly that.

Afterword

The Cat's Pyjamas is based on three of the clubs in 1920's London that answered the need for late-night enjoyment when successive governments, like any of their kind, proved reluctant to surrender control, in this case on drinking hours imposed during the First World War. The 43, Chez Victor and The Kit-Cat were the most fashionable, providing entertainment, dancing and, most importantly, drink after 10pm, supposedly accompanying tickets and food until 12.30am, but often later. The 43, at 43, Gerrard Street, was the most famous of several owned by the redoubtable MRS KATE MEYRICK, an Irishwoman with seven children, great charm, an estranged husband who did not support her, the organisational ability of a quartermaster and a relaxed approach to the law. Part of her success lay in attracting the upper classes, who found that heavy post-war taxes, particularly death duties, were making the expense of the old large-scale and frequent entertaining at home prohibitive. All the real people mentioned above visited the 43, with the possible exception of Neville Chamberlain: it was this mix of old and new money, of the louche, lively and traditional, that alarmed an Establishment grappling with post-war social change and detecting the hand of Communist Russia everywhere – in the rise of the Labour Party and the trades union movement, and, of course, in the General Strike of 1926.

Winston Churchill, with his vigour and eye for mood and gimmick, is often named as the chief architect of the Strike's defeat. Just as important, though now mostly forgotten, was SIR

WILLIAM JOYNSON-HICKS, the then Home Secretary. Joynson-Hicks supplemented Churchill's flashier gifts with an exceptional eye for detail and planning and an unswerving distrust of trades unions and Communism. He was a striking example of the maverick figure British public life quite often throws up and is never entirely sure what to do with or treat seriously. Often, too, there is a nickname or uncommon first name which acts as a great aid to recognition: Joynson-Hicks became known as Jix in one of his early election campaigns (defeating Churchill), and it stuck. A member of the increasingly influential professional middle classes, he was a London solicitor with a voracious appetite for work and making contacts, a gift for oratory, and the fiercest attachment to the previous century's public morality. In one of those twists of fate and politics, and to general surprise, he was made Home Secretary in 1924, thus allowing free rein to his puritanical zeal. D H Lawrence, Radclyffe Hall and Boccaccio, authors of 'Lady Chatterley's Lover', 'The Well of Loneliness', and 'The Decameron' respectively, fell foul of Jix, along with works on birth control, all categorised by him as part of 'this tide of filth coming across the channel'.

The London nightclubs were an obvious target for this righteous wrongheadedness. In the words of a biographer, 'His most publicised and farcical moral policing was the attempt to shut down, or sanitise, the nightclubs which had mushroomed in central London after 1918, where he smelled unbridled and unmentionable vice, much of which was only doubtfully against the law, and a great deal of drinking out of hours, which decidedly was'.

His most obvious opponent was Mrs Meyrick, who refused to be cowed by repeated police raids, opened another club as soon as one was closed down, and served at least three jail sentences; the last, which broke her health, was for bribing a London detective not to raid her clubs. She died in 1933, a year after Joynson-Hicks, by then Viscount Brentford. Her clubs had paid for her sons to go to Harrow and her daughters to Roedean. One daughter married the 26th Baron de Clifford (who was 19 at the time), another, the 14th Earl of Kinnoull. She features, as Mrs Mayfield, in Evelyn Waugh's 'Brideshead Revisited' and 'A Handful of Dust', where the 43 is called The Old Hundredth. Readers may notice a similarity between Willa Wellington and William Boot, of Waugh's 'Scoop'.

Joynson-Hicks was a man of varied and eccentric interests. He was fascinated by machines, studied the workings of telephones and aeroplanes, and was at various times Chairman of the Automobile Association and president of both The National Traction Engine Association and the National Threshing Machine Owners' Association. He was also a fierce defender of the Book of Common Prayer against its revision in 1928, which he saw as an attempt to reintroduce Papism. He was guilty of anti-semitism, and, for reasons best known to himself, defended the action of General Dyer in killing at least 379 unarmed Indians and injuring over 1,200 more in the massacre at Amritsar in 1919.

He seems, then, an unlikely promoter of women's rights. Yet on February 20, 1925, in a debate on the private members' bill introduced by the Labour MP, William Whiteley, Jix committed the Government, without any Cabinet consultation, to lowering the enfranchisement age for women from 30 to 21 at the next general election. It is still unclear why. His old friend and foe Churchill was clear that Jix had reacted off the cuff in the heat of debate without proper authority. Inconveniently, I am compelled to note that those enemies of the fiction writer, revising historians, have suggested that Churchill was in error and that this was Government policy. Whatever, one of the last significant acts of Jix's career was to move the second reading of The Equal Franchise Act in 1928, bringing in what was dismissively known as the 'Flapper Vote'.

Many notable people appeared in the lists of people arrested in the raids on London's nightclubs, including aristocrats and politicians. This is a report of a raid at the Kit-Cat Club in Haymarket:

'One member, who was noticeably and happily absent on that historic occasion, for instance, is Sir William Joynson-Hicks, the Home Secretary. It is whispered, however, that when the raid was being planned nobody informed him, and so very nearly involved the good man in a most embarrassing situation, for it is also whispered that Lady Joynson-Hicks was at the Kit-Cat during the excitement, and was gotten down a fire-escape and out through an unsavoury back alley just in the nick of time'.

I cannot vouch for the whisper, and respect for the truth narrowly compels me to point out that the raid described took place in 1927.

The Kit-Cat also hosted Edward, the Prince of Wales and future King Edward VIII, the night before an earlier raid. Jix's familiarity with the club is confirmed by this report from The New York Times in 1925:

'LONDON — Sir William Joynson-Hicks, Home Secretary, enjoyed his first visit to a London night club a few nights ago, it was revealed to-day [May 17]. There had been so much agitation against the night clubs that the Home Secretary had decided upon personal investigation. He selected the newly opened Kit-Kat club, which has a large membership chiefly among professional people. Apparently he had a good time and found nothing to criticise, but he gave no indication that his experience might result in more freedom for London night life'.

Lady Joynson-Hicks, who was from a Manchester industrial family, lived on until 1952. The raids forced the closure of Chez Victor, in Grafton Street, where, among much else, Edwina Mountbatten cavorted with Leslie 'Hutch' Hutchinson, the West Indian cabaret pianist and singer. The owner, Victor Perosino, moved instead to Paris, where he also enjoyed great success. He invited Sir William and Lady Joynson-Hicks to the Paris opening; Jix replied in friendly fashion, promising to attend if they were in Paris. They didn't.

There is no exaggeration, though (well perhaps a little), in the shooting incident. The London underworld took quite as much interest in Mrs Meyrick's activities and profits as corrupt police officers. In her memoir, she writes:

> 'One of our members, overhearing the refusal of a party of gangsters to pay for their drinks, shouted out, "Cads!". In a moment one of the men whipped out a revolver and fired two shots across the club, shattering a pair of mirrors on the opposite wall. By sheer good luck nobody was struck by the bullets, though one of them whistled past the ear of a man standing near me and the other ploughed a deep furrow in the piano'.

Mr Gatsby did not visit The 43, nor Mr Colombo, who readers may remember from 'Some Like It Hot', the excellent Billy Wilder film with Jack Lemmon, Tony Curtis, Marilyn Monroe, and George Raft as the coin-flipping Spats. Mrs Meyrick nevertheless did play host to strikingly similar visitors from the United States:

> 'Even our old American bootleggers we loved. Perhaps they were just a trifle rough and noisy; perhaps there were times when we saw our English visitors leave soon after these more demonstrative spirits put in an appearance – we loved them just the same. If anything happened to upset them in the least, knives flashed or shots were fired. Then all the women would scream or go off into hysterics. But to me the bootleggers were just nice, dear boys. I could always manage them. A few calming words were all that was required; they only needed to have the position explained to them politely and good-humouredly. Then for a while peace

would reign once more, and whoever had transgressed would either apologise or disappear. Drinks all round would follow. Everything would be all happiness and joy again. And there you have the secret of nightclub management. It is all a simple matter of knowing how to treat people'.

Indeed.

One last glimpse of a raid:

'*The Evening News commented on the extraordinary scenes of those arrested as frequenters of the nightclub upon being led out by the officers, "They roared out with laughter and song, and called to one another as they were pushed into the vans. 'The never-stop railway to Vine-street!' someone shouted, and another retorted, 'All aboard for the Bow-street express!'"..*

What larks.

Miss Tumbleweed and Miss Stubb are fictional examples of the many American heiresses who continued a long-standing trend of marrying into English and European nobility. My favourite example is Princess Afonso of Braganza who before her marriage was Nevada Stoody Hayes. The Golden Guinness Girls, Oonagh, Aileen and Maureen, daughters of Arthur Guinness, second son of the first Earl of Iveagh, led for the rather more boho-aristo home side, along with, a little later, the Mitfords, Nancy, Deborah, Jessica and Unity.

One of the other real people encountered, not strictly chronologically, in The Cat's Pyjamas, JIMMY WHITE was born in Rochdale, Lancashire, and graduated from bricklayer and navvy to large-scale London property speculator via owning a circus, boxing promoting and bankruptcy. Only his straightforward Lancashire charm could explain the willingness of others to back schemes that had a consistent habit of overreaching themselves.

These included trying to buy the Covent Garden Estate with his friend, Joseph Beecham, the awkward but very wealthy pill manufacturer and another Lancastrian, from St Helens. Beecham died in the midst of problems buying the estate during the First World War; rather to pattern, White moved on, leaving others to remedy the trouble. Joseph's son, Thomas Beecham, the great conductor, remained friendly with him, and he continued to be chairman of the Beecham family trust while other involvements with the Dunlop rubber company and the Lancashire cotton industry also came to grief. White continued to make money from his property dealing and moved into theatre ownership, all marked by the same extravagance he brought to the Turf. He ran a successful stables near Swindon, but was not invited into the Royal Enclosure at Ascot, even more of a sign of social acceptance then. He was finally brought down in 1927 when demand for payment from a large share deal coincided overwhelmingly with another for his proposed purchase of the Wembley Conference Centre. On June 29, he poisoned himself at his large country home with chloroform and Prussic acid. His death was much regretted by friends and the public, more than 5,000 of whom attended his funeral and, for different reasons, by his disappointed investors and his family, who were left destitute. He left a note for the coroner, 'Go easy with me, old man. I am dead from prussic acid. No need to cut any deeper. – Jimmy'.

TALLULAH BANKHEAD was an Alabama socialite and actress in theatre and occasionally film but mostly the outstandingly outrageous symbol of the hedonism of the 1920s. There were few addictions she didn't enthusiastically indulge, including drink, drugs, 120 cigarettes a day and sex almost as often, with either sex, whether, allegedly (as is so often the case with legends) the young girls queuing up to share her bed outside her hotel room, or motoring down to the Cafe de Paris hotel in Bray to canoodle 'indecently and unnaturally' with six boys from Eton. She also supported civil rights, supported foster children and helped families escape both the Spanish Civil War and World War II. My favourite Tallulah story remains her watching the 1938 'Free World Versus The Third Reich' heavyweight world championship fight in New York between the great Joe Louis and the Hitler protégé, Max Schmeling: when Louis knocked out Schmeling in the first round, she jumped to her feet and shouted at the Schmeling fans behind her, 'I told you so, you sons of bitches!'

Albert and His Original Orpheans are, sadly, invented; The Rocky Twins, remarkably, are not. 'Norway's Outrageous Jazz Age Beauties', Leif and Paal Roschberg, androgynous and beautiful in and out of drag, were a popular attraction on and off stage in London, the USA and Paris, where they were taken up by the legendarily enticing soubrette, Mistinguett, who said that 'they were so ravishing that each night after the show they would allow themselves to be kidnapped by beauty enthusiasts of both sexes'. It is difficult to imagine even Waugh improving on this image of 1920's hedonism, only enhanced by the affair of one of them – it was never entirely clear who was who – with a tin mining millionaire from Bolivia.

FURTHER READING:
Secrets of the 43 Club, Mrs Kate Merrick
The Last Victorians: A Daring Reassessment of Four Twentieth Century Eccentrics, W Sydney Robinson
A Handful of Dust, Scoop, and Brideshead Revisited, Evelyn Waugh

1935

One Last Draw

THERE WAS NOTHING ESPECIALLY NOTICEABLE OR immediately significant about the two elderly men sitting at a table in the saloon bar of The Highwayman this midsummer day in 1935. But if any of the other and few patrons had cared to look a little closer, which they didn't, just a hint of the unusual would have suggested itself: the cut of the shabby clothes, which were also of a considerable vintage, perhaps; the paleness of the blue eyes of the smaller, livelier man, or the edgy restlessness of the other, whose jacket's suede was now just a shiny memory.

The edgy one wasn't happy, and there was nothing about The Highwayman that was likely to improve his mood. The other patrons wore expressions which could have been described as morose if that didn't convey too much of a sense of gaiety. 'Hellfire,' he said. 'So this is your home town. Dull doesn't quite do it. Dirty, wet, no money. Why didn't we stay in London? And this beer.' His eyes narrowed and his lip curled. It was clear he didn't like the beer.

The livelier man crinkled his eyes into an affectionate smile at what was not the first complaint he'd heard in the 30 years they'd been friends. 'What about that church I showed you? St Walburge's?' He produced a small, battered book from his side pocket, and put on a pair of spectacles that came from his top one. 'That's the tallest spire in England not on a cathedral.'

The other shook his head and gave him a look of pained disbelief that was clearly just as well-practised. 'I'm going to see if they've got some other beer,' he said, getting to his feet with a sigh that could have been exaggerated for his friend's benefit, but wasn't. Arthritis can do that to a knee.

He made his way to the bar, its dark wood providing little contrast to the colour of the walls, which cigarette smoke had left at least six shades darker than what must once have been cream. The overall effect was a shade best described on the tin as Melancholy. The barman was determined in his silence, polishing glasses and contemplating noncommittally every possible direction other than where his potential customer stood.

'What does a man have to do to get a drink round here, friend?' he asked, eventually, in a level but loaded tone which had worked well for him in the past.

'A man has to come back in three hours,' said the barman. 'We're closing now. Didn't you hear the bell?'

'I thought that was for a funeral. Yours, too, if you don't give me a beer that tastes like beer, and now.'

'Sorry, cocker,' said the barman, 'those are the rules, and it's more than my job's worth to break them. On your way.'

It's an interesting thing, how much depends on reputation. There had been many places over the years where a barman would have decided without difficulty that it was more than his job's worth not to serve this man, who had now taken a step back from the bar. His left hand hovered at hip height and his eyes had narrowed and grown as cold as their colour, a darker, less friendly blue than his companion's.

'Hold up there, old friend.' His friend was at his side, his hand over the other's. 'We'll be moving along, then. Charming establishment you run here, sir. Puts me in mind of a little place I know on the Rue Girardon in Montmartre, with a touch of the Number Ten saloon in Deadwood thrown in, roughly. Good day to you. Come on, Sundance.'

As they left, a wizened little man who had been nursing a glass of stout as if he intended it to survive into its teenaged years, said, without removing his gaze from whatever imaginary disaster was occurring in the mid-distance, 'Welcome to Preston.'

IT HAD BEEN QUITE SOME TIME SINCE ROBERT PARKER AND Harry Longabaugh, otherwise and sometimes known as Butch Cassidy and the Sundance Kid, had found themselves heavily outnumbered in a shootout with troops in San Vicente, Bolivia, just across the border from Argentina. Around 25 years, in fact, since they'd slipped away into the South American night, leaving the embarrassed soldiery to report that the two dead bodies were the famous *bandidos yanquis* rather than troopers slain by friendly fire whose relatives would be bribed for the purpose.

The years that followed had been not without incident. The working passage on the tramp steamer across the Pacific that ended prematurely in Kiribati after the second mate took exception to being found out cheating at cards. The time spent beachcombing on Nonouti which was also abandoned abruptly after Sundance became over familiar with the European copra trader's native wife. Paddle steamer up the Irrawaddy interrupted by Butch cheating at cards. Working passage to Sydney and lucrative employment as consultants to a gang of bushrangers at Toowoomba terminated by the termination on the scaffold of the bushrangers. Passage to Marseilles via Suez, short stay in Cairo as unsuccessful tomb robbers and pyramid salesmen before becoming bodyguards to chief white slaver, Pierre 'Quatre Doigts' Le Brut, until Butch fell in love with one of the white slaves. First World War service as piano player (Butch) and bartender with extras (Sundance) in the best brothel in Rouen. Roaring twenties in Paris meeting and cheating the Lost Generation, showing Hemingway how to draw (a gun; Butch) and suggesting *The Great Gatsby* to Fitzgerald (his face: Sundance).

But depressions and recessions also affect outlaws. Butch, who now studied the financial pages of the newspapers with a keen interest, especially, for old time's sake, bank and railway stocks, decided that the cost of living might be less challenging somewhere less glitzy than Paris. As he pithily put it, 'Artists starve, outlaws are savvy.' Then, when he was telling Sundance (not for the first time) over a glass of absinthe about his roots in northern England, how his grandfather had taken his family to America from Preston, proud Preston, the finest town in all of Lancashire, his friend responded (not for the first time), 'Holy cow, Butch, not that again! If this here Preston and this Lancasheer are so damn fine, how come you all left?'

And so a plan formed. 'Just think of it, Harry… [Harry was what Butch called Sundance in their more intimate moments and when he was trying to persuade the curmudgeonly gunslinger into a course of action regarding which Butch himself wasn't yet entirely convinced] …we'd be among the friendliest people this side of the Pecos. Why, my grandaddy used to tell me you only had to walk down one of their quaint little streets and they would be queueing up to take you inside their humble homes and give you a cup of java or whatever it is they drink. Couple of friendly hombres like us could live for next to nothing.'

Sundance was so generally opposed to most things that Butch had long ago concluded his nickname had nothing to do with the town of that name in Wyoming but was in fact ironic. 'But how are we going to rob banks and trains when there's no money? I've made the mistake of leaving this sort of thing to you too many times before, Butch, mostly because you've got glasses and you can read. But even I've heard about England having nearly as tough a time as the States. And this north of England is the pits, I'm told.'

'Well, Harry, there's something in what you say. But it's not all mining. Cotton's in trouble, too, and has been since the Rebs were taught how to behave. And I'm sorry to bring this up again, but our days of robbing banks and trains are long gone.'

This was another bugbear of Sundance's. Butch had been trying to tell him for years that their armed robbing was over, thanks to a debilitating combination of advances in their years – the arthritis, for example, the eyesight ditto – and technology that had produced far better protection and detection. Unfortunately, none of his subsequent money-making schemes had been nearly as successful as the robbing; consequently the need to find somewhere to conserve their dwindling finances in the sunset years. And Lancashire, largely for sentimental reasons, seemed to fit.

The Sundance Kid did have his softer side, but it was as well protected as any of the hideouts where he'd lain low over the years, from the Hole in the Wall and Robbers' Roost to a rather damp cave which had come in useful after the unpleasantness in Penang. It had been many years, for example, since the comely Etta Place had not been able to take any more of it, but he still thought of her fairly often and fairly fondly, even though she had taken a large amount of their South American earnings with her and had not been heard of again. He himself had no wish whatever to return to Phoenixville, Pennsylvania, still less to somewhere in Westphalia, home of his German ancestors, but he did understand that old Butch was a whimsical sort of fellow, and that he needed to be humoured, as he did the thinking for both of them, partly because Sundance himself couldn't be bothered, partly because it allowed him free rein to grumble when things went wrong, and partly because, on the whole, their time together had been rather more interesting than staying in Phoenixville, Pennsylvania.

Besides, the sun was now shining in Preston, Lancashire, and the locals, although not noticeably as friendly as advertised, were showing no signs of considering the cheering rays a rare phenomenon by looking up at the sky and such. The pair strolled through the centre of the town, with Butch pointing out with pride some more of the finer features, including the splendid cathedral of a town hall and the striking neoclassical museum. Butch was all for visiting the museum, but Sundance wanted to take a look at the banks. Anxious to humour him, Butch followed into the imposing establishment of Oldmondroyd & Arkinstall's Providential Lancashire Savings Bank (1847).

The hall of this solid composition of brass, dark oak and money was attended by Mr Makinson, the chamber superintendent, an imposing figure of charcoal, pinstripe and side whiskers who immediately spotted the pair and marked them as less than prime depositors. Approaching them with intent, he enquired with that loftiness special to those whose job title is their only claim to importance, 'Gentlemen, can I help you? The nearest public house is several doors further down the street, on the right.'

Butch, who was not unused to this kind of reception, smiled amiably while Sundance scowled. 'Does the public house take large deposits, friend? Excuse my modest dress – it is a precaution. You see I am only lately returned to the town of my fathers from America, having sensibly withdrawn the fortune I made in acquisitions and murders before the market crashed.' (Butch always enjoyed this little joke; it delighted him that everyone always heard mergers rather than murders.)

The superintendent had not encountered the likes of Butch before and fell, just as so many had done in the past. Before you could say Oldmondroyd and Arkinstall, the two men were sitting in the office of the manager, Mr Coote, who, on the strength of previous positions in both Chorley and Lytham St Annes, fancied himself a man of the world. Butch introduced himself as Mr Vandefeller and Sundance as Mr Rockebilt and explained they were looking for somewhere to deposit large amounts of money, 'Forgive me, Mr Coote, but being American and accustomed to lawlessness and bad men, I should like to know how secure my money will be with your bank?'

Mr Coote assured him that his money would be guaranteed whatever, but, as an amusement to his foreign visitors, he couldn't resist offering to show the pair the bank's security system, 'the safest in all the north of England with the possible exception of Grimtyke & Clutchwedge in Harrogate, but those Yorkshire people do know how to hang on to their money.'

And so it was that, after a blank response to the last little attempt at levity, which required far too much intimacy with northern culture and rivalries, Mr Coote conducted possibly the two most notorious outlaws in the world on a brisk tour of his bank's security arrangements. They seemed particularly interested in the new Allreet Cop-A-Robber alarms hidden in the seats of the tellers' chairs. 'A teller has merely to flex his right buttock three times in quick succession,' said Mr Coote, proudly. 'The alarms are silent in the banking hall, but will set off a flashing red light in my office, allowing me to call for the police so that the would-be felons can be immediately apprehended. If for any reason I am unable to get through, I will run a red flag up the pole outside my office window and wave.'

'Now that's fascinating,' said Butch. 'Presumably the tellers have been properly trained to offset accidental flexing?'

'Rigorously, with six monthly refreshers. Another key feature is that their tills are locked between transactions with a daily code known only to them and myself.'

Excellent. The safe looks strong, too. What make is it?'

'That, Mr Vanderfeller, is a Bulldog Imperial Impervious Combination Mark 2,' said Mr Coote with equal pride.

'The Mark 1 was clearly not quite so,' responded Butch. 'What's the combination?'

'1010… oh, very good, Mr Vanderfeller, you nearly had me there! And I'm the only one who knows the combination, which is of course changed regularly and irregularly.'

'Easily done, Mr Coote, easily done. Mr Rockebilt and I will now retire to consider our options.'

'Splendid, gentlemen. And I should also mention that every new depositor receives a free set of Oldmondroyd and Arkinstall superior wax crayons. The only colour not included is… red!'

Still smiling at another joke he never tired of, Mr Coote led the way to the large and solid bank doors and bade them farewell. Sundance had neither smiled nor spoken during the entire encounter. 'Mr Rockebilt is clearly the silent partner,' said Mr Coote to Mr Makinson, who, as usual, failed to appreciate his good fortune in having such a witty fellow as his superior.

SUNDANCE TALKED A LITTLE MORE AS THEY CONTINUED their interrupted stroll, which, although he didn't know it, was now bound for Victoria Road, where Butch's father had lived as a child before leaving for America with his parents. 'See, Butch? That bank is just crying out to be robbed. It's asking to be robbed, Butch. It's begging. We could rob that bank with our eyes closed. Come on, Butch, then after we've turned that over, we can go for one last train!'

Butch sighed. 'Harry, Harry. Can I remind you for the 100th time that this is exactly what got us into all that trouble south of the border? We didn't know the local situation well enough, and we don't know it well enough here. Nobody can really be as gullible as the Coote guy... it could be a trap... and just for one, how are we going to get away? We don't have any horses, you can't run anymore, and we're sure not driving after what happened last time. So what are we going to do? Time the raid to coincide with the omnibus timetable? And don't get me started on trains. Or trams.'

'That's how it always is with you, Butch. Where I see possibilities, you see problems. That's why we're almost broke. Your nerve's gone, Butch, you might as well as admit it.'

'And your brain's gone, Harry. My nerves are fine because I've learnt, a little late perhaps, what they can stand and what they can't stand. And what they can't stand is a badly planned bank raid in a place we don't know anything about. Now come on, I'm going to find out more by visiting the house where my daddy was a boy.'

Sundance fell silent again, and scowling, but the nagging creaks in his knees were telling him that old Butch might have something of a point, possibly, although it wouldn't do to admit it, as that would lead to a number of other inconvenient truths, mostly age-related.

They turned a corner. 'Howdy, ma'am,' said Butch to an elderly woman who was on her knees busy cleaning the front step of her small terraced house with a scouring stone. She looked remarkably like every other elderly woman Butch had seen in Lancashire so far, hair tucked under a headscarf tied at the front and a floral patterned crossover apron protecting her dress.

Continuing with her scouring without looking up, she said, 'You talking to me, cock?'

'Can't see anybody else, ma'am,' said Butch, amiably. 'That's a fine looking step.'

'Should be, I've stoned it weekly for 30 years. Not like some in this street.'

Butch decided varying front step conditions would not be a fruitful line of discussion. 'My name is Robert Parker, ma'am, and this is my associate, Mr Harry. Can you direct me to Victoria Road? It's the case that my daddy, Max Parker, and his daddy, another Robert, lived in that here road, and I wondered if you or anybody round here remembers them.'

'You're *in* Victoria Road, you daft 'a'p'orth.' (Although he got the drift, the last word was lost on Butch; it is a contraction of halfpennyworth and is a fairly friendly Lancastrian insult.) 'Remember the Parkers?' continued the old woman. 'Oh aye, my dad used to talk about the Parkers. They were quite famous, the Parkers. They was them Morons, strangers, got caught up with all that missioning and baptising and shouting, then left for America to find God. If you're their grandson, looks like it didn't 'appen, 'appen.'

'Mormons, ma'am, Mormons. That's right, they travelled by sea and rail and ended pushing a handcart for hundreds of miles. Hard times followed by harder times, but they did believe that they had found the Saviour. As for myself, I chose a different path, one which involves easing the Almighty's burden by helping myself a little. But they were strangers, you say? I did not know that.'

'Of course they was strangers, the Parkers, they hailed from Accrington, must be at least 20 miles away. Some of the Morons stayed here, which seems fairly sensible, as you're as likely to find God in Preston as anywhere, without the travel cost. You'll find them over the other side of town. But if you're looking for the Parker house, don't bother, it fell down soon after they left.'

'A sign?'

'No, runaway milk cart. Terrible mess. Left a bit of a sour taste, Dad said. No use crying over it, though.'

The woman gave no clue whether this was a joke. She had still not looked up. It was a pensive Butch as they retraced their steps. Sundance wondered if they were heading to see the Mormons. 'Not on your sweet life. Mormons don't use tobacco, alcohol, coffee and tea. They don't hold with getting something for nothing, of taking money without giving fair value in return, which also kinda counts me out. And I never got on with one wife, never mind six. Let's have a drink.'

He led the way into a bar and sat down. Sundance took his cue and approached the bar. 'Two whiskies, friend,' he said, which set off a fairly similar routine to The Highwayman and ended in the purchase of two glasses of milk. Sundance was beginning to wonder if Preston was indeed as good a place as any to find God.

Butch looked at the milk in astonishment. 'Tarnation, Butch, are you trying to remind me of the loss of the family home?'

'It was this or something called Dandelion and Burdock, Butch, and I didn't think you'd be keen on that. This is a Temperance Bar, like Prohibition, only more wholesome. Barman says they're very popular round here. Wyatt Earp drank milk, Butch.'

'You don't want to believe everything you hear, Harry. We'd be dead, for example. Wyatt drank, all right, but it wasn't milk, liver disease when he died in Los Angeles. Only a few years ago, times had passed him by.'

'That's what I mean, Butch. All this looking back as time goes by. We've got to keep going. Robbing banks has never gone out of fashion. Let's have one last crack, then we retire, with money not regrets.'

Butch stared at his milk. Things were not going to plan. No warm welcome. Not a place to settle. Not a place to live on the cheap, either. No jobs. Or perhaps one last job.

'OK, Harry. Maybe you've got a point. That bank should be a pushover. It's just the getaway. Must be an answer to that.'

'That's more like the old Butch. We need something we know for the getaway. Not too many horses about, though, more's the pity. You knew where you were with a horse. Automatic, none of these shifting gears, just point it and go.'

Butch was staring at his milk again. 'That's it, Harry, genius! The old woman and her story, the family home, the milk cart! I've seen a few of those around, perfect! We borrow one of those, leave it round the corner, and escape slowly. Everyone will be looking for a fast car, no one will notice us, clean hooves, away!' It was an elated Butch, the old Butch, who now took his first swig of the milk. 'Not bad, but it'll never catch on.'

THE BANKING HALL, IT NOT BEING A MARKET DAY, WAS pleasingly quiet, with only a few potentially troublesome depositors occupying the tellers. Mr Makinson greeted the outlaws with great enthusiasm. 'Welcome back to Oldmondroyd & Arkinstall, gentlemen! What can we do for you today?'

'Is Mr Coote free? I should like to make a deposit of 50,000 dollars, and my friend Mr Rockebilt has a similar intention.'

Mr Makinson beamed, asked the pair to wait and left to alert Mr Coote in stately but accelerated fashion. The four tellers in their booths seemed alert and efficient in the way it is when times are hard and jobs scarce. Flecks of dust sparkled gold in the shaft of bright sunlight that followed Mr Makinson to Mr Coote's door. Butch recognised the old adrenaline; Sundance welcomed it.

Mr Coote was all attentive amiability. 'Mr Vanderfeller, Mr Rockebilt, how good to see you again! Please come in and we can conduct the needful little formalities.' He ushered Butch and Sundance into his office and closed the door behind him. 'Now—'

Butch saw little point in delay. 'Thank you, Mr Coote. This is a stick-up.'

Mr Coote's sunny expression became only slightly clouded. 'I'm sorry? A stick-up? I'm afraid I'm not over familiar with American banking terms.'

Butch had never enjoyed the unexpected at moments like this. He saw Sundance giving him the fierce look. 'C'mon, Coote. It's a bank-job. Open the strongbox before you get a one-way ticket to Snoozeville!'

'No, sorry, still not really with you. Could I perhaps offer a cup of tea?'

Sundance, now royally frustrated, took matters, or rather a large Colt, into his own hand. It didn't appear with quite the speed he'd achieved in his prime but was nevertheless more than enough to alarm Mr Coote, who fainted. Sundance, even more agitated, shouted, 'Damn it, Butch, what are we going to do now? He's the only one who knows the combination and he's out cold, the sap!' They both stared as if for inspiration at the bank manager, who was measuring his length on the fine Turkish carpet and giving no imminent signs of returning to consciousness.

'OK, OK, let me think!' replied Butch, now properly rattled. While he thought, Sundance got down on his knees with difficulty and shook Mr Coote, who still failed to respond. 'He's dead!' shouted Sundance.

'Don't panic, Harry, he's just fainted. Not a great colour, though. Look, we'll just have to get out there and rob the tellers. Coote isn't going to get any alarm in here while he's like this. Come on!'

They moved swiftly to the door, tensed and then threw it open swiftly to challenge the tellers from behind. The success of this was marred by the complete absence of tellers, or indeed anyone, including Mr Makinson, in the banking hall. Instead, each teller's position was closed, with a portable wooden sign facing the customer. Butch rushed over and picked up a sign, struggled to get his spectacles out and on, and read, with difficulty, 'Tea Break. Back in 20 minutes'. 'Sometimes, Harry,' as Butch would reflect later, 'it's just not your day.'

Preston Pronouncer, July 9, 1935, Page 3.

Unfortunate Incident at Bank. Manager Indisposed. Found on Carpet.

There was something of a commotion at the premises of Oldmondroyd & Arkinstall's Providential Lancashire Savings Bank (1847), in Market Street, Wednesday morning last.

Noting that the manager, Mr Stanley Coote, 43, had failed to emerge from his office for an uncharacteristically long period of time, the Banking Hall Superintendent, Mr Thomas Makinson, 59, took the liberty of entering Mr Coote's office unbidden.

There he found the unfortunate manager, who has worked for Oldmondroyd & Arkinstall for some years in Preston, Chorley and Lytham St Annes, unconscious on the fine Turkish carpet with which visitors to Mr Coote will be familiar.

Mr Makinson having applied some brandy from a small flask which he keeps about him strictly for medicinal purposes, Mr Coote revived, and at the time of going to press had reported no ill effects from his collapse, which he attributed to his failure to take a properly sustaining breakfast owing to the sudden termination of the cook's employment following a fundamental disagreement with Mrs Coote over the correct proportions of ingredients in Tripe Surprise.

Preston Pronouncer, July 9, 1935, Page 13.

Milk Cart Mystery. Disappeared. Also Horse. No Milk. Police Confounded.

Police in Preston are looking into the unusual circumstances in which a milk cart and horse belonging to the Wallace & Dommett dairy in Fulwood disappeared on Wednesday morning last.

Milkman Mr Ernest Benhill, 63, returning from his delivery round at about eight o'clock, halted his progress in Goldman Road and entered the premises of W Bine & Son, Tobacconist, leaving his horse, Lightning, and empty cart parked at the side of the road.

When he returned, only a few minutes later, both had inexplicably disappeared. None of the road's residents had observed anything untoward, but several reported the sound of the cart moving off accompanied by a wild cry that can be best rendered phonetically as, 'Yeehaw!'

At the time of going to press, police were following up a sighting of a cart resembling the missing vehicle on the Kirkham road which might have been the same one that was seen parked illegally on the wrong side of the road in Friargate earlier.

Anyone with any information is urged to contact Inspector E W B Childers at Preston Police Station.

The bland nature of the first report was the result of Mr Coote deciding, probably wisely, that a more detailed examination of the incident would inevitably reveal a certain and professionally damaging naivety in his dealings with the outlaws: in particular, the guided tour of the bank's security arrangements previously described. As, miraculously, no loss had occurred, he could see no point in taking matters further. Mr Makinson had also seen the wisdom of this course after the revived Mr Coote had shown his gratitude by immediately pointing out to him that the possession of spirits on duty was a transgression punishable by instant dismissal.

Butch was always lucky that way.

It was shortly after the milk cart was observed by a passing (and tooting) motorist on the Kirkham road that they decided to abandon it, principally because despite all efforts they had failed to persuade Lightning to progress beyond walking pace, his accustomed delivery mode. Sundance had said little since their hasty retreat from Oldmondroyd, Arkinstall and the unconscious Mr Coote; he had no need, as Butch readily acknowledged that it had not been the finest moment of his long career. There had been a time when he would have long, loudly and quite reasonably blamed a remarkable conjunction of very bad luck, but he now knew too well that this would not impress Sundance, so he kept his counsel as they walked into Kirkham, where they discovered a railway station with trains to Blackpool and Preston.

'Blackpool?' said Sundance. 'Black... pool? Seriously? That sounds attractive.'

After Preston, Butch was understandably cautious about overpromising. 'Well, they say it's quite a lively town, on the sea, a kinda less steep San Francisco.' Not that cautious, then. They boarded the next train.

INSPECTOR ERNIE CHILDERS DID NOT HAVE A LOT TO GO on. Actually, if he were to be completely honest, he did not have a lot on at all. As with any job, police work does have its troughs and doldrums, and this was one of them, Preston in midsummer, with only the routine run of thefts and unruliness.

These could safely be left to his juniors; he spent his time when undisturbed indulging his favourite hobby, which was reading about the exploits of the heroes and villains of the American West. There was no shortage of books on the subject, written in an engaging fashion which never allowed the facts to detract from the excitement. The books were a welcome contrast to his reality, and he did, occasionally, picture himself on a dusty street tense and ready to draw his six shooter more swiftly than his stubble-faced adversary while a thousand eyes watched in apprehension from hastily barred homes. In short, Ernie was a man with an imagination, and, on a slow day, the mystery of the missing milk cart captured it. So much so that when the cart was reported abandoned, he went out to have a look at it for himself. (It was a nice day as well as a slow one.)

'Now why would anyone steal a milk cart?' he asked himself as he stared at Lightning, who was still standing patiently waiting to move on to the next delivery. 'Why would they take it, then bring it all the way out here and just abandon it?' And (as it was a nice day as well as a slow one), he decided to deliver it back to the premises of Wallace & Dommett himself. This, as we are now aware, given Lightning's speed, would take quite some time, allowing the Inspector to ponder on the mystery of the cart when he was not following the Santa Fe Trail in his covered wagon in search of a new life.

EVEN SUNDANCE COULD NOT HELP BUT GET CAUGHT UP IN the thrill and fun of Blackpool on a high summer afternoon, Lancashire *en fête and en masse*, the press of the people on the promenade, unconsciously imitating the unrelenting rhythm of the mills that dominated their lives. The bracing air and scene was filled with the cries of the sideshow barkers and the buzz of the crowd on the Golden Mile, the heady holiday smells of candy floss, rock and tobacco mingling enticingly, the shrieks carrying from the amusement rides and the happy splashes in the sea beyond the seething, heaving beach, the piers and the oyster carts and ice cream stands and above it all, except for the buzzing aeroplane tour, the delightful impertinence that was the half-size Eiffel tower.

'Dammit, Butch! Why didn't you tell me how it would be? Blackpool's kind of sleazy, I like it. Frisco's a funeral next to this! Pretty girls, too.'

Butch, planning ahead as ever, suggested they should find somewhere to stay. They turned off the promenade into the network of small streets just behind it filled with boarding houses. Holidaymakers were lounging outside the doors and sitting on the benches at the top of the steps, just happy to be doing nothing. 'No Vacancies' signs were the usual order, but The Happy Memories Guesthouse – 'A Warm Welcome Assured', Prop. G. Rudge – was advertising a room. Butch knocked on the door; it was answered by a large woman who looked the pair up and down without obvious admiration and said, 'Well?'

Butch, as usual, did the talking. 'What a splendid-looking place you have here, ma'am. You must be very proud of it. I see you have a room available.'

'Might have,' said the woman, arms folded, so far delaying delivery of the promised assurance. 'For you two?'

'Indeed it would be, ma'am. Wonderfully handy for the attractions here, isn't it?'

'Five bob a night each, food included. Condiments, sauce, jam, margarine, second slice of bread, tablecloth, pillow, blanket, wardrobe space, mirror, plug and any more than five sheets of lavatory paper extra. In by ten, lights out by eleven, key available with £5 deposit and shilling daily rental. Shoes off at door, suitcase inspection on departure, no funny business. Any questions?'

'How much for a smile, ma'am?'

The crinkle-eyed Cassidy charm was still working; even Mrs Rudge was not immune. Her lips relented and moved in a northerly direction and her eyes almost crinkled, too. 'All right, cheeky monkey, in you come. Shoes!'

INSPECTOR ERNIE CHILDERS HAD FORGOTTEN ABOUT THE milk cart. Apart from anything else, there'd been that bit of a kerfuffle, the robbery from the town's magic shop, Hey Preston, which had given him the opportunity to say to the shop's owner, 'So what's disappeared, then, Mr Sleary?' The Inspector, in the manner of his trade, liked little jokes like that. The mystery of how the robber had gained access was solved with the arrest of a former assistant at the shop, Frank Jupe, promised by the Inspector that he would be 'going inside for a spell'. It was still not quite clear what young Jupe had intended to do with 36 magic wands, eight interlinked metal hoops and three marked decks. Whatever, that evening, after his tea, the Inspector was, as ever pursuing his fascination with the Wild West, reading about the exploits of the famous Hole in the Wall Gang, the desperados who hid out in this remote Wyoming pass, from where they would make daring raids on banks and trains. It was when he was studying pen pictures of the various members of the Gang that he felt a light turning on. 'Butch Cassidy', one of them read, 'was the grandson of a Mormon who had emigrated from England to make the long and arduous pilgrimage into Utah'.

He turned to his wife, who was reading Dickens. 'Cissie, weren't you telling me your mother had mentioned some Americans looking for their family home the other day? Weren't they Mormons?'

'Aye, they were looking for the Parkers. You remember the Parkers, Ernie. Well, their house, any road. It fell down when a milk cart went slap bang into it, whole lot came crashing down.

Everyone said it must have been a sign. They were looking for the house, the Americans, and they asked Mother. Do you want her to come round?'

'No, you're all right, love,' said the Inspector, with a speed reflecting his relations with his mother-in-law. 'But the Parkers, yes, I remember all that now.' He reread the entry: 'Butch Cassidy was born Robert Leroy Parker on April 13, 1866 in Beaver, Utah Territory, the first of thirteen children of British immigrants Maximillian Parker and Ann Campbell Gillies'.

Milk carts, thought the Inspector. And Mormons. He was well used to coincidences in his job, but still. How many of them? And what about the cry that had been heard in Goldman Road? Yeehaw!?

'Bloody hell, Cissie! I think the man talking to your mother was Butch Cassidy!'

'Who? Who's Butch Cassidy when he's at home?'

'Only one of the most famous outlaws ever to draw breath and a gun! Actually, and most unusually, Butch didn't often draw a gun. It was his proud boast that he'd never killed a man. His sidekick was The Sundance Kid.'

'The Sundance Kid? Sounds like an advert for orange juice. What's this all got to do with the Parkers and Preston?'

'Butch's real name was Parker! His father was a Mormon from Preston who was taken out to America as a young boy! Your mother just met Butch Cassidy and The Sundance Kid!'

'Well, she didn't seem that impressed, to be honest.'

The Inspector stifled a riposte that would have mentioned the arrival together in Victoria Road of the Pope, Sigmund Freud and Douglas Fairbanks Junior. 'The thing is, Cissie, they're supposed to be dead. Ambushed by the Bolivian Army in 1908. But there's been sightings ever since. Not many round here, though. None in fact.'

'You do surprise me. And you're telling me two supposedly dead outlaws last seen in Bolivia are now in Preston, are you, just because two men who might have been Americans asked my mother for directions in Victoria Road while she was donkey-stoning her step?'

'Don't forget the coincidence of the milk carts, Cissie. The one parked illegally in Friargate, and the cry of "yeehaw!" when that one I found was taken off in Currie Street. Call it bobby's nose if you like, but there's something fishy going on.'

'Bobby's nose, indeed! What's "yeehaw!" got to do with the price of fish?'

'That's what your cowboys shout when they want their horses to get going, Cissie.'

'They're not my cowboys, thank you. And milk carts, honestly. If you ask me, Ernie Childers, you've not got enough to do. You're spending too much time in the Wild West, my lad. Mind you, as it happens, and I'll probably regret telling you this, Oldmondroyd & Arkinstall's bank is in Friargate, isn't it, and Elsie Makinson at the haberdashers, her husband works at the bank, was telling me that two Americans were in there the other day. But they were probably Jesse James and Wild Bill Hickok.'

The Inspector smiled, and because there is a selfless restraint that keeps happy marriages happy, refrained from telling his wife that both those men were definitely dead, one killed by a treacherous member of his own gang and the other while he was playing cards and sitting with his back to the saloon door for the first time in his life and that his hand, pairs of eights and aces, had ever after been known as 'the dead man's hand'. So ostensibly he returned to his reading, but really he was resolving to pay Oldmondroyd & Arkinstall a visit.

When Sundance was happy, Butch was happy. They strolled in the sun along the Golden Mile sideshows, which really were the most extraordinary collection. In addition to the standard hoopla and the gypsy fortune tellers and the singers plugging the latest songs – 'Love Is the Sweetest Thing' and 'Ain't It Grand to Be Bloomin' Well Dead' particularly appealed to Butch – there were also the bizarre attractions for which Blackpool was famous, or notorious, according to taste. Although the depression had hit the country as hard as America, it didn't seem to be damping the usual high spirits, although there were signs if you cared to look: the most striking was The Starving Bride, a young girl just married who was not eating for a month in a bid to win £250. It was a con, of course, along with nearly everything else, including The Biggest Rat in the World and The Half Man Half Woman ('He's all man down his left side, ladies and gentlemen, and she's all woman down the other side. And if you want an answer to the most pressing question, come in and see for yourselves, it's only twopence and you won't regret it, I promise you!'). Butch also declined the offer to marry The Ugliest Woman in the World, being rather more interested in The Wild West Shooting Range, where a man dressed in buckskins and a stetson with a curiously fringed brim that had never seen Todmorden let alone Tombstone was challenging one and all in an accent that matched: 'Come on, gents, can you outshoot The Sundance Kid? A crisp fiver – that's right a fiver! – if you can. How about you, old timer? You look mean enough to handle a gun. Come and have a go, why don't you?'

Sundance, buoyant mood faded in an instant, was indeed looking mean. 'Give the man his twopence or whatever the hell it might be, Butch,' he said in the tone already encountered that always set his friend on alert.

'OK, fella, after you,' said the fake Sundance.

'No, after you,' replied the real Sundance. The imposter smiled and turned to the stall behind him. There were six small metal silhouettes of cowboys ranged in a row in front of a crude painted backdrop of the main street of a western town with large cacti and the occasional angry-looking Apache dotted around in the distance.

The saunterers and strollers, attracted by the fuss and something about Sundance, had paused to watch. The imitation Sundance turned and swaggered to the front of the stall, drew a shiny and not particularly authentic-looking revolver and fired some sort of air pellet rapidly six times, knocking six cowboys over with loud clangs. The crowd were impressed. The imposter smirked, blew imaginary smoke from the end of the gun, and reloaded it. 'And now pardners,' he said, in the accent that continued to make Butch wince, 'just to ensure there's no possibility of one of them there double-crosses, I will give the same gun to the old timer here!' The real Sundance, face still full of thunder, weighed the pistol in his hand, grimaced a little, and took aim. He fired six times and despite distinct clanging sounds knocked not a cowboy over. 'Sorry, my friend, better luck next time you're in town,' crowed the imposter. 'Seems not every Yankee is a straight shooter!' The crowd laughed and made to drift on to the next attraction.

What happened next happened very quickly. Sundance brushed his old jacket open and almost instantly six much louder reports rang out in far speedier succession, resulting in six instantly supine and comprehensively former little cowboys. At the same time the imposter's fancy hat spiralled up into the air and the backdrop collapsed with a loud crash to reveal a startled woman on one side who had been operating the spring-loaded bolts securing the figures against all presumptive contenders. One of those intense silences that follows unexpected mayhem was broken by Butch quietly advising the dumbstruck stallholder to hand over the fiver: 'Please don't make my partner any madder, friend.'

The pair moved swiftly away and were soon lost in the crowd. Sundance was looking as narrow-eyed as ever; only Butch could have detected the slight movement in the right cheek that meant he was feeling quite pleased with himself. 'Hell, Harry, you amaze me, you really do!'

'Not sure why, Butch. Fourth shot was a little awry, I grant you, only just hit it, otherwise pretty good for an old timer.'

'I thought we were trying not to draw attention to ourselves, Harry. Taking time to carefully consider our next steps.'

'Yeah, after the doogie of a mess you fixed up for us in your home town. You really expect me to do nothing about some tenderfoot native of yours imitating me with a popgun? And then let the grifting snake make a fool of me by fixing the targets?'

They stared hard at each other, eyes flashing just as they had flashed everywhere around the world. Now just two old men on a sunny day by the seaside. Butch, as ever, was the first to see the ridiculousness of it.

'Certainly gave the crowd some entertainment, Harry. Did you see the way his hair was standing on end after you lifted his hat off? He was howling like a coyote with sunstroke. Hell of a shot.'

Sundance was calming down, if a little grudgingly. 'Sure, not bad, was it? You got the money?'

'Yup. Right here in this pocket.'

There was a small silence. Butch also knew Sundance well enough to see when there was a certain hesitation, and it always amused them both to have it teased out, old friends with a usually unspoken intimacy that allowed them to concede weaknesses they knew would be looked on with indulgent affection, most of the time.

'Like I said, some shot.'

'Sure,' said Sundance again.

'Yup. I'll say. Six cowboys, and the hat, and the backdrop, with six bullets. Never seen shooting like it, even from you. How exactly did you do it?'

Sundance watched as two attractive girls walked past, happy and animated in the sunshine.

'Okay, Butch. Ricochet. Twice.'

'Lucky, then.'

'Got to be a good shot to start with, Butch.'

'Ricochet. That Irish fellow again, Harry.'

They were both smiling now as they resumed their saunter. Like most outlaws, they had always enjoyed having their photograph taken, something about celebrity and the thrill of dangerous consequences, and so were attracted to a stall where you poked your head through a frame and took on someone else's body entirely. Thus, somewhere, a picture of Butch Cassidy and the Sundance Kid as Stan Laurel and Oliver Hardy.

As Sundance had noticed, people determined to have a good time on their one week of holiday in a year make for a bracing air already braced by the breeze from the sea. There were some holidaymakers relaxing into the novelty of no job to go to, often reclining in rented deckchairs with eyes shut and mouth half-open like happy mackerel, but they were on the piers and the beach, not on the Golden Mile. There, any offering was given a favourable look by husbands, wives and groups of workmates, male and female, looking to store up some happy memories against the rest of the year and only too happy to egg each other on and into the various offerings awaiting inside the shows and being trumpeted by their barkers outside, the likes of mysterious fakirs resting on beds of nails and charmers beguiling snakes from baskets.

The pair who, after all, were men of the world, felt able to dismiss all this, plus the varying appeal of the Five-Legged Cow, and the Flea Circus – 'Marvel at the strength of these amazing insects! Watch them lift weights and push their own little wheelbarrows!'. They were more attracted to The Indian Temple Dancers – 'Experience all the wonders of the East as these bewitching oriental beauties embrace writhing snakes and offer their bodies to the mighty and mysterious Vishnu!'. Butch felt Sandy The Fortune Telling Labrador might be educational, but was dissuaded by Sundance, who was more taken by Olga The Headless Woman – 'Olga lost her head in a terrible car accident, ladies and gentlemen, sliced clean off… but thanks to the miracles of modern science and medicine, she lives! Come and see how! You will not be disappointed!'.

They paid their twopences and entered into a dark space with some other interested holidaymakers whose chatter stilled at the sight of shapes at the other end of the small room. A soft light came up to reveal two men in white medical coats standing on either side of a table. Sitting on a chair on the table was a woman without a head. Where it should have been, a metal tube was protruding, fed by cables leading to interesting-looking machines. The supposed doctors explained that this was how the body was kept alive.

The woman was wearing a powder blue satin cocktail dress which revealed shapely legs, crossed at the knee. The audience gasped when she raised her arm and stayed silent as the men in white coats fed her with an orange-looking liquid through another tube.

Well, most of the audience. A boy of about eight said loudly, 'It's all done by mirrors!' and started throwing toffees towards Olga. In the gloom, there was what sounded very much like a clip on a young ear, a cry, and a kerfuffle as the boy was led out, followed by his protesting parents. 'Leave our Albert alone, he's got an enquiring mind!' shouted his father, a small man with fiercely parted hair firmly smarmed down.

The taller of the two men on the stage held up his hands for silence after this kerfuffle. 'Ladies and gentlemen,' he announced, 'we know that in any audience there will always be those who are not prepared to trust the evidence of their eyes.' Butch nudged Sundance.

'So, although we obviously cannot expose Olga to any danger – and you must realise that one false move, one trip, one pulled cable could kill her! – we are prepared to let a representative from the audience approach and touch her!'

Bad knee or no bad knee, Sundance was first up. 'Thank you, sir. You look like an intelligent kind of man. I ask you to show some respect and restraint for Olga and for science. You also seem to be a man of mature years who knows the world. Would you now – gently! – touch Olga's left arm and tell me whether in your opinion that is the living flesh of a real woman!'

Sundance touched Olga's arm. 'Yup,' he said. 'That is the arm of a real woman.'

'Harry?!' said a very soft voice. 'It *is* you!'

Butch watching his friend's back, saw it suddenly stiffen.

'Etta?!'

'Yes, it's me! Come round the back at 9.30!'

'ETTA!?' said Butch once they were outside. 'Olga is Etta?! Etta is Olga?!'

'Sure looks like it. Damndest thing. Couldn't be anybody else. Wants to meet at 9.30.'

'Whoa! You reckon she's still got our money?'

'Unlikely, Butch, if she's Olga The Headless Woman.'

'Sure. You going to meet her?'

'Yup.'

'Whoah. Etta.'

They walked along for a while in silence. Butch had always got along with Etta, but in that way it is when two men are very close and one of them takes to someone else. It's not always a woman, but it often is, and that was how it had been with Butch and Harry. Men didn't talk much about friendships, and especially how there are very rarely equal partners. Look at the ones you know, like yours. One friend always needs the other more. Sure, Sundance relied on Butch, but Butch needed Sundance; not in a practical way, for protection, or for companionship, or because he liked an audience, or even because Sundance was just about the only person he felt easy and properly relaxed with, although these things were important. He'd known wiser, wittier, friendlier men than Sundance, but the simple truth of the thing was that he didn't feel complete without him. Well, maybe not the simple truth. But Butch never thought beyond this point; like, for example, why he'd never felt this way with a woman. All he knew was that without Sundance he couldn't be happy. So he'd tolerated, even liked, Etta, but that didn't mean he didn't prefer it when she wasn't there.

'You want me along?' said Butch, eventually.

'Up to you.'

'HELLO, HARRY. HELLO, BUTCH.' Time, outwardly, had been kind to Etta Place. She must be in her sixties, thought Butch, but she doesn't look much over 40, particularly in the summer dusk.

'Hello, Etta,' said Sundance, as if she hadn't disappeared with most of his money in Antofagasta, Chile, 25 years ago.

'Etta, you look wonderful,' said Butch. 'What's a nice girl like you doing without a head in a place like this? And where's our money?'

Etta's laugh was still attractive, too. 'Same old Butch. Same old Harry, also. Yes, it was a pity about the money. I thought I'd make a better job than you of looking after it, which, in fairness, didn't seem that difficult. I was getting fed up with the life, on the run, on the edge, but I dressed it up a bit in the note because I know you both like a bit of drama and so I said I didn't want to watch you die when I knew you two could survive anything which is how it's proved.'

'What note?' said Sundance.

They stared at each other. Butch moved on quickly before they started staring at him. 'So the money's gone, as I'm guessing you're not here for your health or to satisfy some strange yearning.'

'No, I met the guys here at Coney Island. The Olga before me put on weight. It's not exactly a demanding kind of job and you don't have to look your best. And it's got me travel. Paris before this. Good change after teaching for 30 years in Poughkeepsie.'

'We were in Paris,' said Sundance.

'Do you know, I thought I saw you one night in Montmartre.'

'And the money?' said Butch.

'I can't stop now. Got to get back to my lodgings before the old varmint locks her door. Let's catch up tomorrow. We could go dancing.'

'Dancing?' said Sundance. 'Dancing?'

'Come on, Harry, this is Blackpool! Fun! The Tower Ballroom, tomorrow morning, half-past ten?'

'Half-past ten in the morning?'

'Yes, this is Blackpool. Not so crowded then, either.'

'What about your job, the headless thing?' said Butch.

'Simple – there are two Olgas!'

Etta smiled and the years fell away.

Sundance fell again.

Butch felt uneasy.

It didn't take long for Mr Coote to crack. Things had not improved domestically, particularly in the matter of replacing the cook, and food was important to Mr Coote. There was also the unsettling way Mr Makinson had been eyeing him since 'the incident', as Mr Coote referred to it in his thoughts. The weakness revealed followed by the threat of dismissal had diminished Mr Coote in Mr Makinson's eyes, and in his own. So when Inspector Ernie Childers paid a call, Mr Coote quickly, and with some relief, revealed the shaming truth. The Inspector maintained the outward calm of his kind, but underneath he was a turmoil of excitement at this undreamt of coincidence of his profession and his passion.

Only just remembering to admonish the red-faced bank manager for his failure to alert the authorities, he now, like any good detective, began to fit his theory to the crime and revisited the spot where the milk cart had been abandoned. As he sat on a nearby fence, his musings were interrupted by the distant sound of a train whistle from Kirkham Station.

THE BLACKPOOL TOWER BALLROOM WAS, AND IS, A PLACE of wonder. A riot of rococo and reliefs, a paradise of painted plaster, of burnished gold and more tiers than a wedding cake, a miracle of mouldings, an embarrassment of embossment, an exuberant extravagance, a palace for the people where de trop meets over the top and raises it with a cocked snook and two fingers to Messrs Michelangelo, Bernini and Kitsch. A place where daylight is barely permitted to intrude upon the magic, even at half-past ten on a sunny August morning. But not a bad time to appreciate it, not a bad time at all, when the dancers are numbered in hundreds rather than later, when thousands will dizzy and whirl, well and badly; when marriages are made and lives altered to the swing and fizz of music founded upon, yet again, the rhythm of the mill, the rhythm that produced tap music and now the new young star of the movies, Astaire.

Sundance was impressed; Butch, predictably, adored it. 'Something, huh?' said Etta rising to greet them, again fetching in the kind light. Up on the stage, Leslie Shuttleworth and His Swinging Bobbins, a local outfit, were giving 'South of the Border, Down Mexico Way' a vigorous run-out while playing fair by the tune's famously plaintive undertone. The three went to the rear of the ballroom and took some tea, served from behind the bar by a young waitress in full cap, black frock and apron. Sundance had remained silent, but not forbidding. Etta was smiling that smile. Butch managed, eventually, to take his eyes off the remarkable scene. 'So, Etta,' he said, 'missed us?' Sundance watched her closely.

'Of course I've missed you boys. Like I said last night, I never stopped thinking I'd see you again.'

She paused: she was looking mostly at Sundance now, which, Butch thought, was mostly how it had always been.

'I know I shouldn't have lit off like that, but, you know, they were tough days, and you two weren't always the easiest to get along with, were you? I mean, don't get me wrong, but there were times when I thought there were three in this relationship.'

She smiled. Sundance kept on looking steadily at her, then smiled, too. And so did Butch, but he didn't mean it quite as much.

Les and his Bobbins had now moved on to 'Don't Fence Me In', which the dancers were treating with rather more decorum than Mr Porter had intended.

'Kinda know what you mean, Etta,' said Sundance. 'Not going to blame old Butch too much, though. I wouldn't have been much good if it had been the other way round.'

'Yup,' said Butch. 'I think we can all agree, Harry, that you wouldn't have been much good if it had been the other way round. I think I knew, Etta, that you were feeling a bit shut out at times, and I probably didn't do enough about it.' This was handsome in a way, not entirely honest in another.

'All long ago now, Butch, all gone. Like the money. You always enjoyed a joke, so you'll appreciate that I invested it in the railroads, and we were wiped out in 1929. I took up the Olga-ing not long after.'

'Ha, I wasn't really expecting anything else, given your current employment. And seeing as we're here, why don't you two have a dance?'

'Yes, c'mon Harry. For old times.'

Harry didn't take much persuading, really. The Bobbins were playing the Gershwins' 'But Not for Me'. Sundance and Etta looked easy, pliant against each other; she even seemed to have cured his limp. Butch watched them, with as much going on inside as there was with the ballroom decor. 'Cheer up, love, it might never happen,' said the young waitress, smiling at him.

Butch never could pass up a chance to charm. 'Shouldn't you be getting ready for that beauty competition they're having over at the big swimming pool today? Or have you been banned to give the others a chance?'

'Who's a cheeky one, then?'

'Nope, just a gentleman of mature years who appreciates beauty.'

Butch pointed to the first tier above the dance floor, empty at this time of the morning except for a dozen or so women sitting on their own in the semi-darkness. 'Tell me, what's with the old ladies sitting up there?'

'Widows. They come back to remember when they were happy. Or not alone.'

'My, that's one of the saddest things I've ever heard, or seen. Do they ever dance?'

'No. That would mar the memory. I think it's so romantic. But I'll dance with you if you like?'

'You? Aren't you supposed to be waitressing?'

'It's early yet, and the bosses like me to take a turn with some of the old fellows who want to dance.'

Butch looked around and noticed a few elderly fellows eyeing the floor eagerly and carrying themselves as carefully as they'd not been with the hair dye. 'No thank you, honey, I think I'd be better reading.' He got out his book about Lancashire from his pocket and donned the spectacles.

Etta and Sundance came back, smiling. Butch was pleased his friend was happy, but wary, as he couldn't quite see where this was going, and he liked to know where he was going, even if it was backwards. He looked up from his book. 'Well, you two, do you know what Balzac thought about this here Lancashire?'

'Balzac? Did we know him? Sounds foreign.'

'Listen to Harry Longabaugh.'

Etta was still a school teacher. 'Honoré de Balzac, Harry. The famous French writer.'

For the first time since they'd met again, Sundance was reminded of something that used to irritate him about Etta.

'That's right,' said Butch, reading from his book. 'The famous French author Balzac, writing in his novel, "The Lily in the Valley", had the hero's mistress tell him that Lancashire is the county where women die of love.'

Etta smiled. The waitress snorted. A man who had been sitting nearby quietly sipping his tea stood up and said, 'I've killed a few.' He walked off, to reappeared a few minutes later seated at the mighty Wurlitzer organ as it rose up from beneath the ballroom stage, giving his all to a lively rendition of 'The Thunder and Lightning Polka'.

INSPECTOR ERNIE CHILDERS LOVED BLACKPOOL, TOO, BUT didn't get there as often as he might have liked, possibly because it was so close and easy, more probably because Mrs Childers thought it a little vulgar. It was also off his beat, but he knew that his colleagues in the Lancashire Constabulary there would need a little more evidence to persuade them that Butch Cassidy and Sundance Kid were taking a break in Blackpool. Which was why he was incognito, in his civvies, blazer, white shirt, open at the neck, with fashionably wide grey slacks.

Another sunny day of happy buzz and wide smiles: why, really, thought the Inspector, would you want to be anywhere else? He picked up a copy of *The Blackpool Voice*, with its famous slogan blazoned across the top of the front page, 'Welcome to The Biggest Happiest Resort in the World!'. There was the usual selection of happy stories of happy holidaymakers like Mr and Mrs Albert Halsall, who were celebrating their Golden Wedding anniversary, had spent their honeymoon in Blackpool and had come back every year since, bar one, when they went to Morecambe ('It just wasn't the same'). There were the pictures of the stars appearing in the resort, including, of course, George Formby, draped with pretty girls in swimsuits and mugging toothily at the camera under the headline, 'Turned out VERY nice again!'. There were also, but less prominently, the usual complaints about the changing times, and in particular the threat to Blackpool morals. Apparently a Mr J B Priestley of Bradford had complained that American entertainment influences were degrading good old-fashioned English seaside habits.

The Inspector had long ago learnt never to neglect the classified advertisements. And there, in a box, between plaintive appeals for Tom to meet Carrie at 4pm today at the foot of the Tower, and the boy in the Kiss Me Kwik hat who smiled at the girl in the polkadot dress outside the Winter Gardens on Tuesday morning to contact a box number, he read the following: 'THE WILD WEST SHOOTING RANGE! Can YOU outshoot The Sundance Kid?! Mr Les Quirk, operator and proprietor of the acclaimed Golden Mile attraction of the same name, begs to inform holidaymakers that it has now reopened following a short intermission to carry out a refurbishment which will enhance the REAL WILD WEST experience it offers. You are requested to bring this advertisement with you to receive one completely free shot at the BAD MEN! Hurry now!'.

Even if he had not been struck by another coincidence, the Inspector's interests would have prompted a visit to the stall. Had he been before, he would not have noticed a great deal of change: Mr Quirk had replaced the cowboy silhouettes (and the bolts securing them against the impact of any number of pellets from his pistols) and repaired his backdrop, adding a couple of covered wagons and a sun-bleached cattle skull for good measure at the prompting of Mrs Quirk, who was of a more romantic turn than her husband.

The stall wasn't busy, probably because of its temporary closure. The Inspector, having been greeted with a 'howdy, stranger!' by Mr Quirk, took his free shot and five more without success. 'Bad luck, stranger,' said the proprietor, who was still dressed in his approximation of what a fashionable gunslinger would wear, apart from the hat, which Mrs Quirk had yet to darn; the cloth cap he'd replaced it with didn't produce quite the same effect. 'You were getting closer by the end. Try again?'

The Inspector loudly clinked some coins in his trouser pocket and smiled at Mr Quirk. 'Does anyone ever knock one over?' he asked.

'Loads!' responded Mr Quirk. 'Why, only a couple of days ago we had a real American here who had a cracking time! Knocked over all the bad men with just six shots! A crisp fiver was his! Come on, have another go!'

'An American?' continued the Inspector, still clinking. 'Do you get many of them?'

'Not that many,' said Mr Quirk, in a rare instance of honesty. 'There were two of them.'

'Did they both have a go?'

'No just the one. They seemed in a bit of a hurry. So, six again?'

'Not until you release the bolts.'

'Bit of a smart alec, are you? If you're going to cause trouble, I'm calling the police.'

'Already here. Inspector Ernest Childers at your service. Did you catch their names and did you see where they went?'

Mr Quirk travelled from surly to servile in the time it took to smile creepily. There was nothing that was too much trouble for him, but there was also nothing he could usefully add, except that the shootist's companion had been smaller, and friendlier. Oh, and when pressed, that the shootist was using a real revolver, and limped. 'Mad as a bloody snake!' said Mr Quirk. 'Flashing mean blue eyes. Made a terrible mess of the stall. And my hat. If you find him, I want compensating!'

'Really? I'll ask the magistrates to bear that in mind when you're up for defrauding the public,' said the Inspector, glancing up the stall and adding loudly, 'that includes your accomplice, too.' There was the sound of Mrs Quirk shifting.

The Inspector moved as quickly as dignity would allow to Blackpool Police Station, where he found on duty his old friend, Inspector Horace Case, a custodian of a more stolid stripe whose traditional vocabulary was as rotund as his figure.

'So Ernest, if I have the particulars of this correct, what we as guardians of the peace are confronted with here is nothing less than two of the most famous perpetrators of crime on the western side of the United States proceeding at large and carrying firearms without the requisite permissions in England's premier holiday resort presently experiencing its highest visitor numbers of the year. I apprehend that it will represent a more than considerable challenge, Ernest, to, ah, apprehend [here the Inspector paused to smile knowingly] the suspects among 250,000 holidaymakers bent on leisure.'

'Well, yes, Horace, but they are Americans, there are two of them, and one has a limp. The usual way should find them faster than a trail hand after his chow.'

The 'usual way' was the method unique to Blackpool of tracking down persons of interest: ask the landladies. They knew everything, to the smallest detail, that happened in the town. Nothing, from cruet theft to more interesting personal habits, escaped them. It needed just the one constable to ask just the one landlady. No one ever heard or saw the information being passed on, but failure was rare, even at the height of the season. The 88th whispered exchange, impassive of face, inaudible to the uninitiated, reached Mrs Rudge, the outlaws' landlady, that teatime. The Inspectors were alerted, but wary of trouble and reputation, and because Inspector Childers knew his tea would be waiting at home, decided to reconvene outside the boarding house the next morning and then shadow the pair.

UNAWARE OF ALL THIS, BUTCH AND SUNDANCE AND ETTA were having a good time. Well, Sundance and Etta were having a good time, and Butch was pretending to have one, mostly. Still, he did enjoy the donkey ride, which reminded him of his time in South America, where, in true Butch fashion, he had worked with them to guard mines and also to rob mines. He began to expound his theory that donkeys were more intelligent than horses, but Sundance wasn't listening, as Etta was pointing out to him the most famous sideshow in Blackpool, featuring the Reverend Harold Davidson, the Rector of Stiffkey, Norfolk, who was protesting against his conviction for immorality with prostitutes by standing in a barrel. There was a queue which dwarfed those for the two shows next to him, Dick Harrow, the World's Fattest Man on one side, and Mariana the Gorilla Girl on the other.

Inside, the Rector appeared oblivious to the intense and silent staring from his audience. He had perfected an expression which combined suffering, indignity, dignity, martyrdom, stoicism, courage, adversity and resolution. Not on show was the relief he felt at returning to his barrel after a fortnight's stint in the glass oven being prodded by the pitchfork of a mechanical devil. Ah, Blackpool. All the same, Butch couldn't help spotting that the Rector had noticed Etta and had even allowed a hint of a smile to join the suffering, indignity and the rest.

'What was all that about?' asked Butch once they were outside.

Etta giggled, which Butch found less attractive now she was 40 going on 60. 'I've got to know the old boy since I've been here.

He's been badly misjudged, he just wanted to save all those girls. He's doing this to raise money to fight his cause.' Etta paused and smiled at Sundance. 'Perhaps when he's cleared his name, Harry, we should ask him to marry us!'

'That would be dandy,' said Butch. 'I can see it now, The Sundance Kid marries Olga the Headless Woman, witness, Butch Cassidy, officiating, the Rector of Stiffkey, probably in a barrel.'

Etta laughed gaily but Butch could see she wasn't entirely amused. Sundance laughed, not so gaily, but Butch could see he wasn't entirely amused either, and something more besides. They moved on, took in a few more of the sights while the noisy jollity continued all around, but Blackpool's magic had been pierced by the past, and the future. Etta left for the Olga evening shift; after a few yards she turned back to give the pair a look, half a smile, half a question. Sundance stared, Butch raised a hand. She half-raised hers, then carried on, and didn't turn again. Butch looked at Sundance, Sundance looked at Butch. They went to the railings at the edge of the promenade and stared out at the flat featureless sea beyond the bobbing figures close to the shore. After a while, Sundance said, 'Does anybody ever get any answers doing this?'

'Doing what?'

'Staring at the sea. Never worked for me.'

'Nope, not me either. We came from the sea, you know.'

'Of course I know that, Butch. Dover.'

'No, I don't mean that. I mean humanity. Came out of the sea, in the beginning.'

'So?'

'It's interesting.'

'There you go, Butch. Always thinking. Or reading.'

'Both, sometimes.'

'I enjoy that. I might curse you for it, but I like it. So why don't I like it when Etta does it, like this morning with the French guy, Ballsack.'

Butch knew better than to answer the question, and instead went for diversionary action. 'Balzac, not Ballsack.'

'Whatever.'

'Interesting too about the county where women die of love. Etta seems pretty gone on you again, Harry.'

'Yup.'

Butch knew better than to follow that. There was quite some silence before Sundance spoke again.

'Don't get me wrong, Butch. You can be really, really annoying. You talk too much. You worry too much. Your plans are always too complicated. You've nearly got me killed more times than I can shoot at because of them. Like I say, I enjoy you telling me things, but there are days you never stop and I have to shout at you. But, hell, we're getting old and I don't suppose I've got enough time to find anyone else who suits so well. And...'

The sentence was left hanging in another Sundance silence. Butch waited, still staring ahead, not looking at his friend.

'And Etta might leave again. But you'll never leave, Butch.'

'No, I won't leave, Harry.'

It was one of the Blackpool afternoons without a sea breeze. Sounds were amplified in the summer stillness. A mother passed by chiding her child, whose face was covered in ice cream. She stopped, took out a handkerchief, spat on it, and rubbed the child's face vigorously. The child protested loudly; his father took no notice of any of it. A group of lads had one of their periodic explosions of laughter, at the expense of one of them as usual. In the distance, a barker was guaranteeing wonder and excitement. The aeroplane buzzed overhead. The sea stayed much the same, and so did Butch and Harry.

THE PROBLEM, AS INSPECTOR ERNIE CHILDERS AND Inspector Horace Case saw it, was Sundance. Butch was probably unarmed as usual, but Sundance clearly had a gun, and he still knew how to use it, as Mr Quirk at the Wild West Shooting Range, and his hat, would testify. The Inspectors didn't relish a shoot-out in or near Mrs Rudge's boarding house as it presented a clear danger to the guests, any public nearby, and Mrs Rudge wouldn't like it (and neither would Mrs Glower or Mrs Daggers in the boarding houses on either side, The Fun Times Here Hotel and The Golden Memories Boarding House respectively). Inspector Case was especially clear on the inadvisability of falling out with the landladies, for many reasons: 'Not a viable, ah, *modus operandi*, Ernest.'

So they decided to shadow the two supposed outlaws and see if a good opportunity arose to at least question and perhaps apprehend them. Inspector Childers was dressed much as the day before, Inspector Case was in a bowler and a yellow-and-brown checked suit whose waistcoat emphasised his ample proportions. Mrs Rudge generally managed to eject her guests before nine o'clock and discouraged them from returning before dinner time at 12 noon. Butch and Sundance were no match for her, and strolled out just before nine, Sundance as always in the old fringed buckskin coat which reached well below his waist. He was wearing a straw hat, while Butch, being Butch, was in a nifty Kiss Me Kwik number.

'Very well, let us proceed in a cautious manner, striking a judicious balance between a proximity with the suspects too near to avoid detection and too far to maintain contact,' said Inspector Case, imperturbably. Inspector Childers, in deep frontier marshal mode, just nodded and kept chewing deliberately the tobacco he'd bought for the purpose.

It was quite a stroll. Blackpool was so crowded that shadowing was fairly easy, especially at the gentle pace of Butch and Sundance's proceedings. Perhaps the most difficult decision made by the Inspectors was whether to follow the pair to the top of the Blackpool Tower. They compromised, with Inspector Case, who had no liking for heights, waiting at the entrance while Inspector Childers went up behind the suspects. On the viewing platform, 400 feet up in the air, with the Blackpool crowds far below making ants look positively idle, he got close enough to the pair to hear Butch talking to Sundance: 'Apparently, it's so constructed that if it was to collapse, it would fall into the sea rather than on these surrounding buildings.'

'Thanks for that, Butch, really appreciated,' said Sundance, unknowingly confirming their identities to the listening policeman. The Inspector, suppressing his excitement, brushed against Sundance and felt with his thigh what had to be a gun under his jacket. Sundance shot him a look that he would not forget: 'Easy, stranger.' The Inspector apologised, realising too late that he was holding his hands up like every cowboy ever confronted by a drawn gun. 'You can put your hands down,' said Butch, in reflex. The Inspector turned and made his way back to the lift, not looking behind him. If he had, he would have seen Butch and Sundance exchanging frowns, then shrugging.

From there it was on to Blackpool Pleasure Beach, home to some of the most terrifying roller coasters in the world. The Inspectors passed up the chance of a ride, but Butch and Sundance seemed to enjoy these greatly, which did not meet with Inspector Case's approval. 'Pardon me, Ernest, for entering a modicum of doubt, but in my experience your hardened criminal carries himself with rather more seriousness, even threat. Your two characters on the other hand seem to be enjoying themselves a little too much. I have to confess that I'm struggling to see them as desperate men of violence to whom life is cheap. Are you sure you have a correct identification? The smaller one up on the dipper is actually screaming.'

Inspector Childers was a touch surprised himself, but still convinced by the encounter at the top of the Tower, a conviction confirmed by a turn round the Noah's Ark fun house, where the policemen followed the pair over the rope bridge, the tilting floor, the stepping stones (a wet right leg for Inspector Case) and the hall of mirrors (a shock for Inspector Childers when an elongated Sundance appeared suddenly next to him). 'Horace,' he said when they finally got back onto solid ground. 'Those men are Butch Cassidy and The Sundance Kid. I'm going on what I heard them say on top of the Tower, my lawman's instinct and extensive study of the annals of the old West. I'd stake my career on it.'

'I fear you have, Ernest,' said Inspector Case. He left to organise a cordon of officers around the Pleasure Beach and prevent any more tourists entering.

The outlaws bought sticks of rock and began happily licking them on a bench. 'Some place,' said Butch.

'Yeah,' said Sundance. 'Better than Coney Island, I'd say.' That reminded him of Etta, and he fell silent. A small boy approached, eyeing their rock with much interest through his spectacles. Butch recognised him: it was the child who had been throwing toffees at Olga the day before. Today he was wearing a cowboy hat similar to Mr Quirk's and had a toy gun in a holster, which he proceeded to draw. 'Stick 'em up and give me the rock!' he shouted. 'I'm Billy the Kid!'

Butch raised the hand which wasn't holding his rock. 'Listen, little fella,' he said, 'don't you know that a cowboy would rather die than hand over his rock?'

'All right then – you!' said the boy, pointing at Sundance.

'You got me, son,' said Sundance, breaking his rock in two and offering the unlicked half to the would-be desperado. Butch smiled, impressed that his friend could still surprise him.

'Albert! Come away from those men!' The boy's father was calling him. He hesitated, caught between the rock and a hard place. 'Albert!' shouted the boy's father again, and he walked off reluctantly. He had a loud voice for a small man, and they could could hear him as he continued to tell the boy off. 'What have I told you about talking to strangers? I know those two funny old codgers look harmless, but you can't tell. No, that's enough, Albert, stop it. And it would ruin your tea. Now come on, we've just got time to see the lion.' They trailed off, the father still scolding, Albert alternating between shrill and snivel.

'Just like Billy the Kid,' said Butch.

Another silence fell between them which was broken, eventually, by Sundance. 'Maybe we are too old for this business, Butch,' he said. 'I get tired easy, and it makes me ornery. I take too long to recover from things, like the shoot-up at the gun range. Shouldn't have shot the place up, anyway. And…'

Again, there was a wait before Sundance continued. 'The ricochet that took the guy's hat off. Could have killed him.'

Again, the wait. 'Would have been my first. Wounded two in that shoot-out at the Hole in the Wall, but never killed anyone. Got this reputation for being fast, which I am, nobody dared take me on.'

Another wait. The Inspector, stationed nearby, had almost exhausted innocent things to do and was now retying his left shoe for the third time.

'I know, Harry,' said Butch. 'I've always known. Didn't bother me, much less messy, all that blood, you know, and the screaming. Either way, as I keep saying, we should quit while we're ahead, or at least not dead. You're tired, I'm sure as hell tired. They say the Lake District is very pleasant. We could keep sheep. Sheep are pretty amazing, Harry. Did you know their eyes have rectangular pupils?'

'There you go again, Butch.'

The Inspector was now pretending to read a flyer for Gypsy Rose Lee, the fortune teller, for the fifth time. The future was a cinch; you just had to ask her. Butch nudged Sundance. 'Harry, the guy over there, reading the flyer. He's nervous. Something about him.'

'Yup, that's the guy who bumped into me on top of the Tower. He was in the Noah's Ark place as well. With another fellow. And the other fellow's gone. Reckon we'd better be getting along, Butch.'

The friends sauntered off, outwardly as cool and unconcerned as on any of the boardwalks outside any of the banks and the sides of railway lines they had so often frequented. Inspector Ernie Childers, following closely, saw them paying money for a ride on the Ghost Train. Inspector Horace Case returned to tell him that the cordon was tightening and all visitors were being directed without fuss out of the Pleasure Beach. As they watched, Butch Cassidy and the Sundance Kid climbed into a carriage, disappeared into the darkness and were never seen again.

Afterword

BUTCH CASSIDY AND THE SUNDANCE KID became exceptionally well known after the success of the 1969 Hollywood movie of the same name, much helped by the star power of its leading men, Paul Newman and Robert Redford, and the script from William Goldman, a masterclass in mixing misbehaviour, sentiment and comedy.

Goldman kept fairly faithful to the known if not entirely reliable facts lying within the legend. The pair were among the last, and certainly the most famous, to exploit the less orthodox opportunities in banking and railways provided by the opening up of the West before law enforcement caught up. With the help of his gang, The Wild Bunch, a fluid group which included Sundance, he carried out a series of armed robberies in the last years of the nineteenth century. It's now thought that at most the gang robbed only four banks, four trains and one coal company pay office, but these successes led to Butch, the acknowledged mastermind, being blamed for many more. Between activities, the gang either worked on ranches or hid out in various tucked-away places, including Robbers' Roost in south-east Utah, and the Hole-in-the-Wall, a remote pass in the Big Horn mountains in Wyoming. The railway companies unsurprisingly took exception to their exploits, and to their growing fame, and employed the Pinkerton detective agency and other dangerous freelancers to track them down. In 1900, Cassidy, the Sundance Kid and other members of the gang robbed a Union Pacific train in Tipton, Wyoming and then the First National Bank of Winnemucca,

Nevada, Butch and Sundance apparently following a preconceived plan to use their gains to finance a trip to South America. They left soon after from New York, accompanied by Etta Place, Sundance's girlfriend, of whom little is known, including her real name (Place was the surname of Sundance's grandfather; Ethel was more likely than Etta). They bought a ranch in deepest Patagonia, but the old easier ways of making money soon became more attractive. Robberies and raids were attributed to them over large distances in Argentina and Bolivia, with an escape into Chile. Etta Place left them for San Francisco in 1906; there followed an unlikely spell working as payroll guards for a Bolivian tin mine. Then, in 1908, the pair were reported to have stolen a mining payroll near San Vicente, in Bolivia. A few days later, Bolivian soldiers and police confronted them at the house where they were staying. Goldman famously ended his film with a freeze-frame of the two men taking on most of the Bolivian army and making an impossible break for freedom, guns blazing.

The more accepted account has Sundance shot and badly injured in the shoot-out, night falling and then the sound of two shots coming from inside the house. The two men were found dead from bullets to the head. It is supposed that Cassidy shot the fatally wounded Sundance and then killed himself.

They were said to have been buried in a nearby cemetery, but as with many a hero and outlaw, the legend persists that they escaped; alleged sightings occurred for many years, in particular of Cassidy, in Wyoming and back in the family home in Utah, where he was supposed to have died in the 1930s (another location was Washington). DNA tests on bodies in the San Vicente cemetery, a mine in Nevada, and at the Utah family home have all proved inconclusive.

No sightings, as far as I know, have been reported in Lancashire. But it is agreed that Cassidy began life as Robert Leroy Parker: his grandfather, also Robert, was from Accrington, and moved to Preston, where he was attracted to emigrate to America by the curious reverse missionary activities of the Mormons sent over by Joseph Smith, founder of the esoteric religion, to gain converts when his beliefs were failing to find favour in the United States despite one of them being that two tribes of Israel had travelled there.

The missionaries arrived in Liverpool in 1837 and had such success in Lancashire that there were soon more members there than across the Atlantic. Thus the call, enthusiastically taken up by the north-west's dissenting and poorly paid industrial revolutionaries, to come and settle in Utah, just the 2,400 miles from their point of entry, Boston. Neither Mormonism nor Utah appealed to the young Robert, and he took up cattle rustling, mentored by a man named Mike Cassidy, whose name he borrowed in tribute. One other trifling but irresistible claim is that his great-great-grandfather was in the Marshalsea debtors' prison with Charles Dickens' father and that they were related. In what might be a coincidence or not, Dickens visited Preston in 1853 while he was researching Hard Times, in which it became the desperate Coketown.

The Sundance Kid's real name was the less euphonious Harry Longabaugh; he was from Phoenixville, Pennsylvania, of German extraction. He joined Cassidy in the mid-1890s, already with a reputation as a gunslinger. Nevertheless, neither he nor Cassidy are believed to have killed anyone (well, hardly anyone) and made a point of avoiding violence towards rail passengers and bank customers, another reason for their lasting appeal, along with what was universally acknowledged as Cassidy's great charm and even kindness.

Both the 1900s and the 1930s are loaded and laden with what was to come. But whereas that first decade is mostly remembered as an idyll about to be broken, the second is seen as one of economic woe and pain ignored by the prosperous and rulers too callous or feeble to stand up to the growing threat of foreign force. 'A low dishonest decade' was Auden's famous verdict in 'September 1, 1939'.

Every decade, of course, resists its label, but the 1930s have perhaps more justification than any other in doing so. This century's experience in confronting repugnant regimes has made us look far more sympathetically on the well-intentioned and war-weary efforts that made appeasement such a dirty word. The long-familiar and overriding impression of poverty, hardship and unemployment, so powerfully evoked by George Orwell in 'The Road to Wigan Pier' and Walter Greenwood in 'Love on the Dole', has lately been challenged by a rosier view concentrating on the fall in prices and rise in incomes, the consumer boom in attractive novelties like telephones and radiograms, cookers and even cars, charabanc trips and paid holidays. Three million houses, we're reminded, were built in the 1930s. Orwell and Greenwood, we're told, exaggerated and doomily romanticised suffering. The truth, as Juliet Gardiner and others have pointed out, is that both are true, and most often depended on which part of the country you lived. Above a line drawn from the Severn to the Wash, the big industries built and sustained by the industrial revolution were beginning to falter in the face of foreign competition: coal, steel, chemicals, cotton. Ironically, part of the problem was that an improvement in horrendous working conditions, shorter hours, higher wages, paid holidays, were responsible. And so the North-South divide that exists to this day became more pointed, more obvious.

But that wasn't – isn't – as simple, either. Blackpool, for example, the leading resort of the troubled north-west of England, should by rights have been in the doldrums in the 1930s. Instead, the introduction of paid holidays and falling prices, plus some shrewd innovation and promotion, turned it into a boom town – at least in the summer and into the autumn thanks to its famous illuminations (300,000 bulbs!) as the days shortened. Seven million people a year visited the resort in the 1930s. About £3 million was spent on the town's parks, promenade, piers and Winter Gardens. Over the August bank holiday weekend in 1937, some 400 special trains came into Blackpool, along with an estimated 30,000 motor cars and 5,000 coaches. Nevertheless, there was another sharp divide between the unemployed, who couldn't afford a holiday, and the employed, who wanted one at almost any sacrifice. Even before paid holidays were introduced in 1937, holiday savings clubs abounded. 'The miners and mill hands and other thousands who come to Blackpool for their annual holiday have each saved up about £20', wrote Charles Graves, brother of Robert, in an entertaining travel book mostly set abroad in the likes of the South of France. He'd been told that the holidaymakers spent every last penny then took a taxi home from the railway station, paying the fare 'with the 1s 6d left behind the clock for this very purpose'. Well, perhaps, but the point is clear. This was the Mass Observation social survey on workers in Bolton: 'The possibility of a win on the football pools and the certainty of a week's leisure... are the only two releases from the routine of life'.

Why Blackpool? Because, as we've seen, there was nowhere else quite like it. Promenade, piers, parks, pleasure beach and the press of happy crowds; Tower, Winter Gardens for rainy Lancashire days; and the Golden Mile's raucous, rowdy, boggling parade of sideshows, the freaks and the oddities, fattest, thinnest, ugliest, starving, all curated by a curious man called Luke Gannon, from Burnley, the Lancastrian equivalent of a snake oil salesman who took up the entertainment trade after marrying a clairvoyant.

Blackpool was not just a place where bosses, rules, restrictions and inhibitions and all the taboos of British society could be abandoned, and worries forgotten for a heady week; it was also Britain's first resort for the people by the people: a triumph over middle-class morals and tight-lipped taste, an extravagance of exuberant pleasure palaces designed just for fun at a roar up there in a far corner of Lancashire.

Charles Graves reckoned that twopence in Blackpool was the equal of five shillings in Le Touquet, Deauville, Cairo, Biarritz and Monte Carlo. He was flabbergasted by the place, feeling *like 'a cheerful straw in an organised whirlpool of ridiculously inexpensive gaiety' at the world's first pleasure factory.(Plus ça change: Sundance's approval of its sleaziness was in fact the verdict of Bill Clinton, visiting the Labour Party conference there in 2002.)*

HAROLD DAVIDSON, the Rector of Stiffkey, did exist and did appear in Blackpool as described. Eventually, like young Albert Ramsbottom, in the famous dialect poem by George Marriott Edgar, he was eaten by a lion, in Skegness. Olga the Headless Woman was exported to the United States from Blackpool rather than the other way round. It became so popular that in England alone in 1938 there were nine Olga shows around the resorts. It's unlikely that Etta Place was one of them. And yes, it was all done by mirrors.

FURTHER READING:
Butch Cassidy, The True Story of an American Outlaw, *Charles Leehrsen*
The Thirties, An Intimate History, *Juliet Gardiner*
The Long Weekend, *Robert Graves & Alan Hodge*
And The Greeks, *Charles Graves*
Worktowners at Blackpool, *edited by Gary Cross*
The Road to Wigan Pier, *George Orwell*
Love on the Dole, *Walter Greenwood*
Adventures in the Screen Trade, *William Goldman*
Lancashire, Where Women Die of Love, *Charles Nevin*

1941

Thor Doubles Up

SEVERAL PEOPLE SAW THE LIGHT FLASHING FROM THE SEA off Crovie, near Fraserburgh Head on the east coast of Scotland above Aberdeen. None of them took any action though, assuming that the Gardenstown Coast Guard would know all about it. Which argues either a great deal of confidence in the Gardenstown Coast Guard or a dangerous complacency in 1941.

The light was coming from the torch of Thor Dahling, a Norwegian hairdresser. He was sitting, uncomfortably, in a rubber dinghy also containing two bicycles, rucksacks, various bits of kit and Sigrid Lind, an Oslo usherette.

Things were not going that well. There was quite a swell, Sigrid was constantly being sick and Thor hadn't brought proper gloves with him. Consequently, his hairdresser's hands did not enjoy the three hours' hard rowing it took to reach the shore, narrowly avoiding several rocks that suddenly reared up jagged in the dark.

At last, after rowing round a stone jetty, they reached a small sandy beach. Splashing out of the dinghy, they dragged it onshore, with more difficulty and quite a lot of cursing. Dawn was now breaking, grey and discouraging; up steep and ahead, a line of cottages was beginning to appear. Sigrid stayed with the dinghy while Thor walked up the steps cut into the cliff. He went to the first cottage, hesitated for a moment while he caught his breath – Thor was a little overweight – then knocked sharply on the front door. A light went on upstairs, then after a short delay, the front door opened and a short, squat man in a thick fishing jumper and no trousers was standing there, the face beneath the tousled hair a question, wary rather than welcoming.

'Good morning, very sorry to disturb you,' said Thor. His English was fluent, but he spoke with pronounced Norwegian cadences, which travelled from a lower pitch to an above average height. The man continued to stare. Thor continued to talk. 'Goodness me, it is chilly today, isn't it? What a nice place you have here, very handy for the beach. Don't worry, I won't keep you. My friend down there and I have just been dropped off by a German seaplane. Could you by any chance be kind enough to direct me to the nearest police station?'

In St James's Street, in an office building advertised as 'To Let' by a large sign, but which wasn't, Colonel George Frowne was staring out of the window at one of those London days that can't quite decide whether it is spring or winter, dry or wet, sunny or not, fast clouds, whippy breezes. Frowne had completed *The Times* crossword without difficulty and was now thinking what a bore it would be, another summer without first class cricket.

Turning from the window, he executed an elegant imaginary late cut that reached the boundary in the corner just beyond his large desk, which was empty apart from the copy of *The Times* and a manila folder bearing the names Laurel & Hardy. Frowne prided himself on the nicknames he gave his various cases. Coal Man, for instance, concealed a Dutch agent who was as keen as mustard, while Tripod referred to the impressive private dimensions of an amorously enthusiastic Belgian operative (Frowne retained a public school sense of humour). And Laurel & Hardy seemed a good fit for the latest potential additions to his stable, the generously built Norwegian hairdresser and his slender companion.

An interesting stable, Frowne's. Multiple nationalities, extravagant proclivities, exaggerated personalities, united only by a liking for deceit and no liking for Nazis. Double agents. Ostensibly working for one side while feeding it lies from the other side. Managed by another extraordinary collection: academics, soldiers, writers, aristocrats, outward amateurs.

Espionage. Deception. It's wise to be wary of generalities: easy to conclude that the unsubtle Germans lacked the enthusiasm and the attributes for spying, while the British, and the English in particular, applied a native relish for tricks and overcomplicated games, cricket and crosswords and cards and whodunnits, and a willingness to tolerate eccentricity if it yielded results.

Easy, but overlooking the inconvenient fact that British espionage during the Second World War, while retaining and maintaining an interest in the cricket and the crosswords and all the rest of it, was a model of exhaustive, meticulous, relentless, almost obsessive planning in its every aspect.

And this is what was beginning to fill the manila folder on Frowne's desk: statements, interviews and observations which would allow him to decide whether Thor Dahling and Sigrid Lind were telling the truth and, if so, whether they would be useful agents. Taking imaginary guard at the imaginary wicket next to his desk, Frowne cooly surveyed the imaginary field, then sat down and began to read.

THOR AND SIGRID HAD LUGGED THEIR BICYCLES AND BAGS up on to the coast road and were now cycling to the Gardenstown police station by the long way round recommended by Mr McGregor while he, now with trousers, hurried along the short cut to warn officers of his interesting encounter. Thus it was that Inspector Clouston, from Banff, along with Constable Fraser, came across the Norwegians on the road a little later. Thor was a distance ahead of Sigrid, who was being slowed down by the radio transmitter strapped to her bicycle. Clouston and Fraser got out of their car and were greeted enthusiastically by Thor. 'Just the chaps I was hoping to meet! Would you like this?' Smiling broadly, he reached into a pocket of his ski suit, itself not a common sight on the road from Pennan to Macduff, and produced a Walther PPK pistol. Clouston, not a man to panic, relieved him of it. 'Passport?' enquired Thor, and handed it over.

At this stage, Sigrid arrived. 'Hi guys!' she said (her English had similar cadences to Thor's, but had been much influenced by the American films on show at her cinema). 'Do you want me to make with my passport?' She noticed that Fraser had Thor's gun in his hand, and continued breezily, 'I'm packing heat too.'

Clouston took her passport and gun, examined both, then asked them what they were doing in Scotland. 'Well,' said Thor, 'it's all a bit exciting and dangerous. The Germans have dropped us off so we can do some spying and sabotage. But we want to work for you!'

Sigrid nodded vigorously. 'Sure do!'

Clouston looked at them and looked at Fraser, who looked back at him. Not the quiet day he liked. He asked the two

Norwegians to get into the police car, and then, as an afterthought which disclosed his assessment of the level of threat, told Fraser to follow on with the bicycles. 'Take it easy with that big bag,' Sigrid said. 'There's a radio transmitter in there.' Thor and Sigrid smiled brightly at the policemen and got into the back of the car. Clouston sighed and closed the door after them.

Some time before, Doctor Hasselbacher, the deputy head of the Abwehr, German Military Intelligence, in Oslo, had also been considering another manila folder also containing material concerning Thor and Ingrid. Dr Hasselbacher was not really top spymaster material, otherwise he would not have been merely the deputy head of the Abwehr in Oslo. Nor was he a Nazi. But he was not a fighter either. His time serving in the First World War had shown him that. He had not enjoyed killing. It was why he had become a doctor, of sorts. He'd thought saving lives would be some sort of atonement or compensation, but doctoring hadn't been as heroic as that, even if it was preferable to driving your bayonet into a Russian at Tannenberg. So he'd drifted and pottered. He'd thought about emigrating when Hitler came to power, but his embrace of a detachment from reality, supported by whisky, allowed him to dither and haver. He roused himself enough when war came to pull the few strings he had, enough to remove him from any possible fighting to behind a desk in Norway.

His superior, Oberst Wolff, was a Nazi, but a lazy one, a man who owed his position to being in the right beer hall at the right time. He was tolerated by his seniors in military intelligence because, unlike them, he could display genuine enthusiasm for the Third Reich while his laziness prevented him from doing anything. He, of course, did not know this. So he passed his time skiing or sailing when he wasn't entertaining, and passed his work to Dr Hasselbacher, who was the opposite of officious. The consequent lack of results were common throughout the Abwehr and did not become problematic until the German Army began to falter. But for now Wolff and Hasselbacher were safe as long as Hasselbacher initiated the occasional operation and contributed reports, even though they were long on speculation and short of information.

Hasselbacher sighed, turned away from his daily crossword, which he usually allowed to take up the morning until coffee, and opened the manila folder. Inside was a report from one of the few operatives he hadn't invented, Olaf Gundersen, a loafer of some charm who passed his time in the best Oslo cafes and restaurants, the Ritz, the Regnbruen, the Bristol, spending Nazi money and gleaning little of any importance, mostly because everyone knew what he was doing, but, again in the Norwegian way, gave no hint that they did.

Olaf reported that he had been bumping into Thor for some time. Thor was reasonably well known in Oslo, a popular hairdresser with the better-off sort of Norwegian: quite a flamboyant figure, for Norway. He was often accompanied by Sigrid, whom he'd met when she'd shown him to his seat for the second house of *The Thirty-Nine Steps*. Thor had bought an ice cream from her at the interval and become even more excited by her wonderful cheekbones, inviting her for a free session at the Chez Dahling salon, where he worked for his father. He had cut her hair strikingly short and declared her his muse. Sigrid appeared aloof and unobtainable, reported Olaf, although it was hard to get a word in edgeways anyway, with Thor. Olaf had imagined he would have British sympathies, with an English mother, but he said he had never got on with that side of the family, particularly his grandfather, an old soldier of the crustier kind who frowned on any flamboyance wilder than not wearing a tie. Olaf and Thor lived near each other and had often walked home through the Palace Gardens in the long kind light of Oslo summer evenings. Thor, who was surprisingly discreet, became less so away from the bars and cafes: the British were snobs and bullies who wanted to rule the world. They'd mined Norwegian waters in 1940, it was a good thing that the Germans had come to save Norway. On their last walk, he had wondered aloud about whether his fluent English might be used against his mother's country in the service of a better future under the Reich. Olaf wanted to know what to do about it.

Olaf's report ended with a typical flourish – 'Should we not seize this golden opportunity that destiny or chance has provided for the furtherance of our glorious triumphs?' Hasselbacher finished his crossword, took his normal leisurely lunch at the same table at the Restaurant Schroder on the corner of Torggatta and Hammersborggata, then made arrangements for a discreet meeting with Olaf and Thor.

Abwehr headquarters were not far from the Palace Gardens, at Klingenberggata. It was late afternoon on a day grey with the threat of winter. Olaf and Thor went in by a side entrance. Olaf asked for Dr Hasselbacher, and was told to wait while Thor was taken up in a lift and ushered into the Doctor's office. He did not rise to welcome Thor, greeting him with a carefully neutral look before returning to the novel (Russian) hidden by his elaborate pen stand.

Thor betrayed nervousness in the silence, but not as much as the Doctor was expecting. After a couple of minutes, he looked up and said, 'So, young man, you want to help Germany?'

He was speaking German, which Thor, like most educated Norwegians, spoke easily. 'Yes, sir, I do,' he replied, opting for the earnest enthusiasm which had seemed to work so well with Olaf.

'Why?'

'I want to be of use, for Norway, for the New Society and the New Age.'

'You're half-English, Mr Dahling.'

'Not by choice. You cannot choose your background, sir. I'm not happy about my past. I've spent too much time in England and seen too much injustice. The society there is rotten, but it will soon crumble, and then Germany will be hailed as the saviour of the repressed millions. I want to be there on that day, and I want to be on the right side.'

The enthusiasm might have slightly overwhelmed the earnestness. 'Are you a homosexual, Mr Dahling?'

Thor, unsurprisingly, given the Nazi distaste for (and fascination with) same sex relations, was ready for this. 'I am a Norwegian!'

Dr Hasselbacher, who was a homosexual, if non-practising, gave the ghost of a smile. 'And Miss Lind, she is your sexual partner?'

'No. We are just good friends who share the same views. The finances of her family have forced her to give up her law studies. She hopes to pay for them with savings from her job as an usherette. The English and American films she sees there have made her of the same mind as me.'

'Do you see yourself as a spy, Mr Dahling? Do you relish danger?'

'I am prepared to accept danger, but I don't relish it.'

This was the correct answer. The Doctor thanked Thor for his support and said he would be in touch with him shortly. Thor might have been the answer to Doctor Hasselbacher's prayers if Doctor Hasselbacher had been a praying man. He did think that reality in the twentieth century was better not faced, but his solution took a different form of invention and illusion. Nevertheless, Berlin, prompted by the Party and passed on by Oberst Woolff, was becoming increasingly firm that the Norwegian operation should be infiltrating Britain, and while the Doctor had no problem inventing agents in Norway, non-existent agents in Britain presented more practical problems than he felt confident of being able to solve. More importantly, they would create more work for the Doctor than real ones.

THOR AND SIGRID HAD NOT IMAGINED THAT THEIR adventure in international espionage would see them living in Ruislip. But this was the way with MI5. Those less schooled in English ways might think that spies would be more obtrusive in the London suburbs than in the cosmopolitan centre. But although their arrival would certainly be noticed, and often minutely observed from behind lace curtains, no suburbanite would dream of actually speaking to them. And, of course, and most importantly, accommodation was much cheaper, always essential to Whitehall whatever else might be going on, including a world conflict and fight for the very survival of the nation. So there they were in 14, Kandahar Avenue, having learnt to be German spies, now learning to be British spies. Apparently.

It had not been the smoothest passage, from Scotland to outer west London. British intelligence services had proved rather more rigorous than the approximate operation run by Dr Hasselbacher. He had been friendly and willing to believe that they wanted to be spies, as it much simplified matters and, in any case, their capture might not necessarily be such a bad result for the disenchanteds of the Abwehr. The British had been far less disposed to believe that the hairdresser and the usherette had cunningly deceived the Abwehr from the outset and had all along intended to surrender to the authorities when they arrived in Britain and volunteer to feed the Germans false information. Interrogation at Banff police station by an MI5 major was followed by a train journey to London under police guard and transfer to Latchmere House, the security service detention centre at Ham Common, where a panel of nine officers had questioned them separately, formally and aggressively. Then to another centre in Earl's Court and many more interviews, and thence to the safe house in Ruislip.

Frowne was not as relaxed as Hasselbacher about possible outcomes. He believed strongly in his country and its cause (although he would never be so ill-mannered as to say so) and both were threatened with extinction. Hasselbacher was also at risk of extinction but was less concerned about it. All the same, like his German counterpart, Frowne did have an incentive to believe in Thor and Sigrid: they would fit remarkably well into the intelligence service's schemes to use double agents in the coming offensives against Germany, the desperately needed fightback after the all-conquering Nazi onslaught. When you are counter-attacking an enemy, it is best done where it's not expected, and how better to achieve this than by having their own spies tell them it's going to happen somewhere else?

Still. He was not a man given to indulging in stereotypes, but, however and wherever you pitched it, Thor and Sigrid seemed an extremely unlikely addition to the cast of slippery, subtle and worldly-wise operatives under his control. A camp hairdresser and a cinema usherette in their twenties did not bespeak unflinching daring and cool efficiency. Their story was also unlikely. Why would such a pair decide to become double agents? And where would they get the idea from?

And yet they had held up well during the interrogations. Thor had been convincing in his affection for England and his mother and his grandparents. His grandfather had been decorated at Gallipoli; Thor greatly admired him. The oppressive monotony of life under an occupying power had been stifling. 'These people just marched in and took over and we couldn't do anything! The cheek of it! You see them laughing and happy on our streets and in our land while we go without everything. And then they get angry when we choose not to sit next to them on the trams and try to force us to. They have to be stopped. We are a small country, but this is a big one, my country as well, and I wanted to help you help us! And then Sigrid had the idea.'

Sigrid's idea came to her in the darkness of the Saga cinema in Stortingsgata. 'I love the movies, and most of all I love American movies. Gee, I admire their drama, their style and openness and enthusiasm. Do you know Mr Frank Capra? His films are about justice and freedom and the rights of the people, the little guy. *Mr Deeds Goes to Washington* made me want to be a lawyer, to help the little guys. My studies have shown me how important the rule of law is, the thing that the Nazis kiss off, the foundation on which democracy stands, we the people, self-evident truths, the whole shazam.

'When I had trouble paying for university to study law, I took a job as an usherette at the Saga cinema, mostly because I wanted to watch the movies. That was where I met Thor. *The 39 Steps* was showing, one of the spy movies I admire. So does Thor, we are kindred spirits, though not like that. Have you seen *Knight Without Armour*, also starring Robert Donat, as a double agent in Russia? I like Robert Donat, and Ronald Colman, in *The Prisoner of Zenda*. Lots of deception, and spying, they gave us the spark for the move.

'It was easy. Thor spoke to this guy we knew stooled for them, led him on with hating the British, all that. So the Germans sent for us. I thought Thor's grandfather, the war hero, would set the bells off like crazy, but they just accepted his story, that he despised the old man with all the rest of them. And they believed us. I guess if you believe the hogwash they believe, you'll believe anything.'

Frowne was back at his window. The apparently easy acceptance by the Germans of Thor's disowning of his English family was the most troubling aspect of Laurel & Hardy. But he knew that they were having trouble recruiting over there, principally because, in their own often inscrutable and usually undemonstrative (excepting Thor) way, Norwegians were not in the least attracted to Hitler's race theories, even though he saw his northern neighbours as the Aryan epitome. Frowne had his own theories about the reasons for this: first, having already tried it around 1,000 years before, they had no further interest in conquering the world; second, having thus demonstrated their own superiority from the Oxus to the St Lawrence, they couldn't see any point in bringing the Germans into it. But such speculations were for another day, hopefully as the sun played on the ivy and sounds of cricket carried over from The Parks.

Right now, they would have to see how much the Germans trusted Laurel & Hardy. He had done his checks, as far as he could. Local sources confirmed Thor's background; his heroic grandfather, although unaware of his arrival, and too much of an old soldier to ask more, spoke highly and convincingly of him despite a certain unease with his more *outré* aspects. Sources in Oslo confirmed the identity of the pair there and reported little known but nothing untoward. Nor had any suspicions or disquiet come from the large number of Norwegians in Britain, which included the King, his government and armed forces in exile and the refugees who continued to brave the North Sea in small boats to arrive via Shetland.

Thor and Sigrid had brought a radio transmitter which they soon proved they had been trained to use. The clear course – if they could really be trusted – was for the pair to start feeding information to the Germans in Oslo and watch how matters progressed, to see if the Germans believed in them, hadn't detected or discovered that they had been turned. They had also arrived with explosives equipment and were under orders, they said, to carry out a series of sabotage operations which would further terrify a civilian population already brought to the edge of collapse by bombing raids (not even Dr Hasselbacher was immune to Nazi propaganda). The problem was time: Sigrid and Thor had to begin operations as quickly as they could if they were to fit into the larger plan, the first real strike back at the hitherto all-conquering Nazi war machine. Frowne, in the manner of a man at the crease who though sensibly cautious needed to chase runs, decided to take the risk.

After as short a time as was consistent with their establishing a base and supposedly getting a job working as liaison with the Norwegian army (Thor) and refugee welfare officer (Sigrid), they began to send coded messages from Ruislip (using crosswords: another Hasselbacher touch). But there could be only so many details of morale and movements which could maintain a delicate balance between credibility and offering the enemy too much encouragement. In Oslo, meanwhile, the Doctor was coming under pressure to produce more than just reports from the pair. Which, of course, was what Frowne needed as well: something that would convincingly demonstrate to Berlin that Thor and Sigrid could be trusted and so allow them to play their part in the grand deception designed to conceal the true location of the Allied counter-attack, so desperately needed after the years of disaster.

IT WAS CERTAINLY AN IMAGINATIVE PLAN, AND FROWNE was rather pleased with it, although no one would have known (he was a confirmed bachelor in the donnish way). A large explosion was required, something which would attract press and public attention and thus come to the notice of the Germans from independent sources. It would have to inflict severe damage on a reasonably prominent target but, for obvious reasons, one which was not vital to the war effort. This disqualified bridges and railway lines, but left storage and utilities sites and such. There were several old dumps and redundant power stations and sub-stations that might be available, but Frowne would not have been in his line of work if he had not appreciated a touch of drama.

As with so much involving the English ruling class, the solution came at his club. After lunch at The Thackeray, when Bertie Thornfield had finished complaining that his great war had been conducted far better than the current show, he turned to complaining instead about the upkeep of Thornfield Hall, his Yorkshire home. 'I wouldn't mind if it was a thing of beauty, but, quite frankly, Frowne, it's a ghastly, draughty, ugly Georgian pile. Edward VII honoured my papa with a visit in 1908 – cost us an absolute fortune, apparently the Queen popped in as well – but I'd like to blow it up and start again. The problem is I can't afford it.' Frowne was aware that Bertie's mother, Elsie Thornfield, had been a close confidante of the king at one time, but was far too subtle to mention it. He had other things on his mind.

There is a knack, shared by spies, spivs and schoolboys, which allows a conversation to drop below overhearing while retaining absolute clarity between the intended participants; for the next five minutes all that could be heard from the two armchairs was a low hum from Frowne interspersed with the odd intelligible remark from Thornfield, 'Really?'... 'I could?'... 'Collapse of stout party?'... 'Compensation?'... 'Good old Frowne!'

And so the scheme was set. An important feature of the daring destruction of Thornfield Hall was to be its current, fictitious role as an army headquarters with a camp in the grounds, a familiar arrangement for many country houses in 1942. Frowne had thought about stationing a real army company at Thornfield, but decided, reluctantly, that this was too much of a security risk. The fewer who knew of the plan, the less the chance of that knowledge falling into the wrong hands. He then pondered the idea of employing the Royal Engineers' camouflage and deception section, run by a former stage magician, Captain Gavin 'Now you see him, now you don't!' Williamson, to create an imaginary camp. But it made more sense to arrange simply for military debris and wreckage to be found lying all around as in the aftermath of an explosion or fire.

The final key decision was whether Laurel & Hardy should carry out the raid. It would, after all, be easier for the Army's own ordnance people to blow up the Hall. But there was no telling how useful it would be for the pair in later circumstances; Frowne was rather taken, for example, with the idea of getting them sent back to Norway to continue their work, and a thorough debriefing by the Germans would surely be part of that.

Thor and Sigrid were told of their coming adventure, to much excitement in particular from Thor, who, if he hadn't practised restraint among Norwegians, was unlikely to do it among the English, even in Ruislip. There was also some concern about his fitness, as he'd taken a great deal of interest in fish and chips since arriving. An exercise programme had been introduced which Sigrid seemed to enjoy invigilating, especially the press-ups. The pair had been trained in explosives in Norway and it was decided they should destroy Thornfield Hall with their own method, using the fuse wires and detonators the Germans had given them, which had been cunningly concealed in their belts and hairbrushes. They would set off an incendiary bomb, which would be made from sulphur, saltpetre, weedkiller, and sugar. They had been supposed to buy these ingredients themselves, a plan which Frowne allowed to go ahead, as he was curious to see if anyone would become suspicious. Thor bought the saltpetre at the grocer's on Ruislip High Street, where the grocer retrieved it from a high shelf in the corner. 'Curing your own bacon, eh?' he said. 'Not much call for this since rationing started.'

'Yes, I'm aware of that, my dear chap,' said Thor. 'But actually I'm planning to make a bomb!' They both laughed hard; the grocer continued to shake his head with a smile as Thor left, then forgot all about it. Sugar was a problem, being rationed, but they were given a supply they had supposedly hoarded. Sigrid went to a nursery to buy the sulphur and weedkiller.

The nurseryman was impressed. 'You going to murder your old man, then, sweetheart?'

This might have flummoxed anyone who hadn't watched Bette Davis a few times; Sigrid merely replied, 'Yes, and after that I'm coming for you, Buster!' and there was more laughter in Ruislip.

DR HASSELBACHER TRIED TO MAINTAIN HIS DISILLUSIONED detachment, but he was enjoying the Thor and Sigrid escapade. The messages of teetering morale lent him hope that the British might soon abandon their foolhardy stand, allowing him to retreat to anaesthetised obscurity in some small town in Germany while the Nazis exhausted themselves trying to rule Europe. He passed on Berlin's demands for sabotage with enthusiasm and was looking forward to some action. Meanwhile things in Oslo remained reasonably quiet, although Hasselbacher was entertained by the ingenious civil disobedience of the Norwegians, particularly in the matter of dress accessories. He'd enjoyed most the mass wearing of red bobble hats, a tribute to the traditional headgear of the mischievous native goblin, the *nisse*. The paper clip, invented by the Norwegian, Johan Vaaler, and worn on the lapel, was a subtler and more unchallengeable rebuke, as with the sweet pea buttonhole – the Norwegian word for the flower was the same as the English 'tease'. Each week the summary of the latest jokes, laboriously compiled by the Gestapo, was one of the few despatches from that source he bothered to read. One this week was especially good: 'Why do British planes use twice as much fuel as the Germans? They fly back as well'. The German clerk had put two puzzled question marks next to this, which gave Hasselbacher another smile. There was one other, slightly disquieting report: Thor's mother, who had been on the stage before being swept up and away by Thor's father, had been observed singing 'There'll Always Be an England', or rather half a verse of it before her friends stopped her, after a birthday bottle of champagne at the Theatercafeen, the splendid Viennese-style cafe near the National Theatret. Hasselbacher was also aware that Thor's father, the hairdresser, who was separated from his wife, had been making anti-German remarks to his clients. But he was more intrigued by the former Miss May Flower, 'The Norwood Nightingale', now Fru Dahling. But first, there was the crossword in the *Deutsche Zeitung in Norwegen*.

FROWNE LIKED TO KEEP HIS HAND IN WITH THE ODD FIELD trip if he could. It was important that Laurel & Hardy's first performance went well: the larger deception he wanted them to play a crucial part in was getting ever closer. Thornfield Hall was ready. He'd been impressed with the way Bertie had thrown himself into the plan, fired by patriotism and the lure of a grandly designed new home rising from the ashes of the mouldy old. It was a great help that he commanded the local Home Guard: they would be kept away while Thor and Sigrid carried out the sabotage, and turned out afterwards, but not too quickly. The Hall and grounds had been closed since early in the war; the servants had either been called up or diverted elsewhere to help the war effort. Bertie and Lady Thornfield were now living in the less demanding and draughty East Lodge, but her ladyship had been persuaded to take an extended break at her mother's in Filey. Shortly after, army transport was to be seen entering the Hall's grounds, but not to be seen dropping the debris and wreckage in the dip beyond the elm grove. And as publicity for the daring sabotage would be vital, it seemed an especially lucky touch that the *Yorkshire Argus*'s district reporter, Henry Ormonroyd, was most partial to The Rochester Arms in Thornfield village. What could go wrong?

On the night, Thor and Ingrid had been dropped off near the Hall by Frowne, who was now ensconced in The Rochester Arms, which was quiet as usual. He imagined himself inconspicuous in his country tweeds sitting at a corner table, but he had been spotted for a toff at once, confirmed when he became the first man in at least ten years to ask for half a pint of bitter. The only person, in fact, who hadn't noticed him was Henry Ormonroyd, who was at the bar already, cutting a morose figure, even for Yorkshire.

Outside, it was moonlit and mild for the north country in May. The would-be saboteurs, carrying the half-assembled incendiaries in knapsacks on their backs, cautiously approached the Hall's high wall, intending to make their way through the estate's wood rather than risk the exposure of the long drive. Sigrid helped Thor get up on top of it, thanking his exercise programme as she struggled with his weight. She had just joined him on the top of the wall when they were suddenly hailed from below by the village policeman, PC Gove, who was interrupting his stately progress by bicycle on a round which had included several of them at The Rochester Arms. 'Ay up, thee two, what does tha think theer doing up top yon wall? Poachin' ah'll be bound, appen, if ahm not as slow as a Clitheroe whippet.' Unsurprisingly, neither Thor nor Sigrid had any idea what the Constable was talking about. He, for his part, equally unsurprisingly, took their silence for guilt or cheek. 'Coom on naw, les bee avin thee sharpish laark or eets a neet in t'cells no danger!'

Sigrid, still influenced by her American film watching, was now weighing up whether to, as she put it later, 'drill the cop pronto' with the Walther PPK that had been restored to her for the mission. Thor was beginning to feel dizzy, as, unusually for a Norwegian, he did not have a head for heights. Happily, the situation was rescued by the arrival of Bertie on his bicycle (he was a modern Squire) en route to visit Mrs Stubbs, the widow of the local butcher, whose assets went considerably beyond an irresistible way with a steak and kidney pie (not that modern a Squire). It might well have been distracting thoughts of Mrs Stubbs that caused Bertie to collide with PC Gove, who described an almost graceful arc through the night air before landing on the grass verge and his head, the latter of which was not protected quite enough by his helmet to prevent him losing consciousness. Fortunately, this was for only a brief period, but it was long enough to allow Thor and Sigrid to continue unnoticed on their way while a contrite Bertie tended to the felled guardian of the peace. Bertie first reassured himself that PC Gove was recovered, and then assured PC Gove that he must have been imagining the poachers – 'A thin one and a fat one? On top of the wall? Come on, Govey, how many have you had?!' After which, both resumed their journeys, one to his wobbling circuit, the other to a rich pie, although Bertie's finely whistled rendition of 'I'm in the Mood for Love' did hint at certain other concerns.

Sigrid and Thor had now reached the house, and following Bertie's instructions, entered through the kitchen door, which had been left unlocked.

Once inside, they split up. Sigrid was to set off her incendiary in the main drawing room, still chock full of the fussy furniture of its high Victorian and Edwardian days, while Thor would go to the first floor over to the far east side of the Hall and set his bomb to go off simultaneously in a bedroom. It was, however, a pity that no one had given any thought to the whereabouts of the ancient and mostly retired butler, Cummings, who had been in service at the Hall even before the famous visit in 1908 of the King and Queen. In his later years he had developed a marked aversion to travel, even as far as the pub, due to his failing eyesight, and had become something of a recluse, though a loyal one. So it was that just as Thor had lit the prudently long fuse on his incendiary he heard a floorboard in the corridor outside the bedroom give a loud creak. Eager to escape, he opened a window and made his way on to the ornamental ledge that ran round the Hall's exterior. A bold act, given his vertigo, which led to a sudden plummet into the shrubbery below. Cummings – for it had been he – proceeded unaware on his customary visit to the drinks cabinet in the drawing room, where, having switched the light on, he came across Thor's partner in the act of arson. He at first thought she was a man but was disabused when Sigrid, who had not watched so many American films without learning the importance of remaining laconic at all times, smiled and said, 'Howdy, old timer, is that a gun in your pocket or are you pleased to see me?'

Cummings might have been a little deaf as well as short-sighted but he was also an English butler. 'No, it's not a bun, it's a gun.' He produced the old Webley service revolver he always carried against the possibility of intruders or high-jinking house guests bent on bagging a butler, and pointed it at Sigrid, who noted that his hand was shaking rather badly. He noticed this, too, and went to the drinks cabinet, poured himself a generous scotch without taking his eye or gun off Sigrid, and sipped long and satisfyingly before speaking. 'Might I enquire what you are doing here, madam?'

'You betcha, sweet cheeks. I was moseying along when my pet mouse, Monty, escaped from my rucksack and ran into this house through one of the many holes available. Not a shock, this place is like Swiss cheese, if you get me, pally. Anyhow, I found a door open and tracked the little palooka down to here. I was just enticing him with his favourite mix of sugar and saltpetre and some other stuff when you interrupted us, you ornery son of a gun.'

Cummings had drained his glass as he listened to this frankly incredible story. He poured another one and took a large sip before responding. 'Madam, that is a frankly incredible story. Now can you please give me something I can report to my august employer, Sir Bertram, which will not harm my reputation for honesty and reliability.' Sigrid was still thinking when there was a sound from the other side of the room which, surprisingly, Cummings heard. Performing a swift U-turn, he swivelled and fired a shot in the direction of the noise. He didn't hear the squeak, but he did Sigrid's scream. She ran across the room and, admirably maintaining her cover, shouted half in horror and half in wonder, 'You've killed him! You've killed Monty!'

Cummings joined her, bent down and studied the dead mouse closely. 'No, madam, I think you'll find that's one of ours. They're all over the place since the cat died.'

'You rubbed him out too?!'

'No, I ran him over. I haven't driven since. I don't need to be told when my work is done. Have you noticed an acrid smell, by the way?'

'That's your shooter, mister!'

'I don't think so. Observe the smoke.'

It was indeed smoke from the fire that Thor's incendiary had succeeded in starting. Cummings, who had a weak chest, began to cough and was staggering towards a window when Thor suddenly appeared on the other side of it, fresh from the shrubbery, staring in wide-eyed, dishevelled and more than ever resembling Oliver Hardy. This, the whisky, smoke and gunfire proved too much for the aged butler, who now collapsed, overcome. Sigrid opened the window and got him through it with Thor's help from the other side. They carried him a safe distance from the now blazing Hall and put him down on the lawn, where he lay gently groaning. Flames were now also licking the sky from the other side of the elm grove where Bertie, in captain's uniform after bidding farewell to Mrs Stubbs, her pie, and other delights, had started a fire among the military debris. 'We've got to get out of here!' shouted Thor. 'Come on, quick, this way!'

As we have seen, missions of this type require the most minute and rigorous plans. The slightest oversight could lead to the fiasco with Cummings which had almost scotched the entire mission. But Frowne and his team could surely not have been expected to predict that Thor would now lead Sigrid into Thornfield's ornamental maze.

MEANWHILE, THE ROCHESTER ARMS HAD BEEN NO NEARER achieving what might be described as *en fête*. There were times when Frowne could hear the sound of beer being swallowed on the other side of the room by the silent and impassive patrons. A few were accompanied by their wives, who opened their mouths mostly to take another very small sip of port and lemon. Such conversation as there was seemed mainly concerned with the inevitability of things getting worse before they got better, which was still highly unlikely, whether it was the war, the weather, or some remarkably intimate ailments. Frowne felt it a good thing that no genuine German agents were present, as they might not have been sufficiently familiar with the local culture to understand that this represented the highest point morale ever reached. He tried to strike up a conversation with the landlord, but it faltered after he lamented that the war had interrupted Yorkshire's run of three successive county championships, only to be asked, 'What's it got to do with thee?' A similarly friendly greeting to Ormonroyd had been met with a frown, followed by a stare and no more. The spy chief was starting to worry that Thornfield Hall could burn to the ground without anyone taking the slightest notice.

Just then, a small man in a flat cap burst in and shouted, with commendable economy, 'Fire at big 'ouse!' Loud grumbling followed and drinks were finished with resentful haste as the pub emptied, leaving only the landlord and Ormonroyd, who was sticking to his whisky with a deliberation that would have earned admiration on Plymouth Hoe in 1588. Frowne made his way to the Hall, much buoyed by the red sky in the Yorkshire night.

He got there just after the rest of the pub, most of whom turned out to be Bertie's Home Guard. They dashed about as much as they were able with buckets of water from the ornamental pond, but the stately pile was fiercely ablaze by the time the local auxiliary fire brigade arrived. Bertie, who had taken command, was making an excellent fist of bewailing his loss while adroitly hampering the operation: the axe that surreptitiously severed a hose was a particularly telling touch.

Cummings was soon discovered: his tale of two strangers was supported by Constable Gove and noted by Ormonroyd, who had finally made it, out of breath and unimpressed. 'Two mysterious arsonists bearing a close resemblance to Laurel & Hardy?! Why on earth would they want to burn down Thornfield Hall? They weren't architecture critics were they?' He wheezed happily at his quip, which in turn caused him to hiccough, releasing whisky fumes into the smoky air. But he had the grace to look concerned as Bertie approached, accompanied by Frowne.

'Ormonroyd! Terrible thing, terrible, all gone. Not just the home of my distinguished family, but history as well! Important pictures of earlier Thornfields, some fine sporting prints and a striking replica of Mount Vesuvius exploding in marble. Sabotage!'

He shook his fist dramatically; Frowne wondered if this was going a touch too far, but it needed more to exercise Ormonroyd. 'Saboteurs? Saboteurs, Lord Thornfield? Why would they attack Thornfield? You'll forgive me for saying it's not exactly the front line, is it?'

'The front line is everywhere, Mr Ormonroyd!' thundered Bertie. 'And I can assure you that Thornfield has been playing a vital role in helping us win this war. I obviously cannot say too much, as it's very hush-hush.'

Ormonroyd failed to catch Bertie's last words as they coincided with a loud bang that came from the direction of the fake camp. 'What did you say, Lord Thornfield?'

'I said it's hush-hush!' shouted Bertie. He then nodded to Frowne. 'My companion here, Mr Smith from the Ministry, might be able to tell you more.'

'Not much more, Lord Thornfield,' said Frowne smoothly. 'As you know, Mr Ormonroyd, your report must be submitted to the censor to prevent anything being revealed that could aid the enemy. What I can tell you is that fortunately no one has suffered any injury here, apart from Lord Thornfield's elderly butler, Mr Cummings, who is recovering well from the effects of shock and smoke. I am also able to say that we have not ruled out sabotage, as Thornfield Hall has been used recently for vital training. But fortunately, again, the attack took place when our troops were out on exercise and the camp was unoccupied. What you cannot report is that two people are helping us with our inquiries, as this would most certainly aid the enemy. Constable Gove and Mr Cummings have been instructed accordingly. Thank you.'

'And I suppose your couple of halves in The Rochester Arms are also classified?' said Ormonroyd.

'Very much so,' said Frowne, 'As is the most impressive amount of whisky you managed to put away in there.'

What passed for a smile in Yorkshire passed between them, and an understanding. Frowne had told only one untruth. He had not been able to find Thor and Sigrid, who had failed to make the agreed rendezvous point as they were still in the maze.

The final edition of the *Yorkshire Argus* had gone to print some time before, dawn was beginning to break, and Ormonroyd was anxious to get home to his bed if not Mrs Ormonroyd. Frowne, though, was equally anxious that he should see the purported wreckage and debris in the fake camp. He started walking towards it with Bertie, drawing Ormonroyd with them by apologising for not being able to give him any more detail. Ormonroyd was finally impressed. 'Well, they certainly made a bit of a mess of this,' he said, surveying the chaotic scene, strewn about with wreckage and equipment, cunningly detailed but not necessarily capable of withstanding too close an inspection in the broad light of day.

'Bit of colour for you, old chap,' said Frowne.

THOR AND SIGRID HAD NOT BEEN LOST IN THE MAZE FOR THE entire time. True, there was a certain amount of panic at the outset, not helped by their recent encounter with Cummings. But Sigrid proved once again to be the strong link in the partnership, gathering herself and calming her friend, although he didn't react that well to her little joke, 'This is a fine maze you've got me into.' They stumbled around for a little while; there was a bad moment when they came across a whitened pile of bones, until Thor realised they had been secreted away by a dog (Malthouse, Bertie's Lurcher, as it happened). Then Sigrid's usherette training kicked in, the result of having to move around in the dark, especially during gloomy Swedish films. 'You have to keep your hand touching the wall, the hedge, always touch the hedge, follow your hand, and always turn left. Follow me!' After some time they arrived at the entrance to the maze, but decided to wait there until the frantic action at the Hall had died down. Long after dawn they finally reached their rendezvous point, where fortunately one of Frowne's men was still waiting.

Jubilation broke out in St James and Ruislip a couple of days later at the following leading item in the *Yorkshire Argus*, headlined, 'Thornfield Hall Razed to Ground', with sub-headings, 'Historic House Lost', 'Army Training Camp', 'Sabotage Suspected':

'Sabotage is suspected after a fire destroyed historic Thornfield Hall and an adjacent army camp in its grounds. The Auxiliary Fire Service and the Thornfield Home Guard, commanded by Colonel Lord Thornfield, the owner

of Thornfield Hall, battled for several hours with the blaze but were unable to save the historic old house.

It is understood that the camp, which was completely destroyed, with only charred debris and equipment left strewn about, was being used in a vital training capacity.

Fortunately, troops were away on exercise at the time of the blaze, and no one was hurt in the incident except for Mr Cummings, 83, Lord Thornfield, who is recovering from the effects of shock and smoke inhalation.

"I am heartbroken," said Lord Thornfield. "My family's beautiful house and beloved home has been destroyed in troubling circumstances. Remarkable possessions and objects of great sentimental value have been lost, including a most impressive scale model of Mount Vesuvius exploding in marble. Their value was of course beyond price, but we will do our best for insurance purposes.

"The Thornfields have faced disaster before – my father's desperately unlucky investment in around two million shovels and bridles at the same time as the invention of the motor car comes to mind – but we have always dealt with it for the imposter it is. We will pause, reflect, wipe away a tear, submit the claim and build back better!"

Thornfield Hall was built in 1810, replacing an earlier house which also burnt down. Following that disaster, which also took place in suspicious circumstances, the estate was bought by the Thornfield family from the Rochester family, who lent their name to the nearby village with its splendid hostelry, The Rochester Arms, where a warm Yorkshire welcome is always assured'.

DOCTOR HASSELBACHER WAS STARING OUT OF THE window as usual, this time at one of those glittering northern summer days the great Munch loved so. Sigrid and Thor had done remarkably well, he thought, no doubt of that. The successful sabotage had gone down very well in Berlin. Another telling blow to the already crumbling British resolve, the successful sewing of a deep insecurity, the fostering of fear. They had followed it up with information that would not be published in British newspapers for obvious reasons. What they had discovered at Thornhill Camp included white anoraks, heavy cold weather clothing, including winter drawers and woollen hats; skis, ski poles and tins of ski wax.

All pointed towards training for an attack on the Norwegian coast. What he had to work out was whether Sigrid and Thor had done so remarkably well that what they were telling him was unlikely to be true. The timing of the mission, for example: was it possible for them to be so well informed of troop movements? Thor's work with the Norwegian Army had taken him north to Newcastle, and Sigrid had been up there too, working with the refugees who were arriving from Shetland, but beyond that it was a matter of trust. And then there were the skis: did they ski in North Yorkshire?

But most of all what he had to work out was how much he cared. There seemed to be a disposition in both Oslo and Berlin to believe in the Norwegian attack, for a number of reasons. Many of them were the result of the rivalries, competing suspicions, disguised motives and paranoia that evil tends to engender. But there was also the highly persuasive and completely false information being provided by double agents not only in Britain but in Egypt and elsewhere, all pointing north rather than to the south, North Africa, the true location of the first combined counter-offensive by the Allies against the Axis powers.

Whisky could help only so much, and Wolff had been passing on requests for an assessment of the invasion threat in Norway that had now become orders. The Doctor decided it might well be wise to do what he should have already done and delve a little more into the background of his spies. He began with Thor's mother, the former Miss May Flower. The charming Olaf Gundersen was despatched once more to the Theatercafeen, where Fru Dahling proved as coquettish as might be expected of a former actress separated from her husband and locked down in Norway. Conversation flowed as well as the champagne; along with several repetitions of 'I don't mind if I do' and 'perhaps I will, then, just a little splash', she spoke freely of her 'darling boy', Thor, and her worries about his whereabouts.

'Any idea where he might be?' asked Olaf, all friendly concern.

'I think he must be in England, I'm sure that's where he'd want to be. He is half-English after all, and he loves so much about it over there, he loves the stars, George Formby is a great favourite, and Noël Coward, and cricket and custard and milky tea, steak and kidney pie, lovely suet, fog and fish and chips, pie and mash, liquor from the stewed eels, mmm. No, I really shouldn't, you naughty boy. All right, go on then, just a drop.'

Hasselbacher contemplated Olaf's report of the meeting. Certainly food for thought; a confirmation of suspicion. Hasselbacher knew England. He had visited several times and admired much about it, including its nightlife. The Cat's Pyjamas, for example, rivalled any Berlin nightclub. Still. Enjoying Noël Coward and cricket was one thing, but a liking for the ghastlier end of British taste must argue an attachment strong enough to overcome taste in every way. The clincher, though, was George

Formby: anyone who admired this gormless purveyor of high stupidity, rackety sentimentality, unlikely attraction and general chaos must be English to the very depth of his soul. Hasselbacher needed to know no more.

He poured a scotch. Fate, or whatever passed for it or surpassed it, had contrived to deliver the future of the world into the hands (it was not his first drink) of a gloomy disenchanted romantic, a lover of his country but not its current creed, a man who felt the same way about Beethoven, Bach, Schiller and Goethe as Thor Dahling did about George Formby. He could tell Berlin that all intelligence strongly indicated a large-scale invasion of Norway, or he could tell the truth. Setback for their Germany or hope for his. Put in another way, it was a choice, perhaps unenviable, between Adolf Hitler and George Formby.

FROWNE WAS STARING OUT OF THE WINDOW AT ONE OF those London days where the rain drops follow each other down the pane, obscuring yet more the dank greyness. But all was not gloom. Operation Torch had gone well. The allies had invaded French North Africa, not Norway, successfully and significantly aided by his double agents. Torch and Alamein had secured victory in Africa and the Middle East; he was now looking forward to a deception operation on a much larger scale for the Allied invasion of Europe. There was, though, a problem with Laurel & Hardy. News had that morning reached him of a change in the Abwehr's Oslo organisation. The deputy head, a Doctor Hasselbacher, was no longer in post. Frowne's information, provided by a useful agent in Oslo, Olaf Gundersen, was that he had suddenly disappeared. It was assumed he had been recalled to Berlin. This could mean that German intelligence had blamed him for attaching too much significance to their information. But there had been no let-up in the messages from Oslo to Thor and Sigrid, and the urgings for more action of the Thornfield kind. Certainly he had been most careful to ensure that although their activities were entirely fictional, they only ever provided accurate intelligence, albeit often a touch exaggerated. But would they be taken quite so much on trust in future after Thornfield? What had really happened to Hasselbacher? Frowne turned from the window, sketched a rather flashy cover drive, and decided he could not risk it.

Shortly afterwards Gundersen passed on information to the Abwehr allegedly obtained from a contact in the Norwegian Government in exile: Thor and Sigrid had been arrested and were being held at Pentonville. The trial and execution of a man and woman accused of espionage was subsequently announced in a two-paragraph Ministry of Information press release. In fact, Sigrid was rewarded with a job with the British Army Film and Photographic Unit, and worked as a clapper board girl at Pinewood. She returned to Norway in 1945 and became a director, making such notable films as *Det Er Dystre Nordover* ('It's Grim Up North') and *Noen Liker Det Kaldt* ('Some Like It Cold'). Captain Thor Dahling sailed from Britain on HMS *Berwick* in November 1944 as part of a small Free Norwegian Army force which was to assist and then assume control from the Russians of the liberation of Finnmark, in the far north of Norway. He helped organise and lead the local militia and reinforcements that saw Norwegian forces drive the Germans out of his homeland. After the war, Thor took over his father's hairdressing business and became a leading campaigner for gay rights in Norway, ably supported by his partner, Olaf Gundersen.

For his part, Frowne stayed on with the service well after the war until the unpleasantness with Kim Philby and his retirement to Bath. He played at the local cricket club, delivering leg breaks that occasionally and trickily spun the other way, before turning to umpiring in a not-always-impartial manner. Occasionally he would visit his now very old friend Bertie in his fine new bungalow in Yorkshire where the second Lady Thornfield was never happier than when baking. One memory that always gave him a smile, now, was his last meeting with Thor and Sigrid, when Thor had sheepishly produced a message from Oslo with its transcription, which made no sense. 'Sorry, old chap, it seemed like gibberish, and I completely forgot about it. A souvenir for you, perhaps?' Frowne had looked at it the next day, and agreed with Thor's assessment of the decode, which was obviously some sort of test message or glitch. Much later, though, on a slow day in Bath, he found it again while going through some old papers which he should probably not have kept. The message read, 'verschüttetetintedasistschmerzhaftweiseworte! (1,4)'. After some pondering and refreshing of his now rusty German, Frowne worked out that this was, '*Verschüttete Tinte – das ist schmerzhaft – weise Worte!* (1,4)' and was, of course a crossword clue: 'Spilled ink – that's painful – wise words!'. After a little more time and pencil stub sucking, he solved it: 'spilled ink' indicated an anagram of ink: I kn; 'that's painful': ow; all clinched by 'wise words!' and therefore, clearly: 'I know'. So: Hasselbacher's last message. And one secret Frowne was glad he hadn't known.

Afterword

*Much of this is based on the exploits of Helge Moe and Tor Glad,
two young Norwegians who did indeed work as double agents for
the British in the Second World War, giving themselves up to do so
after arriving by dinghy from a German seaplane on the Scottish
coast in April, 1941. Moe had worked for his father, a Norwegian
hairdresser; his mother was an English opera singer, Ida Wade,
who retired from the stage when she married. Her father, Colonel
Herbert Wade, of the Nineteenth Manchester Regiment, was
decorated at Gallipoli.*

*In 1939, Moe was sent by his father to England to train as a film
make-up artist and worked at Denham Studios on Alexander Korda's
The Thief of Baghdad. He returned to Norway at the outbreak
of war, and was in Oslo when the Germans invaded the neutral
country in 1940. He soon began to chafe against the occupation
and look for ways to resist. His friend Glad recommended him for
a job with him in the censor's office, where they warned writers of
subversive letters rather than reported them. He was dismissed after
raising suspicions, which nevertheless did not prevent the Abwehr,
German military intelligence, from recruiting the pair as agents
when they daringly offered their services. (As mentioned in the text,
the Abwehr, under the inscrutable and apparently untouchable
Admiral Canaris, was a much-flawed mixture of inefficiency,
rivalry and disaffection with the Nazi regime.)*

*Following their arrival in Scotland and immediate surrender
to a bemused local constabulary, they were taken to Ham*

Common, where their interrogators were convinced by Moe, but less so by Glad, who was unable to explain to their satisfaction his links with the Nazi occupiers, and was eventually interned on the Isle of Man, where he remained for the rest of the war.

MI5 decided that the pair – named Mutt and Jeff after the popular American cartoon of the time featuring one thin man and one fat man – could be of great use to the Twenty Committee, its double agent operation. Twenty in Roman numerals is XX, double cross: this combination of facetious pun and puzzle was a hallmark of the MI5 controllers. John Masterman, the chairman of the Twenty Committee, was an Oxford history don and whodunnit writer, who later wrote, 'Running a team of double agents is very like running a club cricket side'.

Mutt and Jeff arrived with a wireless transmitter and sabotage equipment. Mutt and an officer who had learnt to copy the absent Jeff's transmission style established a link with the Abwehr in Oslo using a code based on their matching crossword puzzle books. I should like to tell you that the sabotage of Thornfield Hall and its camp is an accurate account of their activities, but it is not. The two sabotage operations the Abwehr believed Mutt and Jeff carried out were in fact the work of British munition experts: Operation Guy Fawkes at a flour store in Wealdstone and Operation Bunbury (after Wilde's fun in the country), at an electricity generating substation in Bury St Edmunds. Neither went smoothly. A vigilant police officer raised the alarm so quickly in Wealdstone that the less vigilant nightwatchmen had to be roused from their slumbers and the fire brigade extinguished the blaze before it could take hold. At Bury St Edmunds, where a small fire was successfully started among unimportant equipment, they concealed a large unexploded bomb so well that the fire investigators had to be led to it by a police constable in on the plan. But both operations were reported, a little grudgingly, with some prompting, in the newspapers, and a German radio broadcast boasted of 'the big East Anglian' sabotage.

Mutt did travel back to Scotland on several occasions so that he could broadcast from there and maintain his cover. The Germans were also persuaded to make air drops of sabotage equipment in Aberdeenshire – Operations Haggis, Oatmeal and Porridge – which also provided the agents with cash in used five pound notes. Reality's inconvenient habit of intruding tragedy into fun and jinks saw the Germans carrying on from one drop to bomb nearby Fraserburgh, solely to disguise the true purpose of their flight, but thereby killing an 11-year-old boy, Lawrence McKay Kerr. Mutt was deeply distressed by the death and dedicated the memoir of his days as a spy to young Lawrence.

The sabotage and drops confirmed the Abwehr's confidence in the pair, allowing them to play a significant role in the Twenty Committee's overall scheme to persuade the Germans that the Allied counter attacks were being launched far from where they were in reality taking place.

Laurel & Hardy's deception is based on Mutt and Jeff's successful part in tying down large numbers of German forces against an invasion of Norway and allowing Operation Torch, the successful Allied invasion of French North Africa in 1942, the first time American forces engaged in the European theatre.

They were also involved in the deceptions aimed at concealing the D-Day targets. Operation Fortitude North, again promoting Norway as the invasion destination, succeeded in tying down 13 German divisions there.

Operation Fortitude South, pushing the Pas de Calais and the Bay of Biscay, featured other remarkable double agents:

Juan Pujol Garcia, codenamed Garbo because he was such a good actor. Garcia, a sometime Spanish chicken farmer, was so opposed to the Nazis after his experiences in the Spanish Civil War that he was feeding them misleading information even before making contact with MI5. Based in Lisbon, he invented 27 subsidiary agents for the purpose, and took the operation over wholesale to the British side, after which German payments to them went into the British Treasury. His imaginary but busy network was probably the most persuasive part of the operation;

Roman Czerniawski, codenamed Brutus, after Caesar's friend and assassin, a Polish officer who began spying in France for Poland before being arrested by the Nazis and sent to England to spy, where, like Mutt and Jeff, he made himself known to the authorities; he played a prominent role in the Operation Fortitude South deception, promoting the Pas de Calais as the invasion point for D-Day;

Dusko Popov, codenamed Tricycle after his liking for a menage a trois, a flamboyant Yugoslav playboy who also contributed to the Pas de Calais subterfuge;

Elvira Concepcion Josefina de la Fuente Chaudoir, a bisexual Peruvian socialite who was recruited by the British and then the Germans, on both occasions in a casino. Codenamed Bronx after the cocktail, she managed to ensure that an entire crack German Panzer division was in Bordeaux instead of Normandy on D-Day.

But, for me, the most startling feature of the entire British intelligence operation in the Second World War – including the Bletchley codebreaking – is that by 1941 MI5 was running the entire German espionage operation in Britain and continued to do so right up to the end of the war, having turned or interned every German agent bar one, who shot himself in an air raid shelter in Cambridge after running out of money.

Altogether, 19 spies and saboteurs were executed after being prosecuted under the controversially draconian Treachery Act, one in an indoor shooting range at the Tower of London by a firing squad of the Scots Guards. Announcement of their deaths was as brief as that for Laurel & Hardy.

Coal Man and Tripod, mentioned as part of Frowne's stable, are as fictional as he.

Also fictional, in a double sense, is Doctor Hasselbacher, who will have been spotted by readers of Graham Greene as one of the leading characters in 'Our Man in Havana', his excellent entertainment featuring James Wormold, a retailer of vacuum cleaners who is lured into espionage trying to keep his beautiful daughter in the style he thinks she deserves. Wormold's fictions, invented to satisfy British Intelligence, have bewildering and tragic consequences, including the death of Dr Hasselbacher, his best friend. Dr Hasselbacher, who is not described as homosexual, had fought in the First World War with the disenchantment described. He says that he left Germany in 1934; I hope Mr Greene would not be too offended, and perhaps entertained, by this alternative route to Cuba. After all, 'Our Man in Havana' was inspired by his time in wartime intelligence, when he came across Garbo and his fictional network and his invented information about Britain. This was in fact written from Lisbon with the aid of a Blue Guide and an Ordnance Survey map; none of it raised suspicion in spite of such snippets as this, allegedly from Glasgow: 'There are men here who would do anything for a litre of wine'. It might also be of interest that Garbo and Greene's boss was Kim Philby.

Mutt, who was stood down from his spying duties before D-Day, returned to Norway as part of the Allied force that disarmed the German forces and returned the country to independence. After the war, he worked as a manager for the SAS airline in Malmo. He married twice and had three children. He broke his silence about his wartime adventure in 1980, publishing his account of it in 1986. Jeff did not fare so well. After his release from internment he returned to Norway and was charged with collaboration amid much publicity, but freed after a late and undisclosed intervention by MI5. He went on to work for Norwegian Television, but never felt entirely free of the suspicion that led to his internment.

The crossword, besides being a favoured pastime and code method of spymasters, also played a curious role before D-Day, when, to the consternation of the intelligence services, names for various aspects of the operation began to appear as answers to clues in The Daily Telegraph crossword. Officers descended on the compiler, Leonard Dawe, a London school headmaster who had been evacuated to Surrey. He managed to persuade them that this was merely coincidence, and no other explanation has emerged, although one of his pupils has said that he often asked them for words, and that they might well have heard 'Overlord', 'Mulberry', and 'Neptune' from the many US servicemen based in the area. 'Mr Dawe,' he said, 'was a disciplinarian and a man of extremely high principle and one could not imagine anyone less likely to be involved in anything incorrect.' Still odd, though.

The method used by Sigrid to solve another puzzle, the maze at Thornfield, is called the Tremaux Algorithm, after its 19th-century developer, Charles Pierre Tremaux, and is far more complicated than Sigrid made it seem. But do keep turning left lest the same fate befalls you as it did Harris, one of the 'Three Men in a Boat', on his famous visit to the Hampton Court version. Mutt and Jeff just about survive in British popular culture as rhyming slang for deaf.

FURTHER READING:
Double Agent, *John Moe*
Double Cross, *Ben Macintyre*
Fighting to Lose: How the German Secret Intelligence Service Helped the Allies Win the Second World War, *John Dryden*
Our Man in Havana, *Graham Greene*

1952

The Waves of Change

THERE WERE DAYS WHEN JIMMY SHRUBSALL LOVED NUTSBY, and there were days when he didn't. Like this one. It wasn't the March weather, exactly, although slanting rain had now joined the rough wind breaking endless waves of white horses on the sandy beach, Nutsby's pride and joy. Not that he agreed with those who declared themselves irresistibly in thrall to the marvellous melancholy of an English seaside resort out of season. Try living here, he thought, beginning to worry about the pier. No, his mood was more to do with life in general. And not just in Nutsby, either, but in a country, in 1952, still trying to get its wind back from 1939, 1940, 1941, 1942, 1943, 1944 and 1945. Grey days, straitened days, tough days.

Too tough for his dad, Frank Shrubsall, who'd been with the Royal Army Service Corps ('RASC – Run Away Someone's Coming', as he loved to put it), helping to supply troops from North Africa to Normandy and beyond. The last straw for Frank had been the return of Churchill in 1951 after five years of a reforming, nationalising, welfare-providing Labour government. 'Churchill?! The man's 77! What's he going to give us? More bloody speeches?'

The ex-corporal had then pulled himself up to his full height of five feet and six inches, looked fiercely at his only son and said, 'That's why we're off!'

This was a bit of a surprise, as Jimmy had only just got back to Nutsby after completing his National Service at an RAF station in Gloucestershire where there had been little else to do other than improve an education which had shown the pressing need for Rab Butler's reforms of 1944.

Exercising his newly acquired wisdom, he nodded and smiled sympathetically.

'Yeah, Dad, of course, wouldn't blame you if you did.'

'No Jimmy, I'm serious. I'm going to be a ten pound pom. I'll be too old if I leave it any longer.'

'What does Mum think? Where is she? She's not left you, has she?'

'Don't be silly, why would your mum abandon the James Mason of Nutsby? She's over at the pier. She's looking forward to it, too, the change, bit of a challenge.'

'What about me? Shouldn't I be the one who's going? Youth and the future and all that?'

'Too late, old son. We got there first. You've got to look after the pier, can't let that go, can we? Not after all these years. Yours now, no, don't bother to thank me. We're off tomorrow. We were going to leave you a note if you weren't back in time.'

AND THAT HAD BEEN THAT. HIS MUM AND DAD HAD INDEED taken advantage of the assisted passage generously offered by the Australian government after the war, which had proved extremely popular with the grey and straitened Britons, who either didn't know or didn't care they were being recruited expressly to keep the Antipodes white. Mr and Mrs Shrubsall were doing quite well, too: Frank had taken a deckchair concession on Bondi Beach while Jimmy's mum was selling Beaut ice creams – 'You can't beat a Beaut!' – in Coogee.

Not the happiest comparison on a day like this in Nutsby, where it had become difficult to make out the sea from the sky, grey-wise. Jimmy had now reached the pier and was applying his screwdriver to allow a slot machine to be slightly more generous with its payouts (Frank had been a terrible skinflint). Nutsby Pier was not among the front rank of its peers; in some reference books it was listed as the shortest pier in Britain, at 95 feet; others dismissively declared it to be a jetty or, worst insult of all, 'a beach pavilion'.

It had not been meant to be like this. The architect, an ambitious young man, was seduced away to build the great pier at nearby Clicton, leaving Nutsby sadly truncated. Ernest Shrubsall, Jimmy senior's great-great-grandfather had put on a brave show, advertising it as 'the great little pier' with the slogan 'you'll never get tired of walking our pier!'. Jimmy was working in the arcade at the entrance. The slot machines were pretty steady during the season, alongside the mechanical grabber machines which were also mysteriously more liberal since Jimmy had taken over from his dad, although some of the chocolate brands were of an antique type. There was also a charming old animatronic display of the Death of Nelson, set on the deck of the Victory; its climax was when the tiny admiral slumped back, expired, and the grief-stricken Hardy's head plunged towards his sleeve to wipe his tears. Sometimes a loose spring would cause Nelson to suddenly revive, but no one seemed to notice. In one corner, in an area which had been curtained off at the insistence of the town clerk, Mr Mogg, there were three What the Butler Saw machines whose pictures were so grainy that they were not capable of interpretation by anyone without considerable experience in the field, and so had little chance of corrupting callow youth whatever Mr Mogg might think.

Jimmy knew that, really, if he wanted to get ahead, he should chuck out all this elderly entertainment and replace it with brave new attractions, convert the arcade into a milk bar and install a jukebox, go for the American stuff, but in many ways he was more conservative than his dad, if not Mr Mogg. Frank's time away, with all the strangeness, excitement and upheaval of war, had made him restless; Jimmy's, in the tedium of a sleepy rural air base, had teased his nostalgia and sharpened his affection for the creaky old pier, and for Nutsby, which seemed to him, even on a day like this, to hold obstinately to something precious of the past, before the great convulsion. Oh, yes, of course, he knew that this past was partial, that it ignored all manner of inconvenient unpleasantnesses and prejudices. But he also felt it was the good part of the past, and worth preserving, somehow. The trick, it seemed to him, would be to coax Nutsby into the present very gently, the better to guard against throwing out its essence with the Admiral, the Butler and the other wider attractions, including Alf Ellaby and his eternally surly donkeys down on the beach, Jum Turtill's tours of the bay on the Tipsy Dancer – 'Look lively – haven't you seen a baler before?' – crab sandwiches at Cayford's Cosy Cafe, and Housey Housey at the

Nutsby Social Club (1927) – 'Every Thursday. All welcome. Cash Prizes (modest!).'

Certainly, it couldn't continue as it was. Clicton was forging ahead with all the new stuff and, in the season, was busier and brasher than ever. Visitors who once would have come to Nutsby were now going there instead. Regulars at The Nutsby Hotel were becoming irregular, reported the proprietor, Mr Alex Beech, known of course as Sandy (these were great days for nicknames; see also the numerous Nobby Clarks and Dusty Millers). Sandy, a man of cravat, blazer, often-combed hair and uncertain antecedents, was the Chairman of the Nutsby Hoteliers and Ancillary Facilitators Association, and also the Mayor of Nutsby. He was, unlike the rest of the town, fierce for progress in the way that only a newcomer (1948) could be, and had just converted the hotel's saloon bar into the Nutsby Cocktail Lounge. His election as Mayor by fellow town councillors unanimously opposed to his progressive policies was explained by his ownership of the only licensed premises in Nutsby. He was still looking for a cocktail bartender but the public bar remained popular.

Jimmy, still pensive, was on his way there when he was hailed by the town's vicar, the splendidly named Reverend Norman Undercroft, out for his daily blowy constitutional along the seafront. Like most of the town, and indeed most of the country, Jimmy was an unquestioning churchgoer; his tended to be much more frequent during the visits home of the Rev Undercroft's lovely daughter, Jill, a medical student at the legendary London teaching hospital, St Swithin's. Jimmy was madly in love with Jill but far too intimidated by her dark beauty and bright brains to tell her.

'Jimmy! How the heaven are you?' said the Reverend, a man so genial he was more of a bay than a cove. 'Mired in the dark days before the year turns towards sunshine and you begin to hear the sound of shillings clinking in the pockets of happy visitors?'

'You might say, Vicar. Bad time of the year for piers. Not that any time is particularly good for them these days. Town's in a bit of a way, if you ask me.'

'Yes, I know what you mean. My collection plate rather reflects it, too. And there's always the roof. Hellfire below and Flood above. Be a pity to turn the place into Clicton, though.'

'Sandy Beech is quite keen.'

'Ah, yes, Sandy. A man in need of direction, I've always thought. The Nutsby Cocktail Lounge! When I want a Screwdriver I'll go to Manhattan. The Cotton Club, now there was a place! Duke, Fats, the Count, what days. All the same, definitely not for Nutsby.'

The vicar looked a little distant and surveyed the beach, empty but for the cross-strutted wooden tank traps still there from the war while a few gulls caught up in the gusts sounded more melancholy than ever. Jimmy was intrigued. Mr Undercroft had arrived in Nutsby in the 1930s with Jill but without Mrs Undercroft, around whom much speculation had swirled, although not even Frank Shrubsall had suggested she'd been a jazz singer. The rather more prosaic truth was that she'd run off with a minor canon and both should have known better.

'Still, it's not all gloom,' the vicar continued, eventually. 'The tide is turning!'

Jimmy glanced out at the greyness and saw no sign of this.

'No, I'm talking about the mood of the country. A new young queen and a splendid coronation to look forward to next summer. And I've an idea that could help us celebrate that and bring people – the right sort of people, obviously, cultured, well-behaved – to Nutsby. Interested? I can't talk now because I've got to go and sympathise with Mrs Arbuthnott about her bunions. Come and see me at the vicarage on Friday afternoon. Jill will be here.'

'I'll be there,' said Jimmy. The vicar had set off at pace and so didn't see the blush that Jimmy had failed once again to fight off at the mention of Jill. He was smiling as he made his way to the Nutsby Hotel, where Sandy Beech was presiding over the public bar. Jimmy asked, as usual, after the new cocktail bartender and received the reply, as usual, that a number of candidates had expressed an interest and were being considered. Various smirks moved around the clientele: Sandy, unmoved, airily announced, 'Don't worry, there will be one very soon. Then you people will change your tune, believe me. Sophistication, that's what you lot are missing.' Jimmy took his pint and joined Jum Turtill, not necessarily the mayor's greatest fan.

'Sophistication,' said Jum. 'Five syllables. Smashed his old record. He's about as sophisticated as my gunwale which, deceptively, has only one.' Jum, despite the beard, boat and a rich Nutsby accent, was in fact a retired actuary from Leamington and something of an intellectual.

Alf Ellaby, who was not, and only slightly more talkative than his donkeys, said, 'Prat.'

Jill opened the rectory door and Jimmy's heart gave one of those happy tickles that only the undeclared and unrequited know. It wasn't just her beauty, but her marvellously brusque manner that he found so beguiling. He sometimes dreamt that she was his doctor and had taken unflustered control of his condition – 'Breathe in for me, would you?' Today was no exception. 'Jimmy, hello, Daddy's in his study, he's expecting you. Are you well?' She was wearing a polkadot dress with a broad belt and wide skirt and looked absolutely terrific, thought Jimmy when he should have been thinking up a bright, clever and interesting answer.

'Top hole, thanks, Jill,' was what he came out with eventually and regretted immediately. Top hole! Who was he? Bertie Wooster?

The blush was not far behind, but – it was obviously a family trait – Jill was off down the corridor and saying over her shoulder, 'That's good – I love your pier!' Jimmy didn't answer this at all, stalled by how near and yet so far this declaration was to his dreams. By now Jill had reached the door to the study and threw it open to reveal the vicar dozing serenely at his desk. 'Gracious me, Daddy,' said his daughter with a laugh perfectly pitched for Jimmy, 'if your sermon sends you to sleep, what chance has the congregation got?'

Mr Undercroft came to with the ease of the practised napper. 'Ah, Jill – and Jimmy, hello – I was just trying to get a little inspiration. Actually, sleep plays an important part in biblical matters. How could Jacob and Joseph have dreamed their dreams without going to sleep first? St Peter was fast asleep when the angel came to rescue him from Herod's dungeon, and the other Joseph got all his messages about Mary and Jesus in dreams. So you could say that I was merely, as usual, following the way of the Lord.' Jill laughed that laugh again, and Jimmy was grateful to be directed to the nearest seat by the vicar, who continued, 'I'd almost finished my sermon, anyway. I'm going to talk about the great choice that faces our little community, and the nation, still faces us nearly ten years after the end of the war. Do we try to recreate what we had before it, or do we try to make a better society, one that's more equal and more tolerant?'

Jill remained in the doorway, poised and fond of her father. 'Steady, Daddy, they'll be calling you a Communist and marching on the vicarage with bad intent and burning stakes. I'd try to save you, but I'm only a feeble woman and in any case I'm too far on with my medical studies to risk being harpooned by Jum Turtill. Vicar's daughter assassinated by Actuary, no thanks. What do you think, Jimmy?'

It was lucky for Jimmy that he had already been thinking about this, or there would have been more gargling sounds and not much else. As it was, he made a slow start before picking up in confidence. 'Well… er… well… to be honest… I think Nutsby's a good example of what you're talking about, Vicar. We've got something here that's hard to describe, that's precious but we'll only properly recognise when it's not there anymore. And we've also got some things that we'd be much better without…'

'Such as?' asked Jill, to his delight at least apparently interested.

'Well… I think there's a lot of fear about. Fear that makes for suspicion of change, almost any change. That's why we've got Churchill back. People are frightened of too much change, even when they can see a lot of the changes we've had have been for the good, like the new health service. But it's not so surprising after what we've just been through, is it? And that's without the Bomb.'

Jill was now looking at him in a way he had often imagined.

'Yes, that's right. You should hear some of the old fogeys we have to put up with in the medical profession, all sniffy and snarky about our big changes because they're worried about their precious standing, and their pockets, of course. Oh, and the very idea of a woman being able to do it, now that's really frightening. Back in the kitchen, ladies, you were far too good out of it. Pompous asses!'

Now she was the one with colour in her cheeks. Jimmy was bewitched. Mr Undercroft was smiling happily.

'And the answer?' he asked, aptly steepling his hands and secretly imagining himself chairing The Brains Trust, that acme of intellectual discussion which had just transferred to the television and which he watched on Mrs Arbuthnott's tiny set when he wasn't discussing bunions.

'Just keep at it!' said Jill.

'Go gently,' said Jimmy, apologetically, but sticking to his guns. 'Or Nutsby will become a little Clicton run by Sandy Beech with his cocktails and soda fountains and American everything.'

'I quite like Sandy Beech,' said Jill. 'Very nice car.'

'But it's only a Hillman Minx Convertible!' Jimmy found himself saying with a touch too much resentment.

'What do you drive?' asked Jill.

'Well, nothing as such – yet,' stumbled Jimmy. 'But if we have a good year, I quite fancy a Triumph, something like that… or a Sunbeam Alpine… or something,' he finished, lamely.

'Don't pay her any attention, Jimmy,' said Mr Undercroft. 'She knows Sandy Beech is my worst nightmare so she's always pretending to like him.'

'Oh, good!' said Jimmy and then realised what he had said. 'Sorry, I mean it's good you have such a good sense of humour… and you know, it's good you don't like Hillman Minx Convertibles… although it's probably not good that you tease your father, not that it isn't, er…'

Jill was grinning at him, which, such is the rare nature of love and attraction, he found exciting and excruciating at exactly the same time. The vicar exercised a tool of the trade and administered mercy.

'But I've just remembered why you're here, Jimmy. The gentle way to drag Nutsby into the 1950s. Now is the crucial moment. Rationing ending, more things to buy, people with more money in their pockets. The Sandy Beeches are circling with their shiny beads and mirrors. So this is my wizard little wheeze. Canute.'

'Canute?' said Jill.

'Canute?' said Jimmy.

The vicar paused, began tamping his pipe, mostly for effect, and then continued, 'Canute the Great. King of England, Norway and Denmark, known as The North Sea Empire, born circa 990, died 1035. Unjustly ignored because he was the wrong kind of European, being half Danish and half Polish, not German, or Anglo-Saxon as the diplomatic euphemism has it. And a Viking to boot. Tremendous warrior, always biffing, took every crown by force, could be just a touch unforgiving, even with hostages, and far too much for Ethelred the Unready and even Edmund Ironside. Christian, friend of the Pope, relaxed approach to certain aspects, seems to have had two wives, one pagan, the other churched. Difficult to follow at times, unclear chronicles, wistful court poets, and lots of names, many the same. Some of them were absolutely splendid, how about Sigurd the Stout, Sigrid the Haughty, Eric the Victorious and Eadric the Grasper for starters, although my favourite for clarity of purpose is Thorfinn the Skullcrusher—'

Jill, who was now perched on the arm of a chair intoxicatingly close to Jimmy, interrupted: 'Fascinating, but what's this got to do with Nutsby?'

'Ah, that's it, you see. What's the only story anybody knows about him?'

'The waves,' said Jimmy, who had at least enjoyed history at school. 'He had his throne put on the beach and commanded the waves to stop so he could show his creeps of courtiers that his power, unlike God's, had its limits.'

'Exactly. And for which the poor blighter has been mocked ever since by idiots who think he was amazed when the waves kept on coming.'

'Again, absolutely fascinating, Daddy. But, again, what's this got to do with Nutsby?'

'Come on: waves, sea, beach, like ours.' As a practised preacher, the vicar knew the power of the pause; he then intoned with best drama, 'In fact, I believe it *was* ours!'

'Ours!' said Jill, disbelievingly, 'Ours! How on earth have you worked that out?'

Mr Undercroft shook his head in mock despair. 'Very good education in the sciences, but sadly lacking in Norse and old English. Depending on your choice of spelling, we are talking about Canute, Knut or Cnut. All pronounced the same, although the British mangle it as usual into Canyoot. The theory is that Canute became most popular because of the danger of Knut being pronounced Nut and the chance of a worrying misprint of Cnut, although some Saxons would certainly have meant it. There's also a theory that Pope Paschal II couldn't pronounce Cnut and so the Latin Canutus was preferred. But you can still see the traditional Norse form, Knut, in Knutsford, Knut's Ford. And, wait for it, stop yawning, Jill, revelation coming up, I have now discovered from assiduous research in the parish registers, that our very own town was also spelt with a K for some centuries before it was dropped! Nutsby with a K!'

'And?'

'Well, could it be any clearer? This is how we build Nutsby's reputation, attract visitors. Tell everyone that this is the place where Canute commanded the waves to cease. Anyone with an ounce of romance will want to come and look at this historic spot. A better class of visitor, too, none of those dreadful Kiss Me Kwik hats you see at Clicton, or, heaven forfend, candyfloss and beauty pageants. They're talking about a swimsuit competition next summer, you know.'

'More progress!' said Jill, with what from anybody else would have been a sneer, thought Jimmy, but in her case managed to be provocatively winning. 'Well, that was really worth defeating fascism for.'

'But it's a terrific idea!' said Jimmy, and then again realised what he had said when two faces looked at him in surprise. 'No, no, not the beauty contest – Canute! I can see it all now: we could recreate the event every year with a proper old-style pageant, with Canute in a long beard sitting on his throne waiting for high tide. Canute could give out awards to local citizens who had done good things throughout the year. There could be longboat races in the bay. The shops could stock tasteful Canute mementos, tea towels, mugs, all with a great motto like… like… "I stopped at Knutsby where Canute couldn't stop the waves".'

'That's the ticket, Jimmy! Absolutely!' cried Mr Undercroft.

'But how are you going to convince people that Nutsby is where it happened?' said Jill.

The vicar did another bit of business with the pipe. 'Oh, don't worry about that. We churchmen have great experience in this area. How do you think most shrines got started? Your monastery or church is short of readies or a roof? Just spread the word that you've got a sliver of the true cross or a toenail clipping from some obscure early Ephesian martyr who was spit and griddled and the pilgrims roll up, ready to pay to view and generally slosh the spondulicks about. Blackpool and Coney Island are full of the modern equivalent, all manner of freaks you can pay to gawp at. We will remain aloof and conform to the older ways.'

'But where's your toenail?' persisted Jill with admirable scientific rigour, thought Jimmy. He also noticed how a lock of dark hair fell across her face when she was exercised by something like this, and the adorably artless way she brushed it out of the way. But the vicar was replying, so he adjusted focus, with difficulty.

'A minor detail. Nothing miraculous, I think, as Canute, although an extravagant benefactor of the Church, did have, as I mentioned, quite a debit account in St Peter's ledger on account of all the killing, and in any case, I've never thought the good old C of E is too comfortable with that sort of thing. Glastonbury just pretended to have Arthur and Guinevere buried there and that seemed to work well. I could announce that I had arrived at my theory, mention my extensive researches while remaining a little vague, and rely on the Governor.' Here Mr Undercroft raised his eyes and jabbed with his pipe towards the ceiling to indicate his ultimate employer.

Very few people, even beautiful women, can get away with 'harrumph!', but Jill managed it. 'Do you think your Governor is the kind of employer who approves of what is essentially fiction masquerading as truth?'

'Well, you're far from the first to accuse him of it,' said the vicar serenely, pushing out, presumably by coincidence, halos of smoke from his pipe.

Jimmy could see Jill winding up for another assault and rather daringly got in first. 'We could start a campaign to restore the K – that would give us a lot of publicity.'

'Now, that is brilliant!' cried the vicar. 'Jimmy, the blood of the carnival Shrubsalls courses through you. Start spreading the whole idea immediately – we haven't much time.'

'Much time before what?' said Jill, still querying but clearly more and more caught up in the plan, and equally clearly beginning to regard Jimmy in a new light.

'Before the Coronation, of course! We'll have our King Canute defying the waves for the first time in a thousand years on June the second. A new queen in Westminster and an old king to celebrate in Knutsby with a K! Let's get to it!'

Even more emboldened, Jimmy looked at Jill and plunged. 'Why don't we go down to the Nutsby Hotel this evening and start spreading the news – will you come, Jill?'

The first sign that your hopes might not be so foolish after all must be the simplest, purest and most thrilling pleasure known to us. Just a nod can be that to a lovelorn swain; and so it was that later the pair of them walked down to the sea front and into the Nutsby Hotel, pleasantly lit against the dark and the waves that could still just be picked out noisily rolling to the beach.

THE PUBLIC BAR OF THE NUTSBY HOTEL WAS COMPLETELY deserted, which was unusual, as were the happy sounds coming from the Cocktail Lounge. Entering, Jimmy was surprised to see the regulars, including Jum Turtill and Alf Ellaby, sitting up at the bar on stools sipping drinks of varied colours while staring fixedly at the figure behind the bar shaking some more in a chrome cocktail shaker.

It was quite a figure, its top half encased in an extremely tight white sweater which accentuated the movements beneath as the shaker was shaken vigorously in front of the platinum-hued head that topped it. The regulars, transfixed, showed no sign of noticing either Jimmy, or, more remarkably, Jill. It was left to a beaming Sandy Beech to effect introductions. 'Ah, Jimmy and Miss Undercroft, how nice to see you! Jimmy, this is the new cocktail steward you have been asking after. Miss Gloria Honeybunch, this is Jimmy Shrubsall and Miss Jill Undercroft. Jimmy owns the pier and Miss Undercroft is the vicar's daughter.'

'Charmed I'm sure,' said Miss Honeybunch, her voice high-pitched, slightly tremulous on account of the shaking. 'A vicar's daughter? My old man works for an undertaker in Woodford Green, so I suppose you could say they're in the same line of business. There you are,' she continued, pouring out something blue-looking for Jum Turtill, who barely noticed, such was his concentration on her chest. 'Now what can I get you, miss? A Mai Tea? Or a Himlet, perhaps? And what about you, handsome? How about a Bonks?'

'Mai Tai, Gloria,' said Sandy, his touch of exasperation, he hoped, vainly, concealed by his smooth professionalism. 'Gimlet, Bronx.'

'Oh, yes, silly little me! Sorry, Sandy dear, I didn't make them mistakes when I was working at The Savoy.'

Jimmy, still recovering from being called handsome, was further intrigued. 'You worked at The Savoy?'

'Oh yes, I did, didn't I, Sandy? A very well-run bar, everybody spoke very highly of the Chigwell Savoy. Some very good films, too. Have you seen *Kind Hearts and Coronets*? Very funny. I like Alec Guinness, but Mr Clark Gable is my favourite. You remind me of him a little, handsome.'

'Yes, yes, very good, Gloria, but let's see what Miss Undercroft would like, shall we?' interrupted Sandy. 'Miss Undercroft? Miss Undercroft, you're not leaving, surely?'

But she was; when Jimmy finally noticed after he at last managed to tear his eyes away from Miss Honeybunch, she was almost through the door. He rushed after her and caught up with some difficulty, as she was moving rapidly. 'Jill, is there something wrong? Have you forgotten something? Can I help?' he managed to get out as he almost trotted alongside her.

'No, thank you. I'm going to be a doctor, not a dentist.'

'Sorry? I'm afraid I don't follow.'

'I don't want to spend my life staring into open mouths, and there were far too many of them in the hotel, including yours.'

'Sorry, what do you mean?'

'Oh, come on Jimmy! That girl! Every man in the room was transfixed by her chest. Just a teeny bit obvious, wouldn't you say? Sandy Beech brings her in and you all have your tongues hanging out and saying "ah". So much for you and the new Knutsby with a K appealing to the more sophisticated visitor. Come back in ten years or when you and the times have grown up, whichever's sooner. Goodnight!'

It was a downcast Jimmy she left behind. He was, as you know by now, a convinced romantic, and he felt his pain. Quite often he imagined himself owning a nightclub in Casablanca rather than a pier in Nutsby, and a line from his favourite film arrived in his head, when Rick Blaine is remembering being stood up by his true love Ilse at the railway station as the Nazis arrive in Paris: 'A guy standing on a station platform in the rain with a comical look on his face because his insides have been kicked out'. He decided against returning to the cocktail lounge on the grounds that, one, it did not seem a fertile moment for promoting King Canute; two, it would be a betrayal of his beloved; and, three, he didn't fancy a Tom Collins, a Mai Tai, or a Bronx anyway. Instead, he went to check the pier, let himself in and moodily trod the boards while the wind blew and the waves broke, a suitable backdrop for a young man to declaim with passion his firm intention to reclaim his girl (as he regarded her) by promoting old King Canute for all his worth. The fanciful might have imagined they heard the slap of the oar, the flap of a raven's wing and a triumphant Norse roar above the waves and the wind; Jimmy went home and had a cocoa. 'Here's looking at you, kid'.

DESPITE THAT UNPROMISING START, THE CANUTE PLAN was being received with enthusiasm. Jill had gone back to London without further contact, but Jimmy bravely busied himself spreading the word. He would not be the first to remark on how quickly and creatively rumours spread. By the time the first story appeared in the *Nutsby News*, at least three elderly residents of the town claimed to have heard about Canute and the town all their lives. 'We was always told the old king chose here because of our fine setting and wonderful golden beach,' Fred Biggleswade (83) told the editor of the *News*, Jum Turtill's cousin, Cedric Greeenshade, a wiry, enthusiastic man never far from his bicycle clips. Elsie Pargeter (91) seemed to remember that the king's throne or possibly some sort of replica stood above the high water mark for many years. Clara Arbuthnott (79), of the bunions, and almost certainly in response to the vicar's prompting, had a hazy memory that 'some bones or something' had been dug up when she was a young girl. 'In considering our fascinating report of King Canute's connection with Nutsby', wrote Cedric in his leading article, 'all should be mindful that history is not a simple recitation of facts. The important thing is where they come from. And that is a rich broadcloth weaved from memory and tradition, from recollection both written and recited. Here in Nutsby, we are indeed fortunate to have outstanding elderly citizens with memories as keen and long as their lives. And if they remember our fine town's links with the great king, who are we to question them? Especially, indeed, when those memories are supported by one of our town's leading citizens, the Reverend Norman Undercroft. Mr Undercroft is not just a man of learning and conviction in regard to religion: he is also a noted antiquarian. And he has declared this of the Canute Connection: "On balance, after study and reflection, it is entirely feasible that our town is where the great king so vividly demonstrated his humility and Man's limits: yes, in my opinion, the waves didn't stop here!" We here at the *Nutsby News* are proud to follow this lead. We say to the naysayers: do the citizens of Rome challenge their founding fathers, Romulus and Remus? They do not! Nor should Nutsbyites challenge their debt to the mighty King Canute. And so the *Nutsby News* is proud to proclaim: carpe diem and let us celebrate the glorious coming coronation of our beautiful young queen with a gracious and colourful tribute to Her Majesty and our old King!'.

Even Sandy Beech was coming round to the idea, although this had quite a lot to do with events at The Nutsby Hotel Cocktail Lounge, where custom, after approaching some sort of mania, had tailed off badly. The reason wasn't hard to find but remarkable to contemplate: Miss Honeybunch was no longer working there, having conceived a most unlikely – to the outside observer at least – passion for Alf Ellaby, and for his donkeys. 'I've always loved animals,' she would tell anyone who would go along to listen at what Alf liked to call his stables but was in fact one half of an old upturned boat at the end of the beach which housed his donkeys and where Miss Honeybunch now worked, preparing them for the coming season. She was 'staying' – this was the 1950s, after all – in the other half with Alf, whose looks had now been revised by Jimmy and the rest of Nutsby to 'rugged' from 'plug ugly' after Miss Honeybunch gave it as her opinion that he reminded her uncannily of 'Mr Gary Cooper'. Alf himself remained familiarly taciturn but those who knew him well, like Jimmy and Jum, detected a previously undetected gleam in his good eye. His deepest confidence, however, was that the sight of Miss Honeybunch on the lead donkey that summer would do wonders for trade (a paraphrase of the longest remarks anybody could remember him making, which included the vivid description, 'like a dead heat between two Zeppelins'). All of which helped explain why Sandy was now talking excitedly about changing the Lounge to King Canute's Cave, with staff wearing fur waistcoats and horned helmets and serving mead in Bakelite wassail cups.

There remained an outstanding obstacle to the ambitions of Mr Undercroft and Jimmy, however: Mr Mogg, the town clerk. A small man of high moral tone, Mr Mogg saw his role in Nutsby as much more than senior administrator of refuse collections, rates, weights and measures and other trading standards, although in this connection his annual inspections of Jimmy's pier, Jum's boat and Alf's beasts were a byword for what he thought responsible thoroughness and they called busybody nitpicking. Where they saw themselves as representatives of respected and honourable seaside traditions, Mr Mogg saw irresponsible corner cutters from whom the public dearly and clearly needed protecting. Furthermore, he saw Nutsby in need of similar protection from the winds of change that would unleash unwelcome advances in holiday entertainment on the town and threaten the moral fibre of its citizens.

No Miss Nutsby Bathing Beauty here. No Knobbly Knees competitions. No Glamorous Grannies. No dancing in the Nutsby Social Club after 11pm, and only on Fridays and Saturdays. No travelling fairs with their increasingly Americanised offerings like shooting ranges, or, local by-laws forfend, dodgems. Nothing at all on Sundays. A small man, but with a powerful force of personality and a forbidding command of the said by-laws. The town councillors deferred to him in every respect, except, as we have seen, in the case of the *force plus majeure* of the necessity of a licence for the Nutsby Hotel. Indeed, Mr Mogg regarded Sandy Beech and his restless innovating as his greatest challenge. Sandy saw himself as a buccaneering and pioneering businessman in tune with the new Elizabethan

Age that was upon the country; Mr Mogg saw vulgarity, and perhaps more importantly, a threat to Mr Mogg and his sway over Nutsby. His frustration at being unable to find anything in the by-laws forbidding Sandy's cocktail lounge can be imagined, and had been matched only by his delight at Miss Honeybunch's defection donkeywards.

Jimmy, a little naively in view of all this, perhaps, had thought that, given the traditional nature and intent of the Canute plan, Mr Mogg would lend unqualified support. He had not entered into the equation three factors: it involved change, Mr Mogg had not thought of it himself, and Sandy's looming King Canute Cave, which Mr Mogg saw as the grim-garish precursor to a tidal wave of tat sweeping over Nutsby.

Naturally not all of this was mentioned when Jimmy arrived at the town hall to discuss the great matter with Mr Mogg, who remained sitting behind his large and oppressively tidy desk in his large and oppressively tidy office, with its large windows giving onto his kingdom below. He waved Jimmy to a chair in front of his desk with a small, well-manicured hand emerging from the cuff of his white stiff-collared shirt and black jacket above the regulation pinstripe trousers beloved of every caricaturist of the bureaucrat, whose dream he was. Spring sunshine reflected off the wire-rimmed spectacles above the small moustache and thin lips as Jimmy waxed as seized and envisioned as it was possible to be in the circumstances. When he had finished, Mr Mogg remained silent, steepling his small well-tended hands in the same way as Mr Undercroft, although that would be the only obvious point of similarity between the two men.

'Well, Mr Shrubsall,' he said eventually in his interesting accent, in many ways the male equivalent of Miss Honeybunch's, overmeasured and constricted around the aspirates, which were emphasised. 'I applaud your sense of civic pride in coming up with this, ah, unusual proposal. I have several comments. One is that your plan for such an event on Nutsby beach would contravene Section 13 of the Nutsby Urban District Council By-laws, which states, inter alia, that "No person or persons shall conduct himself, herself or themselves on Nutsby beach in such a way as to interfere with the quiet enjoyment of any other user of the said beach by any deed, which said deed will include talking too loudly, moving too quickly, waving too wildly, employing any pastime accessories such as a ball, employing too violent a hue of beach towel, and outraging public decency in any way whatsoever. Offences will render the offender liable to a fine or imprisonment". I think you'll agree, Mr Shrubsall, that dressing up as an English king of the 11th century, sitting on a throne brought onto the said beach specially for the purpose, and commanding the waves to retreat would constitute a clear breach of any number of those restrictions.'

Mr Mogg leaned back in his chair with that air of quiet satisfaction also to be observed after a chess player makes a move he's particularly pleased with, or some functionary or other greets your request for assistance with the announcement that the service you seek has just closed.

Jimmy, as we've seen, was a mild-mannered man, but also one with a strong sense of fairness and decent behaviour, both of which were affronted. But he kept a grip on his outrage, and responded as levelly as he could, 'Surely those restrictions are broken all the time on even the average summer's day in Nutsby? What about the Punch and Judy show, for goodness' sake?'

Mr Mogg was of course aware of Jimmy's anger, which he had been expecting, along with his query.

'That is correct. Contrary to popular opinion, the council and its officers are not unreasonable and insensitive to changes in public mores. And so, over the years, we have taken a discreet approach to enforcement and employed the waiver powers granted to it in certain circumstances. But that could not apply in your case, Mr Shrubsall.'

'Why ever not?'

'Because I have decided, by the authority vested in me as the officer responsible for promoting enforcement of the by-laws, with the authority granted to me by the regulations and standing orders of the UDC, that your proposed activity is a breach of such a serious and fundamental nature that the waiver powers cannot be applied.'

Mr Mogg was now Grand Master and Great Panjandrum combined; Jimmy's restraint was magnificent. Although his colour had been moving slowly from terracotta to puce to pomegranate, he confined himself to asking, 'And what exactly is this serious and fundamental breach when it's at home?'

'I'm glad you asked. You seek to commemorate King Canute; as the responsible officer, I believed it incumbent upon me to determine what sort of man the town would be honouring. Imagine my shock then to discover that this man touted as an English king was not, in fact, English, and that he had invaded our country twice before taking the crown by force. Why, after the most terrible tribulations our town and country has only recently undergone, would we want to commemorate such a man?'

'Well, unless I've got this entirely bottom about face, our new Queen's family is German.'

'But the Queen's family were invited; Canute was not. In fact, according to one of the sagas, his express intention on arrival was, and I quote, "to nourish the Viking raven on the blood of Englishmen". And this is before I mention the inconvenient fact that Canute actually had two wives, one Christian and the other pagan. Is this really how Nutsby should be marking the coming glorious Coronation? I think not, Mr Shrubsall!'

Jimmy, with another heroic effort of self-restraint, decided on a more conciliatory approach. 'Oh, I wouldn't take the sagas literally, Mr Mogg. Think of them as more the *Daily Mirror* or *Tit-Bits* of their day. Canute is called Canute the Great, so he couldn't have been that bad, could he? My scheme is to revive Nutsby's royal connection at this auspicious time to give the town a boost in trade and morale. Where can the harm possibly be in that?'

'The harm in that, Mr Shrubsall? Apart from the highly dubious evidence, if any, for this supposed link, have you considered the implications of changing our name? The cost of altering our signage and stationery to make it Knutsby with a K?'

'Well, we needn't do that immediately, Mr Mogg. It could be done gradually, as the popularity of the idea grows. I don't know whether you've noticed, but the pier is now proudly proclaiming itself as Knutsby Pier. Many businesses will follow suit. It's exciting, and fun!'

'Fun, Mr Shrubsall? Chaos, more like! Confusion, more like! And I warn you that it will not be allowed to happen on my watch.'

Jimmy stood up. 'And I warn *you*, Mr Mogg, that we will not let one man decide what is or isn't good for Nutsby, which *will* be spelt with a K. This country didn't fight one dictator and pay more heed to the people to allow ourselves to be pushed around by you and other faceless pen-pushers! Canute *will* command the waves!'

Jimmy turned and left, closing the door firmly behind him without slamming it, and feeling quite proud of himself. Mr Mogg stared after him, his face expressionless. Then he opened a drawer in his desk and took out a package wrapped in greaseproof paper and tied with brown string in a neat bow. He opened it carefully, placed the now redundant string in his wallet, and began to eat his sandwiches, today as ever a thin covering of meat paste over a thinner covering of margarine. Only Mrs Mogg, and then only possibly, would have discerned the thinnest of smiles.

MR UNDERCROFT WAS IN THE VESTRY, POLISHING THE excessively ornate and very large altar candlesticks – at least one lamenting angel too many draped around the bases – which had been among the last gifts of the last Squire of Nutsby, Sir Jeremy Clarkson, before he emptied Nutsby Manor of every last painting, ornament, and stick of furniture in advance of the sale in 1872 of the house to clear some fairly spectacular gambling debts. The old boy had never married, mostly through lack of interest (on the part of potential spouses); the Manor, after some unhappy episodes, including a spell as a temple of love majoring in diaphanous attire and much scampering to the tinkle of bells, now belonged to Sandy Beech, who was waiting for the income of his other wheezes to finance its regeneration as the focus of the Beech Holiday Hotel and Happy Camp.

'Terrible, aren't they?' said the vicar, happily. 'Lord knows what Sir Jeremy Clarkson was doing with them. Probably won them at cards from a dodgy bishop desperate for readies. Couldn't flog them off, I suspect, or we wouldn't have them. He didn't give us anything else, apart from some moth-eaten tapestries that on closer inspection turned out to be of a highly unsuitable subject, and a shotgun-riddled chest with carvings ditto, containing any number of disordered documents including the manorial rolls, which make interesting reading.'

The vicar looked up from polishing and noticed that Jimmy's familiarly sunny features were not so. 'Some problem? I have tried to put in a good word with Jill, but the fair Miss Honeybunch is a definite impediment.'

Jimmy coloured up on cue. 'Blimey O'Reilly, I've only spoken to the girl once,' he protested, 'and that was to order a Bonks, I mean Bronx!'

'It wasn't the talking, apparently, so much as the look.'

'Well, even you must accept that she's a bit of an eyeful. But she doesn't start to compare to Jill. Jill is so clever, so deliciously direct, so beautiful, so—'

'Yes, yes, I've met my daughter. But I can't do more, she stopped listening to me a long time ago, quite rightly.'

Jimmy sighed the sigh that indicates a chronically affected heart and an owner who sees no remedy, but, with an effort, he concentrated on the immediate. 'That's not why I'm here, sir,' he said. 'It's Mogg. He's threatening to put the kibosh on Canute.'

'Put the kibosh on Canute? He can't do that! Can he?'

'That's what I came to ask you. He claims he has the power under the local by-laws to ban anything on the beach he doesn't approve of.'

'But that can't be right! It's undemocratic. We won't stand for it!'

'Well, he quotes chapter and verse, er, sorry, Vicar, clause and sub-clause. He claims that the ceremony would be disrespectful to the Queen because Canute was a bit of a bad hat. Viking, you know, and all that goes with it, the pillaging, the guttural cries, the shadow of the raven, that sort of thing.'

'Nonsense! How many times do I have to tell people that the Vikings were an essentially peaceful people with an admittedly direct trading manner? And Canute was a devout Christian who was a great chum of the Pope, which is more than can be said for most of the rest of our monarchs.'

'What are we going to do?'

'Do? We're going to call Mogg's bluff and go ahead. Courage, Jimmy. Canute didn't let opposition bother him, and he had Edmund Ironside to contend with, not Mr Nitpicker Mogg. Mind you, a lot of his enemies and rivals did die young in slightly mysterious circumstances, including the great Ironside himself, as it happens.'

'You're not suggesting—'

'Slipping something into the meat paste sandwiches? Good heavens, no. There are far better ways to defeat bureaucrats, and ones that the Governor couldn't possibly object to, might even smile at.'

Mr Undercroft had done the upward jabbing thing again, this time with his silver cloth, at the mention of his employer. He now began to whistle, a touch tunelessly but with meaning, 'Onward, Christian Soldiers'. Jimmy, resolve restored, returned to the pier and preparations. He was surprised to hear himself following the vicar's lead and humming, in his case 'Faith Can Move Mountains', last Christmas's hit for the maudlin, melodramatic and tremulous American singer, Johnny Ray. He decided it might have another application, too, in the Jill direction.

NUTSBY WAS FAR TOO DECOROUS TO BE GRIPPED BY
Canute fever, but there was certainly an infectious enthusiasm
around the place. The king's crown had been fashioned from
papier-mâché and finished with gold milk bottle tops by the
senior class at Nutsby Elementary School under the direction
of their imaginative teacher, Miss Grenfell, who had also turned
an old and floral blackout curtain into a magnificent cape.
The king's throne was finished, ready, supplied free by Wally
Grout, Nutsby's carpenter, fitter and, as was more the custom
then, undertaker. Wally had made it out of the finest cedar with
gold fittings and a familiarly shaped back. All he asked for was
a discreet sign fixed to it bearing the legend, 'You Can't Hold
Back Time, Either: Wally Grout for all your carpentry needs,
including that very last one. Call Knutsby 325'. Wally, like many
an undertaker, was a bit of a card. Jimmy had felt this was
something of a dampener, but you couldn't argue with the price,
and Mr Undercroft thought it was amusing.

Who was going to sit on it was more of a problem. Sandy
Beech was keen, and Jum Turtill, but Mr Undercroft pointed
out that, according to the sagas, Canute was exceptionally tall
and strong, and the handsomest of men, all except for his nose,
which was thin, high-set, and rather hooked. He had a fair
complexion and a fine, thick head of hair. His eyes were better
than those of other men. 'Quite a few disqualifications there,'
continued the vicar, 'but let's focus on just a couple: as you're
small, Sandy, and you're short-sighted, Jum, that leaves Jimmy,
who is also young.' Jimmy wasn't terrifically pleased about this,
either, but could hardly complain.

He was proud of his pier, though, which come the great day, June 2, 1953, was a gaudy gallimaufry of patriotic bunting and posters of the young Queen. Alongside were banners of Canute's royal raven and his seal showing the great king on his throne, imaginatively interpreted by Miss Honeybunch, who was proving to have more gifts than might have been supposed. Above the entrance to the pier, stretching from one side to the other, hung the largest banner of all, which, again thanks to Miss Honeybunch, read, 'God bless our young Queen! Welcome back, King Canute, who is returning to the very spot where he first defied the waves 1,000 years ago! Today, Knutsby Beach, 6 o'clock!'.

A smaller sign below it read, 'Those who doubt the King's power to halt the waves may watch the spectacle in perfect safety from Knutsby Pier for a small charge (9d)'.

But first the Coronation, which was being shown by Sandy Beech at the Knutsby Hotel on his mighty new set, with its huge 17-inch screen. After much grumbling, the leading townsfolk had agreed to pay the five shillings Sandy was demanding, considered an extortionate amount even though he was issuing tickets with a voucher towards (!) a celebratory glass of sweet sherry (but in deference to the solemnity of the event, no drink was to be served until after the ceremony in Westminster Abbey).

Business was slow in early summer at the Pier, but Jimmy was quietly confident that things would pick up when the Canute effect began to be felt: there had already been enquiries and interest, some of it from as far away as Colchester, especially after Cedric Greenshade had created a bit of a story by announcing that, from Coronation Day and the great beach ceremony, the *Nutsby News* would become the *Knutsby Knows*. Mr Mogg, meanwhile, had taken no action, and Jimmy was beginning to think that his spirited appeal had brought about a change in that flinty heart. All of which persuaded him to take the plunge on two tickets and invite Jill to the Coronation showing.

Poets and other writers have repeatedly declaimed the necessity of risk in advancing romance. Mr Ira Gershwin, for example, charmingly advised ignoring the mockers and naysayers in his brother's famous tune, 'They All Laughed'. And Jimmy, as we have seen, was something of an optimist. Even so, inviting Jill to the place that had been the scene of their disagreement did seem a touch rash. And so it had proved several days before when he had presented himself on the vicarage doorstep and outlined his plan to Jill, who looked a little flustered at this sudden appearance, but was not exactly melting. 'Are you serious? Do you really expect me to come with you to that garish, tasteless place with its obvious attractions and slavering clientele?'

Too late Jimmy realised he might have made an error. 'Er, well, Miss Honeybunch doesn't work there anymore, and, er—'

'Really. Well I'm sure Sandy Beech has found somebody else equally up to exciting the savage breast of the Nutsby male. Daddy and I are going to watch it on Mrs Arbuthnott's set. It was made for her by her late husband, Cyril, a keen radio ham, who then unfortunately had that fatal accident adjusting the aerial on the roof. It's a small set, and the picture is a little snowy, but at least we won't have any unwelcome distractions. Goodbye, Jimmy.' And with that the door was firmly closed. It is a mark of the power of love and optimism and of both Mr Gershwins that despite wondering what he was going to do with the other ticket, and whether Sandy would give him a refund, unlikely, he still felt encouraged because she had called him by his name before closing the door in his face.

The day itself dawned greyly, but, as Cedric Greenshade would report in his next special souvenir edition, it failed to dampen the spirits of Nutsby. Much has been written about the Coronation and its bewitching mix of youth, beauty, the past and hope for a future free of it. A mix that triumphed over even the curious, perhaps yet more symbolic, chaos of the Nutsby

Hotel's cocktail lounge, currently in transition from New York to eleventh-century Eastern England, with several rows of chairs lined up in front of the gleaming new television, filled by the town's great and good (with the exception of Mr Mogg, who had decided, predictably, that his independence would be compromised by attendance and was listening to attention on his wireless). There was a brief flurry when a plainly still-hurt Sandy pointed out to Miss Honeybunch that her large and floppy hat was hampering vision for several seats around; her look of magnificent disdain as she removed to the rear was almost enough to rekindle that certain feeling in Jimmy, although he could now see the screen and was hopelessly devoted to another. Almost.

But the spectacle on the 17-inch screen was the thing, the sense of history enhanced by the distant happenings in flickering black and white stilling all and uniting them in awe and wonder. Afterwards, as if in release, the lounge became a happy hubbub presided over by a beaming Sandy. Jimmy was very tempted to cash in his sherry voucher, but, aware of Canute responsibilities, presented it to Miss Grenfell, who was already making him regret his generosity in giving her Jill's ticket with coy looks and two meaningful digs in the ribs accompanied by winks. Why he thought giving her two sherries could possibly improve matters, only those distracted and in love will understand.

So off he went down to the beach, noting with satisfaction that whatever might have been the case in the rest of the country, sunshine was breaking out over Knutsby, as we shall write it from now on. People were beginning to emerge from listening to the radio or watching television, and Jimmy thought he'd rarely seen the old place looking so fine, the beach glorious and golden, Alf Ellaby over at one end sprucing his donkeys, who for once seemed happy, and very smart under their Union Jack hats which Alf had artfully slit to allow their ears to poke through. As he approached the pier he was pleased to see knots of visitors already sniffing the sea air along its short length and even more pleased to hear the chink and clink of coins going into his machines. He waved hello to his Uncle Bob, the only other Shrubsall left in Knutsby, a bachelor of advanced years who was happy to help out with admissions and such in return for free access to the What the Butler Saw machines, over which he would sigh wistfully for quite some time. Now, though, Uncle Bob was pointing gloomily above his head at Jimmy's giant welcoming banner, which had slipped and was now reading, 'od bless ur ung een! elcome ack, King nute, who is urning to the very spo ere he first defied the waves 0 years go! Today, Knutsby Beach, o'clock!'. Quickly getting his ladder out, Jimmy was up in a jiffy and carrying out a restretching operation from the left-hand end of the banner. But the jiffy is not always the most secure of modes, especially when your Uncle Bob has forgotten about holding the ladder and wandered off. And so it was that Jimmy stretched too far, and Jimmy's ladder wobbled, toppled and sent him tumbling down on to the beach 18 feet below. K's fabled sand softened the blow, but even still: a small crowd of concerned people formed around him as he lay there, stunned. Suddenly, there was a shout: 'Let me through, I'm nearly a doctor!' It was Jill, the first thing Jimmy saw when he opened his eyes. Very professionally, she began the concussion tests. 'Any dizziness, nausea, do you have a headache?'

'Jill,' said the fallen hero. 'I'm a little dizzy, but then I always am when I'm with you.'

'That's quite enough of that. You've had a fall. Any confusion, memory loss? Who is the prime minister?'

'Don't be silly, Jill. Good old Winston. He'd understand, he's a man of the world. He could tell I love you. Where am I? Heaven?'

'You're on the beach. You fell off your ladder, you clumsy fool. Just lie still. Anything hurt?' Jill was allowing a quaver of emotion into her voice, which Jimmy was not so dazed he couldn't detect.

'Only my heart, Jill. It hasn't been the same since I made a hash of our first date.'

Jill took his face into her hands and very carefully moved it from side to side while staring intently into his eyes. 'How's that?'

'Absolutely wonderful. Can we stay here like this for ever?'

'Don't be silly, Jimmy. Can you feel your toes?'

'Yes, like the rest of me, they're all a-tingle.'

Those closest to the pair might have detected almost a giggle from the nearly doctor, who now turned to the small crowd. 'Please give him some air. He's quite all right, he's been very lucky.'

'You can say that again. To be cared for by the most beautiful woman in the world, how lucky is that?'

'On further thought, you might be slightly raving. Sit up carefully. Good. Now I'm going to help you to your feet. Good, good. Now we'll go – very slowly – to that bench over there.'

Which is how, shortly after Queen Elizabeth's Coronation, Jill and Jimmy had the always delicious pleasure of becoming good friends again, and hoped for more, sitting on a bench by the beach in Knutsby. Now all that remained for a perfect day was a triumphant pageant.

AT THE APPOINTED HOUR, THE GRAND PROCESSION BEGAN to form up on what Knutsby like to call the esplanade, which was in fact much like any seaside prom, with a long slope down to the beach. There was a sizeable crowd; some charabancs had even made it from Harwich. Jimmy, imposing in his blackout cape and under his crown and shoulder-length blond wig borrowed from Madame Revere, Knutsby's leading (only) hairdresser, was lined up behind his throne, which was to be carried down on to the beach by Wally Grout's two assistants, with capes of similar provenance to Jimmy's. Wally was to lead solemnly from the front even though he was a little disappointed that his best silk mourning top hat had been vetoed as not being quite in period. Miss Grenfell had arrived as Emma of Normandy, Canute's queen (given Mr Mogg's emphatically stated reservations, Mr Undercroft, who was dressed as Archbishop Wulfstan, the king's renownedly wise adviser, had decided against a role for the king's other wife, the pagan Ælfgifu of Northampton). Miss Grenfell's outfit was arresting and of her own creation, including the headgear fashioned from a loud hailer with bright ribbons hanging from the shouting end. She was accompanied by her class; the girls were in cunningly adapted Brownie uniforms and the boys wore their dressing gowns. Cedric Downtable was dressed as a herald, with his bicycle cunningly disguised as a horse. It was all quite a sight.

As Jimmy prepared to raise his royal bottletop sceptre to begin the procession, there was a disturbance from the back of the crowd. This proved to be none other than Mr Mogg, accompanied by the town's two policemen, Sergeant Hastings and

PC Wren. Mr Mogg looked dignified and determined, an office holder every inch of the few he had. His police escort, both of them in the round and jolly constabulary mode rather than the lean and pursuing, looked embarrassed. In truth, both of them had been rather looking forward to the pageant when they were informed by Mr Mogg it was their duty to halt proceedings. In truth, too, Ted Hastings and Edgar 'Benny' Wren had very little to do in Knutsby and enjoyed doing it. The only fly in this soothing ointment was of course Mr Mogg; they hadn't made an actual arrest since Alf Ellaby, rather tight, had made a pass at Madame Revere on New Year's Eve. Madame Revere, an imposing woman originally from Romford made even more imposing by the height of her hairdo, was unflustered and seemingly flattered, as she was not as young as she had been, but her husband, Arnold Cuttle, the fishmonger, had taken exception to the Ellaby manoeuvre and there had been an undignified scuffle on the floor of the Knutsby Hotel which Ted and Benny had been ideally placed to deal with, if a little unsteadily.

Mr Mogg had now reached the front of the crowd; he turned and held up his hand for silence. This came grudgingly, with groans. 'It is my duty to inform you,' he announced, with something possibly passing for relish, 'that this event is in contravention of the by-laws of Nutsby Urban District Council, as it will interfere with the quiet enjoyment of those using this recreational facility, viz Nutsby Beach, and will moreover constitute an outrage to public decency and make mockery of our sovereign lady the Queen on this day of all days by celebrating a Viking invader with morals to match. And should any persons or persons attempt to defy this order, I shall be compelled in my official capacity and competence to read the Riot Act of 1714, which makes a refusal to comply punishable by death. Sergeant Hastings, PC Wren, clear the area!'

Restiveness and loud grumbling as Mr Mogg made his announcement came to a halt at the mention of death. There was a movement away, and it seemed that the day might be lost until Jimmy waved his sceptre in defiance and cried, 'No, nobody leave! Yes, this is a day of days, and it's a day to stand up for ourselves! Do we give into these busybodies trying to run our lives, or do we remind them that WE run THEM, that they're the servants of the people not the other way round. Is this what the war was fought for? Here today we have the chance to start something that will put little Knutsby on the map and bring prosperity to us and our children. Are we going to let the likes of Mr Tinpot Mogg with his jumped-up ways and silly little laws stop us? Come on!'

Cheers rang out and the crowd now went into reverse. Mr Mogg, implacable, ordered the policemen once again to break up the meeting. It was at this point that a commanding figure in full Viking fig, including the horned helmet, called for attention. Jum Turtill's hour had arrived. You might recall that this sailor had been an actuary in his previous life, an occupation that had given him a taste for rigorous research. He spoke up, full-throated, commanding: 'Not so fast, Mogg. You will of course be fully cognisant with the contents of the Local Government Act, 1894, the statute which set up urban district councils such as Knutsby's?'

Mr Mogg nodded, but a certain hesitation could be detected by the more astute in the crowd.

'Section 87 of that act,' continued the Viking Turtill, 'deals with its effect on existing by-laws, orders and regulations, stating that they will continue in force unless expressly altered or revoked.'

'Yes, yes, of course,' said Mr Mogg, for the first time betraying some fluster. 'But what is this supposed previous legislation or regulation? Tell me that!'

It is a well-worn legal axiom that you should never ask a question of your opponent if you don't know the answer to it. Mr Undercroft, who had, rather incongruously, been smoking his pipe below his archbishop's mitre as the contretemps wore on, now joined in: 'Ah, yes, Mr Mogg. You will recall that the late Sir Jeremy Clarkson, the last Lord of Nutsby Manor, bequeathed several items to the parish church, including the manorial rolls. I'd like to draw your attention to the by-law therein of 1432 relating to where we are standing today: "No man, whosoever he might be, and no matter how high, save for our Sovereign himself, can deny passage to Knutsby shore and foreshore to any seeking their passage to the sea".' Mr Undercroft carefully placed his pipe on the sea wall, delved under his cassock and came up with a flourish and a rolled piece of parchment: 'And here it is!'

There were more loud cheers. Mr Mogg checked his fluster, and rallied. 'That is as may be. But the by-law I am relying on obviously revoked this supposed and unproven right that has suddenly come to light.'

'Obviously?!' thundered the Viking. 'Obviously?! Obviously revoked a law it didn't know even existed? Is this England or… [and here he paused for maximum effect] Soviet Russia?!'

The loud cheers were now becoming angry. Fluster became bluster. 'Clearly a meeting of the council needs to consider the position,' Mr Mogg almost shouted. 'But until that meeting takes place, my decision must stand. Sergeant! Constable!' Sergeant Hastings and PC Wren, who had been moving forward then halting in an arresting but clumsy rumba during these exchanges, began to advance once more.

'Not so fast, Mogg,' said Jum Turtill, again. 'I cannot believe you're unfamiliar with that part of the Council's Regulations and Standing Orders which states that by-laws can be amended or repealed by an extraordinary meeting of the UDC on the unanimous vote of councillors.'

Mr Mogg was now showing definite signs of unease, as if he knew what was coming next.

'They also state, in a striking example of the democratic principles which so distinguished our earlier town fathers,' continued the Viking, 'that the requirement to give prior notice of the extraordinary meeting may be waived if not fewer than 100 townspeople are present when the decision to hold the said meeting is taken. Over to you, Mr Mayor!'

Shouts of encouragement broke out; it would have taken a much braver (and far less vain) mayor than Sandy Beech to refuse this invitation. His outfit – bright red robe secured by golden tassel – bore a close resemblance to the mayoral regalia and already spoke to his position in the matter. 'Ladies and gentlemen,' he announced in that mix of drama and portentousness more usually employed by boxing masters of ceremonies, 'as Mayor of Knutsby, it is indeed in my power to call an immediate extraordinary general meeting of the council. I see that all our councillors are in fact present. I now require a count of townspeople, and I call on Mr Undercroft to carry it out!'

The Reverend Archbishop was only too happy to oblige, and calling for a show of hands of Knutsby citizens, speedily confirmed that the EGM was quorate. Councillor Turtill then moved that Section 333 of the Nutsby UDC by-laws, pertaining to permitted activities on the town beach, be revoked, together with the discretionary powers granted in regulations and standing orders to the town clerk, which were 'clearly both *ultra vires* and, what's more, *unBritish*'. More cheers from the crowd, who were now treating these events as a diverting extra entertainment.

It remained only for the councillors to vote for Jum's motion and the pageant could proceed. But there was one problem: Councillor Arnold Cuttle, the fishmonger, who, funnily enough, resembled a haddock. It so happened that Mr Mogg was one of his best customers – the town clerk had quite a thing for jellied eel – and Arnold Cuttle was not a man to place principle above profit. He announced in his prissy tones that Mr Mogg was only doing his job, and part of that job was to protect the virtue of Knutsby. He was then taken aback by the vigour of the opposition to this view: boos, catcalls and shouts, at least one of which was clear and angry: 'Let's do up the long bug-eyed streak of misery like one of his kippers!'

Yes, the mood was turning ugly. Madame Revere, who had taken a unilateral decision to dress as Britannia, now stepped in front of her husband and was looking distinctly dangerous. Mr Mogg was blinking more rapidly than usual. Sgt Hastings was feeling his own collar uncomfortably, while Benny Wren was checking furtively for possible escape routes, but not quite furtively enough.

Cometh the hour, cometh Alf Ellaby, leading Miss Honeybunch on one of his donkeys. She was dressed in a long white diaphanous robe, over which tumbled her long blonde tresses. A commanding tug on her rein brought her to a halt in front of the restive crowd, who fell silent at this splendid sight. 'Good day, good citizens,' she announced in a strong confident voice which suggested she had excellent recollection of Flora Robson as Elizabeth I in *Fire Over England*. 'I am Lady Godiva! I have come before you with my husband, the mighty Earl Leofric, chief supporter of our great King Canute.' Here she bowed graciously towards Jimmy and then to a beaming Alf, two actions which many in the crowd could not help noticing revealed a large amount of her considerable cleavage. 'What passes here? Why are we not processing to the beach to witness our Great Dane command the tide to halt? Am I not to be allowed to chase the retreating briny and bathe in the obedient waters?'

Well. Arnold Cuttle might have been a cussed, obstinate sort of a chap, but he did have the sense – particularly after the collective gasp that greeted Miss Honeybunch's last query – to see that resistance was not only futile but also life-threatening. He announced that further reflection had convinced him that the procession was in the best interests of Knutsby. The vote was taken; the affair was on!

Do pageants ever run smoothly? There was now yet another twist: Jimmy had begun to feel a little dizzy after his passionate address, and was not really feeling strong enough even to walk to his throne. Game as ever, he did make a faltering attempt before Jill, dressed to stunning effect as the Abbess of Knutsby in an outfit that owed much to Deborah Kerr in *Black Narcissus*, declared him unfit to rule. Blessed are the Peacemakers. It was Mr Undercroft who saved the waves with an inspired suggestion for a replacement: yes, Mr Mogg! In a stroke, face was saved and unity secured. Those who were surprised by Mr Mogg agreeing to step in and play the king had observed his liking for being in charge but ignored the strong sense of drama that lay beneath the pinstripe. It was indeed this that had brought about his defeat: he could easily have taken steps to voice his opposition and halt the pageant long before the day, but had relished his last-minute appearance.

To resounding cheers for being 'a jolly good sport', Mr Mogg donned cape, wig and crown. He hardly cut such a fine figure as Jimmy, and the spectacles struck a perhaps incongruous note, but a crown, even one made from bottle tops, has a powerful effect. (As it happens, a pair of spectacles has been discovered in a Viking grave, but that was some years later.) And it was certainly a splendid sight as the procession made its stately way down the beach, through the specially moved aside tank traps, the children leading the way, followed by Miss Grenfell, still just a touch pink from the Knutsby Hotel, Alf Ellaby, Miss Honeybunch and donkey, the Archbishop, the Abbess, Turtill the Viking, and Britannia, the mayor attended by Sgt Hastings and PC Wren, Wally Grout sans top hat but for some reason in tails, and finally Canute the second on his throne bobbing up and down on the shoulders of Wally Grout's pall-bearers, followed by the crowd. The tide had very pleasingly got into the spirit of the occasion, with the white frothy waves urged by the whippy seaside breeze towards shore with a truly impressive irrestibility.

At water's edge, the processors fanned out to allow the king's throne to be placed three feet from the tide. Canute Mogg, definitely enjoying himself, let the waves race nearer the throne while all fell silent. Then with a timing wasted on council meetings, he raised his sceptre and cried out thrillingly, 'Waves of the sea, I Canute, King of England, King of Denmark, King of Norway and King of the Seas between them, command you to halt!'

And just for that moment, down on the beach before the waves, against all sense and understanding, every one of those there held their breath waiting to see what would happen.

Which is where, my friends, I abandon strict authorial control and leave it up to you to decide whether the waves kept coming and Knutsby carried on into a few brief years of success before cheap flights, more sun and copious amounts of exotic alcohol converted the Nutsby Hotel into flats and the boarding houses into rehab hostels and another fire and outdated attractions closed the pier and health and safety regulations banned the donkeys and Cayford's Cosy Cafe became Kozy Kebabs and some killjoy historian poured scorn on the town's famed regal links.

Or that the waves did stop and Knutsby was forever caught in that happy time which is but a mostly misremembered memory; unless, of course, one sleepy shimmer of a summer's day you are lucky enough to get lost near Clicton.

But I'm happy to confirm that Miss Honeybunch will gambol – demurely – in the waves whatever happens.

Afterword

There is a famous problem with our tradition of dividing nearer times and their happenings into decades: events and economic and social movements and shifts refuse to conform quite so neatly. This is certainly true of the fifties, which didn't really begin until October 1951, when the great reforming post-war Labour government had run out of energy, and an electorate exhausted by war, recovery and imposed social change turned to the old certainty of old Winston Churchill. There then followed the high metaphor of the death of King George and the accession of his young daughter in 1952. It is this period, when our story is set, that best reflects the popular view of the fifties, of a Britain marking a golden, uncomplicated time as austerity eased and incomes increased and employment was full; before the old Imperial Dream crashed into the new hard reality of American superpower on the banks of the Suez in 1956. The clumsy plot hatched by Britain and France with Israeli help to take back control of the Canal, nationalised by the Egyptian leader, Colonel Nasser, ended in a quick and humiliating retreat after the US exercised its displeasure and economic hegemony.

Thus the abrupt end to that new Elizabethan era. But in any case, for any who cared to notice, those preceding and supposed three golden years were rich in events of almost semaphored symbolism as Britain the influencer became Britain the influenced. A few hold the old line: Hillary of the Empire conquering Everest on the eve of the Queen's celebration, Bannister of Britain breaking the four-minute mile, Churchill's 80th birthday, still as prime minister. But most breach it: in 1953 the Soviet Union successfully tested its hydrogen bomb, while more charmingly if no less significantly in its way, Gina Lollobrigida opened Britain's first Italian coffee bar in Soho; in 1954, Princess Alexandra began wearing jeans (but only for gardening); that year, too, Winston Churchill asked, 'Are we to saddle ourselves with colour problems here in UK?', after the non-white population, predominantly from the West Indies, had reached 40,000. The next year 'Rock Around the Clock' by Bill Haley and the Comets topped the UK hit parade, while commercial television began broadcasting with brash American comedies like 'I Love Lucy' and brash American-derived quiz shows like 'Double Your Money', with the loud and hammy Hughie Greene offering the chance to win £1,024, as opposed to 'Have A Go', the BBC's comfortable touring radio show with the slightly less loud and differently hammy Wilfred Pickles offering prizes of up to £1/18s/6d plus a modest bonus and the chance to take home some local produce. In 1956, Sudan gained independence, beginning the accelerated end of the British Empire as other colonies followed suit. The night, meanwhile, that Israeli tanks rolled into Egypt towards Britain's great crisis of confidence, the Queen was attending the Royal Film Performance at the Empire, Leicester Square, chosen film, 'The Battle of the River Plate'.

Running alongside and beneath this was a curious disjunction: on the upper hand, a ruling class of a disintegrating empire preoccupied with waning diplomatic, economic and military power; on the other and lower, a population at last enjoying a material improvement that was fun while it lasted. As Macmillan should have said, 'You've never had it so good, so enjoy it while you can before our manufacturing industries collapse and large numbers of you become unemployed and we have to go cap in hand to the International Monetary Fund.'

Keen students of film and the fifties will have noticed the uncanny resemblance of the events in Knutsby to those in *the varied, variable but often sublime comedies made by the Ealing Studios. If they have a common theme, it is the people of Britain hankering after a better world in the future and deeply resenting the interference of bureaucrats in the present. Many of Knutsby's characters are from that stock and other broader comedies of the time, most obviously the wonderful Joyce Grenfell, whose gentle and artfully awkward mockery of most things including herself represents an Englishness that disappeared with the fifties, along with Flanders & Swann, Gerard Hoffnung, and Mr Pastry.*

CNUT, as we now write him, despite the misprint worry, is perhaps even less remembered now than in the 1950s, when he was usually rendered as Canute. This comparative oblivion is a curious thing for the only king of England other than Alfred to be awarded the honorific of 'Great'; it is perhaps best explained by the inconvenience of his being a Viking, and thus upsetting the elegant simplicity of an Island Story that likes to celebrate the Norsemen being bravely repulsed rather than ruling. It seems, though, that he was very much an Anglophile, preferring England to the other, more Scandinavian parts of his mighty northern empire. The first appearance of his dealings with the waves appears in the Historia Anglorum, *by the twelfth-century Anglo-Norman chronicler, Henry of Huntingdon. Henry, as with many another of his kind, was not above a little gentle massaging, fabrication and addition, but it seems unlikely that such a striking story should have no basis in fact. Henry provided no location for the event, but several contenders have put themselves forward over the years, including Southampton, Westminster and Bosham, near Chichester, which has a link with one of Cnut's daughters, who was said to have drowned there at the age of eight. No one, as far as I can tell, has pressed their case with the enthusiasm of Mr Undercroft and Jimmy Shrubsall. Miss Honeybunch was absolutely correct with her identification of Lady Godiva's husband, Leofric, as a chief man of Cnut. He was Earl of Mercia, and, as usual, historians* claim him to be not as popularly painted; they even claim her ladyship's famous ride a fiction.

Miss Honeybunch herself is a tribute to every British starlet of the fifties condemned to fulfil every British man's rudimentary desires; her Coronation hat is a tribute to Groucho Marx, in his famous crouch, looking up under a similar hat being worn by Greta Garbo and saying, 'Pardon me, ma'am, I thought you were a guy I knew in Pittsburgh.'

The local authority organisation of Knutsby is broadly in line with the provisions of the Local Government Act, 1894, which introduced the urban and rural district councils, abolished in 1974, except that the council would have had a chairman; it seemed a little cruel, though, to deny Sandy Beech the glamour of mayoralty.

More than a million ten pound poms like Mr and Mrs Shrubsall, Jimmy's parents, emigrated to Australia for the requisite tenner between 1945 and 1972. Everyone, especially in the northern towns of England, knew a ten pound pom; noted examples would be the great England fast bowlers, Harold Larwood and Frank Tyson, the Bee Gees and Kylie Minogue's mum. Restrictions against non-white immigrants (the White Australia policy) were finally abolished in 1966.

The idea that somewhere like Knutsby could still exist is of course entirely fanciful. But J B Priestley, that old romantic curmudgeon, argued – and I'm sure you have felt it, somewhere and sometimes, in parts unfamiliar – that there is something about England and its concentrated size and intense history which lends itself to such speculation; he wrote that he would not be surprised if Camelot was still here somewhere, waiting at the end of a narrow lane, 'with nettles thick around a dusty Round Table.'

FURTHER READING:
Cnut The Great, *Timothy Bolton*
How Cnut became Canute, *Dr Thijs Porck*
Having It So Good, Britain in the Fifties, *Peter Hennessy*
Family Britain, 1951–1957, *David Kynaston*

1966

1966 and All That

OH YES BLIMEY MATE, THE SIXTIES. GREAT TIME, GREAT time, but then the great times are always in your twenties, aren't they? While you've got time to chop and change, do this, do that, before the results catch up on you, with the creaks, the regrets and the rest of the bill. When you go back to places you loved then, they're not the same, are they, something missing, but what is it? Young you, impressionable you, excitable you has left and will never, ever return. The magic has checked out, crowded out by what's happened since.

But, oh my, they were a time. Straight out of school and the fifties into that, imagine. Random: that music, suddenly, wonderfully from here, not from over there or copying over there, bonkers clothes, girls in short skirts who looked you in the eye, fancy French cigs, coffee, proper spaghetti, hair, pubs that weren't sad, King's Road, Saturday mornings in summer Chelsea, Portobello Road and all the other markets, Petticoat Lane, Bermondsey, Afghan coats, boots, being at art school even if you weren't. Got to be London, hasn't it? Old place finally waking up, finding out it had still got it, even Oxford Street, even Soho, lairy bleary handsome wrecks with loud scarves and voices to match, witty partners who'd seen and heard it all but came alive when they hadn't: all sorts, toffs, proles, in-between, gay, straight, both, money, no money, funny, not funny, watch out for the bore-bohos, trying too hard, probably got a proper job, unlike the rest of them, the ones with a bit of the other, fun, an eye for the gap.

Me, I was from the Essex suburbs, Buckhurst Hill boy and loving it. Still never had it so good, plenty of work about, casual, fun stuff, Carnaby Street boutique sort of work, bar work, good work, and a bit of shady work, more Del and Daley than Reggie and Ronnie, lookouts, lock-ups, fixing. I was a good-looking mug, wasn't I? Knew John Bindon, dodgy geezer, busy with it, but charm when he wanted. Nobs loved him, proper piece of rough, flattered to be in on the whole Bailey-Donovan-Stones-Stamp-Toff thing. Giggling London, Swinging London. Buy a Mini and slum it, sweetie, pubs, clubs, you name it. Met them all I did. Well, I say met. But I think I was there the night Bindon showed Princess Margaret his famous trick, the one involving five half-pint mugs or was it six, their handles and his broom handle of a todger. Flies down, monster out, glass after glass, final roar and astonishment like when it hits the back of the net: I'm sure I can see Peter Sellers' face now behind those big specs. Even the little princess couldn't find anything bitchy to say; it was as if she was afraid of opening her mouth, and who'd blame her with that big dick swinging about like a tipsy snake. Exciting, and like I say, fun, what larks, before everything and everyone became too cool to show it. What did that bloke say, oh yes, the sixties, that brief, heady moment between Empire and Irony. Clever but true, even the satirists thought they could change things as well as poke fun at them.

And don't get me started on the films, how mad were they? Jumping cameras, crazy angles, people talking out to the viewer like I'm talking to you, all those fantasy scenes with birds running through fields in slow motion and titles like *I'll Never Forget How I Learned to Love Felicity Doodah and Stopped the World Going Round the Mulberry Bush*. Thought they were fantastic then, didn't we, can't even watch them now. Well, you can watch them, but you need the same amount of the wacky baccy or stronger they were on and wolfing with the thrill and oomph and mischief of the new. That's why I said I think I was there with Bindon; it's the sixties thing, shot memories and no recordings, thumbs just for holding up, was

I told or was I there, does it matter, history now, can't change the fun.

I was a Jack the Lad, of course. Did I say I was good looking? I had the chat and the cheek, too, had my pick of the dolly birds – dolly birds! Listen to me! – and I wasn't doing that bad, either, particularly with the posh ones, not surprising when they were used to their sort of bloke, the ones more interested in shouting loudly and spilling things and slapping their mates on the back, the ones they'd been away at some snob school with, the ones they really fancied not the girls even if they didn't know it themselves and made do with the joshing and teasing and the playful arm punching. What they wanted was your old trick cyclist, not a girl. So like I say, anyone who felt easy with a girl, listened to a girl, wanted to make her laugh, to actually entertain her and not make the lunge at the first available, was quids in with ten bob to spare plus the place money for a punt on the dogs.

The Pill was something, didn't know what was coming then, better say that again, everyone was coming, before we learnt again that if something's too good to be true, it is. Top time then, though. Nothing went anywhere with anyone, and we – them and me – didn't want it to, I certainly wasn't looking to end up in corduroys in the country being nice to some dad with a few acres and bad teeth who thought I was a twat. So come '66, I was still having fun if not exactly earning a fortune. But, a little inconveniently, I had found a smashing girl. Julie. I met her on a job in Surrey. One of my top, how shall we say, contacts, Micky The Fish Metcalfe, diamond guy if you stayed on the right side of him, had found this bloke in Upper Norwood who'd got a cheap load of Hong Kong suits which he was making desirable by the simple method of cutting the collar and lapels off, sticking some black electrical tape round the edges and calling them Beetle Suits (note the careful misspelling). Micky The Fish thought they couldn't fail to excite London boutique owners, especially if he outlined his incentive scheme, which was not to upset

Micky The Fish. I drove out to pick up the said schmutter and being unfamiliar with the leafy environs, had to stop and ask for directions. From Julie. Dark, slender, and tremendous local knowledge. The directions were very complicated and by the time they'd finished I'd got a date. It turned out she really was an art student, but we hit it off in great style after she told me to stop pretending to know anything about art. I'm still not sure what she saw in me, all she'd say was that I made her laugh, which was true, although I didn't always mean it, like when she told me her family had moved over from Kingston, and I said that wasn't really a long way from Norwood, and she said it was in Jamaica.

Although she was an art student – at Kingston, funnily enough – she wasn't ditsy in the slightest. Said she was so fed up with all that girly stuff, head down, cow eyes looking up, mock vulnerable, what's wrong with equal? Made sense to me, same thing I was finding up against the toffs. She studied hard, but she'd see me every Friday night, when I used to meet her off the train at Waterloo. We used to go to a very nice little boozer I knew, The Bent Elbow in Drayton Gardens. Tucked away a bit, locals as much as passing trade, all dark wood and brass and plush floral carpet, top landlord, too, old Frank Flitcroft, miserable as sin like every good gaffer should be, never heard anyone put so much feeling into saying 'Come on, ladies and gents, haven't you got homes to go to?' at closing time. I knew people who would ring the pub just to hear the way Frank answered, 'Bent Elbow. What do you want?' Never a good idea with Frank to spin out your drink, either, as he was likely to say, 'We do have more, you know.' Great days, and the sort of pub that wound itself up to a series of happy hubbubs as different lots of drinkers came and went, the after-workers, the after-tea-and-suppers, the pop-out-for-a-quick ones, the settlers-in-for-a-session ones. Proper pub atmosphere, warm, always on the verge of a smile if you know what I mean.

Good class of punter, but too many Chelsea fans, it being just round the corner from Stamford Bridge. But even Chelsea

– remember when they were called The Pensioners? – were catching on to the sixties thing, with Docherty, the Doc, first job of many, good manager, good for a line, and young Osgood providing the fancy stuff that Chopper Harris couldn't, even if he was a legend whose name produced that fond shrug-smile Londoners do so well and usually reserve for their villains, which Chopper was, in a panto sort of way. I was a West Ham man myself, my side of town, style on the pitch, not off it. Bobby Moore, of course, and Geoff Hurst, and young Martin Peters, and the human chatterbox, Budgie Byrne, wonderful player, should have been playing alongside Geoff for England in the World Cup, rather than Hunt, but I suppose Ramsey thought that three Hammers were enough, and it certainly turned out that way.

There was talk about England's chances all year and before, of course. Host nation, home of football, decent team, got to have a chance, excitement building everywhere. Julie was keen on football when girls weren't supposed to be. She used to go with her brother to Crystal Palace, but you can't have everything, especially as she could explain the offside rule to me. As it happens, her dad was a pillar of the local church, which was a bit ticklish for him, as he clearly didn't approve of me but felt obliged to exercise the old Christian tolerance. When we first met, I didn't help myself by being too clever answering one of his first questions, which was what church did I go to and I said Upton Park, and he said which church was that and I told him it was the home of the Hammers. He looked baffled, Julie looked cross, Julie's mum pulled a face, and Julie's brother laughed unhelpfully. I didn't go round for a bit after that.

There was quite a lot of World Cup work about in the run-up to the finals in July. Only my searing honesty compels me to tell you about having to dress up as the irritating lion mascot World Cup Willie for an instant curry promotion in which I pranced around with a lot of other Willies while handing out little packets of the dehydrated nirvana and free footballs in Hyde Park to the exciting sounds of Lonnie Donegan singing that terrible song over and over again about how we all loved the little bugger. Go on, laugh if you like, but there wasn't much else on that week and the money was actually quite good. But I hadn't bargained for the little sod who wanted another football and objected to my attempts to get him to go away by elbowing me in the groin, at just the right height for him, and stamping hard on my furry foot, which left me hopping up and down in agony as the sound of Lonnie droned happily and remorselessly on. And then his mother had the brass neck to complain about my language. The whole thing actually ended up in the papers, 'Ouch! Willie's Tackle Tackled! World Cup Willie, England's mascot for the finals which kicks off here in July, got more than he bargained for in London's Hyde Park yesterday…'. Yeah, right. Anyway, the crowd started to move on after the fracas, and the girl organising us, desperate to get them back, shouted at us, 'They think it's all over!' And, properly pissed off, I pulled off my Willie head and shouted back, 'It is now!' You tell me Kenneth Wolstenholme wasn't there. Didn't get hired again, though, but there was other stuff, including some activity for Micky the Fish involving 5,000 World Cup Wally (clever, eh?) tea trays – again sourced from Hong Kong – which took some shifting and are now, I see, much prized on eBay on account of the spelling of Wrold.

In March I got a job working for Camp Freddie's security outfit when the World Cup itself was put on display as part of a big stamp exhibition at Central Hall. Freddie, a colourful bloke given to suits of a striking pink, less noticeable then than now, as it happens, was the eldest boy of Frank, the Bent Elbow's gaffer, and a poacher or a gamekeeper depending on who was paying. We had some fun posing for photos with the cup before the show opened, holding it up like winners for one of Freddie's other oppos, Ray Snapper Davies, who fancied himself a bit of a Bailey. It wasn't that impressive, not that big, but stylish, Julie had informed me, gilded silver. Camp but not soft, Freddie. Our briefing was short, 'Don't get it fucking nicked, loves, or your balls will be bolognese.'

So of course it got nicked, didn't it? Two of us were supposed to be beside it every minute the exhibition was open, but we didn't bother on the Sunday when it was closed, which was of course when some villains broke in the back, popped up the stairs, jemmied the display case and popped back out again while we were taking a leisurely coffee break in the office. Never heard a thing. Not sure why they needed to break in the back when all the other doors were open anyway for the Sunday service downstairs, but there you go, that's how it is with villainy, if they were any smarter they'd be in charge, wouldn't they?

Camp Freddie wasn't quite so, how shall I put this, philosophical. He was the colour of his suit and twice as lively. The gist was that we were a fucking disgrace, we'd not just let ourselves down, him down, but the whole country down, the world was laughing at us and if we thought we were getting paid we should go and look at the fucking headlines in every paper. Worse than that, this bloke Freddie worked for, one of the biggest faces there was, he was super patriotic, and had taken it very badly, very badly indeed, and was threatening to put Freddie's suit well beyond 24-hour dry cleaning if the cup wasn't found pronto. The rozzers would take forever, this was one for the robbers. And if it wasn't found pronto, bolognese wouldn't be long delayed and things would definitely be grated.

Julie was sympathetic, but not that sympathetic. It was only what came from mixing with low life and doing low-life jobs, all a bit of a laugh till something like this happened, where was my self-respect, where did I think I was going, if I wanted to keep seeing her I'd better chuck this sort of lark in and get a proper job. Not very sixties, not very art student, and she had a point. My old man, who worked on the ledgers for the local council, had had been telling me this for years, along with some instructive family history, how my granddad had been on the halls but gave it up and ended up nice and safe running a garage in Thorpe Le Soken. We never went into how come then Dad had ended up with the ledgers in Loughton, but I certainly wasn't going to be doing them, that was what had taken me away in the first place, not wanting to get the bus, take sandwiches, walk home if it was a nice day, take off the jacket and put on the cardigan, the boring stuff. I wanted the buzz, and suddenly the easy money was for the likes of me as well, and the fun and games. On the other hand, I was seeing a lot of Julie, a lot, if you follow me, and I really, really didn't want to lose that. And she wasn't dull either, definitely, tremendous mover, what an Afro, what a whizz, what was she doing with me, outtasight, far out, as we said before it was called back in the day and before we realised it wasn't all great to be black because they put up with all the crap and we didn't notice it, apart from the looks we got when the two of us were together which at first didn't bother me as much as they bothered her, I suppose because I knew it was about her, not me, charming. Anyway, Julie sorted me on that, proper, and even people without beautiful black girlfriends were beginning to think how it wasn't quite right blacks couldn't get the jobs and stay in the places we could. There had been that Notting Hill trouble back in the fifties, whites attacking blacks, but we tried to tell ourselves that was over and done with, history, because we do tend to think in decades, don't we? I knew the police were down on them, too, but I was used to the Old Bill being down on people, like me, yes, all right, for other reasons, but still. And no matter how hard people like Enoch tried to stop it, you could feel the change, for the good for once – that really was what was different about the sixties, wasn't it? – everywhere you looked, race relations, gays, women's rights, a great blast of, oh, all right, peace and love.

The cup, meanwhile, was concentrating minds. Freddie's boss was so big that nobody knew his first name and everybody called him sir, including the said Reggie and Ronnie, even the dogs in the street stopped mid-pee when he went by and casual enquiries were likely to end up with you formally stiff. But the net result of his interest was that information stalled because whoever had been stupid enough to take it was now sensible enough to go very quiet. Which wasn't good enough for Freddie, who came up with one of his wheezes. Camp Freddie's wheezes were either very good or very bad. This one seemed promising, sort of. All we had to do, he said, was make a new one, reveal it to the world and the tea leafs would be checked, mated and screwed tighter than a coffin lid. I was playing along, thinking pleasant thoughts of Julie, until Freddie said over to you then, Terry. Thanks, as the nervous man said when they passed him the ticking parcel. Luckily, I was on donkeys, you know, nodding terms, with Benny Cellini, legendary creator of such silverish bonnet ornaments for your motor as Ecstasy of Romford, the Sprite of Epping Forest and Bobby Moore. He was from a distinguished ice cream family, which explained his nickname, Benny 99. More to my point, Benny also majored in sporting trophies from his workshop in Willesden Junction, and was not averse to a little trade in items of a limited provenance, if you follow, jewellery as well. He was very busy, said it couldn't be done quickly, but agreed to take up the challenge when I bunged him a couple of Freddie's monkeys and, most importantly, mentioned the name of Freddie's boss.

I must say Benny 99 made a terrific job of it, working off Snapper's photos and other stuff. Better than the bleeding original was Benny's view, although I told him that wasn't the point. But it was brilliant. The next problem was how to reintroduce it to polite society. Freddie left that up to me, which I was quite chuffed about till Snapper told me it was because I'd be the one who got nicked if anything went wrong. Whatever, I had a good think before coming up with a brilliant scheme which would jelly several eels and some cockles and winkles as well. I needed someone entirely innocent and upright to come across the cup, and who better than Mr Augustus Grant, Julie's dad, earnest churchgoer and pillar of propriety? There was bound to be publicity, too, which wouldn't do his church roof any harm at all, might even be a reward. I'd be tickled, everybody happy, result. Even better, I knew, because she'd told me often enough, that old Gus took his dog, Trenchtown, out for a short walk every night at nine o'clock to allow for the canine back-leg tango. All I had to do was leave it where Trenchtown would find it and Julie's your daughter. I also knew from reading my comics that Dennis the Menace's pooch Gnasher found nothing sweeter than aniseed. So I wrapped Benny's masterpiece in some newspaper, splashed some Pernod all over it, yes, I know, no expense spared, and on the Sunday evening, nice touch or what, hid it under a hedge on Beulah Hill on Gus's regular route, then settled down in the Cortina to wait for Trenchtown to do his stuff.

Which was when it all went a bit wrong. Gus was late, I found out afterwards he'd got distracted listening on his shortwave radio to Garfield Sobers doing some general pulverising of a cricket ball in Bridgetown, Barbados. So blow me down, pick me up with a shovel and spread me over the roses, as I'm sat there in the motor hugging myself with glee at my genius, another geezer altogether comes along and finds the bloomin' thing! It was very big at the time, you might still remember, he was called Pickles, no, the dog was called Pickles. Cue much national rejoicing, happy Freddie, happy Freddie's boss, Benny's cup conned the FA experts, real cup never seen again, real villains snookered and schtum, although some bit of lower life who'd supposedly been acting as a go-between with the Sweeney ended up inside for two years. Trenchtown never knew what he'd missed, nor Gus or Julie.

Anyway, I thought I'd learned my lesson with that, and started avoiding the dodgy little numbers that Camp Freddie, now my best friend, obviously, and all over me like a rash, kept suggesting. By now his dad was almost in World Cup mood and when England swept through to the final, he surprised us all by holding a raffle in the pub for tickets. Yes, I know what you're thinking, but Benny 99 examined them and declared them kosher. Apparently a tout, who Frank and Freddie both preferred to describe as a late booking agent, owed for a consignment of continental lager which had originated in Norfolk and was, well, a little flat. I know what else you're thinking, too, and you're right: yours truly won and Julie and me were off to Wembley. I rather thought I deserved it after being so closely involved.

What a day! What a game! I remember it particularly vividly because all the goals were scored by West Ham boys, weren't they, with a hat-trick from Sir Geoff, one from St Martin and world-class assurance and support from Mooro. But up and down or what? Geoff scored first, then them, and when St Martin stroked that one in to put us ahead again, I was so moved I produced a little gem that Benny had provided, went down on one knee, and proposed. Luckily, she accepted or that would have put a bit of a dampener on the rest of the game, which would have been a pity, as it was an absolute cracker. In the build-up to Sir Geoff's second, the controversial one, Julie flung up her arms and ever after claimed the sparkle from her engagement ring dazzled the German goalkeeper at the crucial moment. Benny thinks this unlikely, given the quality of the stones. But I've never argued, especially as after the Azerbaijani linesmen confirmed the ball had crossed the line and the old place went wild, Julie told me she was up the duff. Anyway, our boy is called Geoffrey Martin Robert Tilkowski (the German goalie) Bahramov (the linesman) Perks, lively young cove, too.

Benny and I still laugh about it all when we meet, especially the moment when Bobby lifted Benny's beauty up to Wembley and the world, but most of the joke has to stay well private, as neither Freddie's or Freddie's boss's sense of humour has improved with time and Freddie now runs the place. Not that I see him much now, the eighties are dull, aren't they? Almost as bad as the seventies, god how I miss the sixties. But I do go back there from time to time, when I leave the bank and head in to meet Julie at Waterloo on a Friday night. She's a jeweller now, funnily enough, makes her own, lovely stuff, got a nice little shop at Gabriel's Wharf, on the South Bank there. But she still seems to like the engagement ring. Thanks again, Benny.

Afterword

The theft of the Jules Rimet Trophy in 1966 from the Stampex exhibition at Central Hall, Westminster, has provoked lengthy speculation ever since, most often at anniversaries of England's great World Cup triumph, which seems doomed never to be repeated (by the men, at least), another distant image of that ultimately disappointing cul-de-sac of a decade whose features and foibles have been far too minutely pored over to need any more rehearsals here. The thieves have still yet to be properly identified despite repeated attempts; the latest, in 2018, by the Daily Mirror, *named a South London armed robber and counterfeiter, Sid 'Mr Crafty' Cugullere. His nephew Gary related how his uncle had stolen the cup while the exhibition was closed on Sunday, March 20. He had then met his brother, and Gary's father, Reg, outside the Central Hall: 'On the street after coming out of the doors Sid lifted his jacket and said, "'Ere you are, Reg, look at this." He opened one side of his jacket and the World Cup was there.' Reg's alleged response has a definite feel of veracity: 'My dad went: "Fucking hell, Sid, what the fuck do you think we are going to do with that?"'*

Which appears to have been the problem for whomever stole it. A petty criminal alleged by Gary to be an associate of Cugullere made a clumsy attempt to extract a ransom from the Football Association, and was caught, without the cup, in a less-than-smooth operation mounted by an Inspector Buggy of the Flying Squad. The man insisted he was merely the middleman and received a two-year jail sentence. The cup was discovered a week later under a hedge on Beulah Hill, Norwood, by Pickles, a cross-bred Collie being taken for an evening walk by a local man, Mr David Corbett, who received a lot of publicity and £6,000 in various rewards, which was £5,000 more than the England players received for winning the thing. How the cup got there and who took it there is still a mystery.

Further complications and confusions arise from the uncertain number of cups and copies in circulation then and since. It's now known that the FA hurriedly and secretly commissioned a replica from a London silversmith after the 1966 theft in case the cup was not recovered in time for the final. This replica was substituted for the real one for security reasons almost immediately after the Queen had presented it to Bobby Moore, prised from the hands of Nobby Stiles, which could have been rash. It was then exhibited round the country for the next four years until the real cup was returned to the organisers, FIFA, for the 1970 tournament in Mexico, when Brazil won the competition for the third time and were awarded the trophy in perpetuity. Perpetuity did not last long, however, as it was stolen again from Rio de Janeiro in 1983, and has never been found. To muddy matters more, it seems that the original cup, made for the first tournament in 1930, might well have been substituted in West Germany after their cup win in 1954. In 1997, the English replica was bought from the silversmith's family (he had kept it under his bed until his death) for £254,500 by a mystery buyer. This turned out to be none other than FIFA, who, as confused as everybody else, seemed to have believed it was the real one, switched at some stage with the copy, a theory borne out by the amount they paid for it. Unfortunately, if that was the case, subsequent tests confirmed it was indeed the substitute. I would submit, after all this, that it's not entirely implausible to suggest that the cup found on Beulah Hill wasn't the real one either, although there are questions about whether Benny 99 or any other silversmith could have made it in a week to such exact proportions.

John Bindon, and his penis, did exist, although there is comparable debate about exactly how the trick with the beer glasses worked. For an exhaustive discussion, see Craig Brown's splendidly unconventional biography of Princess Margaret, 'Ma'am Darling'. It does not include the incident I described, and Terry himself seems unclear.

Camp Freddie is the consigliere of the formidable Mr Bridger, the deeply patriotic crime boss portrayed by Noël Coward in 'The Italian Job' (1969), the enduring portrayal of the Post-Empire striking back at Europe, a sentiment that continued into Brexit and is much loved by that most unquestioning band of patriots, England's football fans, who have adopted its theme tune with enthusiasm. The Bent Elbow, and Freddie's dad, sadly share the fictional status of George Orwell's wonderful pub, The Moon Under Water.

Micky The Fish Metcalfe was a prized if occasionally frustrating and frustrated contact of Arthur Daley, whose later similarly close-winded exploits featured in the TV series, 'Minder'. Benny Cellini shares some of the attributes of his famous forebear Benevenuto Cellini (1543–1571), renowned Renaissance goldsmith and author of a splendidly lively and unbashful autobiography.

Terry and Julie are the wistful lovers in 'Waterloo Sunset', the immortal hymn to the gone glory that was sixties London written by Ray Davies and recorded by his group, The Kinks. It's often been said that Terry and Julie are those two leading symbols of sixties' London, Terence Stamp and Julie Christie, but Ray Davies has denied it. Our Terry's grandfather, Percy Perks, was encountered in the earlier chapter set in the First World War.

Despite his nickname, Sid Cugellere served 25 years in prison for various offences. Mr Crafty indeed. A friend said of him, 'He was very polite, a great thinker and planner. Sid was a thief but never burgled houses, it was always bigger; banks and warehouses. He was also very funny.' You might be further convinced of his claim when you learn that both Sid and Reg had floral tributes *in the shape of the World Cup at their funerals. Sid died in 2005, Reg in 2012. Pickles appeared on television, and starred in the film 'The Spy with a Cold Nose', alongside Eric Sykes and June Whitfield. He was also awarded a year's supply of free dog food by Spillers. I do not know whether he had finished it by the time he died chasing a cat the next year. His collar is on display at The National Football Museum in Manchester, along with the replica World Cup, presented by FIFA. I trust it is well guarded.*

FURTHER READING:
The Theft of the Jules Rimet Trophy, *Martin Atherton.*
Pickles and the World Cup, *Posey Parker.*
The Self Preservation Society: 50 Years of The Italian Job, *Matthew Field.*

1975

Ted and Margaret

TEDDY WAS IN PAIN. IT WAS DARK ALREADY OUTSIDE, A cold London February against the windows of his Wilton Street home. Teddy took another sip of Scotch and continued to stare bleakly at nothing in particular. The voice out in the hall finishing a phone call was Tim, Teddy's parliamentary private secretary, adviser and confidante. Teddy knew he was now hovering on the other side of the door, but he'd had enough of sympathetic looks for one day.

He still couldn't believe it. She'd told him she was going to do it, but he hadn't thought for a moment that it would really happen. He'd always been good – prided himself on it – at just soldiering on, never showing he was hurt. But this! Not even one of his cherished operatic composers could have come up with this, surely. Betrayed by the woman he loved, and not only betrayed: replaced, supplanted, ousted, removed by the woman he refused to believe was not in love with him.

It is customary to say at this point, with these things, that there had of course been other women in his life. But this wasn't true for Teddy. There had been good old Kay, of course, waiting for the spark that never came until she finally gave up and came to rest elsewhere. But he had never, ever felt for any other woman the way he felt for this woman.

This was a man intent on achieving his ambition by guarding against any threat to his painstakingly constructed belief in himself. Contemporaries, peers, seniors, juniors were never allowed within, never allowed to see how he felt, how he felt about them. Still, in the early days, because he was clever, he had managed the difficult trick of making people like him even if they couldn't get to know him.

Women, though, were and had always been a bit of an unknown to Teddy. There had been little obvious opportunity for him to get to know them, to relish the added frisson of difference and the promise of warmth and more. He had a brother but no sisters; he had been to an all-boys grammar school, then on to an all-male Oxford college, and then into the Army in 1939.

In the usual way in such circumstances, the only person he confided in was a woman: his mother. Not entirely, of course, as she was unwilling to accept that there could be the slightest fault in her treasured boy, unquestionable carrier of her dreams, which made him equally unwilling to betray that slightest fault for fear of hurting and disappointing her. Also, she, his father, and his brother were not educated, another impediment to intimacy that affects more families than is generally thought, and used to affect more. She had been in service, a lady's maid; his father, a carpenter, though also loving, was not in awe of him so much as of his intellect. At school, despite the scholarships, there was only a grudging recognition of his abilities, partly to do with snobbery about his modest background, but also with the resentment often felt by those who have not been lucky enough to receive the gift of an alarmingly retentive memory such as his. Don't show you're hurt; don't get angry, get even; and most of all guard, guard, guard against any more hurt, against showing any more of your vulnerabilities, your lack of the ease, customs and understandings acquired by birth into the class to which you aspire.

It never works, of course: that class is at its most adept when spotting the non-belonger. Teddy had realised this at Oxford, and, being clever, had worked out that the way ahead was to make it reasonably easy for them to detect while indicating a deference and respect. So he had constructed an accent that was a tribute to upper-middle-class vowels while still acknowledging its Kentish working-class origins. He had a broad grin and a happy laugh involving most of his upper body with which he greeted their jokes, however funny, or obscure (Teddy didn't have a natural sense of humour but learned to recognise one). Calling himself and having others call him Teddy rather than Edward or Ted struck almost exactly the right class note.

He'd chosen the right college, too: Balliol, as keen on merit as on blood as it was possible to be in Oxford in the 1930s. The laugh, the smile and hard work at achieving what he wanted to achieve saw him president of the Oxford University Conservative Association first and then the top prize for anyone looking for a career in politics as fiercely as he: president of the Oxford Union, with its entrée to the top figures of the day, happy to come down to debate and be fawned over. Girls? Well, as noted, there weren't that many available, and especially not for a man of clear and determined priorities for whom they were not a clear and determined priority; even a first in Philosophy, Politics and Economics was sacrificed to the time devoted to his ambition to make his way to Parliament and power. But he kept up his music – gritty Teddy had won an organ scholarship once he was there after two earlier failed attempts – because it was useful, and because he loved it: it spoke his otherwise concealed emotions, but safely.

The ambition was interrupted by the war, which he enjoyed: it was well suited to a clear and organised mind. He joined the Royal Artillery, fought all the way to Germany, was mentioned in despatches, and ended up a Lieutenant-Colonel. Teddy had become Ted, but it was the right time. And if some of his fellow officers had begun to notice the reserve, less disguised by the smile and the laugh in a war for survival, it did bolster his authority. And with that authority and reserve combined, they also noticed, came perhaps inevitably a clumsy pompousness.

The traditional answer to this was to fall in love. It was not that Teddy, as we shall continue to call him, had no interest in women: he did, although he could not betray it. But if he was to make the very dangerous decision to allow someone inside the castle keep that was Teddy, it would have to be someone remarkable. Someone attractive in every way; perhaps most importantly, someone (nearly) his intellectual equal. But such a woman was (obviously) hard to find. Many were assessed and instantly found wanting, without being allowed any say in the matter. Indeed, Teddy believed himself such a good judge of Teddy suitability that he didn't need to ask them out to find out. And so, in the immediate post-war years, he devoted himself to political progress – searching for a parliamentary seat – while leaving the personal to this long, and lonely, game.

What he didn't see, despite being clever, was the part that his unease about admitting entry played in the exactingly high standards for admitting entry. Or that his carefully constructed character fostered and required an inflated opinion of himself that is not uncommon but which unforgiving psychologists have described as 'Grandiosity', 'Narcissism', and 'Superiority'. Clever, but not that clever, even though it seems to affect most of those curse-blessed in that way.

TIM CAME IN AND TEDDY SUFFERED HIS LOOK, THEN TOLD him to go home. 'He's taking it very hard,' he told his wife, Sally, when he got there.

Sally frowned and shrugged. 'What did you expect? It was the top job, and what else did he have?' She paused. 'Doesn't have even that, now.' Tim walked determinedly towards the drinks cabinet. 'God,' said Sally, 'he must hate that woman.'

MARGARET WAS NERVOUS. IT WAS FEBRUARY, 1950, IT WAS her first general election campaign, and she had arrived to address a meeting in Bexley, the next constituency to the one she was trying to win in Dartford. She was to speak in support of the Bexley hopeful, and he in turn would come to Dartford to support her. St Celia's church hall was quite large for a church hall, and seemed even more so when empty; she had arrived early, the better to be prepared. Margaret was very good at preparation. A 24-year-old woman looking for a career in politics needed to be. Nervous, but not that nervous. She went up to the table at the front of the hall set out for the speakers, and chose the seat right of the centre one, where she expected the chairman of the meeting to sit. All concentration was on her speech, composed with her usual care. Margaret was not a natural speaker – Oxford had shown her that – but she was formidably briefed and combative in the way a grocer's daughter from the Lincolnshire sticks had to be. She worked away and was quite proud of her closing remarks: 'The British spirit has to be recovered! Do you want it to perish for a soulless Socialist system, or to live to recreate a glorious Britain? You will decide!' She tried it out loud, and had just finished its ringing tones when she saw a youngish man approaching up the hall. He was rather good-looking, she thought, blond hair well-oiled and combed back in the sharply neat military style, and slightly familiar.

'Very good,' he said. 'This is my seat.'

She blushed slightly, and fetchingly, he thought, as she realised who he was. 'Oh, hallo, of course, you're Ted Heath, campaigning so strongly here. I've read your election material, very impressive, especially on reinvigorating the Party and taking the fight to Labour. That's exactly what we need if we're going to stop these Socialists giving us another five years of rationing and nationalising.'

This was Teddy, the candidate for Bexley. He was flattered, and attracted. Margaret had a fine complexion and regular features (rather like his own, although, as is often the case, he wasn't aware of it). He knew about her, too: up at Somerville, scientist, president of the Conservative Association like him before, had seen off several ostensibly better qualified men to be selected for Dartford, rising star. Teddy Testing was on full alert, but he didn't lose sight of his priorities. 'Thank you. But, as I said, this is my seat. I should sit to the right of the chairman. You'll have to move.'

As usual, he'd been graceless enough to give a possible friendship little chance. Unusually, though, this time he didn't immediately excuse himself to himself as a man in a hurry, purposeful, no time for niceties, things to be done. His sudden urge to put things right was helped by Margaret, who had found her own way to protect herself from the slights and bruises of sexism and snobbery: while Teddy fiercely protected and hid his imagination and sensitivity, Margaret simply refused to allow it in.

So she had no trouble getting to her feet and removing herself to the end of the table, where she knew she would also show to some advantage. 'I'm sorry, Mr Heath, I wasn't thinking. Of course you must sit there.'

There was something about her voice, its mixture of precision and something else, that Teddy found most appealing, particularly in the slightly throaty way she said 'Mr Heath'.

'Please, don't worry. It's just that there are ways of doing these things. And do call me Ted.' There were quite a few people who would have been surprised by the gentleness of his tone.

'Of course, and thank you. I have so little experience of these things, so it's very helpful to be set right by someone who knows.

You were still a bit of a legend in the Conservative Association at Oxford when I was there.'

'Really? I know you were also president. I've heard good things.' Quite a few people's surprise would now have been moving towards astonishment.

'Thank you. A lot of it's to do with being a woman and young. But I do want to change this country. I'm not saying things were perfect in the old days, before the Socialists. But the pendulum has swung too far, our people must be free to improve their own lot, not have the Government doing it all for them. As Hayek says, "The more the state 'plans' the more difficult planning becomes for the individual".'

Teddy felt a curious thrill. Hayek! He hadn't heard the name of the great economist since before the war. And coming from this alluring creature! 'Good point, but let's not forget that Hayek also argues that a wealthy society such as ours can provide help to the struggling individual without threatening the freedom of the individual.'

It was almost too exquisite. Margaret smiled in acknowledgement of his knowledge of Hayek, and the curious thrill became even curiouser and thrillier. She for her part decided that this might not be the time to expound on her lack of appreciation for the bit of Hayek Teddy was citing, however tempting. Teddy smiled back and their eyes locked for longer than strictly necessary even between would-be representatives of neighbouring constituencies.

Just a touch embarrassed by this sudden and unexpected intimacy, they sat down, in their correct places, and studied their papers especially assiduously. The hall began to fill up with the Conservatives of Bexley and a few who were clearly not, judging by their stern expressions and clothes more utilitarian than the formal informal suburban wear of Teddy's supporters, jackets and twin sets and bows of different type depending on sex. The pattern was broken by the chairman of the local association,

Colonel Dawnay, who had now arrived to take his place as chair of the meeting, teaming a vivid mustard-yellow moleskin waistcoat with a frayed Tattersall check shirt and an elderly sports jacket assisted by several safety pins. Teddy introduced him to Margaret, but long exposure to artillery prevented him from hearing completely. 'How do you do,' he smiled, alarmingly. 'Keeping the seat warm for your boss, eh? Well done, well done.'

'No, Colonel, Miss Roberts is our Dartford candidate, sir,' Teddy explained, with an apologetic smile that he wouldn't have bothered to give to anyone only a few hours previously.

'Dartford? Dartford? Who's Dartford? Missing? Who's missing? Oh, I see... extraordinary, but I suppose they know what they're doing... bit of a popsy, though, isn't she?' The Colonel's volume became progressively lower through this, so that the last remark was as *sotto* as his *voce* ever got, and was heard only by Teddy, who pretended to ignore it but again found himself strangely excited by it.

The meeting got underway. The Colonel proved a surprisingly adept chairman, moving through matters briskly, including chivvying the association secretary, overarticulated in the way of his kind, to get on with his appeal for funds and notification of the next beetle drive, a more genteel form of bingo, now mostly forgotten along with tombolas, sales of work and people who call their car 'a nice little bus'. Margaret was introduced faultlessly, which was not as surprising as it might be, as Teddy had passed the Colonel a note: 'Miss Margaret Roberts, the outstanding young candidate for our constituency next door in Dartford'. He had toyed with 'the outstanding and, as you can see, most attractive young candidate', but that was a bit too much even for this unfamiliarly frisky Teddy.

Margaret spoke confidently but not excitingly; even that rousing last line was a little betrayed by her worthily earnest delivery. Teddy thought it wonderful. His own address was more polished, as was to be expected from a senior debater, and he could tell he was going down well with his supporters, although he knew enough not to make too much of his great ambition, spurred by all he had seen and thought and fought for through the war, to bring the European countries closer together in safety and co-operation ('There are no votes in Paris, Heath,' the Colonel had advised him after he'd outlined his vision too enthusiastically. 'We're better than the Europeans, just because we saved them doesn't mean we want to be in the same club as them, never will.').

Questions from the floor followed. As usual in church halls, it was the vicar who felt obliged to start things off. One of the keen but green ones pushed through too early by the war, the type that Teddy knew far too well from his recent work for *The Church Times* while he waited for a MP's salary. 'What would the Conservatives say to those who argue that Socialism is closer to Christianity?' The audience muttered and shifted; one of the Labour infiltrators let out a solitary cheer. Ted waited a moment, weighing up crushing the upstart against damaging the feelings of the church-going voters. That was all Margaret needed.

'Thank you, Vicar,' she began, voice full of reasonableness and understanding. 'I'm from the Methodist persuasion, where, as you know, we make a close study of the scriptures. And I must say that I have always been struck by the Parable of the Talents. As I'm sure I don't have to tell you, the master went away on a, yes, business trip and left his servants to watch over varying amounts of money while he was away. Two of them had invested his money wisely, and doubled it, but the third had just buried it in the ground and kept it safe for his master's return. He believed he had done the right thing, but his master was angry with him and called him wicked and lazy for not doing anything with the money. So surely Christ's message is that we should care for one another not by stifling initiative, as the Socialists do, but by encouraging the making of money whose benefits all can share?'

The audience received this sermon with enthusiasm. Teddy was lost in more admiration. As it happened, this parable had also intrigued him since he first heard it in Sunday school and felt a twinge of pity for the castigated servant. He was also aware that some on the left argued that this was as fine a critique of the evils of capitalism as existed, and that the parable was a satire; in which case, thought Teddy, Christ was not alone in seriously overestimating the subtlety of thought displayed by his creations. And then, of course, there was Milton, 'They also serve who only stand and wait'. But Margaret had thrown all this aside, exuding a magnificent certainty that Teddy found intoxicating.

It got yet better. A Labour supporter, instead of challenging her explanation, made the mistake of going for the personal: 'What would a posh girl like you know about what people want?' Margaret's look of cold disdain was thrilling. 'Posh girl?! Posh girl?! I'm a corner shop owner's daughter from Lincolnshire, and I know what it's like to go through hard times. But my father taught me not to be frit of life, that England cannot march forward and prosper if we don't first stand on our own two feet!'

More applause. Teddy rose to his feet, and riding it, brought the meeting to a rousing finish about the Party sweeping the South East and driving the Socialists out to sea, where they belonged: 'They're all at sea!' He'd always been fond of a nautical metaphor, having grown up by the sea, in Broadstairs, and still living there, with his parents. Unusual for a Lieutenant Colonel aged 35, but economical.

The Colonel said well done and Margaret was eyeing him with admiration; Teddy hadn't felt this good since he'd won the organ scholarship (he still carried the confirming note in his wallet). He went up to Margaret, who was now dealing with elderly admirers, took her to one side and astonished himself with his boldness: 'Well done! Can I give you a lift anywhere?'

Margaret smiled and nodded. 'Can you possibly drop me off at my digs in Dartford?'

Teddy was on fire: 'Why don't we have a quick drink first to celebrate tonight's triumph?' Anxiously scouring her face for signs of rejection, he was delighted to see the subtlest of pink colouring her perfect complexion.

'Gosh, all right.'

They found a quiet table in The King's Head in Bexley village, Teddy's unofficial HQ. 'Scotch?' he asked, and Margaret said yes in a way that suggested it might be the first she'd ever had. He brought two of them back to the table, and they sipped.

'Mmm,' said Margaret. 'This is good. I could get to like this.' Teddy enjoyed looking at her. She was aware of his gaze, but wasn't flirtatious in a practised way, more welcoming of attention that hadn't always been expected. They chatted; not easily, but easier than Teddy had ever managed before with a woman to whom he felt remotely attracted. To his further surprise, he found himself telling her that he thought her frankness about her roots was splendid and music to the ears of the son of a builder (Teddy preferred this to carpenter). After half an hour, as they made their way to Teddy's car, Margaret had passed the Teddy Test *magna cum laude*, with particular *laude* for taking Tawney, Laski and Keynes in her stride, dismissing the first two out of hand as dangerous leftists and demurring carefully and less than she believed about the third, with his (to her) unnecessary alleviations of capitalism's hard instructive truths. Already, Teddy's engaging ways and views were discovering a softer Margaret, one she thought she could get to like. It was most often her habit to tell people that she disagreed with them immediately and forcibly; with Teddy, she found she could agree a little first, an advance that might be built on.

Teddy, who always wanted too much, was inwardly cursing that his agent had instructed him to swop his prized MG convertible for a dull Vauxhall saloon as more in keeping with the straitened rationed times. They got in, Teddy holding the door for her in recommended fashion, and he prepared to be masterful at the wheel, in cool command. Unfortunately, the car refused to start, and again unfortunately, mechanics were not his forte. 'Don't worry,' said Margaret brightly. 'I went on a car engine familiarisation course for a few evenings in Oxford. The Cowley Works were most instructive. A lack of energy in the workforce, almost a sense of entitlement. The unions as usual. There will be serious trouble there one day. Have you got a flashlight?' Teddy found his torch and stood awkwardly by holding it as Margaret expertly raised the bonnet and took a look at the engine. 'Hmm, I see. Toolkit?' Teddy fetched the kit from the car's boot and presented it for inspection. Margaret swiftly selected a spanner and moved into rapid action, Teddy holding the torch and watching in disguised awe and complete ignorance. 'Need a rag,' said Margaret without taking her eyes off the job. Teddy had only his handkerchief, embroidered by his loving mother with his monogram, EGH. He passed it to Margaret, who took it without a glance. A sharp cry followed: 'No! We cannot use that, far too good! Pass me my handbag!' Teddy retrieved her handbag and passed it over. Margaret took out a piece of cloth and set to more work. 'Try that!' she ordered when her work was done. Teddy climbed back in; the engine started first time. He had been less impressed by army sappers under fire.

'Thank you, Margaret! I had no idea of the range of your gifts. I hope your cloth isn't ruined.'

'No, nothing to worry about. They're actually my spare bloomers, never travel without them. Easily cleaned: you remove any excess oil, then sprinkle baking soda and allow it to sit for 24 hours. Then brush it away, spray with a vinegar and water solution, scrub with soap and rinse. I'll start on it when I get to the digs. Right here, then second right, first right, right after the telephone box and right again and again... go past the next six lamp posts, turn right... and here we are.'

If it was possible for a man to be any more enthralled, Teddy was that man. Beauty, intelligence and practicality! The blush from the bloomer revelation almost dispelled, he hurried round to let Margaret out, but she was already waiting for him, slightly but delightfully smudged. 'Thank you, Ted, for a most exciting trip, and the very best of luck in the campaign.'

'Thank you, Margaret, for a most stimulating evening and for a startling display of mechanical skills. Westminster is waiting!' They walked to the front garden gate of her digs, where she stopped. Teddy, extremely anxious not to do anything which would ruin this moment, froze, then moved towards her, decided on a handshake at the last second and ended up clutching her handbag's strap. The more practised would have laughed at this, but Ted and Margaret disengaged hurriedly and wishing each other goodnight, parted.

TEDDY MIGHT HAVE BEEN A MAN IN LOVE BUT HE COULD not be expected to change his ways in the middle of an election campaign, his first and the key to all he had hoped for, before that meeting at least. In the way of such men – and they are not as rare as you might think – he was perhaps happier holding on to the memory of Margaret rather than risking the next step, with its possibility of disappointment. So, in his ordered way, it was only last thing at night, or when he was alone in his car that he allowed himself to stop thinking of Mr Attlee and the cost of living and the very unpleasant and large dog he had encountered in Corbyn Drive while canvassing; instead he concentrated on a soothing reverie that featured delightful conversation, smiles, adoring looks, rather good home cooking in a cosy Westminster flat, and more perhaps not fitting to be mentioned outside the interior of Teddy or the Vauxhall.

For her part, Margaret was just as disciplined; this, after all, was someone who'd greeted the attentions of a wealthy farmer holding out the prospect of a comfortable life back in Lincolnshire by passing him on to her sister without so much as a backward glance. She was also currently being courted by another wealthy man, a businessman and pillar of the Dartford Conservative Association, who was getting very little response but remained dogged in his attendance, driving Margaret to engagements in his Jaguar (she did admire the walnut veneer and Denis's racy driving gloves, which would have dismayed Teddy, had he known).

A little to her surprise, she found that thoughts of Teddy did quite often get through her anti-distraction iron curtain (a phrase that had become fashionable following Churchill's speech of 1946). So much so that on the frantic last day before the election she found time to send him a telegram. She was rather pleased with the message: 'I hope you Gallup to the top of the poll', punning on the name of the famous pollster. Denis was clearly having more of an influence than she imagined.

Teddy was understandably delighted to receive this, and even, remarkably, broke off to reply. Believing anything relating to himself to be significant, he kept the message along with everything else in his carefully collated archive. Margaret, being more practical and less sentimental, didn't keep his, although it pleased her and was more revealing than possibly either of them realised: 'Thank you. I hope we can do it together'.

Teddy won, just. Margaret, in a much less winnable seat, didn't. Teddy was immediately caught up in the excitements of being a new MP and the satisfaction of a goal so swiftly achieved. It is also the case that the self-obsessed do not always have sufficient space for anyone else, since that person, however attractive, will never be quite as interesting as they are to themselves, especially when they are the first of the new intake to achieve office, as a Government whip. Teddy was very much a coming man. Margaret, never short of determination, continued to nurse Dartford while employing her chemistry degree with work as a research chemist. But she did not see engineering improved contents for Messrs Lyons' pies and cakes as permanently, if you'll forgive me, fulfilling; particularly not when Denis was proving so enticingly persistent. If she spared a thought for Teddy, it was of a surprisingly intriguing episode that wouldn't amount to anything in the real world of Margaret Roberts.

Twenty months later, Attlee and his great reforming government, exhausted by its work and narrow majority and led by the ailing and the elderly, called a snap election. The Conservatives, too, were led by an ailing and elderly hero, but were reviving under the energy of new young MPs like Teddy, less in thrall to the old givens, willing to accept that some change, such as the infant and popular National Health Service, was there to stay, and that increased public spending, sensibly conducted, was beneficial for a country still struggling to recover from the costs of its war effort.

Not that much change seemed evident at the joint meeting in St Celia's church hall. The Colonel was as crusty as ever, and the young vicar as irritating. Teddy had arrived unnecessarily early, but Margaret was not there. She was efficiently in time, accompanied by Denis, but found herself excited in a way she didn't recognise on seeing Teddy again. 'Hello, Mr Heath,' she said, noting the higher octave her voice had disobediently taken on. 'This is Denis Thatcher, who is being a tremendous support to me in the campaign.' What she didn't add was that she and Denis had recently become engaged, but were keeping it to themselves until after the election, as voters might not relish a candidate who would inevitably soon succumb to marriage and a family.

The two men nodded at each other, Teddy with less enthusiasm. Denis was brisk: 'I don't do that much. Just drive her round, tell her she's marvellous, that sort of thing.' Teddy thought he seemed rather old (just the year more than him, as it happened, 36). He was wearing a regimental tie with his blazer and slacks.

'I see you were a gunner,' said Teddy, small talk even more stilted than usual.

'Yes,' said Denis. 'Sicily, Italy, that whole shooting match mostly. Major.'

'I was a gunner, too. Normandy, Germany. Lieutenant Colonel.'

Margaret was aware that one of those uniquely male contests was taking place, and that Teddy had won. She was also aware that she was rather enjoying it, and, to be as frank as she usually was, her secret engagement. 'No need to hang around, Denis,' she told him. 'There's plenty of envelope stuffing back in Dartford.'

Denis looked a little taken aback, but not as if it was the first time, Teddy thought. 'Oh, right-ho, jolly good, bumf-bothering it is, Thatcher's your man. Shall I pick you up afterwards?'

Teddy, in Lieutenant Colonel mode, saw his chance. 'I'd be happy to take you back. It worked pretty well last time.'

Margaret's fine complexion was made finer by that hint of pink he remembered so well. The two men waited, expectantly, deliciously. 'Thank you, Ted. It would save you a trip, Denis.'

'I really don't mind, Jag and Thatcher always at the service of the best and prettiest candidate, nothing personal, Heath.'

Teddy didn't respond to this. Margaret told Denis his services would not be required in a tone she would use 30 years later with Cabinet ministers. He left, making vigorous but imaginary backhand tennis strokes as he went and whistling something indeterminate but jaunty. 'That's DT,' said Margaret, with the amused forbearance that spells affection, and, in this case, something rather more. Teddy wasn't alive to such nuances, and dismissed Thatcher as a threat. He and Margaret then fell immediately into an intense discussion about the way forward for the Party. Teddy had been a founder member of the One Nation group, taking its name and philosophy from Disraeli's coining the previous century of how the Conservatives could appeal to the increasingly influential and enfranchised working class. Margaret was as instinctively opposed to compromise as a member of the class immediately above would be; a class to which she was loyal in a way that Teddy wasn't to his. But she listened to him with an obvious and genuine admiration that was prompted by rather more than the size of his intellect. There was something about Ted's mixture of confidence and vulnerability that she found deeply appealing. And there was something about Margaret's mixture of unapologetic intellect and traditional femininity that similarly moved him.

The meeting began, with very much the same audience as before, the stolid bulk Conservative with a smattering of Labour supporters. The vicar again asked the first question. 'As this is a church hall, I would like to ask the candidates a question based on Christian principles.' The Colonel groaned, audibly, but the vicar ignored him. 'Would you say the Good Samaritan was a Conservative or Labour supporter?'

This time, Teddy didn't hesitate. 'I should say he would certainly have been a Conservative. Socialism has no monopoly on helping those in need. We wouldn't walk past anyone. We feel for the needy as much as any Socialist. But we also know we have more sensible ways of helping them. The Good Samaritan didn't just throw money at the poor robbed and beaten man, he gave him first aid and organised his care sensibly and practically.'

He paused to allow his point to sink in. Margaret, who had no time for such rhetorical devices, took the opportunity to interrupt. Teddy was once more confounded by his admiration for such brassness.

'But the important point,' she declared with force, 'is that the Good Samaritan had money! It's no good just having pious intentions, you've got to be able to put them into action! And you've got to be able to afford them!'

The hall loved this. The chair scraping of the few Labour supporters – all men – who walked out with disgusted looks on their faces was lost in the cheers and applause, applause which Teddy found himself joining as enthusiastically as anyone, although the next day, in the absence of the marvel that was Margaret, he began to worry about her emphasis.

For now, though, he was delighted to form something of a double act, he more thoughtful, she more forceful, appealing to the broadest Tory instincts. The Colonel was not keen on meetings 'banging on and on', as he frequently put it. Teddy, realising they were now preaching to the converted, apart from the disapproving vicar, was equally keen to escort Margaret elsewhere. The Colonel closed after about an hour, to prolonged applause, apart from the vicar, who was affecting one of those pained but brave smiles modelled on some saint confronted with the sixth deadly sin immediately after seeing off the fifth.

They were soon sitting in The King's Head, with Teddy once again listening intently to her with an expression he didn't remember having. He wanted her to join the One Nation group, but Margaret pleaded her prior membership of the Vermin Club, formed after Nye Bevan had described the Tories as being 'lower than vermin' for 'condemning millions of first-class people to semi-starvation' in their previous administrations. Teddy had recoiled a little from this as too bombastic for his taste, but knowing Margaret was a member made it seem immediately more attractive, like her certainty, something he had learnt to suspect intellectually but found emotionally stimulating at the same time, like chocolate or Charles Dickens. Why she had it and he didn't, he came to think much later, was probably to do with their backgrounds, ostensibly alike but distinguished by Anglicanism, Methodism and Alfred Roberts, a man not troubled by self-doubt, as befits an Alderman; Teddy's parents were less so.

His mother, Elsie, was dying, quietly at home. Every night of the campaign he had driven back to Broadstairs to be with her rather than stay in Bexley. There he would play the piano for her, the old songs she loved, 'When You Come to the End of a Perfect Day', 'In Sweet September', 'When We Are Old and Grey'. Not exactly the metier of a Balliol organ scholar, but he was happy to do it for her, although she being upstairs in her bedroom while he and the piano were in the sitting room below was a metaphor not lost on him.

Being Teddy, he had told only his agent that his mother's last days were upon her. So he could only guess why he now told Margaret. But he saw it had been a good choice when tears welled up in her eyes as he for some reason went on to describe his evenings on the piano.

'Oh, Ted, I am so sorry,' she said. 'This, at such a time. But at least you can be there at night, that must be such a comfort for her – and you. We used to sing at home, too, on a Sunday, hymns of course, with me on the piano and Father and Mother joining in. Families are so important, aren't they?' She took another sip of her scotch and continued to look at Teddy with a sympathy that avoided the pity he hated.

'Do you still play, Margaret?'

'No, no time now, and I couldn't afford one at the moment anyway. I wasn't that good, actually, but I enjoyed it. I even learnt to play the organ.'

'Did you? I was an organ scholar at Balliol.' This usually came out as a boast, but with Margaret it was more an eager try for common ground.

'As well as everything else? Yours was a glittering Oxford, Ted.' This sort of remark usually conveyed a brisk judgment before she moved on, but with Teddy it was different for her, too.

'Have you heard of John Roberts?'

'John Roberts the famous organ builder?'

'He was my great-uncle.' Again, a gentle reaching out, not a claim to vicarious fame.

'That's extraordinary! I've played on a Roberts organ! At Oxford.'

'Yes, at St Simon's, I had a go as well when no one was around.'

They paused happily, looking at each other with the delight of attraction confirmed by things shared.

'We must go to a recital when all this is over,' said Teddy, meaning the election but including his mother's death.

'Yes, we must,' said Margaret enthusiastically. She looked at her watch. 'But hadn't you better be getting back to Broadstairs?'

Teddy was one of those suitors more on guard for discouragement than the opposite: he immediately interpreted this to mean that Margaret wanted him gone rather than a sign of the genuine caring that prompted it.

'Yes, you're right. I'll drop you off on the way.'

'No, don't worry about that. Have they got a public phone here? I'll call Denis.'

'No, that's fine, I don't want to trouble him.'

'DT won't mind. He's on call for me, sweet man that he is.'

Teddy's heart sank a little farther. Another failing of the swain unsure of his allure is to praise the opposition. When Margaret returned from phoning to announce that Denis was on his way, Teddy said, 'He seems a nice chap.'

'He is, he is. Kind, surprisingly thoughtful, and willing to put up with me. I know I put a lot of people off with my directness, but I prefer it to all this faffing and dancing about and insincerity and false modesty that the educated English classes seem to consider a condition of membership. There's too much to do for that, I haven't got the time. Denis is a tremendous faffer, but he seems to find my straightforwardness refreshing and endearing.'

She took a sip of her whisky. Teddy wished he hadn't asked and, as is also usual with his type, was too busy welcoming the gloom of rejection to take proper notice of what Margaret said next, or how wistfully she said it. 'I suppose he could be a bit more exciting.'

Conversation was less easy after that, with Ted distracted and Margaret, who was not one for subtleties, understanding something had changed, but unable to work out what. Any chance of recovering their earlier intimacy left with the entry of Denis, loudly slapping his driving gloves into his other hand and generally beaming until he spotted Margaret, when he waved overenergetically and came over. 'What-ho both,' he said, still beaming. 'Made very good time in the Jag. Could I interest you in a snorterino, Heath? Margaret? On the scotch, eh, hoots man, och aye, another? I'm going for a large G&T, ice and slice myself, worked up a bit of a thirst licking envelopes.'

'Ted has to go, Denis. But I'll have one with you, it's the least you deserve for flogging over here. Off you go for the drinks, there's a dear.'

Teddy was grateful to her for not spelling out why he had to leave. Many people would make the mistake of thinking Margaret uniformly unfeeling. She was impatient with the prolix and the woolly, and with sensitivities she didn't share, but when she cared about someone, she was as capable of subtlety and sympathy as anyone. And Teddy in particular had a vulnerable quality that appealed to this part of her.

Teddy's mother died in the early hours next morning. He was surprised by how much her death affected him, as he often was by his emotions. Margaret wrote a letter of condolence: 'I am so glad your mother saw your initial success and the way you followed it up with a steady ascent to great things'. The loss of his mother seemed somehow to confirm his loss of Margaret. He was re-elected in a bit of a blur; Margaret failed again, against tough odds.

BUT HE SAW HER AGAIN ONLY ONE WEEK LATER, IN slightly unusual circumstances. A fellow whip had been forced to return to his northern constituency on urgent business – a Tory local councillor had taken it on himself for some unknown reason to lower his trousers at the constituency ball and oil was required for troubled waters. As it happened, the whip had two tickets to the opening night of *South Pacific*, the latest Rodgers and Hammerstein musical, and had offered them to Teddy, who had a weakness for this lower art form that he only reluctantly indulged. But this was too good an opportunity to miss, and spurning the chance to take a partner, had settled into the stalls to enjoy the tale of Americans in the wartime Pacific finding love and losing lives, saved by the brash sub-operatic magic of composers at their confident energetic sentimental peak. Just before the house lights went down Teddy, rather to his amazement, spotted Margaret, with Denis, in the front row, who was looking round wildly and grinning, but thankfully didn't see him. Typical flashy Thatcher, he thought to himself grumpily, but it meant he could watch Margaret as the spectacular unfolded above them.

Sometimes, a book, a play seems to have sought you out. Seeing Margaret disturbed in some ways his convenient and safer decision that she was not to be. As usual, he was unprepared for emotion, this time the kind brought on by the potency of cheap music, made even more so by her presence, near but unattainable. The first jolt to his protecting shell was the young romantic lead, an American navy nurse, singing 'A Cock-Eyed Optimist', featuring one of those Hammerstein lines that refuses to leave you, about a dope who still hopes. By the time the lead tenor, playing the role of the romantic, but older, French planter, was giving his all to 'Some Enchanted Evening', the song celebrating the moment he first saw his young love, Teddy had tears running down his cheeks, feelings about his mother and Margaret combining with the repressed stress of the election. Relieved even more that he had not brought a companion, he let them continue to course, and stared at Margaret through them. She turned to look at Denis, and instantly the remark of hers in the pub came to him with a force it had lacked at the time: 'I suppose he could be a bit more exciting.'

At the interval, Teddy made his way against the mass exit for the bars to Margaret and Denis, who was bobbing up and down in his eagerness to get to a 'snorteroo'. 'Hello, Margaret,' said Teddy, who had carefully attended to his tears with a handkerchief while the lights were still down but could do little about guarding his shining eyes from those who noticed, like Margaret.

She beamed at him, and went that remembered and delicate pink which had first entranced him. 'Hello, Ted,' she said. 'How lovely to see you!'

'Hello, Heath,' said Denis, fighting a losing battle with his need for refreshment, eyes darting over Teddy's shoulder to the exit. 'Aren't you going to congratulate me?'

'Congratulate you? Why?' said Teddy, turning to look at him, equally distracted.

'On my engagement to the prettiest cleverest young lady in the Conservative Party.'

Ted's beam died in the face of Denis's.

'We announced it on the election eve. Did you miss it?'

Margaret was looking at Teddy, yet pinker. As was often the case, his quick brain ran through a range of responses and rejected them all.

Denis, who wasn't really paying attention between speaking, broke the silence. 'Coming for a drink? The interval will be almost over.'

'No,' said Teddy. 'I have to get back to my friend. Goodbye. Goodbye Margaret.'

Margaret was left silent for once, and was ushered cluckily by Denis towards drink, looking over her shoulder, the smile now agitated, as she went. Teddy didn't stay for the second half, which was probably just as well, as the tenor's heartfelt lament when he thinks he has lost the girl, 'This Nearly Was Mine', might have proved too much.

WHAT HAD HAPPENED? HOW HAD IT GONE SO WRONG? These were questions Teddy agonised over in the time he allotted for personal matters, now confined to the moments before sleep in order to accommodate his new responsibilities as a Government whip, but no less troubling for being concentrated.

He failed and failed to come up with an answer, but it was quite simple. In his need to protect himself, he hadn't given enough, risked enough. Margaret thought he seemed attracted to her, and she was certainly attracted to him, but she couldn't understand why he didn't make an attempt to take things any further. She accepted that he had just lost his mother, but didn't understand how fierce a blow this was to him, mostly because he hadn't told her. And if a girl was to contemplate breaking an engagement, even a secret one, she did need more than a hint or a sign. Would she have responded if Teddy had ardently declared his love? Who knows? She certainly didn't. She had accepted Denis's proposal because she realised that once again she really didn't have a chance of turning over the large Labour majority. And Denis might be a little elderly, neither exactly handsome nor exciting, but he was clearly tremendously fond of her, and rich. He could support her while she had children, which she wanted, and while she continued her search for a better seat. He did what he was told and she was quite happy for him to consort with his hearty chums. Teddy would be far more of a soulmate, but he didn't have the resources to keep her in the style an aspiring Tory MP and enjoyer of the best middle-class benefits desired, such as a flat in Chelsea. And Teddy never tried.

Margaret and Denis married on a cold December day at Wesley's Chapel, City Road, London. The bride's family considered it too grand; Denis, who, described himself, typically, as 'a middle-stump Anglican', agreed to it, not least because he had been married before, briefly, during the war, to a 'bolter'. Margaret was not so made of iron that being the second Mrs Thatcher didn't always irk a little, until many years later when she became the first Lady Thatcher.

Over the next few years, both Margaret and Teddy kept busy. While the coming man was coming closer and closer, she qualified as a barrister, produced twins the same year (boy and girl, naturally) and kept active in Conservative circles. She missed out on the thumping victory for Sir Anthony Eden in 1955, but in 1958, after her usual bravura assault on the local association hearts and minds, she was selected as the prospective candidate for the safe seat of Finchley.

IN WILTON STREET, TEDDY POURED HIMSELF ANOTHER scotch and carried on brooding. He was thinking about Margaret. It was not that she owed him anything, in that way. After her marriage, and after the initial hurt, he had come to think that there was nothing to do about it, no sensible Heath five-point plan. It probably hadn't been very sensible to conclude, on scarcely tested grounds, that there was no other woman for him, but that was how he had felt and, yes, still felt.

He stopped brooding and just stared. He might have carried further along beyond where this well-travelled train of thought usually stopped, but he never had and was unlikely to start now. Even if he had, he probably wouldn't have realised the truth, as it is tricky, analysing yourself yourself. Well-guarded people guard themselves well for a reason: Teddy, the thinker, the organiser, the man criticised for being a touch wooden, was of course a hopeless romantic who in some ways preferred the tragedy of rejection to happiness and the danger that it could turn out to be mundane.

So he carried no torch for Margaret, and he certainly didn't hate her, but he had, in that unfashionable phrase, hardened his heart against her, protected himself against the thought of her. Such hardening cannot confine itself to its subject, though, and is never entirely successful. His hurt made him curt, more brusque than before. Certainly now being Chief Whip, and privy to the secrets of his fellow MPs and their characters didn't help. Nevertheless, practical Teddy was still dominant, and he disdained to browbeat and blackmail his subjects into obedience, preferring argument and persuasion.

He noticed that Margaret had been selected for Finchley, just as he noted any reference to her, with as near as he allowed himself to wistfulness, momentarily. Nothing, though, quite prepared him for the blush when, a little later, he turned a Commons' corner and almost bumped into her. 'Ted!' she cried, with the added delight that a familiar face receives when encountered in less familiar circumstances. 'Hello! I've just been visiting Alfred Bossom. He's been very helpful to me, wonderful man. How are you? You look a little hot.'

Teddy was fighting his blush and remembering that Alfred Bossom was the wealthy Tory MP who had taken a shine to Margaret and had hosted her wedding reception, to which Teddy had not been invited. 'Margaret, very good to see you,' as near to sounding flustered as anyone had ever heard him. She waited for him to continue, but he was further hampered by the uninvited recollection that Churchill had once said, 'Bossom, odd name, neither one thing or the other.'

'I know you're frightfully busy, Ted,' said Margaret, taking her chance, 'but could you spare a few minutes for some of your incredibly helpful advice?'

It was in fact an unusually quiet moment; the calm competent Harold Macmillan had succeeded the Suez-shattered Anthony Eden, he was between MP indiscretions, and was sauntering off for a sandwich. But he remembered to look judicious, examined his watch, and said, 'Of course, why not come to my office? There's quite a good view over the river.'

They made their way back to his office. They stood at the window admiring what was undoubtedly a good view, and saying so. He was finding her nearness almost giddying. She'd forgotten how attractive he was, and how office and power suited him.

They moved apart. He went behind his desk, and immediately cursed himself for being so damn formal. He waved her to a seat, and distracted, sat down too abruptly. There was the distinct, unmistakable sound of a seam splitting open. His trousers now had a gaping hole at the back. How much more was fate going to throw at him?

Margaret was not in the least disconcerted. 'That sounded like your trousers, Ted.'

A tense nod of assent was all he could manage. She opened her handbag, a superior, larger version of the one that had assisted in the repair of his car those years back.

'Worry not, I've got needle and thread in here. Whip them off and I'll have them repaired in a jiffy.'

'Um, ah, thank you, Margaret, but I'll manage.' Pink became crimson.

'Don't be silly, Ted! You can't go around with your trousers split. The sooner I get started, the quicker it will be done. Come on!'

Discretion, decorum fell away, defeated by her voice of command, which was actually quite thrilling. He stood up, dropped his trousers, took them off and handed them over the desk. Margaret, bright-eyed and never happier than when demonstrating some homely skill to go with her intellect, set to work briskly. They talked as she sewed.

'I'm so very pleased to have been chosen for Finchley, Ted. Everyone seems very kind and enthusiastic. But there are a few old die-hards in the Association who are making life a little difficult and being obstructive. And I just thought that you with your great experience would know exactly what to do.'

This was the sort of thing that appealed to Teddy: a problem needing a solution, nothing emotional or troubling. Besides, concentrating on it would help him forget that he was sitting with no trousers on just a few feet from the woman he loved.

'Margaret, the first thing to remember is that even you couldn't lose Finchley.'

This was not a good start. He really must pull himself together, he thought, a little desperately. Margaret looked up sharply, wide-eyed and questioning. He remembered the trouser deficiency.

'Sorry, that wasn't expressed as well as it might have been. What I meant is that not only is it a solid Tory seat, it also has, as you know, a large Jewish community, and as thinking people who love their mothers they will have less difficulty than most accepting a woman candidate, even one as young as you.'

Better, but not the crisp, confident analysis he was renowned for. What was wrong with him today?

'Of course, Ted, thank you,' said Margaret, looking up from his trousers, with a smile that went to his heart. 'Of course, I'm a mother myself, you know.'

He did know. The announcement had been the cause of another bout of heart-hardening. 'Of course. How are the twins?'

'You remembered. They're both well. Mark still has a bit of trouble finding his way to the potty, but Carol certainly knows her mind. You have very good legs, by the way, Ted, you ought to find something that shows them off more. Sailing, perhaps?'

It was at this point that the door opened and the prime minister walked in to have a word with his Chief Whip. Teddy made to rise, but fortunately Mr Macmillan waved him to keep sitting. He looked at Margaret but didn't appear to notice she was repairing some trousers. 'Hallo, you didn't tell me you had a new secretary, Heath.'

'No, sir, this is Margaret Thatcher, our new prospective candidate for Finchley.'

'Are you? Jolly good. Are you Jewish? Lots of Jews in Finchley. I like Jews. Only ever met one boring one.' He sat down near Margaret and gazed out of the window as if he had all the time in the world.

'No, I'm not Jewish,' said Margaret, putting down her sewing. 'But I like them, too. So civilised. I am trying to get more of them into the Association. There was trouble with not being allowed to join the golf club a few years back which didn't do us any good.'

'Can't think why they'd want to join. Golf's an infuriating game.'

'Who is the boring one?' asked Margaret.

'Keith Joseph. Steer clear. Bright but in an entirely unfocused way. Rare combination of droning on and the ability to put his foot in it. Just finished my book. Who should I go for next, another Trollope or another Dickens?'

'Trollope,' said Teddy. 'Can't go wrong with Trollope. Very good on politics.'

'Dickens!' said Margaret. 'Trollope's such a snob. Narrow, while Dickens climbed his way to success through his talent and energy and really shook things up. Dickens!'

Macmillan looked at Margaret and smiled. 'Well, yes, there's a sly subtlety to Trollope that's not for everyone. But you can shake things up a bit too much, you know. People look to us for calm and stability and the sense and wisdom that comes from experience, from running things.'

'That was all very well, but things have changed and more is now required. If I see something needs changing,' said Margaret, thrilling and terrifying Teddy at the same time with her boldness, 'then I'm going to do it.'

Macmillan opened his eyes fully for the first time since he'd entered, but kept his gentle smile. 'I see. You may well be the future, but do guard against doing anything too rash, going too far. Do you remember how Salisbury defined it? "English policy is to float lazily downstream, occasionally putting out a diplomatic boat hook to avoid collisions." That's the sort of thing. We used to call it noblesse oblige, which was rather condescending, but gives the flavour of service, dutifully offered, for the good of all, the tax on privilege.'

Teddy felt the need to agree with both of them and ended up nodding and smiling and feeling more out of control than is normal even for a man not wearing any trousers.

Macmillan got to his feet. 'I'll let you get on with sewing up the Chief Whip's trousers. Powell spotted me earlier and he'll soon track me down if I don't keep moving. Rather not be harangued by the Glum of Brum today, it's far too warm. Goodbye Heath, goodbye…[there followed a perfectly judged pause]…Mrs Thatcher.'

And he was gone. Teddy and Margaret stared at each other, and after a difficult interval while they waited for the great man to be out of earshot, burst into the delight of unbottling forbidden laughter. She stood up and held his trousers aloft triumphantly, which made them laugh the more. Teddy, without thinking, came round the desk and took them from her, stared admiringly into her eyes, remembered he was not wearing the trousers and retreated rapidly behind the desk. In his hurry to get them back on he was forced into two quick hops, which set them off again.

Just as Teddy had finished adjusting his belt, which is not easy when you are laughing, the door flew open to reveal the said Enoch Powell, honourable member for Wolverhampton South West. He was in his accustomed three-piece suit; the slate grey eyes gleamed with yet more purpose than usual. 'Where is the prime minister?' he demanded in the flat emphatic vowels that would become ever more familiar. 'I must warn him before it is too late!'

Teddy was more used to this approach than Margaret, who, laughter stilled, was staring at him in amazement. He failed to acknowledge her; indeed, it seemed that he hadn't registered her presence. He remained standing at the door, and continued to speak, eyes fixed on some revelation near the top of Teddy's far wall:

'The prime minister must know that the supreme function of statesmanship is to provide against preventable evils. The discussion of future grave but, with effort now, avoidable evils is the most unpopular and at the same time the most necessary occupation for the politician. Those who knowingly shirk it deserve, and not infrequently receive, the curses of those who come after.'

He paused, without taking his eyes off the wall, then carried on, even more gravely. 'A week or two ago I fell into conversation with a constituent, a middle-aged, quite ordinary working man employed in one of our nationalised industries. After a sentence or two about the weather, he suddenly said: "If I had the money to go, I wouldn't stay in this country."'

'I was taken by his seriousness and his certainty, and I asked him why he was so intent on abandoning the land of his birth. He looked me squarely in the eye, and replied thus: "Because in this country in 15 or 20 years' time the woman will have the whip hand over the man. The proper order of things is being disturbed and overturned, Mr Powell. The obedience and respect that it is owed by the woman to the man as an innately superior person is dying and will soon disappear, you mark my words. It started in the war and it is not going away."'

'So I pondered on this, and I thought, this man is right, and not just because he is a man, and he votes for me. No, here, I thought is a cause that needs taking up, and by someone who doesn't fear controversy, or wide public attention. This is a creeping danger of which the nation must be warned. Do you realise women in teaching and the Civil Service are now paid as much as men? Did those who approved of their suffrage envision this? There are, I believe, already some women members of the House of Commons. And only the other day I saw a woman in the House of Lords!'

Teddy forbore to mention that this last was in line with the Life Peerages Act; Margaret, for once, was silent, still stunned by the Sage, who now wound himself up for his accustomed doom-laden finale: 'I must warn the prime minister to put a stop to this before it is too late. As I look ahead, I am filled with foreboding; like the Roman, I seem to see "the River Tiber foaming with much blood". Mark my words, next they will be allowed to answer back.'

He turned on his heel and left, tripping slightly over the door sill as he went. Margaret and Teddy looked at each other and burst into more laughter. 'My goodness, the bloody Tiber again,' said Teddy. 'The last crimson foam was caused by the increasing influence of homosexuals on the good old-fashioned values of British light entertainment. Kenneth Williams was mentioned, and also, I think, sewers.'

'I don't remember that.'

'No, it never really caught on, either. But I expect he'll find something one day.'

The laughter died as it will, leaving them staring into each other's eyes. 'Margaret,' said Teddy.

'Yes, Ted?' said Margaret. There was a pause as Teddy worked out what to say next that would perhaps, possibly, open the door to advancing their friendship without meeting any of the problems in the way of it. But it was just then that the Division Bell rang, and they divided.

STILL THINKING BACK, ALL THESE YEARS LATER, TEDDY sighed, his face falling into a frown that would become increasingly familiar after what had just gone before. At times like these, a man needs to remember his successes. Chief Whip had been but a stepping stone, a proof of loyalty and steadiness. Now he was back in 1960, when Macmillan appointed him Lord Privy Seal, no less, with responsibility for negotiating Britain's late entry into the Common Market. But De Gaulle's churlishly chauvinist refusal to see the sense in his urgings rather scuppered any chance of succeeding Macmillan as leader (yes, he was that high a flyer). However, effective work as the president of The Board of Trade under Alec Douglas-Home placed him in an excellent position to replace the faltered Home in 1963. His luck put him up against another falterer, the clever but damaged Reggie Maudling, and the prophet still waiting to happen, the above Enoch Powell.

Teddy won. The son of a Broadstairs builder had become the leader of Britain's most traditionalist party, a leading sign of the changes of the sixties. It had taken determination, ambition, ability, and a social skill that shrewdly recognised both what people of influence wanted and the importance of disguising with deference what he wanted. Luck played a part, too, of course. Luck that saw him through a landslide defeat in the 1966 general election to a surprising but comfortable majority in 1970 again against the other grammar school boy, Harold Wilson. But then it started to run out, as it so often does for prime ministers, faced with what Macmillan so famously (if apocryphally) described as 'events, dear boy, events'. To which, in Teddy's case, might be added the inevitable consequences of economic forces, geopolitical pressures and the tendency of previous administrations to indulge in preserving-container propulsion, or as it is known more informally, kicking the can down the road.

So he was faced by an economy under sustained attack from inflation given further impetus by the oil crisis which followed the Arab-Israeli war of 1973 and consequent rising unemployment in a labour market dominated by trade union power which a Labour government had tried to reform but couldn't. And not only was trade union power dominant but it was exercised by wily and determined leaders who proved adept at playing to their strength. Workers from an industry with no future intent on maximising the clout they had left and supported by the rest of the national workforce would have defeated any leader, and the miners defeated Teddy, who had also the accelerating Troubles in Northern Ireland to contend with while at the same time managing the wearing fulfilment of his European vision and taking the country into the Common Market. But even that last, a truly substantial achievement, failed to capture the public mood, which was at peak positivity where Europe has been concerned, grudging.

By 1974, he was exhausted, not least because he was almost ideally unsuited to circumstances which demanded confrontation and ruthlessness if he was to succeed. His whole political belief was to be inclusive, uniting of the nation; his heart simply wasn't in strategic strong-arming, whether it be against the miners or the angry and lethal people of Northern Ireland. What was required was nimble footwork and implacable conviction, and Teddy, decent, sensitive, Teddy, with an instinct for compromise for the greater good, had neither. And so his confrontations were inevitably too late, and clumsy. And so crisis, three-day weeks and powerlessness, in every sense, defined him, never left him. In February, 1974, in response to his question, 'who governs Britain?', Britain decided it wasn't Teddy and then told him again in October. The other grammar school boy had taken over; his side, always happy to leave sentiment until later, decided that twice was certainly once too many and demanded a leadership election. Which he had just lost. To her.

It was raining now in Wilton Street. He was still sitting at his desk in his study. He would have preferred his elegantly imposing drawing room but that had been blown up by the IRA in an attempt to kill him six weeks earlier which Teddy had brushed aside, or rather buried, to show it was an incident of no consequence which had no effect on him and would not deflect him from the fight against terrorism. Even that had not been enough to save him.

The irony, of course, which Teddy would never recognise, was that there was someone who could have helped, could have shared his travails, stiffened his sinews, suggested a little trimming and turning of the sort she was so good at because she managed it before anyone noticed (until hubris took over). Someone who could have been there for those lonely nights in the Downing Street flat with red boxes and hard thoughts. Someone who had just abruptly terminated his leadership.

He was still in love with her, of course. As much as when he helped her win hearts and minds in her first fight for Finchley by sending in big names and guns to speak for her and tickle the base. He helped her when she first entered parliament and he helped her, unobtrusively, nobly, to her first junior ministerial position. He'd even tried, once, to rekindle the past: he'd followed her suggestion and started sailing, progressing from a dinghy to a rather fine 32-footer which he'd named, secretly in her honour, *Pink Lady*. And then, after much deliberation, even drawing up a list of pros and cons, he'd taken the enormous step, for him, of inviting her down to Broadstairs to sail. She'd accepted, and although it meant having Denis and the twins along as well, he was almost beside himself with excitement. On a fine summer

Saturday morning, they arrived in Denis's typically flashy Rolls-Royce Silver Spirit, Margaret looking most fetching, Teddy thought, in white slacks and a striped matelot's T-shirt. He was less impressed by Denis's blazer and by the constant whining of the boy twin, but his sister was more fun, even if her spirited rendition of "What Shall We Do with the Drunken Sailor" became a tad repetitious. But at least his gruff warning that they would all have to help with the sailing persuaded Denis and Margaret to take off their matching Captain's caps, a distinct improvement, Teddy thought, at least for Margaret. His plans for regular visits that might lead to something more solitary and less collegiate, were doomed, however: once out of the harbour, morning cloud gone and a friendly, gentle wind blowing, Teddy, still eager to please, made the mistake of allowing the boy twin to take the tiller. The wretched child had immediately swung it vigorously to one side, with the result that Denis, clearly distracted by something from his duties, was sent hurtling over the side of *Pink Lady* into the drink. The boy started screaming and the girl thankfully stopped singing, but it soon became clear, from his peculiar thrashing movements, that Denis, who had spurned the offer of a life jacket, muttering something about needing access to his pockets, was not a strong swimmer. Teddy and Margaret, equally calm, arrived at the nearest lifebelt simultaneously; for one dangerous, delicious moment they stared at the floundering Denis and then into each other's eyes before Margaret grabbed the lifebelt and hurled it expertly at the struggling figure. Teddy had to concede that Denis took it all pretty well, apart from complaining that he'd 'lost his bloody hip flask', but it was clear that there would be no more sailing.

Nevertheless and perhaps more, he still didn't stop loving her, even though he began to wonder if he'd imagined that shared look across the lifebelt when she decided she would vote for Maudling in the leadership election. Ambition coinciding with longing, he invited her to his office to talk it over but as usual disguising his hurt far too well. 'We've known each other a long time, Margaret, haven't we?' he said to her. 'We know we disagree about some things, but we agree about more, don't we? It's mostly a matter of approach, isn't it? You are firmer in your views, more uncompromising in putting them across, than I am. But I would welcome that, I think it complements my way of working. Reggie is a charmer with a clever mind, but I think we understand each other better, with our backgrounds. We know he's the sort that our fathers used to say thinks the world owes them a living. We're workers, you and I. And we're friends, good friends. Or at least I like to think so.'

This, for Teddy, amounted to a *cri de coeur*. This, for Margaret, amounted to a little of what she wanted, why she had let it be known she was for Reggie in the first place. 'You're right, Ted,' she said, her voice taking on that breathy throatiness that always surprised her and entranced him. 'Could I really not vote for a man with whose trousers I'm intimately acquainted?' Each blushed, then laughed.

His secretary, a matronly figure, opened the door. 'Enoch Powell would like to see you, Mr Heath.' They both burst out laughing, leaving the secretary puzzled at such behaviour from her usually rigidly correct employer, which made them laugh all the more. Ted shrugged ruefully, which set off his shoulders far more attractively. He was about to suggest another, more informal meeting soon when they both heard a familiar high pitch and flat vowels in the outer office. They both placed a finger to the lips and Margaret left with thank yous to Teddy and a hello to Enoch, who stared after her with a wary puzzlement that didn't bode well for his election chances.

He sat down and stared at Teddy. 'Heath,' he intoned finally, 'I propose to talk to you on a matter of grave moment.' This proved to be the advisability of Teddy standing down so that Enoch could become leader, mostly it seemed on grounds of national destiny. There might have been more, but Teddy was more occupied in wistful thoughts of Margaret. He nodded firmly, but for a different reason, when Enoch wound up with, 'Mark my words well, Heath, this is an opportunity which, if not seized in the manner of that other Roman crossing that river other than the Tiber, will be lost for ever and grievous failure assured.' And so it proved for the heart of one of them and the sanity of the other.

ON THE MORNING OF FEBRUARY 12, 1975, AT 10.30 precisely, there was a knock on the Wilton Street door. Teddy heard it but let Tim answer. He heard her voice, and she was ushered into his study. He stood up as she came in and they continued standing, facing each other over a desk once again. 'Ted,' she said.

'Margaret,' he said.

'I'm sorry it had to be like this,' she said. Last night, she had been confirmed in a second round of voting as the new leader of the Conservative party.

'I'm sure,' said Teddy. There was a silence while she worked out what to say next and he continued to wonder how she could have done it to him. To him, the man who had loved her for 25 years; to him, the man who had helped her, promoted her, put her in his Cabinet, trusted her.

'I could see you were struggling, Ted. But I could also see that you were too proud, too committed to what you saw as your duty to your Party and your country, too noble – yes, noble! – to stand down. And when everyone was too self-serving and timid to do the right thing, I decided I had to do it, for your sake as much as mine. Do you understand?'

Teddy stared at her. 'Why didn't you come to me, tell me all this?'

'I did! I came to you and told you I was going to stand for leader. And what did you do? You just said, "You'll lose." You didn't even bother to look up! Was I really supposed to tell you how much I cared for you after that? When you have never given me a sign, never risked yourself to say or show you cared for me? You think I haven't noticed how careful you've been not to show the slightest affection for me in front of others? Even drumming your fingers while I have been trying to make points in Cabinet?'

Teddy was silent. What she said was true. And although he loved her, she could be a little repetitious in making her case. He knew he had behaved badly when she came to see him and told him she was running. And he knew why. But could he tell her now, in such circumstances and against the habit of his lifetime?

'You never showed me any sign either,' he said.

'Never showed you a sign! What did you want? It in writing? Ted, Ted, what a pair we could have been! I would have given up anything for you! But you never offered so much as a dalliance!'

'Is it too late?'

'Is it too late? Is it too late?! Of course it's too late!'

Margaret was flushed, with eyes blazing. He thought she'd never looked so magnificent.

'But we can still work together! We can be a tremendous team, with our different skills and attributes perfectly complementing each other. We are both determined with strong beliefs, but we can temper each other's convictions where compromise is necessary because we so admire – I'll go no further – each other. My tactical ability with your ability to analyse. My instinct to impose what I believe to be right with yours to find common ground. My instinct to fight with yours to reason. My outrage with your understanding. My rashness with your reserve. My strength with your sensitivity. Please, Ted. Join my shadow team! Chancellor, Home Secretary, Foreign Office, what would you like? Join me!'

Quandaried Teddy. Two-minded Teddy. Hurt for another against wounded love for oneself. Duty against peeve. Personal against political. The attraction of being close to the unavailable. The sweet and bitter against the endless ache of an incurable condition. The subordination to an (only just, possibly not) equal. Margaret scanned his face but couldn't detect any of what was passing behind the frown.

The frown turned into a grimace and then something else. He returned her anxious look and smiled. 'Yes,' he said, more shocked than she was. She smiled, a smile of relieved gratitude and warmth and affection. He had made her happy.

'What job?' she said, almost skittish.

'Shadow First Secretary of State,' he said, still smiling: her deputy. He came round the desk and they embraced, for the first time, and kissed for the first time, a botched job that ended up between his cheek and her mouth.

And so, in the sweet and heady world of what might have been, Margaret and Ted swept to power in 1979 after a period of vigorous opposition and faltering Labour government. Thus began a blessed period of sensible stability and sympathetic solutions: for twenty years, confrontations avoided, the economy cleverly reformed, old industries gradually replaced with new ones, old prides and followings respected, young and new ones encouraged, no small wars (the Argentines loved Teddy), leading all of Europe into a new era of gentle assimilation, subtle diplomacy and sensible sublimation of national sovereignties to the common good of care for people and planet.

But they remained just good friends.

Afterword

The basic facts laid out in this story are true: Ted and Margaret's backgrounds, early history and candidacy in adjoining constituencies are reported faithfully. They did speak in support of one another, but the events there and which followed them are imagined, including Margaret's impromptu use of her bloomers. Margaret did pass on a local farmer to her sister and married Denis in December 1952, but as far as I know did not meet Ted at the first night of 'South Pacific'. Nor did Ted own a yacht called 'Pink Lady', or go sailing with the Thatchers, but it was difficult to resist. The Kay mentioned is Kay Raven, Ted's only acknowledged girlfriend, who tired of waiting for him and married another. I have absolutely no evidence of any tendresse between Ted and Margaret, and there is a lot to the contrary, but I contend it might explain much. The meetings with Margaret, Harold Macmillan and Enoch Powell are imagined but draw on some fact. The last one at Wilton Street did take place, but the recollections of Ted and Margaret in their respective autobiographies do not tally in the slightest detail, allowing for various speculations of which mine is almost as feasible, apart from the outcome.

The reality, of course, was Ted's Great Sulk, which lasted until his death. There has been much speculation about the depth and source of his chronic and simmering surliness and, indeed, his determinedly bachelor status: I would argue that my explanation is at least as likely, and far less fetched than the disgraceful stuff peddled and believed after his death.

The politics of the seventies have been much studied, with the conclusion that it was a time of crisis unparalleled since 1939–45. Brexit and the pandemic of the 2020s are now clear, tempering and probably superior rivals, but perhaps the first jolt is the strongest, conveying a sense forgotten since the 1930s of a nation divided, angry and literally in the dark. There can be little argument either with the mistakes made by Ted and his government, but they were often prompted by his stubbornness in support of his ideal of One Nation, and some of the deft mix of certainty and the less noticed tactical cleverness that Margaret introduced would have been very helpful much earlier. Moreover, it surely does remain the case that Ted was confronted with a range of problems wider than any subsequent prime minister has so far had to face, and deserved better support than he received or was perhaps prepared to accept.

But this story doesn't claim to encompass and explain the wrapped enigma that was Ted any more than it does the seventies. His autobiography, for example, is a near 800-page work of intense self-justification and record defending, and yet you cannot dislike him (Margaret's is in two volumes, even longer, and can read like it was dictated over her shoulder, at pace). His way with an anecdote, too, would be impossible for someone without a well-developed sense of humour, something very few people would ever have expected from his public persona. My two favourites both involve Harold Macmillan: once, when Ted as Chief Whip approached him with a matter of concern, and the then prime minister gestured to the book he was reading and said, 'Can't you see I'm trying to finish 'Dombey and Son' before I go off on tour in the morning?'; the other when, on the night he became prime minister, he decided to take a break from choosing his Cabinet, and took Ted with him to dine at his club, The Turf. There was only one other member at the bar, who was reading the Evening Standard*'s report of Macmillan's elevation. He said to Macmillan, 'Have you had any good shooting recently?'; 'No,' answered the prime minister. 'What a pity,' responded the member. When they* *left to go to the dining room, where they were to dine on oysters, steak, coffee and cognac, the member looked up and said, 'Oh, by the way, congratulations.'*

And then there is the photograph taken in a restaurant in Marbella, where Heath went soon after the meeting in Wilton Street to recover from his defeat, staying at a villa arranged by Sir Timothy Kitson (Tim in the story), his erstwhile Principal Private Secretary, and his wife, Sally, one of Ted's several close (and platonic) woman friends: another puzzle. In the photograph, the man who has just suffered a humiliating defeat from which he seemed never to recover is laughing happily and looking for all the world like he hasn't a care in it.

FURTHER READING:

Margaret Thatcher, the Autobiography, *Margaret Thatcher*

Margaret Thatcher, Volume One, Not for Turning, *Charles Moore*

The Autobiography of Edward Heath, *Edward Heath*

Edward Heath, the Authorised Biography, *Philip Ziegler*

Seasons in the Sun, Britain 1974–1979, *Dominic Sandbrook*

When The Lights Went Out, Britain in the Seventies, *Andy Beckett*

1984

Fleeting Times

I REMEMBER FLEET STREET. IT WAS IN THE EIGHTIES, WHEN the whole frantic caravan following the fluttering mayfly of events stuttered, wobbled and then lurched off in different directions, never to have such concentrated daily madness again.

I didn't quite see it like that then, of course. Once you started to apply proportion, to appreciate that today's crucial event was tomorrow's vital report but the next day's vague memory, you were lost and best suited to doing something more sensible.

But, oh, the fun and dash of it! The gathering of news was essentially the same operation then as it is today, but then there was no rolling news, no 24-hour availability of a publishing platform, just one major deadline a day, with a very limited opportunity to update after that. Which meant more time, to wait, to relax, to fret, to enjoy your colleagues and rivals and the whole delicious thing, this mix of performance, fear, seriousness, frivolity and power not always completely in touch with responsibility.

They were enjoyable, too, these colleagues and rivals: my, but they were. You will never find a finer, friendlier, unstuffy, mad, maddening, witty, wise, even heroically dull collection of disparates united by not much more than a talent for turning a quick word or turning quick words into something better. Go elsewhere for rock-steady reliability, unstinting loyalty and ever-available sympathy (these people had, quite understandably, only enough for their really needy selves), but I can guarantee that it will not be half as stimulating, annoying, entertaining or irredeemably unhinged as the company of journalists.

And all of it careering, crashing, spinning, whirling, racing and often foundering on an ocean of alcohol. Alcohol that lent inspiration and gave courage; alcohol that infuriated or calmed, passed or piqued the time, lubricated necks and conversation. Drugs were then a minority interest, drink was the thing. I remember as a law student up in Holborn one evening straying down past the law courts and into what I didn't at first realise was this Fleet Street, caught between the quiet of the less lively end of the Strand and the City, from where the bankers and brokers had long since fled for the day. Cheery lights and open doors beckoned in this sudden oasis, not from the newspaper offices, but from the pubs: The Harrow, The Punch, The Bell and more, including The White Hart, better known as The Stab (In the Back was, fittingly, silent). And above all was the noise, the noise of conversation that was Fleet Street's fodder and delight, not a murmur but a roar of raised voices and laughter that would soon be overtaken by the steady thud of the giant printing presses rolling out the results of the drinkers' earlier activity. Who would not be caught, entranced?

I certainly was, to the extent of abandoning my infant and almost certainly doomed legal career to take up the then highly advisable and near obligatory journalism training in the provinces. I got a job in Liverpool, whose natives, with their remarkable mix of conspiratorial drama, overshared wit and knowing exaggeration provided the finest material in the country on which to practise and practice. My first day on a local paper, I sat down at a typewriter, rolled up the piece of paper in it and read, 'No Grads Here'. The lack of an exclamation mark was somehow more threatening, although it turned out to be (almost) a joke. It's perhaps forgotten that much of the news in those days was produced by people without tertiary and with often patchy secondary education. But they had wanted to do this, and had worked and pushed hard to get it: some were workmanlike, some were more flairful, but all could work with discipline to a deadline with the determined enthusiasm of the unentitled. And they liked a laugh.

Which we needed, in the eighties. Although the seventies are the popular first choice for Worst British Decade of the Second Half of the Twentieth Century, there's a good case to be made for the next one. Intense terrorism including the near assassination of the prime minister, hunger strikers serially dying, highest unemployment, record inflation, riots in English cities, the longest miners' strike, the steel strike, and a small but vicious foreign war. No wonder the romance, engagement and marriage of the Prince of Wales and Diana Spencer was embraced so enthusiastically, and unquestioningly. Yo-yos were popular, too.

When you're reporting the news, though, a detachment develops, not necessarily cynical but rather in the manner of a photographer behind the camera or a surgeon behind the scalpel. And everything seemed bigger in the eighties, from all of the above to shoulder pads and the collapse of the world order. And when all that is going on, all seems less remarkable. Besides, I was distracted, intrigued by the Fleet Street beast, and in particular by the organ of it that had, a little unexpectedly, hired me, The Daily Cable.

The Cable was very much a Conservative newspaper, read mostly by lower orders of class and accomplishment than those rather fewer who took 'the top people's paper', the Epoch, a complacently worthy production until recently, when, in the new sharp-elbowed and -suited spirit of the entrepreneurial eighties, it had been acquired by a chippy, amoral Australian, Dan 'The Lion' Burdock. This was a worry for the Cable, as the Epoch was now beginning to trespass upon its rival's previously exclusive field of entertaining, often racy, material camouflaged by respectably dull presentation. Its third page, in particular, was, once the grey and lengthy columns were penetrated, a straight-faced so all the more entertaining chronicle of British bad behaviour, often involving clergymen, animals and aristocrats, not always separately. Such matters were of course noticed by the more popular papers like the Daily Hail, the Daily Reflecter, the Daily Expect and Burdock's brash newcomer, The Light; but the Cable gave them much more space and didn't suffer from the eccentric prudishness of the populars, which permitted photos of women with bare breasts but couldn't possibly allow the spelling of bollocks, bastard or bullshit without employing all sorts of coy symbols.

The changing Epoch had no such qualms, but the Cable's concern was mitigated by its much larger circulation, confidence in a successful formula even it didn't really understand, and the devotion and deep pockets of its owner, Lord Hindmost, with whom a more contrasting character than Dan Burdock could not be imagined. Hindmost was a shy and retiring man even though he commanded an entire floor of the paper's Fleet Street offices, a magnificently Mussolini-style piece of architecture that featured an extravagant relief above its front entrance showing two wing-hatted messengers poised to race off in opposite directions to gather in the news. It seemed somehow typical of the Cable that they were chained at the heels and so would fall over the moment they started. Lord Hindmost's copiously panelled floor was up on high, set back behind a balcony and, improbably, a small lawn which one of his staff would mow with an old-fashioned hand mower every Wednesday. Rebellious staff had pondered launching moles with tiny parachutes down on to this immaculate sward, but, as with much else at 531, Fleet Street, had never got round to it. The printers of the Cable, on the other hand, were far more focused on pursuit of their goals. Their unhesitatingly exercised leverage on such a perishable product as a daily newspaper was seen as a little rich by even the mightiest trade union baron increasingly engaged in a climactic battle with a Government stiffened by the righteous resolve of the grocer's daughter from Grantham.

Lord Hindmost was not only shy but given to fainting at moments of high stress. Such a one was the reception for the journalists returning from the 1939–45 war. As he crumpled, there was an unseemly rush to become the first person he saw when he came round. This was won by the High Court reporter, whose ministrations secured him, unspokenly, the position for life (he was still there, now 76). But His Lordship was an assiduous proprietor, taking a very keen and active interest in the minutiae of his newspapers (the Cable had a Sunday edition). He retained a butler on his floor, who would receive the inky proofs of the next day's pages with an aloofness worthy of Mr Wooster's primary carer. Occasionally, one might encounter Lord Hindmost in the lift, an uneasy experience featuring only ever one question, as to the quality of the food in the staff canteen, which went some way to explaining why this never changed.

It would be fair to say, though, that shyness was not much in evidence on the other floors, particularly the basement, thunderous with the noise of printers typing metal lines of type and the roll of the presses, and especially the first floor, almost as noisy with reporters on banks of desks in the newsroom shouting into phones and typing and cursing ever more feverishly as the Cable came grudgingly towards edition under a deep haze of cigarette smoke, while in the midst of it all was often the Cable's religious correspondent, a distinguished man of the cloth, writing his copy in longhand, smiling benevolently. Even though I had come from a large provincial paper printing a morning edition and numerous evening editions, I was taken aback by the size of the Cable's staff. Eventually I worked out that this was because at any one time a third would be off, a third would be working, and a third would be in the pub. Did I mention there was quite a lot of drinking? A typical early evening would see at least one reporter dictating his story to another one because he was incapable of typing it. I once watched one of the paper's most distinguished correspondents, a man with the ear of Cabinet ministers, archbishops, dukes and captains of industry, type furiously for some ten minutes, at which point he left to relieve himself. Curious to see what bombshell was being primed and loaded, I took a look at the copy in the typewriter. It was complete gibberish: senses scrambled by excessive intake, he had placed his fingers on the wrong keys when he started and had apparently still not noticed that all was not well. I myself was not averse to a drink but I knew I was out of my league when in my second week, just before 11am, I was passed a note which read simply, 'Heart starter?'.

On the other side of the vast open-plan room sat the subeditors, the journalists who edited the variable output for sense, style and length. They were an entirely different but no less fascinating breed, many of whom had chosen the regular if dark hours better to pursue other interests. Novelists were two-a-penny, successful ones less so, but interests were cast much wider than that. The Cable had a Chief Bard of the Eisteddfod, the proprietor of a sausage shop, several scratch golfers and a sprinkling of aristocrats, including one French baron who seemed more English. Encountering him one Sunday in the pouring rain on his way into the office, I asked this haughty figure in splendid tweeds why he wasn't using an umbrella. He responded with perplexed disdain: 'What? With country clothes?'

I see I have mentioned only male journalists. They were indeed in the great majority, but Fleet Street was distinguished by some tremendous women correspondents who had to be: they were tough, ambitious and twice as good as the average man but also highly skilled in dealing with hacks whose opinion of their magnetic appeal to the opposite sex was matched only by their powers of self-delusion and the clumsiness of their approach. I remember, for instance, an overwatered but height-challenged reporter confiding to one of the grandest of the Street's *grandes dames,* dressed as ever in the useful but misleading camouflage of a figure-hugging outfit, 'Do you know, I've always wanted to screw you.'

Literally looking down on him, she replied, 'And if I ever find that you have, I will be very, very cross indeed.'

That was in The Keys to the Kingdom, the pub that was so close to the Cable's offices that it was part of the building. Here all life, drama and romance played out: scoops, scoops that got away, scoops that weren't appreciated, my editor doesn't understand me, your editor doesn't understand you, did you hear about old Gerry, that's nothing, I was told what really happened, why did they give that story to Frank, I could have done it better, you could have done it better, my editor is a bastard, yours is too, is that the time, all right, then, just a quick one.

The Keys was handy and often attracted friends and rivals from other papers, always good for some heavy joshing and hints about upcoming exclusives that would leave egg over all sorts of faces, but no one came for the decor, which was consistent with all the other pubs in Fleet Street, where shabby chic had long been enthusiastically pioneered, if more in the adjective than the noun. Even the posh wine bar, Le Plonc, frequented by the gentlemanly (women were discouraged) journalists with a column or editorial rank, had some sort of brown linoleum on the floor. When the landlord finally replaced the carpet in The Keys, it was cause for regret: as one regular put it, 'Just when the old one was starting to take spin.'

Scoops, though. That was what every real reporter was after. But not just any scoop, not just an exclusive story, a story no one else had. And the kind of that story depended on the real reporter's newspaper. The upmarket press liked scoops with a bit of heft, a bit of consequence, Governments shaken, inquiries ordered, corruption exposed, that sort of thing. The tabloid press liked scoops with a bit of sex and celebrity, betrayal and humiliation. The mid-market press liked scoops that mixed all that up together, had a little more significance than celebrities behaving badly and was less complicated than doggedly pursuing and patiently unravelling misdoing. Instant impact was the thing, the simpler and wider the appeal the better.

I wasn't a real reporter. True, I had been inspired to become a journalist by Bob Woodward and Carl Bernstein bringing down Richard Nixon, but I soon discovered that my gift, if you could call it that, was more, how shall we say, gossamer. I had what the trade called 'the touch', the ability 'to cook up a soufflé'. I was the man given the 'light and bright' stories, the 'colour writer', called in to use my descriptive powers in the sort of article that appeared with the main story, bringing the event, hopefully, to life.

I could see what was a good story and relish tales about the getting of it – 'So there I was, lying horizontal behind the front hedge as old Buggins from the *Reflector* walked past on the pavement on the other side, I could have touched him' – but I lacked one talent of the three famously nominated by Nicholas Tomalin as necessary in the best reporters: 'ratlike cunning, a plausible manner, and a little literary ability'. Tomalin himself was rather better than that and was robbed of becoming yet better by a Syrian missile on the Golan Heights in 1973; his verdict is endlessly repeated because it deserves to be. The very finest example of it at the *Cable* was our legendary chief reporter, Richard 'Dickie' Dasher. Dickie was then in his mid-fifties and at the height of his powers of shameless gambits and sharp practice, a Londoner, with all that entails, masquerading just less than convincingly as a gentleman, with a hail-fellow-well-met manner and dark blue pinstripe suit. His customary term of address was 'dear boy' or 'darling girl'; he was a bundle of nervous energy and relentless in pursuit of 'a good tale'. He might have served as the model for the old Punch cartoon where two journalists are discussing a third, 'Old Whatever would sell his grandmother for a good story,' while just round the corner from them another is standing next to a sweet old woman, holding a placard which reads, 'Grandmother for Sale, £10'. That was Dickie.

He was in the Editor's office when I entered, a little nervously, as no one liked being summoned to see this august grumpy figure. Mind you, journalists are insecure by temperament. If, for example, I greeted a friend at the *Cable* with the usual anodyne, 'John, how are you?', he would invariably reply, with genuine concern, 'why, what have you heard?'. But, this time at least, the Editor was, if not exactly bonhomous, not frightening, either. In fact, he seemed quite excited, although not as excited as Dickie, who was hopping from one leg to the other while his neat moustache had taken on a quivering life of its own. 'Ah,' said the Editor. 'Got something for you. Terrific colour piece. You're to go with Dickie. Tell him, Dickie.'

'Dear boy, dear boy, do you know Ralph Edmondson?'

I adopted my best keenly interested look and lied. 'Hmm, sounds familiar.'

'You must know Ralph, you must have heard of Ralph, old hand, good operator, real professional, worked everywhere for us. He's now living in Arrmiati, retired but still with an ear to the ground.'

'Of course, Ralph,' I said, which was all I could say, as I had no idea where Arrmiati was. I should have stuck with that but I'm not very good at bluffing. 'Yes, Ralph Edmondson. Doesn't he have a parrot or something?'

'No, no,' said Dickie. 'That's Sidney Nickle, in Amman.'

'Get on with it,' said the Editor.

'Yes, yes, well, old Ralph has given us a very, very good one, a great one, a hot one. He says he knows where Lord Archcon is!'

Well. Lord Archcon. Even I knew who Lord Archon was. But then few sentient Britons didn't. Jeremy Archcon, man of many parts, all loud. Eton-educated, he had thrown up more conventional occupations to become one of the country's top National Hunt jockeys. He then went into television where he won an even wider audience, not least because of his clever touch of wearing a crimson trilby during racing coverage. Becoming a Tory MP seemed an obvious step, and he performed equally colourfully in the House and on wider television until he resigned over the imposition of VAT on straw. An imprudent investment in air-conditioned horse boxes with piped music left him with money to make, which he secured through writing acclaimed if breathless bestsellers set in and on the Turf.

Reconciled with the Tory party, he played a leading part in the 1979 general election and was rewarded with a life peerage. All seemed set fair for continued and increasingly self-satisfied success. But then, in a remarkable turn of events, it was revealed that his books were written by his wife, Jolene, a retiring Australian-born academic lecturing in Medieval History at Oxford. That might not have been enough to torpedo his career entirely but the bizarre circumstances surrounding the exposure certainly were. His personal assistant, one Johnson, had threatened to go to the newspapers with the story for motives which later became all too clear. That evening, Johnson had heard a loud report followed by a howl near his home in Hampstead Garden Suburb. Shortly afterwards, his pet, Boris, an incontinent sheepdog, arrived in a nervous state, bleeding from a nick on his leg consistent with being hit by a bullet of small calibre. Nearby was found a piece of rump steak; Johnson concluded that Boris, being a vegetarian, had rejected the meat, thus narrowly avoiding death. Outraged, he carried out his threat, selling his account to one of Burdock's Sunday newspapers for a large sum of money. Archcon was approached by the newspaper immediately prior to publication and, unable to face the humiliation of bogus authorship and more besides, had vanished. A pile of his clothing, with the scarlet trilby neatly placed on top and weighed down by two large pebbles, was discovered on the beach at Frinton; matters were muddied even further by the disappearance at the same time of his favourite horse, the legendary steeplechaser and high-earning stud, Sonnygar, a nation's favourite. Newspaper coverage, understandably, had been huge. Lady Archcon, to much surprise, had seemed positively to enjoy the notoriety, abandoning medieval history with alacrity, confirming her authorship and her relationship with Johnson, whom she soon abandoned for a hirsute Hungarian antique dealer in Chelsea, where she was now living in some style, amply supported by the publicity-filliped sales of her books, which had departed the Turf to racier climes, with titles like 'Now, Sailor' and 'The Heart Burns'. Of her errant spouse, whom she had divorced on grounds of desertion, there had still been no sign, five years later. Until now.

'Ralph's heard from a very reliable source that Archcon's living upcountry near the border with Miradora and passing himself off as a German from Paraguay. He's got a ranch – with horses,' said Dickie, particularly enjoying the last implication.

All Fleet Street would have been giddily agog at this, and although not exactly an exception, I was always a little in two minds about these 'foreign jollies', as we called them. Flying was never a joy, accommodation could be iffy, and was bound to be ghastly upcountry from Arrmiati, wherever it was. Communications in those pre-mobile and online days were always a nightmare, often demanding more ingenuity than getting the story itself. Then there was the tendency of superiors to shoot the messenger if it all went horribly wrong. And this was before taking into account mosquitoes and that sort of thing, like the language. It would never have done to reveal this reluctance, though, so I settled for what I hoped was a professional cavil: 'How reliable is this very reliable source? Long way to go on a tip.'

'Ralph says the source is very reliable, and that's good enough for me,' said Dickie. 'This is the man who found Shabassa, after all.' Shabassa was the African dictator who had disappeared in his private jet after being ousted, leaving the heads of several of his enemies in his refrigerator ('Fridge Fiend', 'Heads Cold', 'Iced!'). Ralph, acting on another tip, had tracked him down to Basingstoke, much to the embarrassment of the Foreign Office.

'The important thing,' said the Editor, 'is to make sure no one else gets wind of this.'

'Well, there's not much competition out there,' said Dickie. This was true: British newspapers, particularly the popular ones, had never been much interested in Latin America, beyond the occasional foray into the larger countries, and then only for something disobliging, revolutions or some such. The quality press, as it liked to be known, no longer made enough money to staff more than a few of the world's capitals, and to contract coverage in a few more. The Cable, which was in reality a 'pop' pretending to be a quality, was fortunate in being owned by the last proprietor careless of budget, and so had a remarkable range of stringers, freelance journalists retained on a small fee who would clatter into life on Telex copy transmitting machines irregularly and rarely. Thus Ralph, who had retired on the proceeds of a life of outrageous expense claims, and was living where they might go furthest, in Buccan, which, Dickie revealed along with this in the pub later, was the Central American country that had Arrmiati as its capital.

'It's here that worries me,' said the Editor. 'We all know everywhere round here leaks more than the bloody Bismarck. This must be kept on a need-to-know basis. You'd best get away as soon as possible. Photographer?'

'Clive,' said Dickie. 'Got to be Clive.' Clive Stiffley was an exception to the usual Fleet Street photographer, possibly the most terrifying group of people in the country, in that he was suave, cultured, bouffant-haired, almost languid. He was no less effective but far better suited to a story that would involve some subtlety and food not necessarily improved by brown sauce.

This was Friday: we were on our way by the next Tuesday, after some heroic refusals to have another drink and be drawn on anything by another group almost as terrifying, Fleet Street colleagues and rivals who sniff that something is going on and exercise all the wiles of possibly the most skilled interrogators in the world to find out what it is. We took separate flights from Heathrow to Madrid and flew to Miradora to fox any of the excellently inquisitive freelances who covered the airports in those days and would have tipped off favoured newsdesks if they saw as distinguished and distinctive a pair as Dasher and Stiffley off somewhere interesting.

I LIKED CENTRAL AMERICA. SOMETHING JOURNALISTS OF the jobbing and general variety are very good at is quickly acquiring a confident, sweeping, overall view unmuddied by too much research. Mine took place in the *Cable*'s library, a multi-aisled and comparatively hushed repository of endless newspaper cuttings and mostly out-of-date reference books. It was staffed by librarians of a familiarly Fleet Street eccentric turn, masters and mistresses of its arcane workings and holders of priceless nuggets of abstruse information. 'Ah, yes, Buccan,' said Edwin, a pale man with the manner of a fallen Jesuit. 'Captured by Drake in 1595 and never given back. The diplomatic posting equivalent of the Chiltern Hundreds. The last news we had from Buccan was in 1968 when Burton and Taylor sheltered there after the gilded couple's yacht was blown off course by a tropical storm. Slightly disobliging about the place, as I recall. Flies, no air conditioning, no one seemed to know who they were, you know the form.' This turned out, as far as I could see from an old Foreign Office handbook and a handful of cuttings, to be Edwin's usual impeccable summary. Buccan was indeed a British colony whose vital importance as a grower and exporter of mahogany had ceased almost overnight as iron and steel took over from wood in shipbuilding and other industries. As there wasn't really anything else there worth exploiting, it had faded from notice, which suited its inhabitants, mostly Maya, descendants of a sophisticated culture who had been unimpressed by first Spanish then British customs, which seemed principally to consist of slavery, something they themselves had abandoned several centuries earlier. Quite soon, Buccan's hitherto largely unnoticed advantages as a tax haven, tourist idyll and convenient conduit for the drugs trade would spoil all this, but for now it continued to snooze its dreams of lost empires and echoing forests.

We travelled from San Jude, the decaying but charming old colonial capital of Miradora, to the border with Buccan, passing some splendid Mayan ruins on the way which Dickie and Clive resolutely refused to have a look at. 'Got to keep moving, dear boy,' said Dickie, who was cutting a natty look in a white linen suit, apt Panama and a regimental tie to which he was not entitled. 'The hunt is on and there are no expenses in ruins.'

'He's right,' said Clive, immaculate in blue linen shirt, khaki chinos and one of those beige photographer waistcoats with endless pockets which he pioneered. 'Eye on the prize, young man.' They were in the back of our car; I was up front with the driver. This was Chi, a grave fellow who claimed to have links with both Miradora and Buccan so, naturally, I decided to pick up some of the local griff using the trusted method that makes the taxi driver the most influential source of opinion in the world. Nuggets of obscure information hinting quite falsely at in-depth knowledge are particularly useful to the colour writer: someone had long ago left in my flat an account by Aldous Huxley of his travels in Central America, and this made quite interesting reading on the flight over, particularly in the matter of the character of the locals. Huxley seemed to think that they were rather miserable and closed; in my brief experience, the grave faces hid broad smiles ready to respond to any invitation to marvel at the idiocy of the world. While Clive slept and Dickie worried endlessly out loud about getting to Arrmiati as quickly as possible, I asked Chi about a ceremony Huxley had observed, The Dance of the Conquistadores, where the participants went through solemn stately movements in antique costume and elaborate false mustachios. Old Aldous seemed to think this was a unique example of the conquered celebrating conquest;

Chi's face split into one of those smiles as he said, 'It's a joke! They're making fun of them!' I began to think that the Central American viewpoint and that of Fleet Street were quite similar.

We reached Arrmiati after a drive of a couple of hours along a straight road which was of excellent quality, having been built some time ago by some Royal Engineers with nothing else to do. While Dickie and Clive dozed, Chi enlivened the monotony of the endless forest on either side by revealing the etymology of the name Arrmiati. The freebooters who had followed in Drake's wake, he said, had never properly named their rackety settlement on the Buccan coast, being more focused on grog, plunder and arguing with each other. They dwindled and disappeared when Britain decided their anti-Spanish usefulness was outweighed by their lawlessness and sent in the Royal Navy. The colonisers who succeeded the pirates were of a slightly more legitimate turn, and, anxious to foster good relations with the indigenous population, thought they would adopt the Mayan name for the area. Thus Arrmiati, which Chi invited me to pronounce slowly while thinking of pirates. Another tease. 'And Buccan, too?' I asked.

Chi smiled his smile again and suggested adding the 'eer' sound. No, he said, this was not generally known, and certainly not by the colonial authorities. 'They've never asked,' he said.

I myself had been wondering about those worthies, and in particular whether Archcon wasn't taking a risk concealing himself in a British territory. 'Don't be silly, old chap,' Ralph Edmondson said to me in the bar of the Hotel Arrmiati later that day. 'Safer here than anywhere. The administration is composed almost entirely of leading colonists descended from the original founders, although nature has taken its course and they are now brown rather than white. They are interested only in maintaining the status quo. Exports of forest products provide just enough to secure that – any innovation and industry would bring all sorts – Americans! – down here and upset everything.

They're assisted in this by British career diplomats with their careers behind them who prize peace and quiet above all. No one wants to rock the boat by coming across one of the most famous fugitives in the world.'

Dickie and Clive nodded sagely at this and continued to sip their drinks, a cold beer for Dickie and, remarkably, creme-de-menthe with ice for Clive. 'Not many pickings for a hack, then,' I said.

'Exactly,' said Ralph. 'I'm retired and don't want any temptation. I've been through all that, now I just want to sit and read Dickens. Bit of a bother when this fell into my lap, to be honest, but it is a cracker.' Ralph, as befits a correspondent of the old school, was dressed smartly in shirt and slacks that conformed to a general impression of frayed edges. He drank some more of his whisky, which he was drinking in our honour and at our expense.

The hotel was civilised in a fading way. We were drinking at one of the tables on a terrace with those colonnades the British had taken with them everywhere, not quite as convincing as the Roman originals, rather like their empire. Dickie was still anxious about competition. He had been shooting worried glances at a group of men on another table: 'There's definitely something familiar about them, Ralph,' he said. 'Do you know them?'

'Yes,' said Ralph. 'They're a little group who come over from Britain every year. Friends of the hotel's owner. You might have heard of him. Jack Shoe.'

'Jack Shoe? Jack Shoe!' Dickie was even more excited. 'Ex-Detective Superintendent Jack Shoe, former head of the Flying Squad? Here?!'

'And I suppose,' said Clive, 'his friends over there are all ex-detectives as well?'

'Yes. Amiable bunch.' Ralph raised his glass to the men, who raised theirs and smiled back.

'But why is Shoe here?' demanded Dickie while nodding and smiling back at the other group. 'Is he undercover? He knows me, Ralph.'

'Don't be silly, Dickie,' said Ralph. 'Jack's well retired. He's like me, looking for peace and quiet and somewhere that'll make his pension go further. And he was never that good at recognising people, was he? You must remember the time he let Scarface Tomkins through the cordon at Stepney.'

I was a touch concerned, too, at this unexpected development. 'But doesn't that make it a bit awkward with Archcon, having all these large policemen about?'

'Not really,' said Ralph equably. 'For a start, as I understand, the only crime Archcon has committed, at least that we know about, is – allegedly – conspiring, unsuccessfully, to shoot a dog. Second, those chaps are not only retired, they're on holiday. Third, Yard detectives of that vintage, you won't remember, before your time, weren't, how shall we put it, very good.'

Clive nodded, Dickie continued to keep an eye on the former guardians of the law, and I asked Ralph, 'Kidnapping a horse?'

'It was his horse,' said Ralph, making a fair point.

'So where is he?' asked Dickie, reasonably if impatiently.

'Couple of hundred miles north-west of here. Unpaved road, six hours' drive.'

'How did you find him?'

'Really, Dickie. Contacts sacred and all that.'

'But we're paying, Ralph.'

'Well, a few weeks ago I went for a spot of fishing up the Mopan river. Snappers, Tarpon, you know. My guide, nice chap, took me off for some *aguardiente* in one of the villages. There was another bloke from farther up the river, more chat-chat, and then talk about this new arrival, pretending to be German but obviously a Brit, careful with his spending in the nearest town, rides in on his horse, tells anyone admiring it that it's nothing special, just a horse, but can shift a bit.'

'Ha, excellent!' said Dickie, clearly relieved. 'Tell us more. What is his place like? Is it easy to find?'

'I don't think it will be too difficult, with the guide.'

'Don't think? Haven't you been there?'

'Not as such.'

'Not as such?! We've come 6,000 miles for this, and you're telling us all you've got is some tittle-tattle about a man and a horse? Bloody hell, Ralph, I've staked my reputation on yours for being reliable! Even Lord Hindmost's going to kick up if this isn't Archcon!'

'Calm down, Dickie. Who else is it going to be? Don't fall into the usual trap of underestimating the natives, old boy. The Mayans were inventing zero while we were still counting on our fingers. These are their descendants and they're just as clever, although they mostly choose to hide it as it makes life simpler with all these jumped-up colonials around. They can tell when a Brit is pretending to be German, just as they can spot when he's being shifty. It's Archcon, age, description, timing, everything.'

'I expect he's wearing a red trilby, too,' said Clive.

'Funny you should mention that,' said Ralph.

I could see that Dickie was about to explode, but fortunately or not, we were interrupted by a short bespectacled man in his forties wearing a crumpled linen suit who looked hot. 'Ah, Edmondson,' he said with an attempt at authority undercut by his appearance. 'Got friends visiting, eh? Who are you? Old journalist chums on the trail of a scoop thingie?'

Some short silences feel longer. This one seemed longer than Ralph's bar bill. Eventually, Clive broke it: 'Ha, very good, wish we were! In fact, we're members of Ralph's old stamp collecting club come out for a spot of fishing and to see how the old rogue's getting on.' Dickie and I nodded enthusiastically while Ralph, more subtly, smiled enquiringly at the man, who was now mopping his brow with a disreputable handkerchief and eyeing the drinks on our table. 'The Papamalil's the one for you, tarpon's as big as taxis. Join you?'

'That would be splendid, Tench,' said Ralph, 'but the chaps have only just got in. Going off for a siesta before dinner. You can buy me one if you like. Large Scotch?'

'Is that the time?' said the man. 'Just realised, can't stop, got to see His Nibs. Another time? Happy fishing, chaps, don't let them get away.' He left quickly, still mopping.

Ralph answered our looks: 'Ah, yes, a little confusing, given the fishing context, but that is Tench, Gerald, First Secretary to the Governor. Peak of his achievement after Pitcairn Island, nothing to worry about, especially the slightest chance of getting him to open his wallet.'

'His Nibs is the Governor, I presume,' said Dickie.

'Ah, yes, even less to worry about there. Sir Dingle Ferry hasn't been the same since the husband of the wife with whom he had been canoodling introduced a Jumping Viper into his lavatory.'

'Stamp collecting, Clive?' said Dickie.

'Sorry, best I could come up with at short notice. I thought it was more likely than water colours or rambling, looking at us.'

'Actually, the Buccan Penny Dreadful is worth quite a bit,' I said. 'Came about after an unfortunate slip left Queen Victoria's head off. Used to collect stamps when I was a kid.' I added the last bit after getting familiar 'colour writer, not a real journalist' looks from the rest.

'Hello, Ralph.' Another man had now joined us. 'Friends from back home?'

'That's right. Frank, Brian, Chris, this is Jack Shoe, owner of the hotel.' Jack smiled at Chris and Brian, or Dickie and Clive, both of whom I was surprised to see were now wearing dark glasses. I hadn't thought of it but I wasn't too concerned, as I'd never met Jack Shoe before. He was tall, with a military bearing and a moustache to match Dickie's. We smiled a greeting back.

'Don't I know you two from somewhere?' said Jack. His voice had been honed and stilted by a lifetime of giving grim statements and deliberate evidence. 'Probably not, you know what old coppers are like.'

'No, I don't think so,' said Clive. 'We're old stamp collecting chums of Ralph, over for a spot of fishing and a catch-up.'

'I didn't know you were into stamps, Ralph,' said Jack. 'After a Buccan Penny Dreadful, are we?'

'That would be something,' said Clive. 'But we wouldn't lose our heads over it.'

'Very good, Brian. My friends and I are off for a spot of fishing, too. Up the Papamalil. We might bump into each other.'

'Yes, we very well might, that would be fun,' said Ralph.

'Mind how you go,' said Jack, going off to join his chums.

'Brian?' said Clive to Ralph.

WE SET OUT EARLY THE NEXT DAY, WITH RALPH GRUMBLING, Dickie insistent and still worried about Jack Shoe, Clive dozing and me up front in an elderly long-wheel-base Land Rover with Chi. The Land Rover was apparently owned by some cousin or other in Chi's extensively extended cross-border family, and he said he knew the way to Lubaantun, the town where Ralph's contact was waiting. I wondered if Ralph's contact might be another of Chi's relatives but I kept it to myself as I didn't enjoy the world-weary looks and mutters about the Pope's religious affiliation that were my usual lot when working abroad.

It took us eight hours to get to Lubaantun. The last few miles were difficult, but two hours had been taken up by lunch: whatever else, Dickie was keen on maintaining standards. Lubaantun did see some tourism, so we were not as conspicuous as we might have been. To further the impression, Ralph had arranged that we should meet in the church, which was quite substantial and unlike any other I had been in. The Catholic Church in Central America had begun by being as intolerant as usual and burning Mayan writings and insisting on baptisms but it had also worked its other, subtler, trick of allying with older beliefs. Thus, Chi informed us, the church sat on steps of an earlier temple: there were 18, the number of months in the ancient Mayan year. On them, shamans were burning incense and praying to whom they chose. Inside, it was dark, with low stone altars up the centre of the church, irregularly lit by candles. A sombre and murky Spanish oil painting of the crucifixion was splashed and stained with *aguardiente*, the Mayan favoured offering. At the altar rails, a Mayan couple were praying to whom they chose. Ralph's contact materialised out of the shadows in the same way as Chi. He confirmed via Chi that the German Englishman was still out at his ranch, and, after a negotiation with Ralph and Dickie, provided directions. Because it would take a couple hours and the sun switched off like a light early in Buccan, it was decided, after more rumination about Archcon's likely reaction to a Land Rover full of hacks, to spend the night in Lubaantun and set off early in the morning. After a meal which prompted Clive into unkind and lengthy comparisons with some of his favourite spots in Paris and New York, we retired to shared bedrooms. I drew Ralph and fell asleep to yet another Fleet Street story, about old Bob causing a terrible stink by getting tight on a royal tour and putting a Buck House assistant press officer over his knee and biting her bottom at a reception at Government House in St Kitts in 1981 or was it 1982? This did not help my dreams, which majored on teeth.

It was tense the next morning. Dickie gave Chi another lecture on the necessity for secrecy: 'Nobody must know we are journalists, *non periodistas, comprende?*' Chi, whose English was excellent, nodded gravely as usual. Ralph looked terrible, Clive immaculate with matching camera bag and a striking red *keffiyeh*, the Arab scarf much favoured by foreign correspondents for its touch of knowing swagger. No clues there, then. We reached the alleged Archcon's ranch after an hour or so along some pretty rough tracks which explained his preference for riding into town. It was an unremarkable collection of wooden buildings, stables, barns and a bungalow with a verandah, where a man looking very much like Archcon was sitting. If he was surprised by our arrival he didn't show it.

'*Guten Tag,*' he said, coming towards us with a smile. Dickie had obviously rehearsed his opening line. 'Fancy seeing you here, my lord. Long way from Kempton Park. Do you remember me? Richard Dasher of The Daily Cable.'

'Excusing me? Vot is dis? Kempton Park? Daily Cable? You are not the *veterinari?* Herr horse doctor? *Donner und blitzen!*'

Dickie didn't falter. 'Oh, come off it, Jeremy, the comic book German isn't fooling anybody. How's tricks?'

'Jeray-mi? Jeray-mi? Vis Jeray-mi, vot is he? I am Count Otto von Sputelhanger and I must ask you to leave my property,' said the alleged Archcon, before continuing: 'Bugger it. Not any better for seeing you, Dickie, old son. How on earth did you find me?'

'This is Ralph Edmondson, the legendary Daily Cable correspondent who, unfortunately for you, Jeremy, thought he had retired to a deserved quiet life in Arrmiati until he heard about you.'

'Good day, my lord,' said Ralph at his most fruity. 'Nice spread you've got here. Love to have a look at the horses.'

I had to give Archcon his due: he had taken all this in his stride and was now pouring out the rueful charm like a geyser. 'Ha, very good, Ralph. Actually, there's only one horse here, and I think you know his name. I'm well rumbled, aren't I? Still, I'm not sure I would have stayed up here that much longer. It is a bit primitive. All you can get is the BBC World Service and their racing coverage is dreadful.'

'Lord Archon, I'm Clive Stiffley, the photographer,' said Clive a little redundantly, seeing as he had already shot off half a roll.

'Of course you are, dear boy. I suppose you want a snap of me with my darling Sonnygar? Now he quite likes it out here. All the same to him as long as he can stretch his legs and get his oats. Not much stud work around, though. Obviously.'

Clive, whom I'd heard announce coldly on more than one occasion, 'I don't take snaps,' managed to overlook this insult, and we walked to the stables, where Sonnygar, a magnificent beast, was looking as perky as advertised. His Lordship happily complied with Clive's instructions, offering a range of expressions from angry to remorseful. By now we had been joined by several locals who clearly formed part of Archcon's retinue, including a strikingly beautiful woman whose position appeared somewhere beyond the strictly clerical and domestic.

Dickie then finally introduced me and suggested that we should sit down together and Archcon could tell us all about it. 'Yes, why not?' said the unabashed peer. 'Chel, could you arrange some chocolate on the verandah?' The beauty smiled assent and moved on gracefully ahead of us. We settled on the verandah and Archcon smiled that smile again. 'Tell you what, chaps, before we start,' he said, 'I'm wondering what all this might be worth to you.'

We were not unprepared for this moment. 'Ah, yes, Jeremy,' said Dickie. 'I expect you know that we at the *Cable* never pay for stories.'

'Yes, yes, Dickie, I know that. But there are certain expenses you might be able to help me with?'

This was slightly tricky: it was true we could pay some expenses to someone who helped us with a story; a small 'research fee' was also often available. There was also the matter of securing willing co-operation. But Dickie was an old hand at this sort of thing.

'Yes, I'm sure we could help out there,' he said. 'Now let's get started with this absolutely fascinating story. And you have my personal guarantee that you will be able to tell your side and get your explanation in first to our readers, who after all are your main readership, too.'

'How much exactly, old boy?' said Archcon. 'I don't have any access to funds since Jolene's little swine of an antique dealer discovered my backdoor account via the Virgin Islands.'

'We can iron out details like that later,' said Dickie. 'The important thing is that you will get a sympathetic platform in a serious newspaper and there will be no taint of money paid or partiality.' What he didn't say was something they both knew – paying even suspected criminals for stories was increasingly infra dig and certainly nothing Lord Hindmost would get involved in. Or that certain newspapers might not be so scrupulous and would inevitably come up with that old slippery sleight of words making no distinction between what interested the public and what was in the public interest.

'Well, I do think people will think differently when they hear my side of the story. The provocation I took from that sheepdog, for example, you wouldn't believe. What happened to it, by the way?'

'Had a seizure in the act of a particularly vigorous copulation last year, never recovered,' said Clive. 'I had to cover the funeral.'

'Well, that's certainly the way he would have wanted to go,' said Archcon.

'A moment, please,' said Chi, which was a little odd, as we had no need of an interpreter; I hadn't even noticed that he had come with us. 'There is also the question of recompense to the local community for the disturbance and notoriety this will bring upon it.'

'Yes, yes,' said Ralph, impatiently. 'We'll sort that out later too. Now leave us alone if you wouldn't mind, old fruit, off you go, chop-chop.'

'No,' said Chi, not in the least ruffled. 'I think it would be better if we sorted it out first. Otherwise our culture's code of hospitality will force us to prevent a guest being molested.'

'Molested? Molested!' said Ralph. 'Lord Archcon is talking to us because he wants to. And we are guests too, being molested by you! And what's this "us" all of a sudden – you're from Miradora, aren't you?'

'The distinction between Miradora and Buccan is comparatively recent, and one we only pretend to recognise as long as it doesn't inconvenience us. And in our culture, guests do not arrive unannounced in stealth and force themselves upon a host. What say you, Lord Archcon?' And here Chi, certainly to my astonishment, winked at the fugitive.

Whatever else he might have been, Jeremy Archcon was not slow on the uptake. 'Well, you know, this chap might have a point. The people round here have been very good to me, and I would hate to offend them.'

There followed, understandably, a silence while Chel poured chocolate exquisitely, willowing down next to each of us in turn. I noticed that the verandah was now surrounded by even more locals, a grave and heavy presence. But whatever else he might have been, Dickie Dasher was not a quitter. 'Well, I suppose we could manage some recompense, and we as a newspaper are very keen on supporting local communities. Obviously we don't have very much money with us, but we can make arrangements once we're back in Arrmiati.'

'I'm afraid that won't be good enough,' said Chi, who, interestingly, had also been served chocolate by Chel. 'There is a history of, how shall we say, broken promises between us, beginning with El Pirata Drake and the "just a loan, my hearties" of some of our artefacts. You must get our recompense wired to the Lubaantun branch of the Buccan Bank and hand it over before the lord talks to you.'

Archcon was rueful once more. 'Does make sense, I suppose. You press chappies don't exactly have a reputation for rectitude and probity, do you?'

This was remarkably rich coming from the source it did but Dickie was not a man to be sidetracked when he was on a job. 'Tell you what. Let us write the report of finding Lord Archcon, get it over to London, and then we'll go to Arrmiati where it will be much easier to sort the money out, leaving him as a surety.'

It will be no surprise to learn that 'him' was me, or that I was not in favour of this plan. You will recall Dickie's alleged relationship with his grandmother. I could hear him saying to me some time in the future, 'Took one for the team there, dear boy. Don't worry, Lord Hindmost will take care of you.' Fortunately, Chi was equally unconvinced that they would come back for me. 'No, the money first.'

Dickie was beaten, for now. 'Very well, how much are we talking about?'

'Let us say twenty thousand pounds for our compensation. And then there's the fee for taking you and Lord Archcon and the horse back to Arrmiati. So twenty-five thousand in all.'

'Twenty five thousand! That's much too much! Ten thousand.'

'No,' said Chi.

'Fifteen thousand,' said Dickie.

'Yes,' said Chi.

Dickie turned to Archcon. 'Do you have a phone?'

''Fraid not, old chum. That was one of the attractions. Line stops at Lubaantun. There's a telex machine at the bank.'

'I'll drive you,' said Chi.

'I bet you will,' said Ralph.

It was decided that Ralph and Clive would stay with Archcon while Dickie and I went into Lubaantun with Chi. The telex was despatched without trouble after the helpful operator smiled and nodded at us, and I realised later, Chi in particular.

THE TELEX CAUSED CONSTERNATION IN LONDON (I reconstruct imaginatively). 'Ex Dasher, Lubaantun, Buccan. Object met. Happy to oblige. But little local difficulty. Transmission problem requires outlay pounds 15,000, repeat 15,000. Please wire to this bank. Await early reply'.

'Good news, Lord Hindmost,' said the Editor. 'We have found Archcon!'

'Excellent,' said Lord Hindmost, who never required exclamation marks. 'When will we see the copy? Are we going to run it tonight?'

'I think we should wait so we can give it maximum coverage. And that will also help us iron out a problem that has arisen with the details, my lord.'

'Problem? Difficulties in transmitting? Archcon requires assurances? What?'

'Dasher wants us to send him fifteen thousand pounds, my lord.'

'Fifteen thousand pounds,' said Lord Hindmost, very close to an exclamation mark even so. He stared out through the window into the gathering dusk, where he fancied he could make out a slight bump in one corner of his lawn. Earlier that day he had received the latest circulation figures, which showed the decline in circulation accelerating.

'We trust Dasher?'

'He wouldn't be asking if it weren't necessary, my lord. He can't say too much in a telex, obviously, but the money must be to placate or ease the way with someone up there, my guess would be a tribal chief, bells and beads and mirrors, that sort of thing. He makes it clear it's not for Archcon, so we're fine on that point. And it's small beer compared to what the tabloids would pay.'

It was time to draw in horns, or charge. Lord Hindmost was not entirely cautious and sensible: he owned a newspaper. 'Send it,' he said.

Around the same time, in Government House, Arrmiati, Gerald Tench was also reading the telex. He became agitated, and made a couple of local telephone calls, and then one rather further afield, to London.

After authorisation came through and Chi's draft was cleared, we returned to Archcon Towers, where Dickie and I interviewed the noble lord lengthily on the verandah. He was very co-operative, and most forthcoming about his literary skills and the minimal role Lady Archcon had in fact played in his success. 'Very talented woman, Jolene, don't get me wrong, but her part in the books has been taken sadly – badly – out of context. I mean, yes, she did often take one of my ideas, well, drafts you could call them really, and, well, perhaps flesh it out at a little, coax it a little, you know, how should we say, tickle the vision. But that was the extent of it, apart from adding the odd little squiggly things, what do you call them, semicolons. And she typed it all up, obviously.' Archcon gave us his familiar lopsided smile, the one inviting us to see him as a trusting innocent in a treacherous world of cynical exaggeration and cruel distortion, then continued.

He said that he had taken Sonnygar because he couldn't live without his beloved horse; claims that it had anything to do with insurance, joint ownership, tax arrangements, or spite towards his ex-wife were simply very wide of the mark and, frankly, grossly insulting. He was equally clear about Johnson: 'The fellow is an absolute snake in the grass. Completely untrustworthy, pathawotsical liar, can't keep his hands off women, boastful, slovenly, idle – in short not the sort you expect to have been at your old school. What on earth Jolene saw in him, I can't think, although her judgment could be questionable in several areas. I've never been quite sure, for example, that she appreciated what a gem she had in me – fiercely loyal, gentlemanly, well-regarded, talented, modest. Still, at least she had the sense to dump him pdq. But then she only went and took up with that odious rat-like Hungarian antique dealer. I shall always love her, though, and I forgive her.'

True or not, this was certainly what we called in the trade good copy. And he was no less direct about the incident with the dog in the night. 'Where Johnson got the notion I had anything to do with it, I can't think. He's always been a fantasist though. I mean to say, the idea that I, a man who truly loves animals, would try to kill one is crazy. He had a grudge against me because I was such a good writer and he was in love with my wife. He probably made it all up, but if he didn't I would point you in the direction of a car backfire and that disgracefully spoilt dog spurning rump steak because he prefers sirloin. Vegetarian indeed! Ghastly creature. I don't know about the leg wound but I do know that strange things happen in Hampstead Garden Suburb, although of course I've never been there, and certainly not on that night.'

Yes, he had made a silly, silly mistake running away, which was completely unlike him, as any of his friends could tell you. Jeremy Archcon was a fighter. When the intrepid correspondents of the Daily Cable had come to visit him, he had already made his decision to return and face the music. He knew his readers and viewers would support him. Archcon was coming home!

And with the Daily Cable. This sort of stuff wrote itself, aided by that prime journalistic skill of 'shepherding the facts'. In no time we were ready to file, Dickie with the lead story of 1,000 words, me with 2,000 more, no colour spared – jungle hideaway, how we found him, the first encounter, dense forest, howling monkeys, screeching macaws, sheer drama. Feeling very pleased with ourselves, we piled into the Land Rover, and Chi, not betraying the slightest change in status or relationship, drove us to the Telex in Lubaantun.

If you're a sports fan, you will be very familiar with a game that is going very well for your side when suddenly the other one scores completely against the run of play. A moment of stun, slump and incredulity. Thus it was when we returned to the Baccan Bank, strolled happily over to the Telex operator and were told that it was out of order. No service today. You might not be so familiar with the feeling of a journalist who has got a story, has written it but is prevented from getting it to his or her newspaper by a sudden unexpected turn of events, like a broken Telex machine. A moment of stun, slump and incredulity.

Dickie recovered first. 'We'll have to get to Arrmiati. Can't file today – let's get back to Archcon, overnight there and set off with him in the morning so he'll be ready to leave with us for Blighty. But some drink and a meal first, I think.'

The drink was welcome but the meal proved no better than the previous night; Dickie's mood was not improved by Clive greeting us on our return with tales of Chel's cooking: 'Amazing. I haven't tasted Chateaubriand like that since Saigon. And she gives receipts.'

The Archcon guest accommodation didn't quite match up to the catering: we were all together on camp beds in a large hut. After Dickie had finally stopped grumbling and Ralph had temporarily run out of stories of the old days, there looked to be a chance of some sleep at last, but the silence within (save snoring from the well-fed Clive) allowed a better listen to the jungle noises without, which were not reassuring. When I questioned nervously one particularly rumbling kind of grumble that seemed very close, Ralph said, 'Jaguar, old boy. Hungry by the sound of it. Good thing you're nearest the door.' Highly amusing, you'll agree.

Early next morning we started out for Arrmiati, Dickie, Clive and I in the Land Rover with the inscrutable Chi, Archcon and Ralph in a jeep driven by the exquisite Chel with Sonnygar in a trailer behind. Chel had now changed into jungle fatigues which produced the opposite effect to their description. The long journey was blessedly uneventful.

Ralph had assumed command of communications but we were still a little surprised when he led the way to the Hotel Arrmiati before explaining he had an arrangement to use the Telex and phone there. Dickie was understandably perturbed: 'But what about Jack Shoe? And won't Jeremy be recognised?'

'Don't worry, Dickie, old boy. Much safer than the General Post Office, away from official prying eyes, quite popular as you might imagine. Jack's past all that, anyway, different ball game out here.'

So it proved. Dickie and I hovered while Ralph hunkered down on the Telex machine in a back office. At one stage, Jack Shoe popped his head in, but seemed quite satisfied when Ralph said, 'Hello, Jack. Stamp collecting waits for no man.' Clive meanwhile wired over two photos, Archcon grimly contrite with Sonnygar and Archcon grimly contrite with Dickie. Receipt confirmed from London, the next thing to do, obviously, was to have a drink or several. It was all going with quite a swing, especially when Dickie got back from a check call: 'They love it! Herograms all round! Apparently, Lord Hindmost smiled!'

Archcon was joining in without seemingly a care in the world. 'Well, I suppose I am quite important. Funny to be going back, though.'

Even the arrival of Gerald Tench couldn't spoil it. 'Tenchy!' shouted Ralph, as if greeting his best friend. 'Bubbly?'

Tench, when I thought about it later, was looking smug as well as hot and crumpled. 'I'd love to in normal circumstances, but not when I have a warrant for the arrest of Lord Archcon here with a view to deporting him back to Britain.'

'Arrest? What on earth for?' It was part of Archcon's charm that he seemed to be genuinely surprised that anyone would want to do such a thing.

'Her Majesty's Governor of Buccan has determined that you should be removed from this country under the provisions of the Buccan Deportation Ordnance of 1958 as you are facing charges involving violence and kidnapping in the United Kingdom and so should be removed there in order that these matters be resolved.'

'Violence?' said Dickie. 'Kidnapping? The violence you're referring to amounts to a scratch on a dog's leg and is in any case denied by Lord Archcon. And he can hardly have kidnapped his own horse!'

'I'm not clear what this has to do with a stamp collector,' said Tench.

'I am Richard Dasher of The Daily Cable and I warn you I will not let this matter rest!' said Dickie.

'I trust you have the correct accreditation from the Government of Buccan to work here?' replied Tench. 'No? Thought not. Now if you'll excuse me, these officers here will escort Lord Archcon to secure premises while arrangements are made for his removal. And that of his horse. Where is it?'

'Steady, old boy, it's a he, not an it. But I'm not answering any questions until I have consulted my lawyer,' said Archcon, far less ruffled than we were. Sonnygar was in fact safe at some stables Ralph had arranged, owned by a man who owed him a favour for some quite punchy advertising copy he'd written for his Canter brand tinned meat, 'Enjoy a Canter – it's lengths ahead!'. ('Nothing can go wrong there then,' as Clive put it.)

The party, or what remained of it, felt a little flat after that, as was the champagne (or more strictly Privateer Sparkling), although we did congratulate ourselves on getting our stories and pix away and consoled ourselves that Archcon would still be going back to Britain, if not exactly with us. So we filed an update on this unexpected twist and awaited developments. It was getting hotter as the day wore on, and Jack's complaining roof fans weren't really up to the task, but waiting is just one more underappreciated journalistic skill. As is learning to be surprised by nothing, but we certainly weren't expecting Archcon to walk back in, smiling broadly and accompanied by Chi and Chen.

'They've let me go!' said Archcon, grinning from ear to ear. 'And it's all thanks to my amazing lawyer here!' We looked around for this august personage, then realised this was in fact Chi.

'Yes,' he said, grave as ever, 'I am an associate attorney, expert in Buccan customs and practices, and recognised as such by the Buccan Department for the Affairs of Indigenous Peoples.'

'Of course you are,' I said.

'Bloody Hell,' said Dickie.

'Wonders never cease,' said Clive.

'I thought I'd seen you before, now you come to mention it,' said Ralph.

'After Lord Archcon requested me to attend,' continued Chi, 'I pointed out to the authorities that his deportation was barred under local Buccan law and custom and under Buccan Government provisions allowing precedence in certain circumstances to the said local laws and customs over conflicting United Kingdom law and thus vitiating the Doctrine of Repugnance.'

'Didn't have a clue what he was on about but by jove he was good!' said Archcon admiringly, drawing up seats for Chi and Chen.

'Certain circumstances?' said Dickie.

'Yes,' said Chi. 'In this case the local law and custom recognising the primacy awarded to care for children in our culture, and specifically, the prohibition of the removal of a father from his wife and child to sea or beyond the sea even when that father stands accused of crime.'

'Uh oh,' I said.

'Hmm,' said Ralph.

'Ah,' said Clive.

'Father? What father? What child? What are you talking about?' said Dickie.

'I am going to have Jeremy's baby,' said Chen, smiling and looking rather wonderful.

'Yes, it's true,' said Archcon, managing to seem even a little embarrassed. 'I'm delighted, absolutely delighted, although I only found out when Chen produced the shaman's letter at the police station.'

'But I thought you were determined to return to Britain to clear your name, to remove this smear and stain on your character brought about by these scandalous falsehoods!' reproached an agitated Dickie seeing the next glorious stage of the scoop being dashed away.

'Well, yes, there is all that of course,' said Archcon, now less embarrassed. 'And nothing would stop me in my fight against these disgraceful falsehoods with the simple sword of truth and the trusty shield of British fair play – nothing, that is, but my love for this woman and my child and my duty to care for them.'

'And the prospect of chokey,' said Clive, the only photographer I'd ever met who could manage *sotto voce*.

'Bravo,' said Ralph, with the air of a man who had regained his mojo and was now seeing the opportunity for good copy for some time to come.

Dickie's shoulders slumped. 'Very well,' he said. 'But if you change your mind – decide to bring your wife and child to support you in your fight, for example, I know you will contact Ralph first.'

'But of course, Ralph, keep in touch with my agent.'

'Agent?' we all said together.

'Chi. Although I'm not sure it would be fair to put my wife and child through something like that. Hey-ho, we'd better be off, I suppose, long way to go, little lady to look after, you know the sort of thing. By the way, I bumped into an old friend of yours at the police station, Dickie, at least he said he was an old friend of yours, Tench introduced us. Ronnie Teasel of The Epoch.'

'Ronnie Teasel? Here?'

'Yes, just got in. Nice chap, very interested in my case.'

'Did you talk to him?'

'We had a bit of a natter. Couldn't see the harm in it, not as if you'd paid me anything, after all. And he was most generous.'

Archcon, Chi, Chen and the incipient Archcon left. Our shoulders were down, too, and our chins: it was all we could do to force down drinks. A little later and no happier, we were approached by Jack Shoe, which was all we needed, really. 'Who was that chap you were just with?' he said. 'Never forget a face, seemed familiar. And how was the fishing?'

'You've just seen the one that got away,' said Clive.

AND THAT WAS JUST ABOUT THAT, I SUPPOSE. ARCHCON DID go back to Lubaantun, and has remained a minor celebrity ever since the typical seven-day hoopla over his discovery. He is apparently blissfully happy with Chen and their son, Ixil Jeremy. The money from his revelations and other resolutely opaque sources funded a swimming pool for him and the Jeremy Archcon Library for the community. The library is run by Chi and is an important resource for Maya writings and culture. It also features a shelf of his (or Jolene's) books, which are in much demand, as the Maya are a gracious people. His subsequent autobiography, 'What Happened to Me', for which he was also paid a great deal of money, has been much studied, too, along with the follow-up, 'Archon', 'Lord of the Jungle', which didn't do quite so well. But his other later works, which included 'The Buccan Buccaneer and the Mayan Maid', and 'The Forest Shall Not Have Them', sold well and were praised for their growing maturity. Chen smiled. Sonnygar was a great attraction, until he disappeared again a couple of years later. He has never been found, and no motive ever discerned; Archcon, although expressing great sorrow, professed himself baffled and, as so often with him, was neither entirely consistent nor convincing. Some suggested that an unlucky demise at the fangs of a jumping viper was not as good for the Archcon brand as the mystery. Whatever, the disappearance had the effect of pausing the continuing questions over Sonnygar's ownership. The possibility of any proceedings over the attack on the dog, Boris, also receded when Johnson was successfully sued by Zoltan Karpathy, the Hungarian antique dealer, for making untruthful claims about his potency and the provenance of an antique fire scuttle.

Poor Dickie never really recovered from a debacle that was hardly his fault. Ralph dined out on it for many years, and would tap Archcon for a new story whenever his bar bill at the Arrmiati Hotel became too oppressive (the one featuring Archcon's discovery of a Buccan Penny Dreadful had a predictable outcome). Clive was taken on by a rival whose new presses were better able to show his photographs and talent. This was of course *The Era*, taken away from Fleet Street by Daniel Burdock and relocated in London's Docklands with state-of-the-art computerised equipment and machinery and without the inconvenient trades unions. This started off a general stampede away from the cluttered confines and restrictions of EC4 and the old ways; soon the Cable was the only national left there, a stranded leviathan that Lord Hindmost could not save without the outside investment and internal ruthlessness it required. Finally, amid a genuine sadness which explained to the most sophisticated of his employees the strong attachment of family retainers, he sold it to a minor version of Burdock, another colonial, Canadian, who saved it but was not as clever as the Australian at either running newspapers or evading jail.

The Cable followed to East London and another anonymous office block in a dock lined with identical glass and concrete, leaving behind the clatter of the typewriter, the roar of the printing machines, the thunder of the presses, and the pubs (often in favour of other, more solitary stimulants). The silence of the word processor and the gradual replacement of that growing growling relentless progress towards the evening deadlines in favour of endless ones put paid to most of what had been: I remember one distinguished foreign correspondent showing me his first mobile phone and saying, 'That's it, really. Now they can get hold of me whenever they like.' It was also the beginning of the end of the traditional media's dominance as an outlet, which had the unforeseen consequence of promoting mass gullibility for unmediated online prattling. Newspapers survived, of course, but for all the new sobriety and technological improvement, the interesting thing is not that the product has become better, but that it has become so little better.

Me? As you can tell, I lost my enthusiasm, borne home hard to me when I decided not to push two nuns out of the way on the airplane steps to get to an assignment. And it was an end: nothing like the pursuit of Archcon would ever be allowed to happen again; indeed it was a matter of endless veteran discussion as to how it had been allowed to happen in the first place. But this reckoned without a newspaper losing its way coinciding with the enticement and magic and reckless reality-defying bravado of old Fleet Street fighting for its life. I went freelance and I've since rubbed along, supplementing journalism with the odd book. Ghost writing can be quite profitable, for example. But this would clearly not be an appropriate moment to discuss the authorship of 'What Happened to Me', 'Archcon, Lord of the Jungle', or that other bestselling memoir, 'The Beat I Walked', by Jack Shoe.

Afterword

The more astute will have noticed certain similarities between *The Daily Cable* and *The Era* with newspapers that actually exist. This is of course the case but it would be a mistake to conclude that all is true. Some of it was worse. Certain elements of the story are far-fetched but I would also point you in the direction of the credibility originally given to the publication of the fake Hitler diaries, the alleged discovery of Hitler's deputy, Martin Bormann, in Argentina, and, perhaps most pertinently for our purposes, the continued sightings of the disappeared peer, Lord Lucan, one of which confused him with a banjo player from St Helens called Barry. A disturbed man named Michael Ryan managed to hoax Fleet Street consistently in the 1980s because a very small amount of time spent in newspapers demonstrates that however unlikely something may be, it may also be true. One of Ryan's minor coups was the revelation that Shergar, the racehorse famously kidnapped never to be seen again, was alive and well and resident in Jersey. Other memories that might be prompted by Lord Archcon include the exploits of Dick Francis, Jeremy Thorpe and John Stonehouse.

The greatest debt, though, is owed to the legendary RONNIE BIGGS scoop secured by the Daily Express and vividly chronicled by Anthony Delano in a classic of the genre, 'Slip-Up'. A tip-off to an Express reporter led to Rio de Janeiro and Biggs, one of the Great Train Robbers of 1963 who got away with £2.6m from a Royal Mail Train. The Express took far more care to establish that

Biggs was in Brazil, and that he was Biggs, than the Daily Cable managed with Lord Archcon but still fell foul of bad luck and Brazilian law, which blocked his deportation back to Britain on the grounds that his girlfriend was pregnant and he was about to become the parent of a Brazilian citizen. Principal among those also caught up in the affair was Detective Chief Superintendent JACK SLIPPER, of the Metropolitan Police's Flying Squad, who, alerted by the Express, flew to Rio and arrested Biggs with the celebrated line, 'Hello, Ronnie, long time no see.' The extradition failure meant that Slipper had to fly back to Britain without Biggs; Michael Brennan, an enterprising photographer for the Express's great rival, the Daily Mail, joined the flight and waited patiently for the detective sitting next to Slipper to go off to the loo, allowing the arresting and exclusive photograph of the Detective Chief Superintendent and the empty seat which should have been for Biggs.

The colony of Buccan has of course similarities with Belize (as does Miradora with Guatemala). The failure to secure Lord Archcon's extradition from a British colony for a similar reason to that in the Biggs case is not without some legal basis. It was well accepted that the Doctrine of Repugnance, which disallowed local ordinances in conflict with English law, could be overruled in certain sensitive situations. Queen Victoria herself, for example, in a proclamation of 1858, promised that British authorities would 'abstain from all interference with the Religious Beliefs or Worship of any of [her] subjects'. I have also sought to correct the popular view that the Maya mysteriously disappeared towards the end of the first millennium. They did not disappear: they are still there in Mexico and Central America. The majority of the population in Guatemala is Mayan, as is a significant minority in El Salvador and Belize, formerly British Honduras, disparate but distinguished by a determination to maintain their culture with passion, subtlety and humour. Belize is more complicated than our fictional Buccan, with a rich, shifting mingle and intermingle *of Maya, Caribs, African Caribbeans, Europeans, American religious fundamentalists and the descendants of Confederates who emigrated after the South's defeat in the American Civil War.*

As for the eighties, the divisions they demonstrated, between solutions believed harsh but vital and inevitable and the more obviously compassionate consensual approach favoured by the Heath (qv) and Blair administrations, continue to be the essential contention in British politics. Indeed, it might be argued that the present preoccupation with identity and the rights of minorities is the result of the heavy-handed approach of the Thatcher (qv) government in the eighties. The journalistic view was as well expressed as well as any by the Reuters subeditor of the time who used to announce regularly, 'Well, whatever happens, there'll be no justice in it.'

FURTHER READING:
Slip-Up: How Fleet Street Caught Ronnie Biggs and Scotland Yard Lost Him: The Story Behind the Scoop, *Anthony Delano*
Not Many Dead: Journal of a Year in Fleet Street, *Nicholas Garland*
Paper Dreams: Story of the "Independent" and the "Independent on Sunday" by One of the Founding Fathers, *Stephen Glover*
Rejoice! Rejoice: Britain in the 1980s, *Alwyn W Turner*

1995

It Could Be You!

PEOPLE LIKED KIT PARROTT. KIT HAD THAT GENTLE WEST Country way which can be deceptive but wasn't in the case of Kit. What you saw in Kit was very much what you got: amiable, genially well disposed; calm, practical in a deliberate way, not in a hurry. At other times in the twentieth century, he might have been the NCO heavily relied upon by inexperienced, jumpy officers, or high up in service, a butler or head gamekeeper or some such. As it was, in 1995, aged 26, he was the senior sales assistant at Davey & Cray, the premier gentlemen's outfitters in Fromerton, eastern pearl of Somerset's greenly glorious Mendip Hills.

Actually, the only gentlemen's outfitters: the others had gone with the wind of change that had brought casual dress and chains with short indeterminate names like Next or Gap and very keen prices. DCs, as everyone knew Davey & Cray, had survived with a concentration on country clothes attractive to the local farming community and the growing number of weekenders and incomers who were discovering Fromerton's quaint charms, its winding streets up steep hills lined with buildings of local stone, mellower and less posh than Bath's. Small shops staggered on in the face of supermarkets and such, barely sustained by the DFLs (Down from London): 'Do you know, it's even got an ironmongers! We buy all our nails there.'

There had been a cattle market in the centre of the town, a rich, clamorous, messy weekly affair, but it had now joined the supermarkets out of town in a new concrete, more sensible setting. Kit still liked Fromerton, though. Born and bred, attended the local comprehensive, enjoyed it despite everyone saying it had gone to the dogs since 'that Shirley Williams' stopped it being a grammar. Not a brilliant student, nor a great thinker, steady rather. 'Kit is a diligent pupil but needs to find in himself the spark that kindles learning', wrote the form teacher, a failed novelist. His dad worked in the big local printers, his mum in the factory that had once been called a dairy.

The position at DCs had seemed ideal. Kit was quite interested in fashion, provided it was neat. Spotting a likely prospect, Mr Davey took him on. There was no need to consult anyone else as there hadn't been a Cray since 1927, when Arnold Cray and William Davey had fallen out irrevocably over turn-up lengths. Arnold had gone into hatting, with an inevitable outcome.

Kit, unsurprisingly, did well. A manner naturally well placed between attentiveness and respect, a ready but gentle smile, far removed from the smarm being so cleverly and currently lampooned in the television hit, *The Fast Show* – 'Suits you, sir!' – along with other familiar social types the nineties were leaving behind, like lascivious foreigners and drunken aristocrats. He had achieved his senior status on the recent and sudden death of Mr Nutkin, a DC stalwart for 30 years, who had tripped and impaled himself on his umbrella outside the Somerset Bank in the Market Place. 'The show must go on, Kit,' was how Mr Davey had put it when he appointed him to take poor Mr Nutkin's place, also advising him always to check his umbrella was the right way up.

And so the show did, with the ups and downs of busyness that were the lot of the gentlemen's outfitter. This left Kit with plenty of time for thinking, which it's fair to say he did not use all that wisely. Last century, before the mobile phone, there was something known as daydreaming. Kit was an adept. They were not deep, these daydreams, but they were beguiling, and almost always featured a setting sun, palms, a bay, a drink with a little paper parasol in it, and Daisy. Once there had been quite a lot of football as well, but recently he had been forced to concede that he was getting a touch too old for his first England cap, particularly as the rest of the Fromerton Town Reserves did not always share his vision of midfield generalship.

Ah, yes, Daisy. Daisy Rae. How long had Kit been in love with Daisy? Since Year Nine at least. When had he told her he was in love with her? He hadn't. Not yet. Daisy had always been the most popular girl in the class, and Kit had never been the most popular boy. Too gentle, not alpha enough, not like Norris Jakeway or Ricky Bardgett. They'd been out with Daisy, of course. But not for long. She had very high standards, Daisy, which was why she was still unmarried and why Kit had never dared even to ask her for a date, let alone tell her he was madly in love with her. His encounters with various Daisy substitutes had never got very far, mostly because they were Daisy substitutes. Still living at home might also have been significant.

Something was going to have to give. Not least because Daisy had recently returned from a spell away in London and was now working three shops up from Kit in Trickle Street, the picturesque pride of Fromerton, with an open leat carrying clear water down from the fountain at St Jude's, the old town's original water supply, to the delight of children and tourists, who share many characteristics. There didn't seem to be a great deal of information about Daisy's spell in London, but she certainly looked very attractive in the tailored teal suit with white pussy-bow blouse she wore to befit her role as a travel advisor at the Friendly Zephyr travel agency.

'Hallo, Daisy!' he had said, meeting her on the street on her first day there. 'You're back then?'

Daisy had smiled the smile he remembered so well, as delicious as ever. 'Don't tell me,' she said. 'It's Chris Sidefather, isn't it? How are you?'

'No, Kit Parrott,' he'd said, smiling bravely. Chris Sidefather had been a quiet boy very keen on Super Mario, chemistry and chips, so the confusion was not necessarily encouraging. And it hadn't got much better over the following months, either. Daisy was always friendly when they met, but she never asked him anything about himself, and she greeted any enquiries of his with a 'fine' or a 'cool' and a perceptible edging towards The Friendly Zephyr. He'd seen her out with Norris Jakeway a couple of times but nothing seemed to have come of it. He'd also discovered that Chris Sidefather was now a top City trader. Kit was quite good at adding up the prices of a pair of socks and a Tattersall shirt but not a man with a yen for leverage and shorts unless they were khaki and to the knee. And he would certainly never be seen in wide scarlet braces and boxy suits, a prejudice shared by Mr Davey. Nevertheless, the return of Daisy Rae had definitely disturbed Kit's contentment. The daydreams were no longer quite so satisfying; the termination of his international footballing aspirations also pointed to other signs of time passing. Even Norris Jakeway, for goodness sake, was doing well selling conservatories.

AND THEN KIT WON THE LOTTERY. HE'D BEEN DOING IT since John Major's great wheeze had been launched the year before amid worries about moral fibre, effect of easy money on same, and whether a proportion of the ticket money going to good causes excused gambling or posed a moral dilemma fit for Plato, Sartre and Michael Buerk to mull. As it turned out, the mood of the nineties, heavily influenced by widespread change and the freedom of the individual evidenced by the triumph of US capitalism over Soviet communism, had no difficulty choosing practical advantage over ethical purity, just as it did the same year when Sunday trading restrictions were eased. These were curious triumphs for Mr Major, a man declaredly in favour of taking Britain back to a richly imagined time of probity and decency when the only movement on a Sunday came from old maids bicycling to communion through the morning mist.

Such considerations weighed little with Kit, especially as Mr Davey had declared that DCs would open on a Sunday over his dead body (an accurate prediction). No, Kit's interest was in activating his daydreams, although they often prevented him from remembering to buy a ticket. Prudently, in view of this, he had no regular numbers but invented a different system each time. The winning formula proved to be, in order: his street number; how many peas were left on his plate; the amount of times during the meal his father said 'I don't know what's up with people today'; his mother's mention of certain people, usually female, in Fromerton who were no better than they ought to be; how many ties he'd sold that week; and an estimate of how many times he'd thought of Daisy that day: 29, 11, 5, 2, 3, 89.

It was funny, really, how things turned out. He never watched the National Lottery Draw on television on Saturday nights, preferring the programme on the other side at the same time, *Match Me!*, where a young single man or woman would listen to three of the opposite sex behind a screen promoting their charms and attractions with an enthusiasm untroubled by modesty. One would be chosen, and the pair would go off on a luxurious holiday and report back the next week. It was coy and suggestive and innocent at the same time, kept firmly the right side of prurient and kept distant from the shows that would follow the next century by its hostess, the friendly Liverpudlian singer and personality, Penny Vayne. Penny had a laugh like a draining bath but Kit, being Kit, rather fancied her, much more than he did the Lottery presenter, a pert young blonde called Anthea Lerner whose simple charms would similarly not survive the coming cynicisms. This evening, while his father dozed in his chair and his mother nodded in hers, Penny was putting one arm round Dean from Staines and the other round Gill from Wisbech, giving that laugh and telling them, 'Well, chucks, guess what, you're off to Torremolinos!' And Kit smiled gently, unaware that his numbers had just come up and he'd won £6.5 million. After that he watched *Casualty* and *Match of the Day*, then went to bed and, unusually, didn't dream.

There were reports the next day that the winner lived in Somerset but Kit didn't hear or see them, as he was busy tending to his beehive. It was over at his dad's allotment, on the edge of town, rhubarb and beetroot a speciality. Kit liked bees, their sense of order and their honey, and he often thought that the life of a drone was not that bad. Short, sure, but comfortable: fed by the workers and lots of laughs waiting in the drone congregation area to fulfil your one and only job: mating with a Queen. And you did it in mid-air: fancy that! Of course, the odds were against you scoring – about 100-1 – but they were much better than winning the Lottery, which he'd seen put at a ridiculous 15,000,000-1.

On the Monday, he managed by dint of careful timing and observation to come across Daisy as if by chance as they walked up Trickle Street. 'Hello, Daisy,' he said. 'Exciting weekend?'

Daisy smiled her smile and fluttered a finely manicured hand with fashionable plum-coloured nails. 'Exhausting. Too much socialising! Didn't see you at Ricky Bardgett's party, were you there?'

This was bitter-sweet: on the one hand, Daisy was giving him more than the usual syllables and had actually or apparently been looking out for him; on the other, this was the first he knew about Ricky Bardgett's party.

'Ah, no,' he said. 'Took a bit of a tumble playing for Town. Nasty foul by one of the Radbury guys as I was closing in on goal. Casualty for me, I'm afraid, stitches and I felt groggy after that. Good party, was it?' Some of this was partly true.

'Oh, poor you! That must have hurt!'

Kit grimaced in what he hoped was a dismissive way which conveyed the toughness and bravery demanded of the dedicated footballer. He also started to limp a little.

'The party was fun. You'll never guess who was there – Chris Sidefather! He's rather big in the City, well according to him. Who'd have thought little Chris would be a success? I was pinning my hopes on the Lottery but now they're saying someone round here's already done it, won £6.5 million on Saturday, apparently. Ah, well, back to the wonderful world of travel, I suppose. Bye, Chris.'

Quite a lot more bitter-sweetness, but at least it prompted Kit to check his ticket.

Publicity or no publicity? A big decision. The first he'd had to make, really. Everything had been a bit odd up to then, strangely automatic. Checking the numbers, checking the numbers again, checking the numbers again. Waiting for the lunch break to phone the organisers, Havalot, from the phone box at the top of the street. Puzzled glances from Mr Davey. One shirt, one scarf, one pair of gumboots, two no-buys, all taking place in a bubble, voices at a distance, listening to himself, 'Yes, very hard-wearing, sir, countrymen swear by them… shall I wrap it or will you keep it on? Looks very good with your jacket… it *is* a vibrant check, no doubt, but you can carry it off, this way, sir, a cheque, yes, that will be fine, just put your address on the back, thank you, oh, yes, that's a very pretty village, isn't it?' More puzzled glances from Mr Davey, a little short with the assistant, young Paddy Belper, who could be a bit slow on the uptake at the best of times. Mr Davey off to lunch, it being Monday (Mrs Davey's casserole from yesterday's joint), then telling Paddy to mind the shop. Phoning Havalot, running out of change, having to give way to Mrs Bell from the cake shop, not a woman to cross, finally getting through, convinced all the time something would be wrong, but no, Mr Truss of Havalot would be over to see him at 5pm. Asking Mr Davey if he could leave a little early as he was feeling a bit funny, not a word of a lie. Told mother, she still quiet in shock when Mr Truss, big, genial man, turned up prompt at five, followed a little later by Mr Parrott senior, who had to have it explained to him three times, and then had to have a glass of the Spanish brandy he'd brought back last summer from the package to Majorca. Offered one to Mr Truss but not to Kit, or his wife.

Mr Truss was very calm. He suggested that Kit do nothing major for the time being, perhaps take a holiday to think things over. Was he single, did he have a partner? Kit said he'd think about that, and about his job. Publicity? He would have to decide about that. Some people didn't want it, stopped all the hoo-hah and the pointing in the street and the begging letters. On the other hand, meant you couldn't really tell anybody and they find out eventually anyway. Publicity could be fun, meeting a celebrity, could be on the telly, that kind of thing, and all organised by Havalot to take the pressure off, everything done for you, could be fun. Need to know now, though, said Mr Truss, smiling, encouraging. Kit looked at his mum and dad. His father was smiling vacantly, nursing his brandy and occasionally repeating, 'Six and a half million! Who would have thought it? Our Kit!' Mrs Parrott was beaming at Kit and kept on beaming when he asked her what she thought but didn't say anything. All that Kit had heard apart from 'everything done for you' was 'on the telly', which played into a favourite daydream where he was rattling off witty one-liners about his latest film. 'Let's give the telly and all a go,' he said.

Mr Truss was pleased with his choice and said they would arrange for a press conference to announce Kit's win the next morning. He opened a large faux crocodile skin case he'd brought with him and produced a bottle of champagne and four fluted glasses in different colours, popped the cork and announced, 'You'll get used to this, Mr Parrott!' Kit's dad was getting into the swing of things, helped by the brandy; his mum was now adding giggles to the beams.

Kit joined in enthusiastically, then had a sudden thought. 'What about work tomorrow?'

'I expect your employer might see his way clear to giving you the morning off,' said Mr Truss, who was used to these sorts of reactions. He took his leave, looking forward to the next day and once again promising to take care of everything.

As he got to the door, Mrs Parrott spoke for the first time: 'Wait a minute, you're going without your nice champagne glasses! Give me a second and I'll rinse them.' Mr Truss assured her they were a gift and was gone.

'Well, it's a bit inconvenient, Kit,' said Mr Davey on the phone. 'I'm due off the tee in the Fromerton Traders' Mixed Foursomes at two and Mrs Bell is not a woman to be crossed. Are you still feeling off colour?'

'No, I've won £6.5 million on the Lottery,' said Kit.

There was a long silence at the other end of the phone. 'I see. Well done. Be back before twelve,' said Mr Davey, eventually.

IT WENT PRETTY WELL THE NEXT DAY, ALL CONSIDERING. You will, hopefully, recall those times in your life when you've woken up in the morning, blinked a little, thought about going back to sleep, and then had a delicious realisation: so with Kit on one of the first fine days of Spring, pale sunshine piercing through the gap in the curtains, suspiciously, actually, when he thought about it. Ah, yes, the morning off, that's why no alarm, good. Hold up, £6.5 million! His parents, seeing no reason not to, had gone to work. Leisurely breakfast, musing on possibilities – holiday, Daisy, new slacks – interrupted by Mr Truss with news of the press conference, to be held at 12 noon in Fromerton's largest venue, the Market Hall. 'And,' said Mr Truss, with a touch of drama, 'an exciting guest!'

This being the early days of the Lottery, there was much media excitement about Kit's win. The Market Hall was buzzing. Both big television channels were there, and most of the regional correspondents that the national newspapers employed in those long-lost days. After some thought, Kit had gone for a formal look, check sports jacket and shirt, horse-head tie, red corduroys, mustard moleskin waistcoat; he looked a good ten years older than 25. Mr Truss, who met his car at the Market Place, was torn between the novelty of the outfit and the need to attract the ordinary punter: he settled on advising Kit to take off his jacket and tie. This produced headlines in the tabloid papers like 'Wurzel Winner!' and 'Big Lottery Oo Arr!' Mr Truss was quite pleased, but more so with 'Tailor Suits £6.5m' and 'Hello Girls! Single Kit Bags Lotto Millions'.

Mr Truss had told Kit to try to relax and just smile if he was having trouble with any questions, but he coped with the ease of a man who had been rehearsing for some time, which he had. 'Over the moon? You can throw in a couple of planets as well!'... 'Shocked? Almost as much as if Bristol City won the cup!'... 'Well, obviously I'll be doing some saving – the receipts!'... 'No, the right girl's never come along – I bet she does now!' Cue, 'Young Tailor Measures up Spending Spree', 'Lotto Kit Looking for Love', and 'Anyone Attracted to Millionaire Lottery Winner?' (this was a reference to Mrs Merton, the spoof chat show host, and her recent enquiry of Debbie McGee about her elderly magician of a husband, 'What first attracted you to the millionaire Paul Daniels?'). After a while of this, Mr Truss made an announcement. 'Ladies and gentlemen, here to present Mr Parrott with his cheque for £6.5 million is none other than, yes, she's more than a match for anyone, Britain's Cuddly Cupid herself... Miss Penny Vayne!'

'Here's a shock, pets!' shouted Penny, appearing from the wings with the catchphrase from her other top-rated show, where fun and good things happened to unsuspecting nice ordinary people. Trademark alarmingly auburn hair firmly in place, she was wearing a (fun, obviously) fur coat, tottering on heels and holding her arms out in front of her. 'Where are you, chuck?' she shouted, heading towards Kit with the determination of a show business pro. 'Where's the handsome young man who's won a lorra lorra lolly?'

Despite all his daydream practice and previous admiration, Kit began to shuffle away, startled by this apparition and particularly the noise. But Penny was on him, clutching his arm, and still shouting, 'Is this the lucky fella, fellas? It is, it's Kit!' She then lunged and landed a big kiss on the unnerved outfitter's cheek. 'It's the new King of Fromerton! Where are you, girls? Form a queue behind me!'

Kit, further taken aback by the sight of Penny quite so close up, said the first thing that came into his head, which was, 'Actually, Penny, it's pronounced Froomerton, not Fromerton.' Penny paid no attention and seized the traditional and enormous cardboard cheque for £6.5 million now brought out by Mr Truss. Kit knew what to do and took the other end as the click and whizz and flash of the press photographs went into overdrive.

Mr Truss produced a bottle of champagne, gave it a shake and opened it, expertly diverting its frothy spray away from Penny, in line with an earlier warning in the wings, 'If a drop of this cheap stuff gets anywhere near my her, I'll twist your bollocks till *your* cork pops, chuck.' ('Your her?' a puzzled Mr Truss had queried; Penny had pointed significantly to her arresting coiffure and then threateningly at him.)

But that was then; the nation's Cuddly Cupid had now taken Kit by the arm and was once again in full happy flow. 'Kit, chuck, if I wasn't already taken by my dear husband Billy, I wouldn't ever let you go, I wouldn't! It's not the money, honestly… well, maybe a little bit, eh, fellas?! No, it's because you're so sexy! Honestly! He is, isn't he, girls!? Kit was so embarrassed by this that he began almost automatically to shake the bottle of champagne that the generous Mr Truss had also presented to him. This unwittingly secured Penny's instant retreat to a safe distance. 'Got to go now, chucks!' she cried. 'Don't forget to watch *Match Me!* – we might even have our Kit on soon! Oooh, what am I saying? Byeee!'

And then she was gone, off to the previously arranged engagement in Bristol (opening a flagship Fabflix video rental store) which had fortuitously secured her appearance in Fromerton (along with a substantial fee and some rather better champagne). There was that silence, often welcome, which immediately follows the departure of large, noisy people; the event soon broke up, with Mr Truss promising to keep in touch and advising Kit again to take a holiday before making any big decisions. He walked over to Trickle Street, at once getting to know how a celebrity feels, with the added disadvantage that everyone seemed to have known him before he was famous and felt entitled to remind him of his or her friendship. It took him a good half hour to cover the short distance to DCs, a handle of calm in this teacup of tumult. Mr Davey greeted him with a 'good afternoon, Kit', which placed an emphasis on the second word, and then went off to his golf without adding more. Paddy Belper was silent, too, when he wasn't staring at Kit and chuckling at regular intervals. Footfall began to pick up noticeably, but without any purchasing. Eventually, Kit, rather fed up with all his new-old friends, told Paddy he was taking a short break and left the shop, smiling but saying nothing. More of them were outside. There really was a limit to how many times you could say, 'it hasn't really sunk in yet', 'I don't know', 'random numbers, actually', 'they're very pleased', 'good idea, I'll get in touch when everything's sorted out', 'did I really?', 'and a Lamborghini as well, probably', 'of course I remember you'. Looking around for escape, he saw The Friendly Zephyr travel shop. He'd been trying to work out what he would say to Daisy and hadn't got any further than rehearsing in a casual way, 'Hello, Daisy, I've had a spot of luck, do you fancy helping me celebrate?', but that sounded too corny. He went into the shop: she was there, looking as cool and pretty as ever. She saw him and smiled. 'You've had a spot of luck!'

This reversal of the routine threw him. 'Yes,' he said. 'Do you fancy selling me a holiday?'

'Of course! Where would you like to go?' She motioned him over to a desk and they sat down on opposite sides.

Where would he like to go? He'd not been abroad since the football club trip to Amsterdam, when he'd been ill on the ferry and ill again after drinking too much Dutch lager, losing the rest of the team and walking around for miles until he'd sobered up sufficiently to find the way back to the hotel, where he was locked out. He was ill on the way back, too. And the only time before that had been with his parents on their first trip to Majorca (they went every year) when he'd been ill on the plane, both ways. He wasn't sure he really liked abroad, and he certainly didn't like flying, or sailing. He quite liked camping but a trip to the Lake District wasn't going to impress Daisy, even more so now that for some insane reason, obviously brought on by the shock of all that money, he'd decided it would be a good idea to ask someone he'd never been out with to come with him on holiday.

'Where would you recommend?' he asked her.

'For the man who's won £6.5 million? You can have anything you like!'

'Well, almost anything,' he said in what he hoped was a meaningful way. He wasn't entirely sure Daisy took the point.

'Well, if it was me,' she said, 'it would be somewhere hot – the Greek Islands, or the Caribbean or Florida. If you want culture, Italy, fun, the Costas and the Balearics. If travel's your thing, there's India and Asia. Have you got family and friends down under, Australia, New Zealand?'

Kit was conscious he was nodding like a donkey, which was obviously not a good look, and more importantly, that he didn't have a clue where he'd like to go. He settled for smiling brightly with a touch of expectation.

Daisy smiled back. It was a nice smile, with a touch of amusement, even, possibly, probably imagining it, affection. 'You haven't got a clue, Chris, have you?'

That again. But perhaps it meant she wasn't taking much notice of the big win. Or perhaps she meant the clue thing generally, which wasn't so good. For something to say and to give him time, he said, 'Kit.'

'Sorry?'

'It's Kit, Daisy. Not Chris.'

Daisy blushed, which although it was very fetching made him blush as well. 'Sorry, Kit, I can't think where that came from. I'm usually good with names, too. I've got an idea. Why don't you have a short holiday to decide on your long holiday? What about a few days in London, best hotel, take in a show and the sights, the parks are lovely in the spring. Good idea?'

It was a good idea. Daisy was so clever. 'That's a good idea, Daisy, yes, let's do that.'

'Brilliant. How many is it for?' she asked.

'Sorry?'

'How many of you will be going? Are you taking anyone?'

Ah. 'Two,' said Kit, then started panicking. He'd have to ask her now. He wanted to ask her now, but Penny Vayne, the champagne and the attention were wearing off. Kit hesitated, and you will be familiar with what happens to he who does that.

'Are you all right, Kit? See, got it right this time! But you do look worried,' said Daisy.

'No, I'm fine, fine. It's just been a bit sudden, all of this. I mean you can't object to being given £6.5 million but it does take getting used to. That's why they advised me to take a holiday, to think about it… Daisy, I know it's sudden, a bit of a rush, but this weekend, would you like to, er, you know, would you like to, it might be fun, er, would you like to… book the trip for me? One room, please.'

Flunked it. Pathetic. Imagine how many lives could have been changed by a little more recklessness, by less faint hearts. But, it should be recorded, on behalf of the shy, the gentle and the meek, changed for the bad as well as for the good. There were a couple of days left for him to ask her, but he knew he wouldn't. Daisy had the quizzical, amused look on again, but she told him she'd have it all sorted out by the end of the day, she had in mind the Megalopolitan in Mayfair, five-star luxury, wonderful bathrooms, slippers and everything.

Kit went back to DCs, where Paddy Belper was mostly fending off people looking for him. The afternoon carried on as before, Kit increasingly less responsive to the curious and the hopeful as he mulled over his present condition: was it possible to be unhappy when you've just won £6.5 million? Apparently so. Still, there was London to look forward to, and somewhere after that. Perhaps he should buy himself a house as well, nothing too fancy, obviously. And he could give his parents a nice trip. And, who knows, he might meet someone who wasn't Daisy. Mr Davey returned in a not particularly good mood. He and Tabitha Comfort of Gloria's Glamour Gowns had been beaten 10 and 8 by Ralph Brisket the butcher and Mrs Bell, who had not been gracious in victory, suggesting, among other things, that his slices were remarkable enough to be on sale in her shop, with vanilla on top. The Kit well-wishers did not improve things. Mr Davey, as we have seen, was not a demonstrative man; he wasn't unkind, either. But he did lack a little imagination, which seems strange for a tailor and outfitter, whose province is the future style and comfort of his customers. Some might have seen an opportunity for a sale followed by comfortable retirement if an employee suddenly came into funds, or, perhaps, to adopt a new approach to the said employee. Not Mr Davey, who instead began to get grumpy about all these unprofitable visitors. When Kit came over and told him he wanted to take a few days off to think about his changed circumstances, he said, 'I suppose you'll be leaving us for good anyway, now you've come into this money.'

'Well, I don't want to leave you in the lurch.'

Mr Davey relented a little. 'That's all right, Kit. Only to be expected, I suppose. With all that money. Don't know what I'd do if I wasn't here, though. Could you be back on Monday? It's my bowls afternoon.'

The Megalopolitan was luxurious, and large, Arabian amounts of marble, columns and floors, endless clusters of sofas and glass tables, many occupied by people in business suits looking conspiratorial. This was fine with Kit, who liked the anonymity large brought, particularly after his recent experience of celebrity in Fromerton. Daisy had booked him in on the Thursday, with a show on the Saturday. 'I've got you into *Ain't Misbehavin*', she'd told him. 'Should be fun.' Kit went out for a stroll, thought about joining the queue for the Hard Rock Cafe in Piccadilly but decided this was beneath the dignity of a Lottery winner. He crossed over to Green Park, wandered down to have a look at Buckingham Palace, then decided on a small outlay for a deck chair in the afternoon sun, falling asleep to dream about Fats Waller trying to buy a padded green shooting gilet from Mr Davey but they didn't have a big enough size. When he got back to the hotel there was a message from Mr Truss at reception, asking Kit to ring him. He sounded excited. 'Kit! It turns out Penny Vayne wasn't joking – they do want you to appear on *Match Me!* What do you think? You two got on so well on Monday, didn't you, it should be great fun. You'd be in the studio tomorrow. They do everything for you, all you have to do is enjoy it.' Kit had always wanted to be on a show like this, but his fantasies had been given quite a buffeting since his win. Still, he was intimidated by being alone in London and even just seeing how they made the programme would be exciting. And he was feeling disappointed with himself over the Daisy disaster. So he said yes, and then went into one of the hotel bars, also dotted around with whispering conspirators next to their briefcases, and, once he'd been condescended to by the waiter for trying to order a half of bitter – 'We only serve continental lager here, sir' – started sipping steadily at something Dutch for old times' sake.

It was then that he saw a man waving and smiling at him as if he were his oldest and dearest friend. This turned out to be none other than Chris Sidefather, the other talk of Fromerton for his financial success in the City. He was of the business suit persuasion, but Kit's expertise noted a more expensive cloth and a cunning double-breasted cut which concealed the convex contours that had contributed to his school nickname, Wobble. His once unruly hair was now slicked back and there was an air about him far removed from Super Mario and chemistry, if not chips. 'As I live and breathe,' he said, 'it's Fromerton's most eligible bachelor apart from me! How are you, Kit? It's been ages.'

It had; the last time they'd talked, Kit remembered, was when Chris had refused to let him have a chip. But he wasn't a man to bear a grudge. 'Wobble! I'm fine, thanks, how are you? Didn't expect to see you here.'

Chris had already slipped into the chair beside Kit; the expensive cloth did not prevent his bottom making one of those squeaking sounds on the leather, which he ignored. 'Be grateful if you didn't call me Wobble, Kit, nobody does now. Just been doing a spot of hot business, old chap, say no more, confidential. But tell me about you, tell me about all that lovely money. What have you bought so far?'

'Well, not much, really. New pair of shoes. Might buy a new car, although the Fiesta's still got more mileage in it yet. Going to buy a house. This holiday, perhaps one abroad, you know the sort of thing.'

'Interesting. I'll have a vodka and cranberry, please,' said Chris, although Kit hadn't asked him. 'I think you need to raise your sights, Kit. I realise the size of the win probably hasn't sunk in yet, but £6.5 million is one hell of a lot of smackeroonies. Have you got a plan?'

The waiter, summoned by Chris, returned with two vodka and cranberries. 'Try one of these, Kit, much better for your image.' Kit sipped and decided he preferred beer. But he was happy to go along with Chris. The money had been playing on his mind; he'd been very pleased with his smart answers at the press conference, but he was having trouble translating them into reality.

'No, nothing more than that planned at the moment, Chris,' he said. 'Are you going to make me even richer?'

'Well, I certainly could do. £6.5 million doesn't actually go that far these days if you want to enjoy a decent lifestyle. Look at your watch, for example. Did it come out of a cereal packet? Plastic strap, digital display? Sends out a terrible message. A girl looks at that and says to herself, "He might be rich, but he's not spending it". What you want is an Alpha Masterful Conqueror VII like mine. Chris shot his cuff to reveal what looked like a small power station on his wrist, in gold. Kit was impressed, particularly with the bit about girls. The Daisy encounter had convinced him that he needed to, as Chris would undoubtedly describe it, 'up his game'.

'Same about the car,' Chris continued. 'A Fiesta? Come on! Do you want to end up being called the Lottery Loner? A couple at least, Range Rover for the practical stuff and a Lambo for showing off. House, need some land for privacy, pool, tennis, the works, polo's fun. Do you sail? Anybody who can afford it should be in San Trop in August. Another house down there, and one in the Caribbean, obviously. Time to enjoy yourself, Kit! Thanks, I'd love another.'

Chris ordered another two vodka and cranberries and asked for them to go on Kit's bill. The waiter was looking at Kit with a new respect. Kit was beginning to enjoy himself, and Chris's vision.

'As I say, all this needs servicing, or you'll run out of the moolah before you can say usual table, The Cipriani. That's where

I might come in, Kit, as an old friend, and for a very reasonable commission. I can take the worry off you, guarantee you an income to provide all you need day to day while the capital sum is invested in some spectacularly high growth products. I'm pretty good at this sort of stuff, and when I say pretty good I mean very very good. I've got an associate who specialises in the Asian markets, one of the shrewdest guys around, derivatives, futures, options, shorts, straddles, strike price, all that stuff. You could just leave it to me, take all the worry off you, leave you to enjoy yourself.'

'That's very interesting,' said Kit, who had not understood all that Chris had been saying but found himself liking the sound of it. 'Of course, I've been thinking about doing some charity things, but I haven't decided what's best.'

'Again,' said Chris, 'leave it to me. I can produce money for your chosen charities like you wouldn't believe. Is that the time? Sorry, I've got to go, Jakie Rothschild doesn't like to be kept waiting. Here's my card, call me!'

Kit sat back, toying with his vodka and cranberry and trying out this beguiling new daydreaming material. Good old Wobble, eh?

THE METROPOLITAN TV STUDIOS WERE ON THE SOUTH Bank. Kit was picked up and taken there quite early the next day. The reception foyer was fairly typical of such places, the usual mix of confident people breezing through and the non-confident feeling out of place and showing it, the receptionists giving loud friendly greetings to obvious celebrities and instantly switching off the grins to deal with the nons, who were despatched to wait on the sofas. Kit despite being very smart in DCs best, including a yellow paisley cravat, got the switch-off but was reprieved into almost-friendliness when he turned out to be one of the contestants on *Match Me!* A man about his own age called Matthew in jeans and crewneck sweater arrived busily with a clipboard and big smile and took him down to the studio, where he met the other two male contestants hoping to be picked out for the date. Simon was a floppy-haired estate agent from Kensington; Kevin was a hairdresser and part-time disc jockey from Doncaster; they had clearly filled in questionnaires and were discussing them with one of the researchers, Lucy, amid much laughter and knowingness. Kit felt rather intimidated by their ease, and had to keep saying '£6.5 million' to himself quietly. A man in a leather jacket and black turtleneck came up, introduced himself as Neville, the assistant producer, and took him to one side. 'Don't worry about the questionnaire, Kit, we know all about you!' he said with the unlikely intimacy common to his world. 'We want to do something a little different today. We're not going to tell your prospective date that you're a multimillionaire! We're not! No, we want to see if you get chosen for being Kit, not being rich, great idea, eh? Some of the audience might recognise you so we'll let them in on the secret before we record and ask them not to get too enthusiastic about you. It'll say much more about your date than you, won't it? What do you say? OK? It'll be fun! And we'll write what you have to say for you, so there'll be no problem there. OK?'

Kit felt he had gone too far to stop now, and Neville somehow managed to convey subtly that the whole show would collapse if he didn't agree, so he did. 'Great, super,' said Neville. 'We'll get on with it. And there's Penny. Penny, come over and say hello to Kit!'

The pre-prepared Penny was quite as arresting as the prepared one. 'Kit, chuck! How's my filthy rich young friend?!' she shouted from a distance as she homed in, hair in a towel, eyes behind dark glasses, the rest of her in a scarlet velour jumpsuit with silver flashes on the shoulders. 'Has Neville told you? It's my idea, we need to pep things up round here and you, Kit, are the answer, isn't he, Nev? Don't worry about Neville, Kit, he's a poppet, aren't you, chuck!?' She continued on her way, folksy, imperious, impossible. The day passed as TV days did, rehearsals, technical stuff, rewrites and long periods of waiting around. Kit met the director, Alan, a humourless man, and the producer, Anna, a lively woman. He tried his script out, written by Lucy and Neville, and sensed a lack of satisfaction, met by more rewriting and more trying out. Simon and Kevin seemed better at it than he was, and, now they knew who he was, wary. Of his intended date, there was no sign: she was being kept well away for spontaneity's sake.

Came recording, Kit was fairly nervous, and the wait behind the set as the audience filed in and settled didn't help. The warm-up man, though, a minor northern comic called Frank Speke, did make him laugh. 'Good afternoon, ladies and gentlemen, and welcome to *Match Me!*, the answer to many prayers, including, "Please God, really?" If only I'd got on here when I was young and handsome. Excuse me, madam, I was young. If I'd come on here then, I could have avoided the wife. What a woman! An absolute treasure! She is, she is, someone asked me the other day where I'd dug her up! And what a cook! Remarkable. We haven't had a clean plate in the house since the dog died. I saw a cockroach in the kitchen the other day sucking a Rennie! I did!

'Seriously, though, she's a wonderful woman, and that's not just because she's in the front row. No, not that front row, the front row here! Smile, luv! And, our lovely audience, I do have some hints how you can help us make this a great show today. See that man over there with the headphones? That's Graham, the floor manager. Give us a wave, Graham, thank you, don't get your hopes up. He's called the floor manager because that's where we have to help him get up from a lot of the time. But no, seriously, ladies and gentlemen, we know you'll love the show and you'll want to show how much you're enjoying it, so if during the show the lovely Graham holds his hands up like this – thank you, lovely Graham – we want you to clap as loudly as you can until he brings them down again, like that. So let's give it a go – lovely Graham, please! What was that? This isn't a wet Monday in Blackpool listening to Des O'Connor singing, you know, this is *Match Me!*, with the incomparable, the one and only, your host tonight, Miss Penny Vayne! So let's give it another go! That's much better! Now, if Penny's talking to one of the contestants and then turns and gives you one of her looks, where she raises her eyebrows like this, follow Graham's cue – like this – and try a little mock booing…

'…And there's just a couple more tips. We love audience participation, but let's keep it to what lovely Graham asks you to do, ok? No shouting out, you might not think I'm very funny, but I can assure you you'll be worse, especially after we've taken you into a side room afterwards. No, that's just a joke, possibly. And the last thing is that some of you might recognise one of our happy handsomes hoping to win the fair lady's hand today… it's that lucky lad from the West Country who's just won all that lolly on the Lottery! We thought it would be a lot of fun if the beautiful lady – and she is a lady, let me tell you! – choosing her perfect partner didn't know about the money! So please, keep your sniggers to yourself and let's see who the lady chooses without interference!'

Moments later, recording began with the usual introduction and appearance of Penny, sleek in a black suit, pausing at the top of the flight of stage steps to acknowledge the loud applause by executing a half-curtsey and then making a rapid and worrying descent in very high heels. Graham, well out of sight of the cameras, signalled for the clapping to stop after Penny had smilingly soaked up a bit more. 'Good evening, you lovely ladies and gentlemen,' she announced in her familiar de-aspirated tones, 'and welcome to *Match Me!*, the show that loves love and knows how to find it! And let's get right on and meet tonight's handsome hopefuls!' Simon, Kevin and Kit came bounding on as rehearsed while Penny stepped around the partition that would conceal the aspirants from their object and vice versa. They were now perched on high stools and were interviewed by Penny in turn. Simon confirmed he was indeed an estate agent – Penny turning to the audience and raising both eyebrows to receive the requested booing – and added that he had some very attractive features and considerable potential, which achieved laughter despite his slightly laboured delivery. Kevin, encouraged by Penny to turn up the Yorkshireness even higher, said he could give his date a discount on a hairdo and other services and as a deejay knew exactly the music to turn her on. Kit, concentrating hard, said he was proud to be a gentleman's outfitter but could also fit any girl's dreams, which was well received.

Then Penny tottered her way round to the other side of the partition and introduced the girl who was going to have to choose to go out on a date with these variously enticing prospects, guided only by their answers to her questions. 'Ladies and gentlemen, are we having fun? Oooh, we are having fun! Now I'm going to ask you to meet the lucky lady who's going to meet these lovely fellas. And, ladies and gentlemen, this lady really is a lady – it's Lady Katy!'

A tall attractively vivacious blonde strode confidently onto the set and greeted Penny like an old friend. 'Katy!' said Penny. 'I wasn't joking, was I? You are a real lady, aren't you?'

Katy tossed her hair back, laughed and said in manner-born drawl, 'Of course I'm a real lady, darling! Can't you tell?' She smoothed her tight-fitting dress down to further applause.

'No,' said Penny. 'I mean you're a nob, aren't you?' More laughter. 'A member of the aristocracy?' Penny elongated the last word in a mock posh voice and added an h to its front.

'Well, if you mean I'm the daughter of an earl and Daddy owns a castle, yes!'

Further amusement. Penny pressed on. 'Well, perhaps one of these lucky lads will end up owning it!' she said. 'Now you've got some questions you'd like to ask them, haven't you? Let's hear the first one. Who do you want to ask first?'

'This is for Number One. Do you know how to give a girl a good time?'

Simon was ready. 'I most certainly do! I'm an estate agent so I'm used to dealing with hot properties! I'm also a keen balloonist so I'd take you into the skies and give you champagne and caviar.'

'Hot air makes sense, certainly,' said Penny to the audience, who loved it.

'How about you, Number Two?' asked Katy.

Kevin was more than ready. 'Well, Katy, I'm a hairdresser so I certainly know how to make the best of things. And shampoo and sets means something entirely different with me, not just the champagne either! I'm a disc jockey too, so I'll really be music to your ears. And even though I'm a Yorkshireman I won't expect you to go halves!'

Penny and Katy both went raised eyebrows on that one. Things were going so well that Graham was relaxing on the sidelines. 'Well, Kevin,' said Lady Katy, I'm also from Yorkshire so I won't expect you to go halves either!'

'Can't understand why you haven't met already,' said Penny. 'Hunt Ball perhaps?' She emphasised the H, gave the look and the audience responded on Graham's cue.

'Pardon me, Penny,' chipped in Kevin, 'I must have misheard you there.'

'Number Three?' said Penny quickly.

Kit cleared his throat, not necessarily a good start. 'Hello Katy. I'm a gentlemen's outfitter and I think you'll find I'm a good fit for you too! I'll certainly measure up to your expectations and I'm very good with checks!'

This produced the best reaction yet from the audience, some of whom were clearly in on who Kit was. 'Well, they like you, Kit chuck – and your checks! How about you, Katy?'

'Ya,' said Katy. 'Number Three's a bit of an imp, isn't he? Very interesting, but I have more questions.'

'Indeed you do, my pet, sorry, lady,' said Penny. 'Ask away!'

Katy's second question was what they liked and disliked. They had been given free rein with these answers. Simon said, 'Likes, a beautiful girl and the moonlight,' and 'dislikes, boring people and small cars.' Kevin chose, 'Titled ladies with broad tastes,' and 'estate agents and gentlemens' outfitters.' Kit chose, 'Love and friendship,' and 'bad manners and cruelty, especially to animals.' Another hit.

'So, before you make your mind up, Katy – ooh, can I call you Katy!? – one last question.'

'Okey dokey,' said Katy. 'Why would I like you?'

Simon said, 'Because I'm handsome, charming and witty and my Death by Chocolate cake is to die for!'

Kevin said, 'Because you'll know exactly where are you with me, I speak as I find and like my turntable, I'll have you in a spin.'

Kit had been given a prepared line involving a combine harvester but said, 'As you can tell from my accent, I'm a West Country boy, so I'm not sharp and slick like these other two, I'm gentle, kind and fun, and I would give you everything.'

That got a delighted 'aahh' and loud applause from Penny and the audience. Simon and Kevin looked sheepish. Kit smiled modestly. And Katy chose Kevin.

After the uproar had subsided, Penny said to Katy, 'Lady Katy! What have you done? Why have you chosen Kevin and not lovely Kit?'

Katy was haughtily unabashed and unrepentant. 'Well, actually, Penny, Kevin just seemed more fun!' Penny gave that laugh, again.

The camera went to Kevin smirking, Kit smiling ruefully, and Simon looking like the sale of a Holland Park four-storied double-fronter had fallen through just before completion. 'All right then, chucks,' said Penny. 'Can we have the two unlucky Romeos first please!' The partition slid back to allow Simon through. He gave Katy an incredulous look and spread his arms wide to demonstrate his blazered and bejeaned self, they air kissed and he went off. 'Now, then,' said Penny, 'it's lovely Kit!' Thunderous applause and some cheering took even Katy aback. Kit came through, still looking sheepish, and Penny seized him by the hand. 'Katy, what you didn't know but what the audience knew is that there's something else about Kit. What is it, Kit?'

Kit, boosted by the audience, rallied. 'I'm the most handsome man in Somerset!' More applause, with Katy sportingly nodding her head vigorously. 'And,' said Kit, with pretty good timing for an amateur, 'I've just won six and a half million on the Lottery!'

Breeding has its positives as well as negatives. Katy took it well, jumping up and down and whooping, then putting her hands to her face and throwing back her head in faux despair. When the noise finally died away, she said, 'The castle needs a new roof, too!' Kit was even more taken with her, but he formally shook her hand and left to an ovation, feeling pretty good despite it all.

'Ooh-ay!' said Penny. 'What a to-do!' Katy, still playing the game, was looking forlorn, and actually rather felt it, as there was no denying Kit's uncomplicated charm, or his money. 'So you turned down Simon, Kit, and the possibility of a lorra lorra lolly, even though that's not really what it's about, is it, ladies and gentlemen? And here he is, your choice, Kevin from Doncaster!'

Breeding also has its limits. Katy gazed upon Kevin and her smile froze halfway to full formation, leaving her mouth fixed half ajar. He was wearing loose high-waisted white jeans, fluorescent yellow clogs, a lime green jacket with sleeves rolled up to bare forearms and an orange T-shirt bearing the legend, 'This Way Girls!'. The ensemble was topped off by blond streaked hair styled in an obvious tribute to the Chuckle Brothers. He smiled at Katy, who was still on pause, and said, 'Gorgeous! And that's just me!' Penny, who was enjoying herself hugely, did the laugh, twice.

'Well, chucks, I bet you can't believe your luck, can you? So who's going to open the envelope to find out where your date will be taking place? Lady Katy?'

Katy was still on pause. Kevin, without waiting, seized the envelope, opened it, read the card inside and shouted, 'Result! A weekend on a desert island!' Katy had now come to and was smiling bravely.

'Yes, chucks, you're going to fly to the Virgin Islands and stay on a tiny one, just the two of you in a luxury villa, no distractions but the crash of the surf and the mating calls of the exotic wildlife!' Kevin was now getting out of control; his wink accompanying the pumping of his arm and shout of 'wahey!' at the mention of the Virgin in Virgin Islands was matched only by Katy's look of horror, even if the audience much enjoyed it. Penny ushered them off and they exited stage right, Kevin gurning at the audience as he went and executing another vigorous pump of his arm with clenched fist, Katy, several inches taller, maintaining as much dignity as she could. Back in the Green Room, Kit and Simon, who had exchanged no more than a few words – 'bad luck', 'thank you', 'lucky bastard' – were waiting, but for what they weren't quite sure; meanwhile they'd watched impassively as the large monitor showed Kevin and Katy meeting. The previous episode's match, Mark and Melanie, were still kissing in the corner, although they had managed to break off long enough to give Kit and Simon a brief sympathetic smile when the two losers had come in. The only other occupant of the room was a small, morose-looking middle-aged man with a hairstyle far too young for him, reading the racing pages of the evening newspaper in a corner. Matthew, clutching clipboard, came in next. 'Bad luck, guys!' he shouted over his shoulder as he made his way to the entwined. 'But Kevin is a lot of fun, isn't he? Priceless haircut! Now then you two lovebirds, unclinch, it's time to tell the world about your date!' As he escorted the pair out, still holding hands, Kevin and Katy arrived, not holding hands.

They were guided by Neville, who made his way over to the drinks table. 'Right, let's get this party started!' he announced in an impressive impression of Penny's accent. 'Come on!' Kevin needed no encouragement and was soon clutching a bottle of lager; the others were a little slower but after some chivvying from Neville, Simon and Katy had a glass of white wine and Kit poured a lager into a wine glass. Neville was standing in the middle of the room watching Mark and Melanie on the monitor. They were holding hands on a sofa while Penny was clucking over them from a nearby chair. Clearly their weekend – in Skegness, one of the less attractive venues the programme liked to throw in – had been a great success, even though it had been out of season up on the Lincolnshire coast. There were pictures of the pair giggling in the rain and running up and down the wide windswept beach then collapsing in a cuddling huddle on the cold sand. The dodgems had been persuaded to open up specially for them, cue more shrieking and laughter, followed by a candlelit supper in the traditional fish and chip restaurant.

'What do you think, chucks? Do I have to keep any dates free?' This was Penny's code for a wedding, gleefully recognised by the audience (for whom, like all of them, happiness is nearly as good as humiliation, providing it's all supposed to be in good fun).

Finally, recording was over, and Penny appeared in the room more quickly than seemed scientifically possible. The room was now filling with the innumerable people and their associates necessary to the making of a television programme. 'Come on you lot,' she shouted, 'let's hold hands and contact the living! Billy! Where's my bubbles?' The man from the corner came up to her, carrying a yellow container which proved to be a cool box with two bottles of Veuve Cliquot inside. He opened one of them in practised fashion and poured Penny a glass, waited for her to down it in one, refilled the glass and retreated to his corner and newspaper.

'What a great show!' said Neville to Penny. 'You were terrific!'

'Thanks, pet,' said Penny. 'That Kevin, eh? And where's poor Kit?'

Kevin, already on his third beer, came up. 'Penny, my love, I want to thank you for fixing me up with such a top piece of top totty! I can't wait to get her to that island!' He turned to Katy, who was in animated conversation with Lucy the researcher.

Snatches could be heard: 'Unbelievable!'... 'Not funny, Lucy!'... 'Do you know, I think I've lost my passport.'

Kevin, whose hearing had clearly been affected by his deejaying, shouted to her, 'Don't worry, flower, I'll be back in a second. Just getting some romantic tips from this little cracker.' Penny made a vigorous hand movement behind his back; Katy smiled fixedly at him until he turned back and then repeated Penny's gesture, with more feeling.

'Are you all right, Kit, lah? Lovely girl, but you've still got all that money. And you were so sweet,' said Penny, grasping him hard by the arm. 'How did I do?' Kit was taken aback by Penny's question and her worried stare into his eyes.

'I thought you were very good, Penny,' he said, with the careful spacing and deliberate pronunciation of a man who had now had several glasses of lager. 'And the audience loved you.' Penny didn't really register this, but her grip on his arm weakened and she began to look around for somebody else to talk to. Billy came up with the champagne and filled her glass. They didn't talk. She espied Anna, the producer, and launched off in pursuit.

Billy watched her go and said to Kit: 'I'll give you two pieces of advice. Never go into show business and never back a horse with an R in its name.' He then returned to his corner.

Lady Katy, ducking under Kevin's encircling arm, no mean feat given their difference in height, came over to Kit. 'I really don't know why I chose him,' she said. 'It must have been the heat of the moment. I do like to have fun and he sounded like he did as well. It's supposed to be a fun show, isn't it? But when I saw what I had let myself into, I couldn't believe it. I should have chosen you, Kit. Crikey, I'd have been better off getting creepy Simon, but it should have been you!'

She looked at him appealingly; she really was very attractive, thought Kit. 'Tell me you'll come and see me in the country, though, Kit, won't you, when this nightmare is over? I'm sure Mummy and Daddy will adore you!' Kit might have had a few beers, but he did remember her roof.

Kevin arrived to reclaim Katy: 'Come on, flower, let the dog see the rabbit! Old Kevin might not be a posh git, but we deejays know how to get the ladies jumping, if you follow me! Tough luck, Kit old lad, but you were never going to get in over a Yorkshire lad, were you?' Kit was about to defend West Country ways but Kevin had already dragged Katy away. Billy was still in his corner. Penny was now all over Alan the director. Simon and Lucy the researcher seemed to be getting on very well. Neville was laughing uproariously at Anna's sarcastic quips, clearly aimed at Penny, who was asking Matthew the runner if she'd been all right. Kit thought he might go, and did.

THAT WAS PROBABLY THE HIGHLIGHT OF THE EARLY DAYS OF the win, Kit thought later, when it had all calmed down. He hadn't gone back to Davey & Cray except to tell Mr Davey he wouldn't be going back. Mr Davey took it quite well, all considering, and even offered him his hand, after an uneasy few moments staring at the shirt drawers. He'd followed Chris Sidefather's advice and bought a Ferrari and a Range Rover, but he found the suspension of the Ferrari too hard for country lanes and it was difficult getting anywhere to park the Range Rover outside his parents' house. So, following some more of Chris's advice, he bought a large house in a village outside Fromerton, mostly so he could park the Range Rover and keep the Ferrari in the garage. His parents didn't want to move or stop working, so he gave them a new bathroom. He also took Chris's advice about investing his money, and had entrusted it all to him, apart from a comparatively small amount which he placed with the local building society, a farewell suggestion from the wise Mr Truss. His social life had become rather more quiet, which was not unwelcome and coincided with his new-old friends discovering that Chris had secured his business. Daisy? That was not going as well as it might. No two ways about it, she'd definitely been upset when he decided he wouldn't be taking any foreign trips just yet. But she had agreed to go out with him when he finally managed to ask her, in a rush of stammers and starts, at the end of the holiday discussion. A series of dates hadn't really got very far. Given his local celebrity, he had taken her outside Fromerton, in the bumpy Ferrari, to some pubs serving a variety of things still in baskets, with chips. She'd been friendly and chatty but hadn't really given much hint of more, and Kit was not a man to force a relationship. But he was gaining the confidence that several million pounds can give a person and decided, in his old-fashioned way, that the way ahead would be Sunday afternoon tea in Bath. First they took a turn round the Roman Baths, which Kit hadn't been to in years, and enjoyed the calm warm wonder the centuries brought to what remained. Daisy, who arranged coach trips to Bath, seemed happy explaining some of the details – 'A million litres of water comes every day up from 4,000 metres under the ground, the temperature of it here is 46 degrees celsius!' – and Kit was happy to see her so enthusiastic. It was a fine day in early June and they took a long walk to reinspect the Georgian glories of a city made for strolling. Daisy was pleased and pretty and Kit began to think he might be on the verge of a breakthrough, especially when the man dressed as Mr Bennett outside The Jane Austen Centre gave him a conspiratorial wink of encouragement. They went to one of the finest hotels and took tea on its terrace, cucumber sandwiches and a well-filled cake stand. Kit, after some chat about the marvels of the Bath, took, if not exactly the plunge, a step off the edge. 'It's really nice seeing all this stuff with you, Daisy. You're so knowledgeable you make it come alive for me. Actually, Daisy, you make me come alive, too. I've always liked you, right back to when we were at school, but I've never dared say so.'

He looked meaningfully at Daisy, but she seemed a little distracted coping with a scone. Some crumbs had strayed onto her chin, along with a smear of strawberry jam and she was attending to it with her linen napkin. 'Sorry, Kit, I must have looked a mess! What were you saying?'

Kit was disappointed by the response but bravely pressed on: 'I was saying about liking you right back to when we were at school. I suppose winning all this money has changed things, but it also makes you think about the things that haven't changed.'

Another meaningful look. There was a silence while Daisy finished dealing with the scone, and then she said, 'I think I might try that slice of Victoria sponge, could you pass it please, Kit?'

Kit smiled and obliged, but his heart was heavy. Too soon? She began to talk, between bites of the sponge, about the hotel decor – 'very stylish, classic but with a contemporary feel' – and the beautiful honeysuckle on the terrace trellis – 'I bet that needs some watering!'; then, after a short pause, she turned to him and smiled. 'Could you pass that piece of strawberry layer cake, please?'

No, not the right time, clearly. Conversation, with further cake interruptions, continued, and Kit began to notice that she was mentioning Chris rather a lot. 'You're good friends, you and Chris?' he asked.

'We've been out a few times. He's very funny, isn't he? And so clever. And charming. I can't think why I didn't know him better at school.' Kit knew the answer to that, but chose not to supply it, or to tell her about his investment with Chris. As they drove back to Fromerton, he was beginning to think his chances with Daisy were very slim if he couldn't compete with Chris, or cake.

And, besides, Lady Katy Cruste had been in touch, with an invitation to the family seat, Upshawes Castle, near Ilkley. Kit, being a sensitive man, had not watched the episode of *Match Me!* featuring her trip to the Caribbean island with the hairdressing disc jockey, but his parents had told him about it, particularly the moment when Lady Katy emptied an ice bucket over Kevin's head and then kicked him hard below the lower stomach area; Kevin, soaked through and doubled up, had still managed to wink at the camera and confide, 'I think she's beginning to like me!' Kit was in two minds about going, but in truth he was getting bored with his new lifestyle, which involved no work and repetitive conversations when he ventured out. His new house was a worry, too, because it needed filling with things in which he had no real interest, like furniture. But he had brought his beehive, and added another two, and took solace at the bottom of his large garden (his footballing had ended after the team captain asked him to stand down because the other players always passed the ball to him).

There was also the quandary of whether to take the Ferrari or the Range Rover. In the end, he decided to go and to take the Ferrari. This had been a mistake on both counts, as the Crustes were snobs of the county order for whom a member of a lower one might just have been acceptable in a Range Rover, but certainly not in something red, foreign and flashy. Nothing was said, of course, especially in view of the state of the castle roof. The house party, for such it was, had not gone that well, although Lady Katy, by far the least stuffy there, had tried her hardest to make him feel welcome and at ease after his initial error in mistaking the butler for the Earl of Upshawes when he'd arrived. Lady Katy had warned him, for example, in a friendly phone call, that they would be dressing for dinner, but hadn't thought to advise further. DCs had never stocked evening wear, and so, left to his own lively sense of colour, Kit had chosen a magenta pleated cummerbund, an emerald green dress shirt with white lace front and a jumbo velvet bow tie. Still, he'd just about managed his way through the various cutleries and small talks, which had tended to falter when his limited knowledge of hacking, flies, fixed tenancies and the iniquity of Mr Tony Benn was exhausted. Unravelling began after dinner, when, his nervousness having contributed to far too much claret, he chose to stand up and follow Katy's mother, Lady Celia and her sensitive rendition of 'We'll Gather Lilacs in the Spring' with an a cappella 'I Am a Cider Drinker' with particular emphasis on the 'ooh arrh, ooh arrh ay'. Charades had gone no better: *Practical Beekeeping* had not been a wise choice.

He was happy to go to bed, and after some difficulty, located his room. He slept for a time but then woke with a terrible thirst.

The sophistications of Upshawes Castle not extending to tumbler and carafe, he made his way, with more difficulty, to a bathroom tap. He had even more trouble finding his way back, and ended up in the room which contained the Earl and Countess, who were not amused. More misfortune arose several hours later when the volume of claret and additional water demanded urgent bladder action. He didn't dare leave the room again, and took the desperate remedy of urinating out of the window. The next morning, he looked out and saw that his emission was warming in the sun in a disconcertingly large puddle on the awning over the table on the terrace set for breakfast. He left immediately and as quietly as the Ferrari allowed, and never heard from Lady Katy again after an awkward phone call – 'Your poor mother, I do hope she's out of hospital now. I had no idea housemaid's knee can strike so suddenly… no, no, people are always bursting in on Mummy and Daddy… in a way I'm glad you missed breakfast as it was then that we first noticed a sewery smell that we're still investigating, you know what these old houses are like…'

Kit wasn't terribly upset, as he'd decided quite early on that a life with the English aristocracy might not be ideal; the embarrassment of how it had turned out had been excruciating but did pretty firmly end any chance of the relationship progressing further. Monotony can have its attractions after such an adventure, and Kit continued quite happily with his bees and – new interest – asparagus. There was the occasional dalliance – inevitable with all that money – but nothing to disturb him. So placid and unadventurous had he become that his heart barely missed a beat when Daisy called him after at least a year of silence, which was just as well as she sounded formal and a little strained. 'Kit, hello, I need to have a talk – can we meet?' Kit suggested she come out to see him and she agreed to come at six that evening. Remembering their last encounter, he popped down to the village shop and bought a Battenberg cake and, of course a Victoria sponge. When she turned down a slice of either he knew it was serious. 'Kit, I have bad news, I'm afraid.'

'What's happened, Daisy, they haven't sacked you, surely?'

'No, it's not about me, it's about you.'

'Me? What do you mean?'

'And Chris.'

'Chris? Is he ok? Why couldn't he get in touch himself?'

'He's not around.'

'Not around? What's happened? He's not dead?'

'No. He's gone missing. Have you read about the Asian stock markets?'

'Ha, fat chance, why?' said Kit, beginning to cotton on.

'They're in trouble. That's where Chris was doing his investing. With your money and a lot of other people's. The trouble is, he lost your money and theirs a long time ago and built up debts trying to get it back, but this crash ended any chance of that, so he's done a runner. He's gone and so has your money.'

The mind goes to less important matters in situations like this. 'How do you know all this, Daisy?' he asked.

'He told me this morning. We've been going out for ages.'

'Oh, I see. All of it?'

Daisy looked upset, which touched him. She also seemed a little larger than he remembered. 'Yes. He might be caught, but you'll never get the money back, it's gone. I'm so sorry about this, Kit. It was me who told him where you were staying in London when he bumped into you accidentally on purpose.'

'Ah. He didn't take you with him, then. I suppose he wanted to protect you.'

Daisy laughed. 'Yes, that'll be right, I don't think.'

'Are you sure you won't have a slice of cake?'

Daisy hesitated. There was a suggestion of jowliness about her jaw that Kit hadn't noticed before. 'No, thank you, Kit,' she said.

'Goodbye, Daisy.'

CHRIS SIDEFATHER WAS ARRESTED IN FRANKFURT SHORTLY afterwards and extradited back to Britain where he was given a four-year jail sentence for false accounting and theft. Kit never saw his money again, and was relieved. It had been too much and had imposed a burden of expectation that he didn't want and couldn't cope with. All that he did want, really, was the comfortable cushioned life that the English without it had always aspired to before they were beguiled into the pursuit of more. He was left with enough to buy a small house with room and time for his bees, asparagus and – new interest – an Apple Mac PowerBook 100 on which he mostly played games. And to buy DCs from Mr Davey. So on December 31, 1999, while they lengthily queued in confusion at Stratford tube station for their tickets to the Millennium Dome extravaganza which like every celebration failed quite to live up to epochal expectation, Kit sat cosily and content at home reading a gardening magazine. It's true that the Fromerton Association of Amateur Apiarists had recently gained a new member who looked particularly fetching in her white beekeeper's suit with integrated veil, but that is a story for another century.

Afterword

READERS OF NOW UNFASHIONABLE COMIC NOVELS WILL *recognise this story's debt to 'Kipps' and 'The History of Mr Polly', both portrayals by H G WELLS of English society in the 1890s while its structure struggled with change as Victorian certainty faded with the Queen herself. Arthur Kipps and Alfred Polly (hence Kit Parrott) are, like Wells himself, working-class boys who begin in drapery shops and progress through life with varying success (and nothing like that of their author, leading literary lion of the first half of the twentieth century, acclaimed science fiction writer of 'The Time Machine, The War of the Worlds', etc, social commentator, historian and apparently effortless philanderer). Kipps is the closest to Kit Parrott, coming into money unexpectedly, floundering among the higher classes and finding contentment in a more modest life after being defrauded out of his windfall.*

Chris Sidefather should evoke memories of NICK LEESON, the city trader from a Watford council estate who broke Barings Bank in a scandal which foreshadowed many more in the next century. Working in Singapore, he made unauthorised speculations on derivatives that at first brought the bank great profits but soon began to build up enormous losses which he concealed while taking equally eye-watering risks to get the money back. In 1995, he gambled that Japanese stock would not move overnight, and lost when the Kobe earthquake did. Abandoning further failed attempts to recover, he fled leaving a note which read, 'I'm sorry'. Leeson's losses were £827m: Barings, Britain's oldest merchant bank, collapsed. He was arrested in Frankfurt, deported back to Singapore and tried and sentenced to six years in Changi Prison. At school, he had failed his Maths A level. After his release, he exploited his infamy in best 21st century manner by appearing on 'the global corporate circuit'.

Fromerton is based on Frome in Somerset, but is not entirely faithful to it. Similarly, 'Match Me!' is based on 'Blind Date', imported from America, highly popular and a pioneer of the invasion of one's own privacy that would be immensely accelerated by the coming of social media and provide an unquestioning welcome to encroaching mass surveillance. Penny Vayne shares some but by no means all of the attributes of Cilla Black, the wholesome host of 'Blind Date', determined if exiled Liverpudlian. Ours were edited highlights of a lengthy recording.

Kit and Kipps might also serve as a wider metaphor for the 1990s, when the liberal West was presented with but lost a startling opportunity to encourage and implant its values in the wrecked economies and ruined societies that the failed Marxist experiment had left behind. There was a very recent and highly successful precedent – the Marshall Plan sponsored by the United States after the Second World War to help Europe recover – but Western governments chose not to follow it. They could not argue that they were too beset by other crises and considerations: from 1989 to 1991, from the fall of the Berlin Wall to 2001 and 9/11, there was what seems today an eery respite from major wars and disasters. Resolution was in the air – the end of apartheid in South Africa, the Good Friday agreement in Northern Ireland – but wider gains were lost amid the distractions of Consumerism, Celebrity and technological advance. And so Russia's tumble into brigandry was largely ignored, while we all – mostly – settled for enjoying our good fortune, even believing that 'Things Could Only Get Better'. The Britain of Tony Blair and Gordon Brown did try to provide moral leadership abroad and invested strongly in social provision at home, but it also took a relaxed approach to *unsustainable and divisive methods of making profit – this was the era of 'Greed is Good' on Wall Street and the 'Big Bang' in the City of London, with its new brash classless traders and their unabashed enjoyment of 'loadsamoney'. The best-remembered text of the time is Francis Fukuyama's catchily entitled study of the upheaval, 'The End of History', but a better title for the decade is Jonathan Freedland's 'A Holiday from History'.*

Thus the twentieth century, a time of terror, chaos and change of a hitherto unrealised order. With the occasional laugh.

FURTHER READING:
Kipps, The Story of a Simple Soul, *H G Wells*
The History of Mr Polly, *H G Wells*
The End of History and the Last Man, *Francis Fukuyama*
A Classless Society: Britain in the 1990s, *Alwyn W Turner*

Acknowledgements

First, as ever, i should like to thank my dear wife, Liv O'Hanlon, for applying her professional editing skills to these stories and offering crucial improvements with such perception and patience, but as I have noted before, even she can't work miracles: any mistakes that remain are all mine. Two writers gave free and friendly advice beyond their excellent books: David Martin, author of 'Death of a Division', 'Eight Days in March 1918' and the 'Untold Story of the 66th (2/1st East Lancashire) Division', checked 'Gus Hits the Front' for accuracy and made some clever suggestions; W Sydney Robinson, author of 'The Last Victorians: A Daring Reassessment of Four Twentieth Century Eccentrics', helped me with one of them, William Joynson-Hicks, the Home Secretary determined to clamp down on London's nightlife, who appears in 'The Cat's Pyjamas'. Debts are also owed to the authors whose works, already credited, I have gleefully and gratefully pillaged, and to those others whose styles, plots and characters I have similarly shamelessly adopted: PG Wodehouse, H G Wells, Evelyn Waugh, F Scott Fitzgerald, Graham Greene, and all involved with the Ealing Comedies. My efforts to trace the holder of permission to include short quotes from Lena Ashwell's moving account of troop entertainment in the First World War, 'Modern Troubadours', have so far proved fruitless; I trust he or she would have no objection to their use in this context: I would be delighted to include a full acknowledgement in subsequent editions. Some of the names of characters, but none of the characteristics, have been taken from past and present players of St Helens RFC, unrivalled exponents of the wonderful game of Rugby League. Thanks also to another fine team, at the Book Guild, who were as splendid, wise and heroically patient as ever, Fern Bushnell in particular. And to S Faulks for the fine crossword clue in Thor Doubles Up and to D Keech for the translation. Lastly, thank you, too, the twentieth century, for producing, inspiring, infuriating and challenging this writer, and for not, unlike so many others who experienced you, killing me.